"Beyazh," Brim yelled, hauling in the little ship's helm. "Get that last torpedo ready. NOW!"

■ ■ ■

"We're not going to fire this one," Brim warned, holding up his hand, "instead, we're going to jettison it."

"Jettison?" Beyazh exclaimed. "An armed torpedo?"

"Yeah," Brim said through clenched teeth; the Leaguers were catching up fast, "...but set the fuse for proximity—at about five hundred irals."

"A space mine!" the Fluvannian whispered. "Of course."

"If they'll just hold off firing a few more clicks," Brim grunted, his eyes glued to the aft view display. The bastards had to be *just* where he wanted them. "Ready..." he warned. A whir behind the aft bulkhead told him that the number five torpedo-loading hatch was open. The Leaguers were nearly on top of him. He dared not wait another moment.

"Let 'er go!" he bellowed, then shoved the thrust dampers into MILITARY OVERLOAD.

No sooner had the ejector mechanismn cycled than both League ships fired ranging shots—and space itself erupted in a binding inferno of raw energy...

Also by Bill Baldwin

THE MERCENARIES
THE TROPHY
THE HELMSMAN
GALACTIC CONVOY

Published by
WARNER BOOKS

A Time Warner Company

WARNER BOOKS EDITION

Cover illustration by John Berkey
Cover design by Don Puckey

Warner Books, Inc.
1271 Avenue of the Americas
New York, NY 10020

 A Time Warner Company

Printed in the United States of America

First Printing: August, 1992

10 9 8 7 6 5 4 3 2 1

CHAPTER 1

Back to Gimmas

ASHF234812-19E GROUP 198BA 113/52011
[TOP SECRET]

PERSONNEL ACTION MEMORANDUM,
IMPERIAL FLEET,
PERSONAL COPY

FROM:
BU FLEET PERSONNEL;
ADMIRALTY, AVALON

TO:
W. A. BRIM, CAPTAIN, I.F., IVG
AVALON
<0893BVC-12-K2134MV/573250>
SUBJECT: DUTY ASSIGNMENT

(1) YOU ARE DETACHED PRESENT IVG DUTY AS OF 205/52012.
(2) PROCEED MOST EXPEDITIOUS TRANSPORT GIMMAS STARBASE, HAEFDON. REPORT REAR

ADM B. GALLSWORTHY, 11 GROUP, HOME FLEET, DEFENSE COMMAND, AS WING COMMANDER.
(3) SUBMIT TRAVEL EXPENSE VOUCHERS DIRECT ADMIRALTY
C/O H. DRUMMOND, REAR ADMIRAL, I.F.

FOR THE EMPEROR:
TANDOR K. KNORR, CAPTAIN, I.F.

[END TOP SECRET]
ASHF234812-19E

"Hands to landfall stations! All hands man your stations for landfall. Secure from HyperSpace operations. . . ."

Frigid, cloud-swept Haefdon, third planet of the dying star Gimmas, filled the forward Hyperscreens as Imperial destroyer *Jacques Schneider*—eight days out from Avalon—shut down her interstellar Drive and thundered in toward landfall using gravity generators alone. On the cramped flight bridge, Captain Wilf Brim, I.F., leaned forward in a jump seat between the two Helmsmen, listening to sounds of thudding feet, the dull bang of airtight doors and hatches, starsailors hurrying to their stations, and the general cacophony associated with securing a starship from deep space. It was never easy for an active Helmsman to ride as a passenger, but at least he wasn't staring at a bulkhead as the powerful little warship settled purposefully toward the thick undercast—he hated riding that way.

The deck trembled slightly as stumpy Zinu Corbeil in the left seat turned up power in preparation for the roiling storms that were part and parcel of entry to the planet-girding Imperial Fleet base below. Brim chuckled. Corbeil—a Lieutenant Commander—spoke with a Rhodorian dialect you could carry in a bucket. The man had a lot of rank for commanding a mere destroyer, and an elderly one at that. But drastic starship reductions in the past meant that often senior officers skippered the few ships that remained in service. Keeping an enemy at bay while rebuilding (and recrewing) a sadly neglected fleet was only one of a myriad of problems facing the Grand Galactic Empire of Emperor Onrad V after his recent declaration of war. And not all of those troubles came from his perennial adversary, the League of Dark Stars.

"Gimmas Tower Nineteen, Imperial V981 is with you out of twenty-four and a half for twenty-four," Sada Takanada broadcast to the Sector 19 Controller. Clearly younger than Corbeil, the diminutive Takanada looked as if she had recently graduated from the Helmsman's Academy—but she was probably nearer Brim's age of forty-seven than that of a cadet.

"Imperial V981:" the distant tower replied, "Sector Nineteen Control reads you. Continue descent and maintain one zero thousand. The altimeter nine two nine five."

Brim listened to the discourse with real interest. Approaches to Gimmas Haefdon were *routinely* difficult, even for old-timers like Corbeil. Storms kept Helmsmen busy with simple basics—like attempting to stay on course. Whenever traffic permitted, Controllers here kept close track of landing starships, especially little ones. And with *very* recent reactivation of the base, traffic was still light. Certainly not the madhouse he remembered from the last war, more than eleven years ago. He shook his head sadly at *that* thought—what wouldn't the Admiralty give to have that madhouse of ships today!

"Imperial V981: suggest a heading of two five zero two five to join the Blue-10 zero one zero radial inbound."

Corbeil put the helm over. "Imperial V981 turning two five zero," he answered. Only clicks later, the flames of reentry died in their wake and the little starship shuddered as her trilon-shaped hull met the first of Gimmas's famous turbulence. Soon they were driving along through the first ragged cloud tatters. At least four more layers of dirty-looking, wind-frayed clouds defined themselves below before perspective itself was swallowed in the murky undercast of the planet's dismal afternoon. As the starship descended into solid cloud, Corbeil and Takanada began their final checkout litany.

"Warning panel?"

"Check."

"Altimeters?"

"Verified."

"Landing lights . . ."

"Imperial V981: radio check," the distant Controller interrupted.

"Loud and clear," Takanada answered, "—and the lights are ON." Corbeil had now concentrated most of his considerable facilities on the helm. *Jacques Schneider* was tossing like a leaf in a millrace while rain and hail thundered against the forward Hyperscreens, instantly turning to steam on the outer layers of crystal still heated by their reentry.

Brim turned up the power on his seat restraints, then tightened his shoulder belts. He'd been through this particular soup a thousand times at least.

"Start the approach check, Sada."

"Ten degrees lift enhancers. . . ."

"Ten degrees."

"Auto flight panels. . . ."

"Imperial V981:" the tower Controller interrupted again, "reduce speed to one eight zero and descend to five thousand irals altitude."

"V981—speed to one eight zero and down to five thousand. Zinu, say again the auto flight panels."

"Checked."

The litany continued until, just short of two thousand irals altitude, little *Jacques Schneider* gamely plunged out of the overcast into a mounting gale and driving snow—ancient Gimmas was living up to her hard reputation for weather. Below in the gray afternoon murk, Brim could see ice-flecked rollers tossing wildly in column against slender causeways dotted with Karlsson lamps. Almost at the limit of his vision, a long goods train gave off tremendous sparks as it seemed to crawl across the arcing spans. *Relativity.* Brim knew it was doing at least five hundred c'lenyts each metacycle.

"Imperial V981: you're six c'lenyts from the marker," the

Tower announced. "Turn left to heading nine seven one and join the localizer at seventeen hundred. You are cleared for instrument approach one seven left."

"Fleet V981 acknowledges all of that," Corbeil answered. "Thank you. . . ."

Ahead, a land mass was materializing out of the gloomy mists. Here and there, beacons flashed indistinctly, and reflected daylight—such as it was—defined a maze of canals. Massive, silver-domed reactor towers dotted the snow-covered landscape. Brim shook his head. It was almost as if eleven years had suddenly compressed to nothing. Little more than a year ago the great sector harbor had appeared to be completely abandoned—frozen over and lifeless. Now, as they approached, thousands of Karlsson lights glowed everywhere among a myriad of buildings and odd-shaped structures that had once been buried in a hundred irals of snow.

"Sector Tower One Nine to Imperial V981: you are cleared to land three-seven left, wind one nine zero at fifty, gust to one one twelve."

"Thank you, Tower. . . ."

While Corbeil turned onto final, a point of ruby light burned through the mist at them—the landing vector. Moments later their own triangular shadow moved in beneath them and they were level, skimming just above the tops of the huge rollers. From long years of instinct, Brim glanced out the quarter window, judging their touchdown as if he were at the controls. The generators surged for a moment as the ship rotated slightly nose high, then great cascades of white water soared skyward on either side of the hull as Corbeil "plastered" the ship onto her "gravity foot," the hull-shaped depression in the water starships made when they were on the surface. Four orange lights appeared on the instrument panel as he shifted the generators into reverse, and a succession of graviton waves sent clouds of spray forward until the ship came to a halt a regulation twenty-five irals above her foot, pitching moderately in the ground swell.

"All hands secure from landfall operations. All hands secure from landfall operations,'' the blower announced. ''Go to your stations, all landing parties. Stand by mooring and fender beams. . . .''

''Nice landing, Commander,'' Brim said. The words were no mere courtesy. Corbeil had actually made the whole thing seem easy—which was, after all, a good bit of what Helmsmanship was all about. But nothing was particularly easy on Gimmas Haefdon. He knew. Years ago, he'd called the huge, frigid base ''home.''

Corbeil turned and grinned. ''Thanks, Captain Brim,'' he said. ''I watched you bring in those tricky little Mitchell Trophy racers a couple o' years back—so I take those words as quite a compliment.''

Brim nodded, feeling his face flush. ''I never had to land a racer on Gimmas,'' he returned as Corbeil taxied the little ship past a glowing buoy tossing in the swell and headed toward two age-blackened monoliths that marked the entrance to Sector 17's harbor. The horrible weather was what made the frozen planet such a perfect Fleet base. Nobody else but starsailors could be persuaded to go there.

Negotiating a maze of wide, stone-walled canals lined by rows of gravity pools—many occupied by huge freighters from all over the Empire—they headed through driving snow for a forest of massive shipyard cranes and a huge structure of ancient, age-blackened brick that Brim recognized as a finishing bay where recently completed starships were fitted out in preparation for Fleet duty. Clearly, this part of the great base would soon be in the business of building a fleet again. On either side of the canal, causeways were alive with scurrying vehicles of all kinds and shapes. Past a sharp curve, beacons began to strobe astride one of the gravity-pool ramps curving up from the water. Through the snow, he could make out two bundled figures on a corner of the old stone seawall, holding their ears against the noise as the starship approached. The taller was clearly a Sodeskayan Bear, splendidly dressed in his country's distinctive *papakha* (a tall black hat shaped like a woolly pillbox), high boots made of black leather so soft they bagged at the ankles, and a long, deep maroon Fleet Cloak cut on the lines of its Imperial counterpart. The other figure, dressed in the dark blue greatcloak of the Imperial Fleet wore an officer's cap and significant bands of gold above his cuffs. Both waved as Corbeil applied the gravity brakes and swung the starship's nose over a glowing Becton tube that led up the curving stone ramp to a gravity pool.

Outside on the obsidian hull, parties of deck hands in magnetic boots and clumsy-looking antiradiation mittens were already racing here and there to open hatches to activate the mooring systems. Generators surged for a moment as the ship's mass transferred from its gravity foot, and moments later, they were coasting onto the pool. Below, on the age-stained cobblestones, six spool-shaped repulsion generators filled the great, open cell with a reassuring yellow glow. Corbeil eased the ship into reverse for a moment while mooring beams leaped out to optical bollards along the pool's walls, surging and flashing as *Jacques Schneider* settled to her moorings. Then he glanced at Takanada, who grinned and nodded in return while a weathered brow clanked into place abaft the bridge and connected to the boarding port with a great rush of air.

''All hands stand by for local gravity,'' she announced as six jewels in an overhead panel switched from red to orange. ''All hands stand by for local gravity.''

Brim braced himself, watching Takanada reach up and touch each jewel in turn, turning it from orange to green. A momentary wave of nausea savaged his gut and he fought his gorge to a draw. During all his years in space, he'd never quite gotten used to The Switchover—just the momentary discomfort it brought. He shook his head wryly as the feeling rapidly passed. A lot of people never had any problems at all. . . .

''Finished with generators,'' Corbeil announced to the bearded visage of an Engineering Officer that appeared in a globular display.

''Aye, Captain.''

Simultaneously, the background rumble of gravity generators

died to the first silence Brim had encountered since the ship lifted off seven days previously.

They were down.

Brim had departed Avalon in such a hurry he had little in the way of baggage as he descended through the brow, dodging busy crewmen running past in both directions. He pulled his Fleet Cloak tighter around his neck and turned up the heat against blasts of cold air surging up from below. As he stepped outside into the snowy air, two figures resembling the pair he had spied on the seawall stepped forward. He recognized them almost immediately. "Dr. Borodov!" he exclaimed, first saluting the Sodeskayan officer, who returned the salute, then immediately engulfed him in a traditional Bear hug.

"Wilfooshka!" the Bear replied. "Seems like year of special holidays since I last laid eyes on you." Grand Duke (Doctor) Anastas Alexi Borodov was master of vast baronial estates in the deeply wooded lake country outside Holy Gromcow on the G.F.S.S. "Mother" planet of Sodeskaya itself, and—for Brim—as close to family as anyone alive. He was also perhaps the greatest Drive scientist in the known Universe. Both collars of his maroon Fleet Cloak were tipped in the black leather of the Sodeskayan Engineers and bore three stars, denoting a Colonel General. Graying fur on his great muzzle would have been chestnut-colored in his youth but was now as much silver as brown. Somewhat bowed by the years, he stood only a little taller than Brim's six-iral height, but his tiny eyes sparkled with youthful humor and prodigious intellect behind a pair of old-fashioned horn-rimmed spectacles. Enormous sideburns provided him with a most profoundly academic countenance despite a huge, wet nose of the sort that gave most Bears a slightly comic look in humans' eyes—until they'd seen one angry. They were the only warm-blooded beings in the galaxy who could enjoy Gimmas's weather. If anything, the original seed planets of the Great Federation were often colder.

Grinning, Brim emerged from the Bear's embrace only to encounter another old friend and mentor, now a Rear Admiral with a broad and a narrow gold band above the cuffs of his dark blue Imperial Fleet Cloak. Bosporus Gallsworthy—no one else in the Universe had *that* combination of dark complexion, thin, dry lips, pockmarked jowls, and eyes that could drill holes in hullmetal. Though Brim had long since surpassed the man's skills at the controls of a starship, he still considered Gallsworthy the greatest Helmsman of all times. An astounding Atalantan who had started out as a ground soldier, fighting in the first Imperio-Leaguer Wars at Ilepillag (947th Sector), Gallsworthy was wounded at the Emmos Confrontation, and then, by purposely losing his own medical records, transferred to the Fleet and became a Helmsman who helped destroy twenty Leaguer starships. "Hmm," he joked, returning Brim's salute. "Seems to me Alexi and I once shipped out with somebody who looks a lot like you."

The three starsailors originally met aboard the old T-class destroyer I.F.S. *Truculent* at the beginning of Brim's first tour of duty. "Interesting, Admiral," Brim replied, wrinkling his brow in mock recollection. "I believe I've heard of somebody like that. A real troublemaker, if memory serves."

Gallsworthy laughed. "A real troublemaker indeed!"

"Couldn't have been me, then," Brim continued, rolling his eyes heavenward. "I *never* make trouble."

"That's good to know," Gallsworthy said. "The fellow *was* about twenty years younger than you, now that I think about it."

"Nineteen, to be exact, Admiral," Brim chuckled. "But who's counting?"

"And here we are, still fighting a xaxtdamned war," Borodov growled. "Except this one we call Second Great War, and we've given ten-year rest period to Leaguer zukeeds."

Brim nodded. "Looks like they've made the most of it, too. Doctor."

"So we have heard," Gallsworthy replied. "And of course you were among the first to sample their new fighting skills, Wilf. Alexi and I are most anxious to hear about your adventures as a mercenary in Fluvanna."

Snow stung Brim's face and he grinned. "As I am anxious to hear about this assignment of mine, Admiral," he said. "And rumors of a new ship, General."

"Aha!" Borodov exclaimed to Gallsworthy, a huge grin baring his gem-inlaid fangs. "If you are no longer trouble-maker, you have at least lost none of your curiosity." He peered over his glasses and nodded to a Fleet-blue staff skimmer hovering nearby in the passenger parking area. "Come, Wilf Ansorivich," he said. "We will first drop you at the Visiting Officers Quarters so you can freshen up. Later, over goblet of Logish Meem in Officers Bar, Bosporus and I will introduce you to many new things—some you may even want to hear about."

"We'll soon be needing all the 'things' we can get our hands on," Brim said, starting off for the waiting skimmer. "Because from what I've seen of the Leaguers and their Second Great War so far, they're going to be tougher to deal with than ever before. . . ."

The period of time Brim and many of his contemporaries already were referring to as the Second Great War existed only as a name. In reality, it was no more than a logical extension of a larger struggle that entered temporary hiatus eleven years previously during Standard Year 52000 with the abdication of Emperor Nergol Triannic, the League-proposed Treaty of Garak, and a concomitant armistice until the treaty could be approved.

Shortly after these three critical events, the Empire found itself divided into hostile camps of war-weary reconciliationist groups and equally war-weary militants. Most reconciliationists coalesced rapidly into the politically powerful Congress for Intra-Galactic Accord (CIGA). Militants, however—comprising various military and veteran organizations—were still required to concentrate the bulk of their efforts on such workaday tasks as securing the farflung bulwarks of Empire. They therefore steadily lost political influence at all levels, and subsequently, after furious debate throughout the Imperial Parliament, the League's treaty—already signed by League Emperor Nergol

Triannic—was pushed through by CIGA Chief Puvis Amherst. It was formally ratified by (then) Emperor Greyffin IV two days prior to the Year's End holiday in Avalon, 52000.

Amid vociferous Admiralty protests and resignations, Imperial Fleet reductions (with resultant base closings) began promptly in 52001 to rigid schedules set forth in the new treaty. Each of the ex-antagonists chose referees to oversee the other's disarmament progress. After two successive Imperial Fleet reductions in 52002 and 52003, out-of-work veterans gathered for a "March on Avalon." Most departed peacefully after Parliament vetoed cash bonuses recommended by Greyffin IV; however, other, more adamant veterans were forcibly expelled by special detachments of Imperial Marines wearing the special CIGA flash on their uniforms and lead by CIGA-aligned officers.

A further reduction in Fleet strength during 52004 completed Imperial disarmament requirements and resulted in the smallest Fleet in the Empire's history. Half a galaxy away in Tarrott, Puvis Amherst personally confirmed similar reductions in League strength, but the scattering of starsailors who remained loyal to the Empire knew the League's claims were little more than fabrications. Unfortunately, a clamor of pacifist emotion sweeping the Empire—though ultimately emotional and uninformed—was nevertheless politically unassailable. And while the League secretly built a new and much more powerful fleet, the Empire continued to sink into impotency.

In 52005, culmination of a three-year study by the blue-ribbon Interdominion Reparations Committee resulted in a report fixing League war liability at 132 billion credits, to be indemnified during the next ten Standard Years. Zoguard Grobermann, League Minister of State, promised that the Chancellery would, "take the sum under advisement," but no further action was forthcoming.

In 52006, the anti-League president of Beta Jago, Konrad Igno, was assassinated by an unknown murderer during the traditional mid-year holiday interval in that dominion. League Minister for Public Consensus Hanna Notrom denied any knowledge of the act, and soon afterward, the League's Supreme

Council even enacted laws forbidding assassination to prove once and for all their peaceful intentions.

Early in 52007, exiled Nergol Triannic published his semibiographical *Ughast Niefft* as a formal declaration of proper League objectives. By Avalonian midsummer, League sympathizers annexed all planets of the Gammil'lt star system at the request of openly League-endorsing Chancellor, I. B. Groenlj. At year's end, CIGA elements in the Imperial Parliament itself passed the Cavir-Wilvo Bill posing stringent limits on Imperial starship manufacture.

Soon after Standard Year 52008 began, exiled Nergol Triannic returned in triumph to Tarrott and resumed the reins of League government wearing the outlawed black uniform of a Controller. Less than one month later, Conrad Zorn, prominent intragalactic traveler and industrialist, was found murdered after accusing the League of secretly expanding its Deep Space Fleet. By midyear, Triannic repudiated the League's reparations debt and reintroduced compulsory military service for all League citizens. At the end of the League's Festival of Conquest holidays (Imperial Standard Date: 2 Nonad, 52008), Controller forces entered and occupied planets of The Torond, enthroned League-sympathizer Rogan LaKarn as ruler, and proclaimed the "eternal" political union of League and Torond.

Midway through 52009, Zoguard Grobermann and Hanna Notrom jointly announced League incorporation of the Zathian planetary system, as result of a plebiscite. Soon afterward, Nergol Triannic issued a stern warning to the dominion of Fluvanna concerning treatment of League citizens dwelling on its planets.

Early in 52010, after CIGA-inspired frustration of numerous Imperial attempts to defend the important Dominion of Fluvanna (supplier of nearly one hundred percent of the Empire's Drive crystals), Emperor Greyffin IV formed the Imperial Volunteer Group (IVG) from the first eleven Starfury starcruisers delivered, "leasing" not only the warships but their crews to Fluvanna for a year. Shortly thereafter, League forces invaded and occupied the Dominion of Beta Jago, ignoring protests from throughout the galaxy. Two months later—on trumped-up charges, Triannic also declared war on Fluvanna, thus supplying a spark that would eventually reignite war itself.

Until well into 52011, CIGAs throughout the Imperial Parliament prevented implementation of the Empire's mutual-assistance treaty with Fluvanna. However, with the abdication of Greyffin IV, Onrad V became Emperor and declared war on the League even as IVG forces destroyed huge League space fortifications at Zonga'ar and set Triannic's timetable for conquest back nearly a Standard Year. Within a month, the new Imperial Emperor dissolved the IVG, ordering his battle-proven crews back to a newly expanding Imperial Fleet, where the veterans would be spread throughout the Home Fleet in preparation for the inevitable Battle of Avalon. Wilf Brim—commander of the Zonga'ar raid—formed the vanguard of this historic migration.

Later, after a luxuriously long shower and shave in a washroom large enough to turn around in, Brim donned the only clean uniform he had with him and headed for the lobby. A hodgepodge of officers in military dress from all over the Empire relaxed here and there in the low-ceilinged room, some dozing in battered couches, others puffing on spice-filled pipes while they idly sifted the news on global displays. Like lobbies of the other thousand-odd VOQs Brim had seen—all painted in the same two tones of wearisome green—it was one of two escapes from the ultimate boredom of a lonely transient's cubicle. He was headed for the other . . .

"Bar's down the road, Captain," a desk clerk said perspicaciously. "Shall I call a skimmer?"

"Thanks, starsailor," Brim answered, "but after a week in a destroyer . . ."

"Aye, sir," the rating said with a smile. "You'd rather walk. I know the feelin.' About a half c'lenyt to starboard on your left. Can't miss it."

Brim nodded and headed for the door. Unless you liked snow—a *lot* of snow—Gimmas Haefdon offered little else than vast amounts of work and drinking. Bars for all ranks tended to be large and crowded.

Outside, the wind had lost some of its intensity and the snow was falling less heavily. He returned the salute of a rating who was operating one of Gimmas's ubiquitous snow shovels—the little machine chirped and scurried off to the side of the parking lot as he passed—then he started down the dark street, boots crunching on the fresh powder. No odors on Gimmas Haefdon, he thought for the millionth time as he walked in the muffled stillness. Smells of all kinds been frozen solid for centuries.

Ahead, through gently falling snow, the street dwindled in perspective to diminishing circles of light cast by a long column of Karlsson lamps placed in military precision along the center divider. Somewhere in the distance he could hear the sound of big gravity generators spooling up. Ancient, shadowed goods houses, one more massive than the next, loomed on either side, darkened reminders of past Imperial might. Here and there, however, lights appeared in odd windows. Onrad V's hoary old Imperial Fleet was once again on the upswing after more than ten years of intentional neglect, caused from within by a traitor's organization, the Congress for Intra-Galactic Accord.

A starship thundered invisibly close overhead, its gravs at full lift-off power. It was already lost in Gimmas's swirling clouds. Brim laughed softly to himself, remembering his early days at the base as a green Sub-lieutenant, fresh from the Helmsman's Academy on balmy Ariel. Even discounting the miserable weather of Carescria, his homeland in one of the Empire's poorest sectors, after four Standard Years on balmy Ariel, he'd found himself quite unprepared for Gimmas's fulsome climate. Yet he'd eventually come to think of the great base as home. He certainly didn't consider his native Carescria as any kind of home. And besides, at the time, Margot was here. . . .

He sighed wistfully as the snowy darkness merged through nearly seventeen years to the night he met Her Serene Majesty, Margot Effer'wyck, Princess of the Effer'wyck Dominions and first cousin to Onrad, the present Imperial ruler. It had been a routine wardroom party aboard little I.F.S. *Truculent*. She was there as an ordinary Lieutenant—a hardworking one at that, he'd quickly discovered. And if the tall, amply built woman were not the most beautiful he'd ever encountered, she'd still appealed to him in a most fundamental manner. Even after all these years, he could picture her that night: artfully tousled golden curls and soft, expressive blue eyes, flashing with nimble intelligence. Skin almost painfully fair, brushed lightly with pink high in the cheeks. And when she smiled, her brow formed the most engaging frown he could imagine. Moist lips, long, shapely legs, small breasts, and . . . He bit his lip.

They'd become lovers long after they'd fallen in love. She a princess of Effer'wyck, the Empire's most influential dominion—he a commoner from the shabbiest sector imaginable. For a while, the desperate absurdity of galactic war had canceled out that awesome gap in status. But reality intervened soon enough, forcing a political marriage between Brim's Princess and Rogan LaKarn, Baron of the Torond—a union designated to cement the bond between his massive palatinate and the Empire.

Afterward, the two star-crossed lovers continued as best they could, carrying on a tawdry affair filled with endless stretches of longing punctuated by brilliant flashes of their own special passion. For a while it had worked—even after ersatz peace forced a return to "normal" canons of class and status. But eventually distance, a child, and Margot's growing addiction to the Leaguers' devastating narcotic TimeWeed ate away their ties until only longing remained, buried deep within Brim's psyche to mask the pain it brought. Now, he didn't know if she were even still alive.

Twin convoys of immense lorries droned past, loaded with massive shapes under billowing tarpaulins; their traction engines whipped the fresh snow into swirling eddies. The rushing columns were gone in a moment, swallowed up by the night and the snow as if it had never existed. Not even tracks in the snow marked the passage of the big gravity skimmers.

He snorted. The lorries were a lot like Margot and himself,

he thought, wryly brushing snow from his face. As if they'd never met. Even the Emperor's sacrifice of their love had come to nothing, for in spite of a marriage linking LaKarn to the royal family itself, the preening bully eventually allied himself with the League of Dark Stars and took Margot to the side of the enemy—or so it sometimes seemed to those who kept track of such things. Until little more than a month ago, that is, when she'd laid her own life on the line to save his, then disappeared from the face of the Universe in the explosion of a giant space fortification.

Grinding his teeth, he put *that* from his mind. Much as he wished to the contrary, there was nothing he could do about Margot Effer'wyck-Lakarn at present, and he had a number of other pressing matters on his mind, not the least of which was his new assignment. . . .

"Hoy! Brim! Only Bears walk on Gimmas when they can ride."

The voice yanked his mind back to the present. Beside him, a command car hovered at curbside with its door open. Inside, illuminated only by instrument lights, he could see a long, thin nose terminating in an enormous mustache. Behind it were the rheumy eyes and painfully thin physique of Mark Valerian, designer of I.F.S. *Starfury,* name ship for a whole class of light cruisers that had revolutionized space warfare. In Brim's estimation, the man was easily the premiere starship designer of his times. "Bears and Carescrians, Mark," he replied with a grin of pleasure. "We're both a little daft."

"I'll drink to that," Valerian said matter-of-factly. "Anybody who'd fly those racing starships I designed *has* to be a little daft."

Brim grinned as his mind went spinning backward in years. Probably he *had* been a little daft to fly Valerian's racers. It all seemed so long ago, but the whole thing had begun only a few years previously—in 52005, if he remembered correctly—when Sodeskayan physicist U.V. Popova theorized the Reflecting HyperLight Drive. Based upon Sheldon Travis's (then) obscure Special Theory Number Six, Popova's hypothesis foreshadowed a whole new generation of starships. Under normal circumstances, practical applications of such a radical new Drive would have required years of experimentation. Instead, the singular rise to intergalactic prominence of a yearly competition for starship speed, the Mitchell Trophy race, spurred Sodeskayan development of the reflecting Drive to such a pace that prototypes were available for use by Imperial racers within three years, permitting Imperial Helmsmen like Brim to win permanent possession of the trophy—while League Drive development continued along a more conventional path. This seemingly arcane technological achievement combined with simultaneous development by Designer Mark Valerian of the classic Sherrington Starfury produced historic results only a few Standard Years afterward.

And despite the Starfury's legendary reputation, there was really no mystique about Valerian's design. It was a straightforward merger of all the technical knowledge of the time into one composite unit of machinery, including its superb Krasni-Peych Drive, that, with the spaceframe, embodied every experience of high-speed starflight gathered from the Mitchell Trophy races. In the case of the Reflecting-Drive Starfury, everything came right at the psychological moment—a rare event in starship and Drive design. . . .

"Daft or not, I'll drive you to the bar anyway," Valerian continued, snapping Brim from his reverie. "How about that for compassion?"

Brim relented; no exercise tonight—again. "You've got a deal," he said, climbing into the warmth of the passenger seat. "And speaking of daft, what kind of new starship brings you to Gimmas this time?" he asked. "Especially when it's summertime back home at the Sherrington labs on Lys."

"Starfuries," Valerian said, easing the skimmer into forward. "At least for the present."

Brim turned and frowned. "But you designed *Starfury* years ago," he said. "Nothing new?"

"Oh, we're kickin' around a few new ideas on Lys, Brim," Valerian drawled with a little smile. "But I didn't say *Starfury*;

I said Starfuries.'' He winked as they pulled into a circular driveway lined by the twisted, skeletal forms of trees that had been dead for centuries. ''New Starfuries, my friend,'' he added. ''Like Starfury Mark 1C killer ships.''

''Killer ships? Mark, Starfuries are light cruisers, not short-range killer ships.''

''One Cs are killer ships, Brim. Trust me,'' Valerian laughed. ''All they share with normal Starfuries is hullmetal. Single helms. No provisions for long-range cruising at all. I've packed every cubic iral with amplification gear for the new disruptors.''

''New disruptors, too?''

''You bet—425s.''

''Four *what*?'' Brim demanded, stepping out onto the snow. ''I thought 406s were the biggest they make.''

''Not anymore,'' Valerian said. ''And the new 1Cs carry *fourteen* 425s in seven turrets. Superfocused, no less; we brought the technology from Theobold Interspace in Lixor.''

Brim held the bar door for his friend as tides of familiar warm odors swept past him into the cold air outside. A thousand subtle flavors of camarge cigarettes mixed with Hogge'Poa, meem, perfume, and life itself. ''The Great Neutrals,'' he laughed at the mention of Theobold Interspace. ''Those Lixorian zukeeds manufacture—and peddle—more weapons than anybody else in the galaxy. Why, they're so peaceful, they almost make me sick.''

''Yeah, you're right,'' Valerian admitted. ''But at least they don't do much of the shooting.''

''They leave that up to their clients,'' Brim said, handing his Fleet Cape to a shapely rating. ''Like the xaxtdamned Leaguers.''

''And *us*, now,'' Valerian reminded him. ''From what I hear, you're gonna like the merchandise.''

''If it kills Leaguer starships easier, I'll *love* it,'' Brim said grimly. ''The bastards we fought in Fluvanna gave us quite a run for the money.'' Through an ancient wooden arch, he could see Borodov and Gallsworthy signaling from the crowded twilight and started into the room.

"Disruptors won't be the only things you'll like about the 1C," Valerian assured him.

"Somehow I have little doubt about that," Brim called over his shoulder. "Like Logish Meem! Thank you, Doctor," he said, taking a goblet from the old Bear. He sniffed its pungent contents. "Excellent, excellent!" he exclaimed, examining the deep ruby liquid against light from an excellently counterfeited fireplace—firewood on dead Gimmas was worth a king's ransom.

"Tastes as good as it looks!" Valerian said, appreciatively sipping a goblet proffered by Gallsworthy. "It once again proves that Drive systems are not the only subjects on which Bears are born masters."

"Is good to be appreciated for truly important things," Borodov chuckled. "No Drive system can compare with excellent Logish Meem."

"And speaking of important things..." Gallsworthy interrupted.

"You going to talk about work already?" Valerian asked with a twinkle in his eye.

"War," Gallsworthy corrected.

"War's work enough for me," Brim observed bleakly, refilling his goblet from a fresh decanter silently placed on the table by a rating. After six Standard Days at Hyperspeed in a cramped destroyer, he was beginning to feel the trip.

"It's war's work we need to talk about, Brim," Gallsworthy said, turning abruptly serious. "All of us."

"Is calling meeting to official order," Borodov intoned, raising his goblet. "To His Majesty, Onrad the Fifth," he toasted.

"To Onrad the Fifth," the others chorused earnestly. "Long may he reign!"

"Now, Brim," Gallsworthy began, "all three of us are here tonight specifically to get you started in your new job. What do you want to hear about first?"

Brim sat back and considered. The meem was warm in his stomach and he was tired. If he really had his choice, he wanted to hear about how to get back to his room and some sack time. "Well," he chuckled, "Mark introduced me to the

Starfury 1C on the way over. So I'm assuming I'll be flying one."

"You've got that right," Gallsworthy said with a smile. "But you'll be doing a lot more than flying."

"I was afraid of that," Brim said wryly. "The Wing Commander thing. . . ."

"Yeah," Gallsworthy laughed, "the Wing Commander thing. You want to hear about that next?"

"I've got a choice?" Brim asked.

"Certainly," Gallsworthy answered. "We can also talk about your new job as Wing Commander. Which one?"

Brim grinned resignedly. "Well then, how about an introduction to my new job, Admiral?" he said.

"Ah! Perceptive choice, Wilf Ansor," Borodov rumbled.

"You always were lucky at thinks like that," Valerian observed with mock gravity.

"Things won't be as bad as you think, Brim," Gallsworthy promised. "You'll get plenty of time at the helm of a starship, believe me. It's just that you'll have a number of other duties, too—with the same importance as Helmsmanship. And you won't be doin' anything that you haven't already done setting up that IVG base at Varnholm Manor for our friend Baxter Calhoun. Mostly getting things done and keeping people out of trouble. It all came out pretty well on Fluvanna, didn't it, now?"

Brim shrugged. "The IVG was a pretty special outfit, Admiral," he said. "All veterans with years of experience. I think anybody could have set up the base at Varnholm—especially with Chief Barbousse to help."

"You'll have the Chief as soon as we can fly him out here," Gallsworthy asserted. "Emperor's personal orders on that."

"And that's all there is to being a Wing Commander?" Brim asked, cocking his head suspiciously. "Just like Fluvanna?"

"A few differences," Gallsworthy said. "This time, for instance, you'll be doing all those 'commander' jobs *officially*."

"And . . . ?"

"Well, you won't start with experienced crews like you did

in Fluvanna, either. This time, you'll have to build an organization from the ground up—and see to their training. We'll get you the best people we can lay our hands on, but aside from being individually talented, they won't be a fighting force by anybody's definition. You'll have to turn 'em into that."

"And," Brim continued, wincing. He'd been waiting for something like that.

"And," Gallsworthy continued, "Baxter Calhoun won't be around to let you off the hook after you've got it all set up. It's a permanent assignment—at least as permanent as anything about the Fleet."

Brim nodded as Borodov refilled his goblet. "Where?" he asked. "Here?"

"Avalon."

"Avalon?" Brim exclaimed in relief. "You mean Avalon as in . . . ?"

"As in the Imperial capital planet," Gallsworthy laughed, "—or at least orbiting *above* it. Now *that*'s not hard to take, is it?

"Not hardly, Admiral," Brim agreed.

"I'd vote for that and lend a hand stuffin' the ballot box," Valerian put in.

Brim chuckled. "The 30 Defense Wing, Admiral?"

Gallsworthy nodded. "They called it 30 Wing during the last war," he said. "Got deactivated right after the Treaty of Garak. This time, it'll have two squadrons: 32 and 610. I've already got 32 Squadron set up in one of the new, orbiting FleetPort satellites under Commander Karen Rumsey. You two met in Atalanta during the Payless Operation years ago."

"Karen Rumsey," Brim said, nodding his head. "Yeah. I remember her. Fine Helmsman if memory serves."

"Fine administrator, too," Gallsworthy added. "Unfortunately, she's not much of a Squadron Leader at the helm. She puts too much emphasis on formation flying—one of those damn-fool ideas the CIGAs pushed so well when they had everybody's ear. Form over function—looks great but doesn't do much for winning wars." He shrugged. "Your problem now. She's running sixteen Defiant-class cruisers in four flights of four and one in reserve. You and she will have to get together by KA'PPA for a while because you'll be too busy helpin' set up 610 Squadron from scratch."

"Who'll I have to command *that* squadron?" Brim demanded. "I've got a strong recommendation if you haven't assigned anybody yet."

"How about Toby Moulding?" Gallsworthy asked with a grin.

Brim laughed. "Since Toby's my recommendation," he said, "I'm in violent agreement."

"He'll be tied up for a while helpin' to shut down the IVG," Gallsworthy said. "But I'll have him here as soon as Calhoun releases him." He laughed. "I used all my 'obs' with Calhoun gettin' you assigned directly."

"'Obs'?" Brim asked.

"As in 'obligations'," Gallsworthy explained. "He owed me a few for supportin' his IVG in Fluvanna."

"Guess I owe you a couple of 'obs' myself, then," Brim acknowledged.

"You'll pay 'em," Gallsworthy said. "You'll take care of quite a few operating 610 Squadron all by yourself."

"We'll be flying 1Cs?" Brim asked.

"Fifteen of 'em," Gallsworthy assured him. "Three flights of four. That'll give you two in reserve."

Brim frowned. "By my count, Admiral," he said, "you're one Starfury short."

"You count well, Brim," Gallsworthy said with a sly smile. "But I think I'll let brother Valerian tell you about your third 'reserve ship'."

"P7350," the designer said. "Killer ships don't get names. She's the first production Starfury 1C off the lines—proved out the manufacturin' plan. And she's *here,* not more than a c'lenyt away in a finishing shed. Skeleton crew from the factory brought her here. They've been checking her out for a week. We'll go have a look in the morning."

"P7350's yours, too, Wilf," Gallsworthy said. "She and her

crew will be your personal responsibility while you're forming the new squadron, so you won't lack left-seat time here at Gimmas. After you get to Avalon, though, you'll be expected to take any available ship into combat whenever you can."

Brim laughed. "Sounds good to me," he said trenchantly, "I become bored so easily. . . ."

"Not much danger of that, Wilf Ansor," Borodov observed, "at least from what friend Nikolai Yanuarievich messages."

"What's Nik say?" Brim asked.

" 'Phony war' will last only so long as it takes Triannic to rebuild what you blew up with space fort at Zonga'ar. Then, Voof!"

"Doesn't take Nik Ursis and the Sodeskayan Intelligence Community to bet that ol' Wilf here is going to be a busy man back on Avalon," Valerian said. "The CIGAs are bound to make a stink about you blowing up one of our own battleships."

"Yeah, Brim," Gallsworthy said with a frown. "Things have been pretty quiet, considering that you destroyed I.F.S. *Queen Elidian* with every hand on board. Even if she was crewed by a bunch of CIGA traitors."

Brim grimaced. "Except for the CIGAs themselves," he said, "nobody felt worse than I did about those Imperial ships we destroyed at Zonga'ar. But . . ."

"But," Gallsworthy interrupted, "you weren't a member of the Imperial Fleet at the time. Right?"

"That's right, Admiral," Brim assured him. "At the time, I was working as a mercenary in the Fluvannian Fleet."

"An' all the zukeed CIGAs aboard the *Queen* were tryin' to keep you from the Leaguers' space fort," Valerian added.

"So the *Queen* had to go. Right, Wilf Ansor?" Borodov observed.

"Pretty much, that's it, Dr. Borodov," Brim said. "But it was still pretty awful." He shook his head. "The old *Queen*. . . For years, she was the largest, fastest, and most handsome warship anywhere. Why, she was the Fleet when I was a kid." He ground his teeth and stared into his goblet as if its dark liquid could hide him from the memories. After more than a month, his decision to destroy the historic battleship still bothered him. And it had little to do with the crew of traitors who died aboard her. When he looked up, the other three were still staring at him.

"Word is that Margot Effer'wyck had something to do with that battle, Wilf Ansor," Borodov said softly.

"The word's right, Doctor," Brim said. "Crazy as it sounds, she was aboard the fort through most of our attack. When we ruptured the doors where they were keeping her prisoner—with her zukeed husband's approval—she escaped to one of the fort's message rooms and began transmitting. Everybody on *Starfury*'s bridge probably saw her in my global display. Nadia Tissaurd—my Number One on *Starfury*—was looking right at her when she told us where to plant the torpedoes."

"You mean *Margot* told you where to hit the fort?" Valerian demanded.

"None other," Brim answered.

"But . . . if the scuttlebutt's true, not a month earlier, she was *also* the big lure in a Leaguer attempt to ambush you in Magor City. . . ."

"That's how it looks to a lot of people."

"Somehow I doubt if that's what *you* think, Wilf" Gallsworthy said.

Brim shrugged gloomily. The meem and exhaustion were beginning to get the best of him. "Probably doesn't matter what *anybody* thinks," he replied with a weary shrug. "It's not very likely she survived when the fort blew up." He shook his head. "That explosion xaxtdamned wrecked *Starfury,* and we were a long way off when the energy wave hit us. Close as she was to it . . . Well, unless she made it to the protection of that asteroid shoal, she's nothing but free ions now."

"Perhaps Lady Fortune was more kind to her than that," Borodov suggested.

"You've heard something?" Brim asked, feeling a surge of excitement in spite of his fatigue.

The older Bear nodded. "When word concerning the Princess first reached me," he said, "I caused certain . . . 'inquiries' to be made through Sodeskayan military intelligence organizations." He smiled. "Sometimes, being Grand Duke has its rewards."

"And you found . . . ?" Brim prodded, now completely alert.

"Almost nothing, at first, my friend," Borodov answered, "Not until last week did I receive any sort of word that held promise of her survival."

"What did you hear . . . ?"

"Last week, Wilfooshka, rumors surfaced in remote part of galaxy concerning golden-haired 'princess' passing along some old trade routes a few Standard Weeks or so following your raid." He sighed. "Not *much* to go on, but enough to keep flame of hope alight, eh? Especially since some reports alleged that she was accompanied by a child."

"*Anything's* better than the certainty she's dead," Brim said earnestly. "At least there's a chance."

"A chance," Borodov said, staring off into another time. "Odd," he mused, "but I can remember evening you two met as if it were yesterday. Nikolai Yanuarievich and I were there, in wardroom of old I.F.S. *Truculent*." He shook his head wistfully. "Somehow, I never dreamed Universe would allow such beauty to end up in such trouble. . . ."

"Thanks," Brim said, refilling his goblet. Margot Effer'wyck was out of his life now, and he *had* to keep it that way, otherwise he'd spend the remainder of his days mooning after her memory. With an almost physical effort, he forced her from his mind. "And how is Nik getting along these days?" he asked.

"Ah, he has been inquiring after you," the old Bear said with a smile. "From correspondence, he seems to be having time of his life working on intelligence projects."

"Nik? In Intelligence?"

"Oh, yes," Borodov said with raised eyebrows. "You know how he loves theoretical work."

"What's his field now?" Brim asked. "I never attempted to keep track of his interests."

Borodov frowned. "Curious," he said. "I do not know

exactly *what* he does there. But you will remember his fascination with remote aiming systems. Last time he visited me at Manor house outside Gromcow, he talked at some length about KA'PPA COMM-based systems that could triangulate two or more beams at great distances with terrific accuracy. My guess is he is working on something like that. But who knows?" He laughed. "As he said himself, 'If you want to keep something concealed from your enemy, you do *not* disclose it to your friends.' So we talked of other things. . . ."

After that, conversation became a lot less structured as the four veteran warriors settled down to rare moments of peace and a chance to reminisce about old times and places. Emperor Nergol Triannic's League of Dark Stars was a fierce, remorseless enemy. Soon enough it would be on the march again through civilized portions of the galaxy. Then, there would be little time for anything but fighting. Tonight, a little repose yet remained in the Universe. A very little. . . .

Brim awoke to the insistent chiming of a communicator from his nightstand. He could recall very little more of the evening—except that he'd collected a considerable meem hangover. Nudging the little device into operation, he heard Mark Valerian on the other end.

"Let's go see a starship, Wilf," the designer said.

"Mark," Brim groaned at the privacy darkened display, "it's got to be the middle of the night." No light emanated from the room's small window at all.

"On Gimmas, who can tell?" Valerian laughed.

"How come you don't have a hangover?" Brim complained.

"Oh, I *do*," Valerian assured him. "But they don't last long once you're outside in the cold."

Brim chuckled in spite of himself. "I can believe that," he said. "All right, I'll be down in a couple of cycles. You're in the lobby?"

"Not yet," Valerian said. "I'm still in my quarters. But by the time you drag yourself downstairs, I'll be there."

Less than a metacycle later, the two were hurtling along

through driving snow in a rattle-packed staff skimmer that was clearly left over from *early* in the last war. The heater was nonoperative, and steam rose in clouds from the PyroMug of cvceese' Brim held in his gloves. Valerian sipped from a similar mug with one hand while he navigated with the other. Riding with the designer was always a thrill for Brim—much like being in a dogfight. He always came out of it with the adrenaline flowing and renewed appreciation for life.

"You say they flew the new 1C in from Bromwich only a week ago?" Brim asked.

"The 'week ago' part's right, Wilf," Valerian said, skidding around a corner at high speed—and just missing the all-too-solid-looking concrete base of a Karlsson lamp, "but they didn't bring her in from the factory at Bromwich. She was built 'way out in the asteroid mining sections of Carescria. In one of the shadow factories old Emperor Greyffin IV funded in secret a couple of years ago."

"Factories in Carescria?" Brim asked in amazement. "They don't make anything out there, except maybe poverty and too many children. I know. That was *my* sector of the Empire. At least it was until I managed to escape.

"Oh, yeah," Valerian said. "I'd almost forgotten. You *are* a Carescrian, even though you don't talk like one." He frowned. "Anyway, Greyffin got *something* in his craw about the place, 'cause from what I understand, he started a number of secret complexes there to build military starships." With no hands on the tiller, he brushed ice from the windshield as they passed the rusting, snow-covered remains of a crashed starship—one of hundreds that dotted the landscape around Gimmas's great starship wharves. The wrecks—both Imperial and enemy—were left over from one of thousand-odd failed attempts by the League to put the base out of business.

Brim sipped his cvceese', the hot, sweet liquid searing his tongue as it came from the PyroMug. "Carescria," he mused, thinking back through what seemed like centuries to his youth in that depressed region—before his family had been wiped out by one of the Leaguers' surprise attacks that heralded the beginning of the last war. Then, the only Carescrian industry had been asteroid mining. Brim had learned to fly starships by piloting the infamously dangerous Carescrian ore barges—worn-out military space barges with huge Drive chambers and oversize gravity generators that could race to the smoke-belching hullmetal smelters that polluted the natural beauty of nearly all (so-called) "habitable" Carescrian planets. He'd been one of the lucky ones who managed to escape—and only because he'd been blessed at birth with extraordinarily keen vision and the quick reflexes of a rothcat. . . . But had he really escaped Carescria? Not if one judged by what other people said. It was always "you *are* a Carescrian," not "you *were*." After years of trying to distance himself from anything even slightly Carescrian, his impoverished youth still seemed to taint him.

"That shut you up, Wilf," Valerian commented as he pulled of the highway, across five sets of glowing, tube-shaped tram tracks, and through the gates of a parking lot beside a gigantic finishing bay—probably the one he'd spotted from *Jacques Schneider.* The mammoth brick structure was surrounded on three sides by rows of huge, roaring generators and squat, finned towers that flashed alternatively in deep blue and reddish orange. Overhead, fat cables arced from great conduits in the surface to connect with dozens of shimmering globes mounted on the building's roof.

Brim smiled distantly. "Memories," he explained. "Some go pretty deep."

Valerian nodded. "I think I understand," he said. "I visited Carescria a couple years ago. . . ."

"You had to *live* there, Mark," Brim muttered, wondering for the ten billionth time what it was that made him love the Empire in spite of what hundreds of years of heartless-but-legal plundering had made of his native dominion.

"Yeah," Valerian replied after a pause, pulling to a halt near two sets of doors under a small canopy, "I'll be glad to take your word for it. . . ."

* * *

Inside, the cavernous building was divided into four huge chambers, each capable of housing at least three cruiser-sized starships. For the most part, two of the mammoth rooms were cold and empty—as they had existed since the great base was shut down by the CIGAs in the first years of "peace" after the disastrous Treaty of Garak. Rusting donkey engines rested ghostlike on darkened tracks beneath old-fashioned gantry cranes that could still lift whole Drive sections from their chambers. Brim and Valerian passed through these rooms aboard a clanking little tram that echoed in the emptiness like some noisy insect caught in the Catacombs of Savnie'er. But long before passing through the door to the third chamber, they could hear the bustle that emanated from the other side. Glare from hundreds of ceiling-mounted Karlsson lamps was almost painful as they emerged from tomblike stillness to the noisy commotion of an active finishing bay.

Two of the room's thundering gravity pools were occupied by what were unmistakably Sherrington Starfury-class starships, attached to an army of monitoring instruments through what looked like thousands of glittering cables. Handsome vessels in obsidian hullmetal, the cruisers were designed to enhance high-speed atmospheric maneuvering by extremely clean exterior configurations. They were tri-hulled, in the Valerian tradition: a main fuselage complemented on either side by "pontoon" units mounted slightly below the centerline. These housed three Admiralty A876 gravity generators each and were connected to the main hull through "trouser" structures characteristic of the racing starships produced earlier by Sherrington HyperSpace Works. Raked, low-set bridge/deckhouse units protruded some way back from their sharply tapered bows, and except for blisters housing the main battery, these constituted the only slipstream disturbances anywhere. The turrets were also the most visible difference between Mk1s and Mk1Cs, for the latter carried two twin-mount turrets atop the main fuselage instead of one. Of course!—new superfocused disruptor pairs emanating from the sheered-off turrets *were* slightly thicker. They'd have to be if the big weapons were to house a boost path close enough to the main feeds for efficient cooling. And . . . *yes*, the forward Hyperscreens *were* raked even further. He nodded. That ought to clear up the ship's nasty bent toward overheat during high-speed landfall operations. By Voot, she was a bit longer, too. Had to be. On Mk1 models, the Drive-chamber hatch line ran just past center on the trousers. This one made it only midway along the fillet. And what else . . . ? In his utter fascination, he forgot all about Valerian until chuckling intruded. . . .

"I take it you approve of how she looks," the designer said, softly nudging the Carescrian's elbow.

"Count on it, friend," Brim said, emerging slowly from his reverie. "You always did have a penchant for handsome starships."

"If they look good . . . " Valerian prompted, holding his hands palm outward in the manner of a popular children's game.

"They usually fly that way, too," Brim finished like a litany. It was the oldest aphorism in the engineering handbook—but it rarely failed. Sherrington Starfuries followed the dictum exactly. They were a pure, delicate pleasure to fly from lift-off to landfall, with a turn of speed that placed them among the fastest ships in the known Universe. And now, at least some of the phenomenal ships were being built in *Carescrian* yards.

Boarding through an open brow, Brim wandered through the ship with Valerian in tow, dodging busy workmen and engineers while taking in all the amazing changes he found *within* the hull. Vastly—incredibly—different from normal Starfury-class warships, Mk1Cs existed on the basis of shooting, maneuverability, and speed alone—in that order. With full exploitation anywhere in the flight envelope. Gone were the comfortable wardrooms, messing facilities, sleeping quarters, and the rest of the facilities necessary for extended cruising. The only elements Brim could see that had been left untouched were the propulsion units. Even the primary plasma generators had been enlarged in the form of Krasni-Peych 2450 units fresh from research laboratories in Sodeskaya. This alone made it possible to slightly increase armor protection over the Drive chambers, a weak spot that had become glaringly apparent in Fluvanna during battles with the League's deadly new Gorn Hoff 262s.

Toward late afternoon, they emerged back onto the noisy floor of the bay. "All right, Wilf," Valerian shouted over the roar of the pool generators, "what do you think?"

Brim grinned happily. "Well," he allowed, "they're certainly pure killer ships, now. I haven't seen enough room aboard for so much as a box lunch. What's the crew size again? With less than ten command stations—and I'll bet the enlisted complement is reduced by at least half."

"Pretty close, Wilf," Valerian said. "We've got it down to a single Helmsman, eight other officers, and thirty-one ratings. No support types at all—except for damage-control teams."

"Probably not a bad idea to keep them aboard," Brim agreed emphatically. *Starfury* had sustained considerable damage during her year in Fluvanna, and had even been shot down once with direct hits in a Drive chamber—an event that, he considered with no little misgiving, led directly to the fathering of his first child.

He'd only learned about *that* within the last week, and still found his new status difficult to comprehend. Especially since Raddisma of Magor, the unborn child's mother, was *also* the favorite consort of His Majesty, Mustafa Eyren, Nabob and absolute ruler of embattled Fluvanna.

He shrugged. *Later*. . . . He'd deal with that once he got all the *other* loose ends of his life sorted out—like setting up a whole new wing of the Home Fleet. The child's mother could provide her with a home, for *he* certainly had none. Anywhere but the fleet.

"Voot's beard, Wilf, *that* certainly took you afield," Valerian said with a curious smile. "I'd heard *Starfury* was shot down during one of her battles with the Leaguers, but I'd no idea it had affected you so. I'm sorry. Truly."

Brim laughed sardonically. "Mark," he said, placing a hand on the designer's shoulder. "Aside from killing a number of fine Imperials—and scaring the bevboots out of *me*—crash landing *Starfury* was no particularly big thing. I've been shot down a number of times before. It was what happened later that . . ." He stopped himself and laughed. "If I ever get it all sorted out myself, you'll be among the very first to know."

"Sounds like a deal to me," Valerian said—still frowning. Then he shrugged, checking the ancient timepiece he carried with him. "Probably time we hie ourselves off to meet Admiral Gallsworthy and Dr. Borodov. They'll be waiting at the Officers Mess. Both of 'em are anxious to hear what you think of the new 1Cs."

Laughing as they boarded the little tram for the parking lot, Brim nodded. "I'll tell everyone they're beautiful as ever, Mark," he promised.

"Yeah, yeah, I know," Valerian said. "You didn't get to *fly* one."

"*Well,*" the Carescrian said, "that would be nice."

"How about tomorrow morning?"

Brim consulted a pocket schedule he'd found in his lobby pickup box. "Yeah," he said, scanning the tiny globe as it displayed complex patterns of color in intricate rhythms and hues. He laughed. "*After* I finish at least four metacycles of appointments with a staff of temporary orderlies they've assigned to me." He shook his head. "Better plan on tomorrow afternoon, Mark. Late."

Valerian nodded. "Give me a call as soon as you have a firm schedule. The Sherrington crew has promised to have most of the cables off your ship by morning."

"Sounds like a plan to me," Brim said, blowing on his heated gloves as he followed the designer through bitterly cold darkness to the skimmer. He sighed to himself while Valerian coaxed the vehicle's tiny grav to life. Wing Commander, no less. An exalted title to be certain. The next step was certain to come with promotion to Commodore, or even Rear Admiral. Yet deep down he wondered if the new assignment was *really* right for a dyed-in-the-wool Helmsman like himself. Then he shrugged. With considerable assistance from his prodigious valet—and trusted friend—Master Chief Petty Officer Utrillo

Barbousse, he'd survived the same sort of assignment when he set up the IVG's first headquarters during Baxter Calhoun's absence, and he hadn't been vetted any help there at all. This time, with *real* bean counters to take care of the details, maybe he could get even more time in space.

Then again maybe he couldn't. . . .

Predictably, it took the long-anticipated arrival of Chief Barbousse to ultimately free Brim from his administrative shackles. But when he did finally slip away to fly his new Starfury 1C, the graceful ship was more than worth his wait. From the moment he taxied out onto Gimmas's tossing ocean for takeoff until he nudged her back onto a gravity pool, P7350 was everything Valerian had claimed—and a great deal more. With the new gravs, acceleration was phenomenal, and the extra speed only slightly affected maneuverability. Above the velocity of light, her characteristics were completely unchanged from the original *Starfury* he had flown in the Imperial Volunteer group.

Over the next three Standard Months, she was joined by others, as new ships began to arrive on a regular basis and crews assembled from all over the Empire in a gigantic training effort. Miraculously, the League of Dark Stars extended the interruption they had inaugurated after the Battle of Zonga'ar, still licking their wounds while they prepared for the next brutal attempt at conquest. And along with other unit commanders in the Imperial Fleet, Wilf Brim took every advantage of the hiatus, feverishly working to forge new organizations that could bear the terrible impact of renewed war when it inexorably came.

Through it all, CIGAs all over the Empire continued to press for peace with the League at any price, chanting their clever, empty slogans and heaping abuse on Emperor Onrad for provoking the war in the first place. But for all their sound and fury, the CIGAs had lost at least some of the popular support they once enjoyed. In the few months since Emperor Onrad's declaration of war over the League's attack on Fluvanna, counterdemonstrations had grown apace until the number of loyal citizens often matched the CIGAs they opposed. Occasionally, loyalist numbers were even larger.

Nevertheless, the CIGA protests made it doubly difficult to organize a workable system of home defense, even though devoted Imperials everywhere knuckled down and worked 'round the clock with whatever resources they could scrape together. Almost miraculously, new defense organizations began to function anyway—haltingly at first, but gaining form and momentum with every moment that passed.

Unfortunately, *far* too few moments remained. . . .

CHAPTER 2

CIGAs Again

On 213/52011—little more than three Standard Months following Brim's arrival on Gimmas—the League began its long-impending attack on the Empire, ending the period of "Sham War" that had extended since their defeat the previous year at Zonga'ar. In a stunning onslaught across nearly 500 light-years of arc, armadas numbering more than 1,880 starships, 570,000 jackbooted Controllers, and 2000 giant land crawlers mounted a colossal offensive. The Imperial dominions of Lamintir, Korbu, and Gannat fell within two Standard Days, their planetary legislatures so weakened from within by CIGAs that their armed forces could offer only token resistance. The flighted people of courageous little A'zurn capitulated only after a bloody struggle—and a wild naval melee during which three gallant A'zurnian destroyers nearly demolished a Leaguer battleship before they, themselves, were wiped out by the big ship's surviving disruptors.

With astonishing speed, Triannic's seemingly invincible fleets and land armies conquered all before them until before long they were poised before the affluent collection of stars and habitable planets called Effer'wyck, a proud and powerful dominion with more than ten thousand Standard Years of history. Once this was subjugated, only the 'Wyckean Void, a narrow emptiness at the origin of a galactic arm, would separate the Leaguers from the great triple star called Triad of Asterious. Collectively known throughout the galaxy as "Greater Avalon," this triple star and its five planets—jointly capital of Onrad V's Grand Galactic Empire—were preeminent among the League's targets of conquest.

A month earlier, in the face of violent CIGA protests, powerful units of the Imperial Expeditionary Forces under Major General (the Hon.) Gastudgon Z'Hagbut had been rushed across the Void to bolster Effer'wyckean Defense Forces. But by the time these forces could be brought to bear, the League juggernaut had already gained tremendous momentum—as well as vast stores of matériel from its new conquests.

On Gimmas itself, Brim was viewing the latest dispatches—all bad news—when Master Chief Petty Officer Utrillo Barbousse stuck his bald head inside the temporary office Brim had designated Headquarters, 30 Wing. "An old friend o' yours, Cap'm," the big rating announced with a great smile.

Brim looked up with a frown. Hadn't Barbousse been out by the gravity pools overseeing a repair detail? Why was *he* here making the announcement. . . ? He'd always instructed the orderlies to let "special" friends simply walk in on him. "Send him in, Chief," he replied warily.

Immediately, a grand, prominentorial nose burst into the room, followed by a pair of humorous blue eyes with a droll, confident sort of smile that fairly shouted old, well-established wealth. Only one person Brim knew looked like that. . . .

"Toby Moulding!" he exclaimed, jumping to his feet. "Great suffering Universe, I'd nearly forgotten you were due here today from Fluvanna." Leaping around the desk, he returned a brief salute, then grabbed the man's out-thrust hand.

Commander Tobias Moulding, I.F., was tall, blond, and essentially the same age as Brim. He was also immaculately attired in an Imperial Fleet uniform that looked as if it had been delivered that morning direct from one of the exclusive shops along Avalon's fabled Crispin Row. Like Brim, he wore the discreet red-on-blue insignia of the Imperial High-Speed Starflight team, and presently held the galactic speed record of 111.97M LightSpeed. He'd set that record in the same Valerian-designed M-6 Beta racing starship in which Brim retired the galaxy-famous Mitchell Trophy two years earlier. "I say, Captain," Moulding drawled, "so long as you're going to call in your friends to help with this new assignment, couldn't you at least locate yourself somewhere in a more temperate climate?"

Brim grinned and shook his head. "Can't blame *me* for this frozen mess, Toby. I just came here following orders."

"Sounds like a Leaguer's excuse from here," Moulding chuckled, "but it's good enough for me—as are you, old friend. I've missed you since we served together, if for no other reason than I've not had to fight for my life in almost four months now."

Brim settled into one of two battered armchairs in front of his desk, indicating the other with a nod of his head. "I think we'll change *that* soon enough," he said.

"Bloody well," Moulding chuckled. "Seems as if someone's been after my hide constantly since I met you."

"Commanding 610 Squadron won't seem much of a change, then," Brim said.

"Why am I not surprised?" Moulding asked with a grin. "Where's it to be?"

"Avalon."

"*Well,*" Moulding said, brightening. "Quite an improvement. From a dominion barely awakened to starflight we're now assigned to the very center of galactic civilization."

"'Very center of a huge target,' is more like it." Brim laughed. "My take is that anybody even remotely near Avalon will shortly be a recipient of the League's finest efforts."

"We saw some fine efforts in Fluvanna," Moulding observed soberly. "Let's hope these aren't *too* much better, or we may not survive the show."

Brim nodded. "I can't say that hasn't entered my mind. . . ."

"Nobody lives forever," Moulding said, a smile breaking across his face.

"Probably won't have to worry about that," Brim assured him darkly. "We've already lost Karen Rumsey—your counterpart who was commanding Squadron 32 back at FleetPort 30. I just heard about it this morning; only got a chance to meet her a couple of times in person. She'd been running things pretty much on her own while I started the Starfury operation."

"I knew her in school," Moulding said. "A real expert in formation flying. How'd it happen?"

"Ferried some Effer'wyckean bigwig back to the capital," Brim explained. "League bastards caught her on the ground during their first raid on Luculent."

"Mmm," Moulding observed. "Well, if the night life over there was anything like I remember, the poor woman probably went out with a smile on her face."

Brim nodded. Luculent, the capital of Effer'wyck, was famed not only for a heroic overdose of pretentious architecture but also for its libertine way of living. "I'll bet things are a lot more subdued right now," he observed.

"You never know," Moulding replied. "People over there probably have a lot they'd like to forget these days."

"Yeah," Brim agreed. It was years since his own family had been wiped out in a single League raid from space, yet his mind's eye could see his tiny sister dying in his arms as if it had happened five minutes ago. "I wish them a lot of luck doing that. . . ." Then he shrugged. "Enough," he said, forcing himself to relax. "There's ample bad news coming from Effer'wyck without dredging up the past—and I'll bet you'd like to hear about the new assignment."

Moulding laughed. "Well," he said, crossing his legs, "I already know it's dangerous. Otherwise, you wouldn't be involved. But *do* let me in on the other details. Squadron Commander is it? Daresay *that* ought to prove interesting. Where might the crews be coming from?"

"That's probably the biggest problem we've got right now," Brim said. "The xaxtdamned CIGAs have been more successful than I ever dreamed. They drove so many people from the

Fleet over the last ten years that trained crews are almost as scarce as ships. We're recruiting anywhere we can."

"Hmm," Moulding said, scratching his chin. "Somehow I was afraid that might be the case."

"We have plenty of warm bodies already, and a lot more on the way," Brim said. "A surprising lot of potentially good people—even Helmsmen, for all that. And individually, they're pretty well qualified for their positions. Universe, I've studied their records well enough and flown with some of them every day. But transforming groups of lone mavens into effective crews, then turning those crews into fighting squadrons isn't something that can be done in a few short weeks. At least, I don't know how."

"Combat," Moulding said.

"Combat?"

"Best instructor in the Universe—if a trifle short-tempered."

Brim nodded with a rueful grin.

"Let me get this straight," Moulding said. "All I have to do is whip a hodgepodge gaggle of independent space virtuosos into fighting teams good enough to compete with an experienced, highly organized, excellently trained and equipped enemy with high morale and absolutely no concept of compassion or fair play. Right?"

"No," Brim corrected, looking Moulding in the eye. "Competing isn't good enough. They've got to beat the zukeed bastards. And I don't mean in formation flying."

"Somehow, I didn't think you did," Moulding said with a little smile. "I suppose you want me to start immediately."

"Actually, no," Brim replied. "Not immediately."

"Oh?" Moulding asked with a cocked eyebrow.

"Yesterday," Brim answered. "Actually, last month would have been even better."

"In that case," Moulding chuckled, "I suppose I'd better be moving."

"Get yourself unpacked, old friend," Brim said, returning to his work. "I'll meet you at Pool Sector Twelve in three metacycles to introduce you around."

"I'll be there with my 'time rewinder,'" Moulding said on his way out the door.

"Better bring two," Brim replied over his shoulder. "The Leaguers aren't going to wait forever. . . ."

The next evening, at the end of a frustrating day consisting mostly of useless paperwork, Brim wearily dropped into the Officers' Bar so late that even Borodov had called it a night more than a metacycle ago. However, due to increased traffic in and out of the great base, the bar was still crowded by transients keeping hours from any one of a thousand-odd planetary systems scattered across the galaxy. Colossal Gimmas Haefdon *was* coming back to life with each passing metacycle, no matter how slow the revival process seemed to impatient people like himself. Perched on a bar stool that was wedged between a huge Sodeskayan Drive Lieutenant and a morose-looking A'zurnian refugee, he was sipping a lonesome goblet of meem—and lamenting his wasted day—when he suddenly found his eyes covered from behind by a pair of warm hands scented by a familiar perfume.

"Guess who I am or *you* buy the meem," a disguised—obviously feminine—voice demanded.

"Hmm," Brim grumbled under his breath, "let's see. Nergol Triannic?"

"Wrong gender."

"Yeah, I thought so. Um . . . Zorfrieda, Queen of Halaci?"

"*Universe,* Captain, she's been dead a couple hundred years now."

"Oh," Brim agreed with a chuckle, "she was kind of boring. Ah . . . the Empress Mother Honorotha?"

"At least she's alive—now try somebody a few hundredweight lighter."

"Hmm. A few hundredweight lighter. . . ." Now he remembered, or at least his nose did. The perfume! How could he have forgotten a hundred-odd receptions in the Fluvannian capital? "If I started moving my hands around back there," he asked with a grin, "would I touch anything familiar?"

The disguised voice laughed. ''Unfortunately not, my ex-Skipper. But we can remedy that any time.''

''Nadia Tissaurd!'' Brim exclaimed, grabbing blindly behind him to capture a tiny, solid waist.

''Xaxtdamn,'' a lilting voice swore in mock rage as the hands covering Brim's eyes slid lower in an embrace of considerable affection, ''I guess I buy the meem.'' At the same time, a pair of moist lips brushed his cheek, then retracted with a feminine grunt of dismay. ''Voot's beard, Skipper, when did you last shave?''

''*Early* this morning,'' Brim replied, slipping off the bar stool to accept a hug that was—as always—a great deal more suggestive than friendly. ''It's been a long day.''

''You never let yourself go like that aboard *Starfury,*'' Tissaurd sniffed, accepting a boost onto the high stool.

''I never had to work so hard aboard *Starfury,*'' Brim groused. ''And I'm *not* letting myself go!''

''If you say so, Skipper,'' she said, humor gleaming in her eyes. A tiny, prematurely graying Lieutenant Commander in her early forties, her round face, large eyes, pug nose, and full, sensuous lips gave a most pixielike countenance. She had a compact figure with large hands and feet—and prominent breasts that rarely failed to attract attention, even when mostly hidden by a Fleet Cloak. As Brim's First Lieutenant aboard I.F.S. *Starfury* in Fluvanna, she had proven herself to be a *most* competent Helmsman who could carry out a myriad of duties with the cheerful willingness of a saint. She was also frank and highly sensual. A strong bond had formed between the two officers, and occasionally they had been at pains to keep their relationship on the ''safe'' side of professionalism. ''I assume you *will* join me in a Logish Meem,'' she said, signaling to the bartender.

''The goblet might be a little crowded, Number One,'' Brim chuckled, addressing her by the traditional Fleet nickname for a starship's First Lieutenant, ''but with you, I'd try anything at least once.''

''Good news, my *ex*-Skipper,'' she said, surreptitiously cupping his hand over her breast. "There's nothing in the regs about a little fun between friends who *don't* share the same ship. Bartender! The Skipper here wants a refill and I'll have one of the same."

A decidedly assertive sensation surged momentarily in Brim's loins as he withdrew his hand. Even as a joke, it had been a long time since . . . "Tissaurd," he said with a grin, "you could be a bad influence on me."

"Finish your drink, Wilf," she said with a mischievous grin. "I lift ship in two metacycles. When I *do* finally drag you to bed, I'll want to enjoy myself significantly longer than that."

"Xaxtdamn," Brim mumbled through a grin. "Always at the wrong place at the wrong time."

"Sooner or later," Tissaurd said over her shoulder while she paid the bartender. Then she turned and saluted with her goblet of meem. "Here's to a future evening of strict purience."

"To future purience," Brim answered, touching the lip of her goblet with his. "But what of Nadia Tissaurd right now? Last time I heard, you were commanding *Starfury.* I didn't know she was in port."

"She isn't," Tissaurd said. "Someone decided that such a famous prototype ought to be placed safely in a museum before she's blasted beyond repair. After all, we *did* put a few dents in the old girl last year."

"Dents and more," Brim agreed.

"So I drove her off to that remote storage yard in the thirty-fifth sector and now I'm flying I.F.S. *Nord*. You've heard of her?"

Brim felt his eyebrows rise. "Universe," he exclaimed, "*Nord*'s a bender, isn't she?"

"The *latest* bender," Tissaurd said, examining her manicured fingernails. "And you wouldn't believe where I've had her already."

"Probably, I'm not cleared to know anyway." Brim laughed. Perfected by the League during the last war, benders were special starships that could, in effect, "bend" the entire spectrum (except "heavy" N rays) around their hulls, thereby becoming virtually invisible.

"True," Tissaurd agreed. "But one of the places I will tell *you* about—in spite of the thraggling regulations—is A'zurn. I had *Nord* there when the dominion fell, and I was able to bring out a number of A'zurnian officials. Including a friend of yours. He's actually the *second* reason I stopped in to see you during my layover."

"The second reason?" Brim asked.

"Well, *of course,*" Tissaurd said. "The first reason was to make certain you were still interested in a little erotic fun some time in the future."

Brim chuckled. "Were I to *back* away from the bar stool right now," he bantered, "you'd have a visual answer to that little question."

"Too bad I'm leaving so soon, then, Captain. But someday . . ." She grinned and sipped her meem. "I do have important business to discuss tonight, though—like the replacement Commander you need for 32 Squadron."

Brim frowned. "How in xaxt did you hear about *that*?" he demanded. "I just found out yesterday myself."

"Oh, I have my methods," Tissaurd said impishly, "and I also have the *replacement* you need."

"For 32 Squadron?"

"Landed him today in my bender," Tissaurd asserted.

"But they haven't even *assigned* anybody yet," Brim protested.

"That's the best part," Tissaurd said. "They won't need to, now."

"Wait a cycle," Brim said. "How could you have a replacement? Didn't you say you just came in from combat duty?"

"That's right," Tissaurd assured him. "From A'zurn."

"Then how in Voot's greasy beard could you have . . ."

"Does the name Aram of Nahshon ring a bell, Wilf Brim?" Tissaurd interrupted. "That's the old friend I picked up."

Brim felt his eyebrows go orbital. "Aram of Nahshon?" he asked. "I heard he'd been killed commanding the group of destroyers that almost got the Leaguer battleship off Magalla'ana."

"He's *here*—at the sector hospital," she said. "I picked up his lifeglobe on the way back. Pure luck. He's a bit the worse for wear, but full of fight as ever—and plenty ready to command a squadron of killer ships, I'd say. Even if he *weren't* a natural, think how it would help post-war relations with A'zurn."

"Universe," Brim agreed. "You're right on both counts. But he's not an Imperial. How would I go about getting him assigned?"

"*You* wouldn't. I thought about that on the way here," Tissaurd said with a smile. "But your old friend and mentor Baxter Calhoun *could*. Vice Admirals can do nearly anything, especially ones assigned directly to the Admiralty."

"Nadia," Brim asked fervently, "did I ever tell you you're wonderful. . . ."

"A number of times, ex-Skipper of mine. But I'm always ripe for more bouquets."

"You're wonderful."

Tissaurd fluttered her eyelids. "I know," she said, preening facetiously. "You needn't tell me."

Brim rolled his eyes. "I've changed my mind," he grumped.

"Bet I could change it back if we were in bed," Tissaurd said impishly.

"Not before you lift ship." Brim chuckled. "But I'll take a promise in the meantime."

"I've already promised, Skipper," she replied with a serious little smile. "Count on it."

"I shall," Brim said, suddenly aware of the fact that something very fundamental had changed between them.

"Wilf Brim," she said, looking him directly in the eye, "you are far and away the best Commander I've ever had—but I'm glad I don't work for you anymore. We've had a professional relationship much too long." Then she glanced at her timepiece and drained her goblet. "Time to go," she said.

Brim pressed her hand gently. "May stars light all thy paths," he said in the age-old salute between starsailors.

"And thy path, Star Traveler," she pronounced in return.

Then she pressed his hand and slipped from the bar stool, disappearing quickly into the crowd.

When she was gone, Brim found himself surprised at how noisy the room had suddenly become. He and Tissaurd had a lot in common, now that he thought about. She too had never mentioned a home—but then again, she never seemed lonely, either. . . .

In the morning, or the grayness that passed for "morning" on Gimmas Haefdon, Brim dispatched a KA'PPA message to the Admiralty in Avalon, then battled his way through a raging snowstorm to the sprawling hospital compound that served Sector 19. Portions of the huge receiving gallery were obviously under restoration from years of neglect, and a few dark corridors still led off into the darkness of abandonment, but the room teemed with evacuated refugees and Imperial casualties flown in from Effer'wyck. Both served as urgent reminders that many important allies of the Empire had already fallen—and little time remained before the League would launch its next offensive, probably against Avalon herself.

A small knot of flighted civilians had gathered outside one of the main corridors and were talking quietly among themselves. Though dressed in battered remains of what once must have been opulent civilian clothes, each held a new Fleet Cloak over his arm; clearly they had been evacuated during a season of warmth and were being issued temporary clothing until they could be resettled elsewhere.

After all these years, Brim had never gotten over a sense of wonder when he encountered A'zurnians in real life. Men and women alike were tall and barrel-chested, normal-enough humanoids except for great folded wings—really a very specialized second set of arms—that arched upward like golden cowls trailing long flight feathers in alabaster cascades that reached all the way to the floor. These extended from "tensils," or down-covered, pillow-sized lumps growing midway between their shoulders. The protrusions, manifesting themselves at puberty, covered an outgrowth of the reflexive nervous system that automatically coordinated complex motions of feather and flesh that resulted in flight.

Peering around the huge lobby, Brim could see that the two clearly harried clerks who manned the administrative desk were already mobbed by at least twenty white-suited technicians, so he made his way directly to the A'zurnians themselves. Raising his hands palms to his chest in the Universal sign of peace and respect, he half mumbled one of the few formal A'zurnian salutations he knew. ''*O' collo sol ammi*. Do any of you speak Avalonian?''

''I do, Captain Brim,'' replied a gray-haired individual—clearly patriarch of the group. His massive forehead and great hooked nose gave him a distinctly fierce demeanor, but his huge green eyes were filled with the gentle wisdom that characterized A'zurnian people wherever they settled. Even stooped by age, the old man stood taller than Brim by at least half an iral. ''How may I serve you?'' he asked with no trace of an accent.

''You know my name, sir?'' Brim asked in surprise.

The elder decorously placed a long, slim finger on the green-and-gold ribbon Brim wore among his decorations. ''In all of our long history,'' he said with great dignity, ''only one nonflighted individual has ever worn that ribbon. Your name is well know among A'zurnians.''

Brim felt his cheeks flush. It had been more than fifteen Standard Years since he—a mere Sub-lieutenant at the time—led a small party of Imperials on a perilous raid against the Leaguers who occupied much of the little domain at the time. For his heroism, he'd been personally awarded the Order of Cloudless Flight by A'zurn's Crown Prince, now King Leopold XVIII. ''I am most honored that you remember me, er . . .'' he stumbled.

''At home, I was known as Knorr the Elder,'' the A'zurnian replied. ''I served Leopold's father as Grand Ambassador to Avalon for many years.''

''Then I am doubly honored, Your Excellency,'' Brim said.

"And so am I, Captain," Knorr replied modestly. "Now, how may I help you?"

Brim smiled. The old man was a true A'zurnian. "You landed last night aboard the bender *Nord,* did you not?" he asked.

"Aye, Captain," Knorr replied. "All of us."

"I seek Aram of Nahshon who landed with you," Brim said. "Can you tell me where they have taken him?"

"I have just returned from Commander Nahshon's side," Knorr said, pointing across the lobby toward one of the lighted corridors. "Ward B-131. Almost to the end, on the right. His bed is the first past the entrance. I take it you met Aram during his racing days, Captain?"

"Earlier, we were once shipmates as well," Brim answered. "But everyone knows of his recent heroism. For a while we feared he had not survived. How is he?"

The old man shook his head. "Only youth and Lady Fortune saved his reckless feathers this time," he chuckled. "But aside from some painful burns and bruises, it appears that he needs only nourishment and liquids to assure his survival."

"Thank the Universe," Brim said with no little feeling; Aram had always been one of his favorites.

"I'm certain he will be glad to see you, Captain," Knorr said, clearly anxious to continue his talk with the other A'zurnians.

Touching his forehead in thanks, Brim set off across the lobby, through a new crush of wounded Imperial servicemen who must have just arrived at the base. He grimaced. The steady stream of casualties boded ill for the defense of Effer'wyck. Unless he missed his guess, it would soon be Avalon's turn.

Except for dark rings beneath the eyes and a large area of badly singed feathers atop his starboard wing, scarlet-haired Aram of Nahshon had changed very little since he and Brim competed in the Mitchell Trophy races. "Wilf!" he shouted, struggling to his feet in spite of clearly obvious discomfort. "I thought you were still in Fluvanna," he added, throwing a plucky salute. "You look great!"

Returning the salute, Brim could only stare in awe at the young A'zurnian who had calmly set his tiny destroyer against a Leaguer battleship and nearly won—then survived nearly two weeks in a lifeglobe with supplies that should have lasted no more than ten Standard Days. "Aram," he said, offering his hand, "you look perfectly awful. What is it that keeps you alive in spite of Voot's best efforts?"

The A'zurnian thought for a moment in feigned concentration. "Maliciousness," he replied with a twinkle in his eyes. "I simply hate Leaguers so much that I can't die until I take a lot more of 'em with me."

Brim shook his head. "For xaxt's sake, sit down before you fall down, Aram," he chuckled. "How do you feel?"

"About half, Wilf," the A'zurnian admitted, settling to the bed. "Not only have I got the grandfather of all headaches, I can't fly until I grow a *lot* of replacement feathers." He shook his head. "The liquid in this glass will get rid of the headache by tomorrow, but feathers grow slowly and you know how I *hate* to walk."

"I believe I've heard about that," Brim said with a chuckle, pressing a locator button on his paging unit as it sent a mild tingling into his shoulder. The two friends soon fell to reminiscing as starsailors are wont to do throughout the galaxy, and had just finished a spirited conversation on the merits of Defiant-class attack ships when Barbousse burst into the room, carrying a briefcase and a large red envelope that he passed to Brim.

"Commander Aram!" the big rating said with a broad smile. "It's wondrous good to see you alive, sir."

Brim opened the envelope and studied its contents while the A'zurnian struggled to his feet again and gripped Barbousse's hand. "It's good to see you, too, Chief," he said, winking. "Sort of proves I'm still alive."

Barbousse laughed. "You A'zurnians are a tough lot, if you'll pardon m'sayin' it. I'd bet that singed wing pains ye some."

''It'll keep me from flying for a while,'' Aram said, ruefully peering up over his shoulder.

''Not necessarily,'' Brim interrupted. ''The Chief's brought a message from our old friend Baxter Calhoun that'll get you a lot of time in a starship if you want it.''

Frowning, Aram turned. ''Time in a starship?'' he asked.

''Absolutely,'' Brim said, handing him a sheet of plastic hardcopy. ''Read it for yourself.''

As he read aloud, Aram's eyebrows rose in apparent surprise. ''This gives you authority to . . . .'' he began. His voice suddenly trailed away, as if he didn't believe what he was reading.

''To commission you on the spot as a Commander in the Imperial Fleet,'' Brim finished for him. ''And to put you in charge of 32 Squadron. You sign up for the duration only; after we win, you stay in our Fleet at your own discretion.''

''Working for *you*?'' Aram said.

''Well,'' Brim said with a shrug, ''there's a down side to everything, you know. But I'm not half as bad as the Chief here claims.''

''I suppose the Cap'm's right, if the truth were known.'' Barbousse sniffed in mock resignation.

Aram rolled his eyes and lowered himself painfully to a sitting position again. ''Chief, I know how much you hate working for the Captain.'' He chuckled, then looked at Brim with a serious mien. ''How do you suppose a group of Imperials would feel taking orders from a foreigner?''

''I assume you'll take orders from *me*,'' Brim countered. ''And I haven't noticed any wings on my back.''

Aram grinned and shook his head. ''You know what I mean,'' he said.

''Yeah,'' Brim said, ''I've done a lot of thinking about it since I heard you arrived. And I can't say there mightn't be problems. People are people, whatever race they happen to be. Everybody's prejudiced to a degree. But overcoming that sort of thing, that's what galactic civilization's all about, isn't it?''

Aram nodded, although he continued to frown.

"You don't have to make your mind up right away," Brim said. "Think about it for a while. "I'll be around the base all—"

"That won't be necessary," Aram interrupted, suddenly wide-eyed. "I mean, I *want* the job! I'm simply trying to think of something significant to say when I accept."

"How about, 'I'll do it.' "

"I'll do it, Skipper. . . ."

"Chief, did you bring the Oath Taker along with you?"

"Aye, Cap'm," Barbousse said, taking a portable warrant board from his briefcase. "Commander," he said, setting the small device beside Aram on the bed and activating its window. "Place your right hand on the window here and repeat after me. . . ."

The next day, after a *long* night of briefings, Aram of Nahshon—Commander, I.F.—was on his way to Avalon and FleetPort 30, where he would assume command of 32 Squadron. As Brim sat in his office listening to the morning starpacket thunder overhead, he smiled. Almost miraculous, he considered, how the excitement of a new assignment could mask the aches and pains of a very dangerous war. And besides, Aram was, after all, an A'zurnian, with a real sense of identity from which he could draw strength. Probably, he thought, that would be more than enough. . . .

Toward the end of the Standard Month Pentad, as Brim and Moulding prepared to move 610 Squadron to its new home at Fleetport 30, Imperial Expeditionary Forces under Major General (the Hon.) Gastudgon Z'Hagbut and remnants of the Effer'wyckean army were forced to retreat from the Torbean worlds toward the center of the galaxy. Hoping to link up with other Effer'wyckean forces, they made a stand on three watery planets orbiting Aunkayr, a fifth-class star on the edge of the 'Wyckean Void, only 160 light-years away from Asterious.

Scarcely a matter of days later, however, fresh Leaguer armadas overran most of the Effer'wyckean Sixth Fleet, and Hagbut swiftly concluded that even his new position was hopeless. To the General's everlasting credit, he immediately KA'PPAed for help—and in doing so triggered an event that bordered on the miraculous.

In no way could the beleaguered Imperial Admiralty muster sufficient transports to effect the withdrawal before oncoming Leaguers totally wiped out their trapped Allied quarry. So the Admirals put out a general call for help to anyone in the area who had an operational starship. And with panache that had saved the hoary old Empire literally hundreds of times in the past, Avalon's private citizens provided the miracle.

Barges, interstellar ferries, space yachts, HyperLaunches, salvage vessels, tramps, smugglers, space drifters, ore trawlers, even a beacon ship halfway through her overhaul, anything that could lift into HyperSpace—plus the Fleet—crossed the 'Wyckean Void to Aunkayr in mass. There, operating loosely under Admiralty supervision, the ragtag squadrons began what was soon called The Miracle of Aunkayr.

Each morning saw a shrinking perimeter around the beleaguered Allied forces, and the lakes that served as lift-off stations became more jammed by the metacycle as interplanetary barges full of soldiers and their gear arrived from the shrinking front. "The ground troops were hungry and thirsty and nearly dead," commented one volunteer with a small rescue craft. "A lot of 'em even wore ripped battlesuits. But they kept in line. I was proud of the poor sods!" Leaguer warships fired viciously on them from every direction, in spite of dedicated efforts from every attack ship the Imperials could get into space. Yet volunteers in unknown hundreds of private starships ultimately rescued nearly 225,000 Imperial soldiers and an additional 113,000 Effer'wyckean troops, transporting them back to Avalon before the operation ended during the first metacycles of Standard date 2 Hexad 52012.

In the local darkness, General Hagbut packed his few items of equipment in a small spacecraft and made a final tour with the Senior Fleet Officer, Captain W. G. Landlord. When they were satisfied, as they remarked in their official communiqué, "that there were no more Imperial troops alive at the lift-off sites,'' they themselves left for Avalon aboard a destroyer. The operation would continue to lift off Effer'wyckean troops before the Admiralty declared an official termination at the end of 4 Hexad.

Brim, Moulding, and 610 Squadron arrived at FleetPort 30 just after midday on the fifth, as the last stragglers were still limping in from Aunkayr. The usually crowded sky over Avalon was mobbed, and since passing through LightSpeed the squadron of rakish Starfuries had been assigned vector after vector to avoid collisions with slower traffic. Lake Mersin was already reflecting light through the haze that obscured the far horizon when Brim contacted a FleetPort Controller in the midst of what promised to be tremendous confusion. ''Imperial P7350 to FleetPort 30,'' he announced. ''I am leading sixteen Starfuries inside your outer marker.''

''Defiant N956,'' the Controller announced to someone else, ''move into position and hold vector two four left. Traffic will cross downrange.''

''Acknowledge two four left and hold, Defiant N956. . . .''

Brim shrugged and held his course. Maybe they hadn't heard his call. However, with sixteen Starfuries immediately behind him—and only the barest experience in heavily crowded airspace—there wouldn't be a lot of time for course corrections. He opened his mouth to repeat his initial contact when . . .

''AkroKahn 725 is ready in sequence,'' a deep Sodeskayan voice interrupted on the same frequency.

''AkroKahn 725: affirmative,'' the Controller announced, still completely ignoring Brim's fast-moving squadron. ''Move up to vector two four left and hold short.''

''Up to hold short, AkroKahn 725,'' the Sodeskayan confirmed.

Brim checked his instruments. ''Sanders,'' he demanded, ''is the radio working?''

''Checks out on this end, Skipper,'' the radio officer reported.

Still *another* voice came on the tower frequency with a burst of static. ''Um, we're on frequency again. Changed radios. Sorry about that.''

"5006: you're back with me?" the Controller asked in a voice dripping with irritation.

"Yeah, and we didn't mean to switch radios. We're now on. . . ."

Concerned, Brim swung high to starboard, avoiding a battered interstellar ferry that suddenly lumbered into his path. The old ship was clearly off course, victim of worn-out navigational equipment or—more probably—damage from a near miss by League disruptors. Ahead, he could actually see FleetPort 30's long-range beacons against the darkness of space. Time was running out. Keying an arrival layout for the satellite to one of his displays, he chose his own inbound vector, one that at least *seemed* to be generally aligned with his present path. "Imperial P7350," he announced, as if she had already assigned the vector to him, "I am leading sixteen Starfuries for vector two four left. Do you read me?" he asked, his voice clearly indicating an end to his patience.

That brought the Controller to life. "Er . . . thank you," she said with more than a hint of surprise in her voice. "Imperial P7350 and sixteen Starfuries are cleared for arrival on vector two four left."

Brim shook his head; the huge satellite was now clearly visible ahead. He would soon have a word with *that* Controller. Drawing more power from the big Admiralty gravs, he banked into his final approach. "Cleared for arrival two four left, P7350," he acknowledged, and passed the message to the four groups of Starfuries following close in his wake.

Constructed in stationary orbit approximately 150 c'lenyts above spinward Avalon, FleetPort 30 was shaped like a flattened glove nearly three quarters of a c'lenyt in diameter. It was ringed about the middle by a transparent mooring tube and pressurized to the standard atmosphere on the surface below. Complex antenna fields on both "poles" of the huge structure furnished clear communications throughout the galaxy; the mooring tube provided forty-five docking portals spaced equally around its margin, each equipped with its own optical mooring system and retractable brow. When docked, Brim's killer ships would protrude bow first from thirty-two of these portals, with a few of the remainder occupied by surface shuttles and transient ships. Both the interior of the structure and its moored ships were supplied with locally generated gravity distributed evenly on every level with "down focus" toward the center of the planet itself.

Using the excellent docking systems provided, Brim had the whole squadron moored less than half a metacycle later. However, with fewer than ninety irals' width at the docking rim, he hated to think what it would be like to moor a full-sized cruiser—or a Starfury with shot-up opticals. . . . Unfortunately, he had little time to worry about such future problems, or even to inspect his new command and space anchorage. Only cycles after his arrival, he and Moulding were on their way to the surface in a high-speed shuttle piloted by Aram of Nahshon himself. Barbousse scarcely had time to pack spare uniforms for them.

"Admiral Calhoun said he didn't care what you looked like after a long ferry mission, Captain," the A'zurnian explained. "He simply made it clear that you were to be at the briefing—and it would be my neck if he didn't see you there."

"Any kind of a bloody friend would have offered his neck," Moulding grumped in feigned wrath. "Six days in a thraggling bus designed for nothing but day trips. Mark Valerian must be a closet Leaguer—maybe even a Controller. I haven't had a proper bath and shave since Gimmas."

Brim laughed in spite of his own discomfort. "Don't listen to him, Aram," he said. "Friend Moulding secretly hates to attend meetings, that's all."

From his seat at the little spaceship's helm, Aram grinned over his shoulder. "I think I know what Toby means," he said. "The way they've stripped down the Defiants we're using, you'd never recognize them—and I'd hate to take any of 'em more than a day's flight away."

"If anybody can tell the differences, you can," Brim said, remembering the days he and Aram had taken I.F.S. *Defiant*, the first Defiant MK1A, aloft back in the spring of 51998. It seemed like two hundred years ago. "How do they handle?" he asked.

"Rather nicely, now that you mention it," the A'zurnian replied with a nod of approval. "They're nowhere near as fast as your Starfuries, but they can turn on a ten-credit coin, and they'll accelerate with the best the League has put up yet. *And,*" he added pointedly, "we've nearly twice the number of Defiants to face the Leaguers than you have Starfuries. . . ."

That sort of half-joking braggado soon had Brim smiling with both pride and relief. It reflected the kind of positive outlook on life that could only come from a person who had little problem with his work. Now, maybe he could worry a little more about fighting a war. . . .

As the shuttle swooped low over the capital, Brim could see that every gravity pool in the vicinity of Lake Mersin was filled with ships from the ragtag rescue fleet, and the overflow spread out hovering over the surface of the lake itself. Moulding summed the scene up accurately when he commented, "I think I could hike across the bay just by stepping from deck to deck. . . ."

Aram set the little ship down on a vector that was kept open only by the hard work of a dozen police launches, then taxied quickly to wharf where they were flagged onto a gravity pad recently vacated by what could have only been an industrial barge, and a dilapidated one at that. It probably had been helping to ferry evacuees from an orbiting starship too old to qualify for surface license. As the clumsy spaceship lumbered out onto the lake, Brim shook his head. *Every* vehicle capable of spaceflight had helped in the evacuation. Little wonder the operation was called a "miracle."

Walking to the staff skimmer that would take them to the Admiralty, the trio passed between long lines of bedraggled soldiers who were giving their names to tired-looking officials with logic scribers, dropping what blast pikes and other weapons they'd managed to save into heaps, and climbing wearily onto hovering omnibuses. Nearby, steady streams of volunteers were bringing and sorting odd clothes, because many of the evacuees arrived with only blankets thrown around their tattered battlesuits. For the remainder of his days, Brim would remember a tall, blond woman heading for one of the buses in the badly scorched bottom half of a battlesuit and a man's formal jacket; the latter accomplishing little to cover a magnificent bust. For all her obvious fatigue, she somehow managed the panache to walk proudly, head up and alert, with the indescribable spirit that characterized Imperial military no matter where—or in what condition—they were to be found.

Probably the most amazing aspect of the operation, however—at least to Brim—was that he knew the scene was being duplicated in more than a hundred similar starports scattered over the Triad's five planets. Most of the soldiers had lost their equipment, land crawlers, siege disruptors, and the like. But equipment could be replaced quickly in comparison to how long it took to gain the experience of actual combat. These ragged professionals had faced the Leaguers in action—and had survived. They would teach new Imperial armies how to do the same thing. And—with a little help from Lady Fortune—new armies equipped with fresh equipment would depart from the same ports, this time headed for victory. *If,* Brim reminded himself, the Fleet could keep the Leaguers from the doors until the new Imperial forces were ready to march. Otherwise, today's inrush of refugees would only be *rehearsal* for what was to come. For a moment he shivered inside his Fleet Cape. It was a tall order indeed, and he knew it.

Brim got his first taste of the CIGA's new sense of assertiveness as his skimmer-pool driver followed a refugee bus through the front gates of the base. At least five hundred obviously well-dressed, pampered-looking men and women of all ages were shouting obscenities, hurling garbage, and waving placards as they strained against cordons of police in full battlesuits. Many carried animated placards proclaiming the CIGA motto, "Contemplate Galactic Peace." One—a fat, cherubic-faced woman with a bad complexion—was using hers to pummel an officer over the head while she screamed incomprehensible peace slogans through a mouth twisted by rage.

"Can't imagine *that* one 'contemplating' much of bloody anything," Moulding commented as the driver pulled around the slower omnibus and accelerated along the refuse-strewn boulevard.

At the same moment, the window beside Brim took a hit by something obscene-looking that landed with a dull splat and dribbled slowly along the curved surface of the crystal. The flying mass startled him, and he flinched, shaking his head the next moment in embarrassment. "Pretty ugly spectacle," he said lamely to Aram. "Try to remember that they're only a small percentage of our population."

"I understand," the A'zurnian said. "They're afraid. You can see it in their faces. They've got it in their minds that *anything's* better than fighting, so they're willing to make up with monsters like the Leaguers on the Leaguers' own terms. We had our own brand of CIGAs—did damnably well until the Leaguers showed their version of 'peace' for what it really was. The CIGAs changed their minds posthaste when the attacks came, but by that time, it was too late to reverse the damage they'd done to the military." He shook his head. "And—at least in the few days I was able to observe—many of those sorry zukeeds were the first the Leaguers executed."

Brim nodded, staring at the floor of the skimmer. "Makes sense," he said. "Leaguers conquer by gaining control—absolute control. You saw what they did to your countrymen in the last version of this war. They tore off people's wings so they'd be easier to keep track of."

"Yeah," Aram said bleakly. "I still have a bad time with that. The bastards really *didn't* do that out of any overt love of inflicting pain—although I'm certain some of 'em do. People who can't fly are simply easier to control than those who can."

By the time Brim looked up, they'd cleared the base entrance and were speeding along a broad highway that paralleled the shore of Lake Mersin. In the distance to spinward, a baroque clutter of towers and domes that was Avalon City dominated the horizon. Off to the right, a thousand-odd starships surrounded the great island structure of Grand Imperial Terminal, a galaxy of mooring beams glittering through the haze as the ships rode to optical anchoring devices. In a matter of cycles, the highway fed into Vereker Boulevard with its famous stands of kilgal trees and traffic began to pick up substantially. The three rode in silence, absorbed by their own thoughts—and the war. Brim settled back in the seat and watched as they passed parks, sparkling fountains, and rococo facades as if the deadly war bearing down on them had no existence at all. He'd seen the damage in Atalanta after the League's great raid there years back. This war would surely change the face of the great city, in spite of any efforts he could bring about to avoid it. But today, great black limousine skimmers decorated by embassy flags still sped by importantly in both directions. Many, he guessed, would be on their last trips in the Empire as one by one, the Leaguers' real allies declared for the enemy camp and departed into the darkness of war.

They passed the shimmering Desterro Monument, still crowded by tourists, hurried over the Grand Achtite Canal just moments before a huge barge closed the ornate ruby span in what promised to be a snarl of traffic, and moments later pulled daredevil fashion into Locorno Square with its traffic charging wildly around the monumental statue of Admiral Gondor Bemus. With a mad series of starts and panic applications of the skimmer's gravity brakes, the driver plunged into a turnoff and stopped at a marble staircase leading to the imposing, ornate structure known simply as "the Admiralty" for millions of light-years in every direction.

"How'd you like to fly a killer ship?" Moulding jokingly asked the driver as he stepped onto the pavement. "That kind of navigation takes real fortitude, in my book."

The driver grinned. "Thank you, sir," he said, "but those of us wot can survive Locorno are needed right where we are. Otherwise, none o' you starship drivers would ever get to the Admiralty alive."

"You're right." Moulding chuckled, glancing over his shoulder at the noisy traffic careening around the square. "I'd rather face the Leaguers anyday."

Brim agreed wholeheartedly as he started up the great staircase beneath wheeling squadrons of dirty, noisy pidwings. The stair treads bore mute testimony to at least five centuries of open warfare between the Admiralty and the birds—which the former had clearly lost. "I take it you're an old hand with the guards by now," he said to Aram as they reached the top and strode toward the massive entrance.

"Watch me," the A'zurnian said, setting a purposeful course toward the ornate entrance. When he was precisely four paces from the center portal, two of the four guards snapped to attention and saluted while the other two yanked open the doors. Returning the salute, Aram led the way through the entrance without breaking stride, Moulding and Brim followed close in his wake. Only experienced Admiralty hands knew how to do that; invariably, everyone else stopped. "Just like downtown, as they say," he chuckled over his shoulder.

Brim winked to Moulding. "So much for picking up local customs," he said.

"You were worried?" Moulding asked.

"Who, me?" Brim answered with a chuckle. But inside, he *had* been worried. Much as he loved Moulding, his blue-blooded old friend was far too wealthy and insulated from the realities of Imperial social protocol even to recognize de facto discrimination when he saw it. Indeed, to a large extent, Brim had become that way over his years in the Fleet, too. But in the beginning, he'd been only a talented Helmsman from Carescria, the most backward, underdeveloped section of the Empire, where the sole industries were poverty and asteroid mining. He *well* knew what it was like to be on the outside looking into a society that—in truth—gave only lip service to the notion of classless integration. It was good to see that Aram had so far soared above these hurdles as if they didn't even exist. Mentally, he blew a kiss to Nadia Tissaurd, who from the beginning had manifested confidence in the young A'zurnian.

* * *

They were late for the briefing and—once they'd submitted to retinal-image and fingerprint checks—tiptoed to seats at the rear of the small auditorium. "Universe," Brim groaned under his breath before he even saw the speaker. The man's grating voice immediately set his teeth on edge and brought back a flood of memories. General (the Hon.) Gastudgon Z'Hagbut, X^{ce}, N.B.E., and Q.O.C., had changed little since Brim first met him more than sixteen years previously during the famous raid on occupied A'zurn that ultimately led to the League's losing control of the small planetary system by guerrilla action alone. Hagbut would also forever bring Margot Effer'wyck to Brim's mind because of a wonderful evening in which she managed to so thoroughly embarrass the pompous officer that he nearly lost consciousness. As if it were yesterday, Brim could still see the buxom Princess costumed in the low-cut, virtually skirtless blue uniform of an Orenwald prostitute leading Hagbut across the dance floor of Avalon's ostentatious Golden Cockerel club.

"What's the matter?" Moulding whispered from Brim's side. "Your face has suddenly gone red."

Struggling to stifle the mirth that threatened to break loose from the pit of his stomach, Brim could only shake his head and mumble, "It's all right, Toby—just a stray memory."

Hagbut had made his share of military mistakes over the years—mainly through an inability to listen when he was offered advice. However, the blustery General had usually proven himself to be more than competent in dealing with Leaguers. A small, intense-looking superpatriotic man of undetermined years, he had a perpetually flushed face and spoke as if he disliked showing his teeth. As always, his uniform was perfectly tailored, although its wrinkled condition left little doubt that he had been intensely busy since his precipitous return to Avalon.

"We are now in the midst of a *MISTAKE* nearly as *GRAVE* as the *DEFEAT* we have just suffered at the hands of the Leaguers," he said in his most boisterous style of speaking.

"I find myself *DISGUSTED* when I see Imperial soldiers walking about in Avalon and elsewhere with an embroidered flash on their sleeve reading 'Aunkayr.' " He took a deep breath, and his face became even redder.

Feelings of humor quickly drained from Brim's mind as he listened to the man's angry words.

"Those people *THINK* that they are *HEROES*!" Hagbut roared on. "And the civilian public thinks so, too. But they are *ALL WRONG*. They fail to understand that the Empire suffered a *CRUSHING DEFEAT* at Aunkayr, and that our five planets are now in immediate danger—as is the remainder of the Empire should we fail to save ourselves here." He pounded on the lectern. "I see no sense of urgency outside these walls—except perhaps in the ranks of the CIGAs—only relief." Glaring, he peered around the auditorium. "Of *COURSE* I look at Aunkayr as a deliverance," he continued. "In that sense, I feel a bit of relief myself. Like anybody else, I have no desire for a Leaguer prison camp—or death, which might well be preferable. But while this feeling of relief remains among the general public, it displaces the true reality that I have seen with my own eyes during a *VERY AWKWARD* retreat across the planets of Effer'wyck. And what is that? The hard, harsh fact to be realized this day is that the inconceivable might now be possible. Those jackbooted Controllers who stamped their way across Lamintir, Korbu, Gannat, and A'zurn—and who are now poised to finish off Effer'wyck—might soon be making landfall right here on our *HOME PLANETS* . . . !"

Later, after the long, impassioned speech, Brim and his two companions happened into the General in the Admiralty's great lobby. It was no surprise to the Carescrian that Hagbut met his eyes with no recognition whatsoever, even though it had been *he* who was largely responsible for preserving the man's military renown in the wake of the A'zurnian raid.

"You *have* met him, haven't you?" Moulding asked as the General and his party of staff-level appendages swept past. "I mean, it *is* rather well known that you saved his career during the A'zurnian raid a few years back."

Aram interrupted with a snort. "It was by no mistake that Captain Brim wears my domain's highest award," he said quietly. "For *his* pains, Hagbut received only the A'zurnian medal presented to all 'foreign' individuals who excel in the domain's service."

Brim felt himself blush. "I wouldn't expect him to remember me—especially with all he's got on his mind right now."

"Perhaps," Moulding said, but he didn't look very convinced. Hagbut was not a popular man among large segments of the Imperial military establishment. Suddenly, the tall aristocrat glanced over Brim's shoulder and winced. "Don't look now," he said with an aspect of distaste, "but here comes somebody who seems to recognize you all too well—with the media, no less."

"Huh?" Brim asked, but before Moulding could reply, he felt a hand grasp his shoulder in a *most* unfriendly manner. Whirling around, ready to defend himself, he found himself confronting none other than Puvis Amherst—in mufti—and a number of his "progressive" journalists with HoloRecorders in hand.

"Well, Brim," the CIGA chief said, posing grandly. "I thought it might be you. War seems to attract your kind, doesn't it?"

"I suppose it does," Brim replied evenly, eyeing the man's pin-stripe cloak, dress-gray business suit, and expensive shoes. "And it seems as if you have *really* gone the other way this time, wearing a civilian getup like that."

"This is *not* a 'getup,' Brim," Amherst sniffed in a disparaging voice. "In case you haven't heard, I resigned my commission a short time ago to protest the *horrible* war in which you and your ilk have embroiled us." He looked toward the HoloRecorders with a pained expression. "Have you *seen* the results of your futile struggles against the might of the League?" he demanded rhetorically. "How many innocent soldiers must suffer or die before callous brutes like you give peace the chance it deserves?"

Brim chuckled, ignoring the journalists and looking Amherst

straight in the eye. "When I see some real peace come along, Puvis, you can be certain that I will be the first to give it a chance." Then he frowned. "But what's all this about your resigning your commission—you actually *did* something like that?"

"I most certainly did," Amherst said, hands on his hips in what he clearly expected was a heroic pose. "Someone *had* to do something about the hundreds of billions that Onrad V is appropriating for weapons and manpower now that he's become Emperor. Running wild, that's what. I had no influence with that dreadful man from within the Fleet, even in my capacity as the leading CIGA. But I certainly can use my position in government to cut off his funds. That will stop all of you war lovers. And then I shall go about earmarking those credits toward efforts to reestablish peace with the League."

"*You* have a position in government?" Brim demanded in amazement.

"Only a guttersnipe like you would be ignorant of that," Amherst replied venomously. "By right of birth, I am also the Earl of Amherst," he sniffed. "I received the title at the time of my beloved father's death."

"I see," Brim said—of course, the Imperial House of Nobles, holdover from a form of government that had outlived its usefulness a thousand years in the past. "And now you're going to start campaigning against military expenditures?" he demanded. *"In the middle of a war?"*

Amherst narrowed his eyes. "We are *not* in the middle of a war, Brim," he pronounced as if he were scolding a small child. "We are only at the beginning. There is still time to stop the horror you beasts have started. And one way to do it is to cut off the resources that fund your cursed war engines."

"You're already off to a good start on that project," Brim stated grimly. "You CIGAs all but stopped defense production years ago. We've been fighting this war at a disadvantage right from the start."

"And I thank the very Universe for it," Amherst intoned in a firm voice, carefully projecting a profile view toward the

HoloRecorders. "If people like you had *your* way, there would be no chance at all for peace with the Emperor Triannic and his League."

Brim shook his head. "Puvis," he said earnestly, "if we weren't dealing with that tinhorn now, we'd be dealing with him later on when he's even stronger."

"Unlike you militants, I deal only in peace," Amherst intoned, gloating as if he had just made a terribly clever comeback.

"That's where you're dead wrong," Brim growled, "and you know it. I deal in peace, too, every bit as much as you."

Amherst opened his mouth to protest, but Brim cut him off with a look of utter contempt. "Even in its best light, Amherst," he growled, "your kind of pacifism is only a hothouse indulgence. And you know it. It's a cozy-comfy state of wishfulness where everybody assumes that the protective walls will stay up. But keeping those very important walls intact is a task for militants—among other hard jobs that nobody else wants. All through history, we militants—whether we slog in the mud, ride in land crawlers, or fly starships—have shielded pacifists like you from consequences of your own shortsighted sermons. When evil beings like Nergol Triannic and his minions triumph, pacifists are among the first to be rounded up and herded off to the death camps. And don't try to tell me you haven't heard about such things. I've been warning you for years myself."

He glared at his ex-shipmate who had now drawn back a step and was listening with an anxious look on his face. "How many peace demonstrations do you hear about in Tarrott?" he demanded. "*Zero*. That's how many. Nergol Triannic has preempted *any* debate about peace. In his League, he is the only 'right' permitted. No matter what the citizens of his empire may *want* to think, it is *we* who are wrong by decree. Except that by the more objective measure of civilization itself, it is *we* who are right, Puvis Amherst—in spite of the ignoble trash your CIGA cowards bleat during their squalid little demonstrations. Don't fool yourself," he said, pointing directly at the CIGA leader, "Leaguers are the real war lovers. They've turned down every chance for peace we've offered since their false Treaty of Garak. The *real* responsibility for this war isn't with the militants here on Avalon, but with Nergol Triannic himself—and the misled traitors in our Empire who support him."

Brim paused for a moment, suddenly aware of what had just happened. The HoloRecorders were now concentrated entirely on *him*. He'd been outmaneuvered. This wasn't the bridge of a starship where he could fight with the best of them. He was now in the very center of CIGA territory—the slippery arena of media-swaying.

Then he looked into Amherst's eyes and saw . . . fear.

Of course! For once, *he* had an important advantage—people everywhere could see what was happening. The truth was out. He turned to face his old adversary, heart in his mouth. "The moment to decide on an Imperial course of action has long since passed," he said, "because the choice of fighting or acquiescing has already been made for us in Tarrott, not in Avalon. Now, it's high time that everyone—you included, Mr. Earl of Amherst—gets himself behind the people whose job it is to fight this war."

He took a deep breath, recalling a wise Gradgroat-Norchelite friar in the Juniper Street Mission of waterfront Atalanta who long ago taught him one of the ancient prayers peculiar to that venerable sect. He peered meaningfully into the HoloRecorders and spoke with all the determination he could muster. "I am not a religious man," he said. "Nor am I certain that I shall ever comprehend anything deeper than the spiritual ties I have to my Empire. But long ago, I learned a few words from a wise man who lives halfway across the galaxy. They have served me well over the years, and I offer them to you, Puvis Amherst, Chief of the CIGAs, for your guidance as you begin your campaign to bring about our ultimate defeat."

He bowed his head. "O Universe," he invoked in a clear voice, his words echoing in the great, still lobby of the Admiralty, "stretch forth, we pray thee, thine almighty spirit to strengthen and protect the soldiers of this Empire. Support them in the day of battle... endow them with courage and loyalty, and grant that in all things they may serve without reproach...."

When he had finished, the HoloRecorders were still riveted solely on him. And Puvis Amherst was nowhere to be seen.

CHAPTER 3

A Last Glimpse of Effer'wyck

As it turned out, Brim never did return to FleetPort 30 that evening. Shortly after the briefing, he and his two companions found themselves "invited" to a wardroom party aboard the Imperial battlecruiser *Benwell*. And it was quite clear that "regrets" were definitely not in order—even for two officers who had just flown halfway across a galaxy and were dressed more for conning starships than joining their colleagues for an evening of relaxation. Brim especially was outraged; he'd been looking forward to getting a fast start in his new command that same day. But, as ever in the politics-charged military arena of Avalon, social duties were often considered as important as one's actual job. The League would soon put a stop to that, he grumped to himself. However, until an actual attack came, Avalon evenings were meant for entertaining—and political posturing. . . .

Benwell had come off the stocks more than twenty years ago, if Brim's memory served. She'd been built to replace *Nimue*, the great battlecruiser—whose destruction during an unequal battle with powerful League forces near the historic battlefield of Zarnathor had also resulted in loss of Admiral Merlin Emrys. As the skimmer drew to a halt at the majestic battlecruiser's entry port, he remembered his own youthful worship for Emrys and the three great battlecruisers, *Nimue, Iaith Galad,* and *Oddeon*. Before the war, the Admiral and his majestic squadron had ghosted in and out of harbors all over the galaxy, showing the colors—and the power—of Greyffin IV's Galactic Empire. Loss of both Emrys and his flagship had been devastating at the time, mourned throughout the galaxy. The former's near-miraculous reappearance after six years of "exile" on a primitive planet and his influence (secret, at the time) on the Battle of Atalanta were more than enough to establish him as a legend in his own time.

"Universe," Moulding whispered as they stepped to the pavement and looked up at the colossal machine before them. "No matter how often I see the old girl, I always find myself surprised at how big she really is."

"And beautiful," seconded Brim. Along a thousand-odd irals of her length, not a single light glowed; moreover the system of mooring beams that secured her had been damped against all but local radiation. Even blacked out, however, the ship's famous silhouette could be clearly seen against the starry firmament of the galactic center. Early on, the big Nimues gained a reputation as the best-looking warships of their day, with none to match their perfect balance of design. *Benwell* was no exception. Fore and aft, her sleek, low-set hull was surmounted by three sets of superfiring disruptors placed into graceful turrets that literally melted into the gentle curve of her decks. A frowning bridge surmounted her raked superstructure and afforded the big ship a malevolent countenance that naturally bespoke her deadly purpose. And if the great ship had never completely replaced the original *Nimue* in the hearts of old-guard Imperial starsailors, she was perhaps even more beautiful than her predecessor by a dint of the many improvements incorporated into her design.

As Brim and his two companions approached the ship's prodigious gravity pool, thunder from what must have been at least fifty heavy-duty repulsion generators filled the night air and made further conversation virtually impossible until all three had identified themselves to a large—*very* thorough—security detachment and were well along the great brow that carried into the ship's spacious boarding lobby. "Voot's beard," Aram commented, making a little frown. "With all that, you'd think they'd invited the Emperor."

Moulding laughed. "*Benwell*'s a bloody important ship, and her skipper, Admiral Dugan, is a most influential man in the Admiralty. I wouldn't be a bit surprised if he *had* invited Onrad tonight."

"Nor would I be surprised if he showed up," Brim chuckled half seriously. The Onrad he'd known as a Crown Prince enjoyed a good party as much as anyone else.

Benwell's wardroom was already teeming with Blue Capes by the time Brim and his companions stepped over the coaming. Lighted for the party by dimmed sidelights only, the large, dark-paneled room was close with the spicy fragrance of camarge cigarettes, meem, perfume, and Sodeskayan Zempa pipes. One quick scan through the haze made Brim thankful for the clean uniform Barbousse had packed for him. A year in relatively primitive Fluvanna had clearly little affected the big man's penchant for working miracles *or* his inclination to discover events that were about to happen long before other mortals knew about them.

Checking his Fleet Cloak with a white-gloved rating, Brim led the way through the crowd toward the bar. The very atmosphere was charged with a cozy hum of animated conversation, musical clinking of fine crystal, and soft, elegant music played on a quintet of stringed instruments. And whoever had laid on the meem did a superb job. Elegantly Logish and aged to perfection, the fine old meem was a tribute to Admiral Dugan's meem chambers—and clearly his purse strings as well. If this were a true sample of the libations to come, Dugan was indeed a wealthy man or expected wealthy guests—or (most probably) both. Brim had just touched his goblet to Aram's and Moulding's in salute to A'zurn when his glance met a familiar pair of gentle perspicacious eyes greeting him from the other side of the room. These were set into a heartshaped face along with a sensuous mouth, wide forehead, and prominent nose, all framed by long black hair cut severely straight at the shoulders and across the forehead. Eve Cartier! She was smiling now that he'd recognized her, and he grinned back, inexplicably filled with delight. Less than a year previously, her unexpected arrival—leading three powerful attack ships—had literally saved his ship and his life following the battle of Zonga'ar. And, of all things, she was a fellow Carescrian. To Brim's eternal consternation, she was clearly *proud* of her heritage, even going so far as to retain the Carescrian burr that he had worked so diligently to erase during his years in the Helmsman's Academy.

"I say, Wilf," Moulding commented, "your mind certainly seems to have wondered."

Blinking, Brim raised his glass once more and nodded assent. "That is has, my friend," he said, nodding toward Cartier who apparently had *also* been resummoned to a previous conversation. "If you two will excuse me . . . ?"

"That's Commander Eve Cartier over there, isn't it?" Moulding remarked offhandedly.

"Either Eve or somebody who looks a lot like her," Brim said over his shoulder as he began pushing his way through the throng of Blue Capes.

With a grin, Moulding raised his goblet once more. Brim heard him say, "To Carescrians . . ." Then he was engulfed in a babbling sea of faces as he struggled toward the other side of the room.

Cartier was one of those exquisite women whose beauty was so completely natural that Brim found it difficult to characterize. Each time he saw her, he had the delicious pleasure of rediscovering her all over again. Tonight was no exception. A small-busted, statuesque woman of middling age, she wore a uniform clearly tailored to reveal her long, shapely legs to their best advantage. "Stunning" was a good description so far as Brim was concerned. Just as she had been the first day he set eyes on her aboard Baxter Calhoun's space yacht *Patriot*.

Presently, she was talking to a tall, athletic-looking Captain whose bull neck and massive physique Brim imagined might start hormones flowing in a granite sprite. And the studied manner in which he ignored Brim's determined approach through the crowd revealed that either he and Cartier had come as a pair or he had staked her out as her personal conquest of the evening.

The encouraging glances Brim was receiving from her were a good indication, however, that she might not entirely share the same feelings. "Eve," he exclaimed as he pushed his way through a last gaggle of Blue Capes. "How good it is to see you again."

"Faith, Wilf Brim," she said, looking deeply into his eyes, " 'tis a ge'at pleasure to see your face again, too. I did'na know you war here in Avalon."

"I wasn't," Brim explained with a grin, "until the middle of this morning when I arrived from Gimmas."

"I suppose I *had* heard that you were coming," she said, her eyes dropping to the floor shyly. Then suddenly she remembered the man with whom she had previously been talking. "Oh, er . . . yes. Captain Brim," she stammered, "I should like to present Captain, er . . . ?"

"Cavindish," the man announced with studied ennui. "Kingsly Cavindish, First Officer of His Majesty's battlecruiser I.F.S. *Benwell*. I, ah, didn't catch your ship, Brim."

Smiling evenly, Brim turned to face the man whose campaign he had just badly interrupted. "Pleased to meet you, Cavindish," he said, extending his hand, "and I didn't give the name of my ship because she doesn't have one."

"A pity," the man said disparagingly as he grandly shook Brim's hand, "but then if we gave names to all the small ones, we'd soon run out, wouldn't we?"

"I never thought of that," Brim replied, fighting back a sudden desire to alter the shape of the man's handsome nose. Instead, he turned to Cartier. "What news of Baxter Calhoun?" he asked.

Cartier smiled. "The Govern . . . er, Admiral Calhoun seems

to be settlin' into his new job directin' Defense Command. I see him noo and again."

"And you, Eve?" he asked, attempting to ignore the angry scowl that was beginning to cloud Cavindish's handsome countenance. "They say you're heading up 617 Squadron."

"'Tis true," she said with a proud little blush. "I've even got my own Starfury noo. The 1Cs started comin' thro' twa' weeks ago."

"And *Patriot*?" he asked.

"I turned her over to the Admiralty," she said with a shrug. "She's a fine auld ship—they'll mak' good use o' her somewhere."

"Yes, well," Cavindish interrupted with a most pointed little cough. Brim guessed the man had little interest either in Cartier's career or the ships she commanded. "I *had* invited the Commander for a tour of the ship. I'm certain that you will excuse us, Brim."

Brim gave a little bow. "By all means, Cavindish," he said with a smile. It was perfect. If he and the lovely Cartier were indeed a pair, this gave both of them an opportunity to be easily rid of him. On the other hand, if Cartier were merely the target of an evening's dalliance, then she would be free to return (or *not* return) as she wished. He turned and took her hand for a moment. "Eve," he said, "I look forward to seeing you again soon."

"I look forward to the same thing, Wilf," she said with an enigmatic little smile, "soon."

For the next half metacycle, Brim found that he knew a number of the guests aboard *Benwell*. During twenty-odd years of HyperSpace activity, one tends to collect acquaintances from all over the galaxy. He even encountered a member of his graduating class at the Helmsman's Academy, noting wryly how things had changed over the intervening decades. During those days, Carescrians had been looked down upon to the point of subjugation. Amazing how Captain's stripes changed people's opinions!

Moulding and Aram appeared to have blended into the party well, too, especially the latter. The young, red-haired A'zurnian clearly had winning ways, especially with a number of A'zurnian ladies from the Embassy. He thanked the Universe Aram's gregariousness seemed to have also worked on the prima-donna Helmsmen of 32 Squadron. It made things easier all the way around.

He had just accepted a fresh goblet of excellent Logish Meem when a hush suddenly came over the room as if someone had thrown a switch. Turning with a frown, he was just in time to watch Admiral Dugan himself step into the room followed immediately by the hefty bulk of a man whose visage now hung in the wardroom of every ship in the Imperial Fleet: Onrad V, Grand Galactic Emperor, Prince of the Reggio Star Cluster, and Rightful Protector of the Heavens.

Dressed in the uniform of a Vice Admiral (a rank he *earned* by his brilliant command of Task Group 16 during the Battle of Atalanta), Onrad was slightly taller than Brim and considerably heavier. A comfortable man of obvious royalty, he had dark brown hair and wore a short, pointed beard with perfectly trimmed mustaches. And even halfway across a room, the man's eyes clearly set him apart. As he greeted the high-ranking guests who immediately surrounded him, he had a way of looking at them that bespoke genuine honesty. Not the kind of bumpkin morality that attempts to please everyone, everywhere. Onrad's mien promised only that he would make the best decisions for his Empire, and if *you* happened to think you could help, so be it.

"Looks as if I was right," Moulding chuckled, joining Brim at the bar. "No wonder security was so tight at the brow."

Brim nodded, sipping his meem. Somehow, the unannounced appearance was just like Onrad—or at least the Onrad that he had come to know over the years. Pragmatic as well as human, the young Emperor would clearly have seen tonight's party as an opportunity to be with the people who would soon be protecting the very skies over his head *and* a much-needed personal diversion. He was an active man who must surely find his own royalty stultifying at times.

With all the high-ranking brass about, Brim expected he wouldn't get within ten irals of the new Emperor, so he found himself considerably surprised when he responded to a tap on the back ....

"It's been a bloody long time, Brim," Onrad said, offering his hand. "I'm sure you think I've forgotten all about you."

Brim grinned and took the Emperor's hand. "Your Majesty," he said, "I think that you've probably been busier than you can remember. And, er, congratulations, I think."

Onrad gave a private little laugh. "Save your congratulations for my father," Onrad joked. "He's the one who really benefited from his abdication."

"I'm glad I'm not running this war," Brim said.

"You'd better be running it," Onrad chuckled, "and the people who work for you, right down to the lowest-level feather merchant civilians. Because the higher I climb, the less I can see. And at my level, all I get is policy, with an occasional fillip of actual happenings."

"In that case, Your Majesty, I'll do my best," Brim joked.

Onrad put a hand on Brim's shoulder. "I know that, Brim," he said. "Don't ever forget that I know. You're not a squeaking wheel, so I won't often get around to personally making a fuss about your exploits—like when you managed to delay the whole bloody war for more than half a year. And you have already been awarded your second Imperial Comet for that, even if it may be a long time before either of us has sufficient time to accomplish the ceremony that awards the medal to you publicly."

Brim shook his head. "I don't particularly need medals," he said. "I'm certain you must realize how much better off I am right now than ninety-nine percent of all the Carescrians ever born."

"Medals make promotions easier, Brim," Onrad said, reaching inside his trousers pocket to retrieve a small leather pouch. "That's why I brought you this." Handing the pouch to Brim, he next drew a thick ribbon from within his formal jacket. "You'll have to wear this without ceremony until bloody Nergol Triannic provides us with enough breathing room to lay on a proper celebration."

Brim emptied the pouch into the palm of his hand. It contained an eight-pointed starburst in silver and dark blue enamel, inscribed with a single word at its center: VALOR.

"Here," Onrad said, handing the sash to Brim. "Slip this on right now—you should have been wearing it months ago. I awarded the bloody thing to you as one of my very first official acts as Emperor."

Brim unrolled the heavy loop of ribbon and clipped the gold disk to a catch sewn into its lower hem. "Onrad V, Grand Galactic Emperor, Prince of the Reggio Star Cluster, and Rightful Protector of the Heavens," he read aloud. "You know I'm terribly proud of this, Your Highness," he said, slipping the ribbon over his left shoulder to rest beside a similar ribbon and disk awarded by the previous Emperor.

"Well, Onrad said, "I suppose I feel rather proud of it myself. It's not that often that someone gets two of these things. I feel pretty good about awarding it."

"Thank you, Your Majesty," Brim said, sensing his face burn. "I'll do my best to make sure I continue to deserve the honor."

Onrad laughed quietly. "That's just like you, Brim," he said, grabbing the Carescrian's shoulder for a moment. "Anybody else would be breaking his arm in an attempt to pat his own back."

"I've got to fly with that arm tomorrow," Brim said with a grin. "Otherwise . . . I'd probably end up with a sling myself."

"Save it till we win the thraggling war." Onrad chuckled under his breath. "By the Universe, I'll proclaim a Wilf Brim Appreciation Day."

"I'll change my name, Your Majesty," Brim joked.

"We'll find you, Carescrian," Onrad returned. "I don't have Secret Police for nothing, you know." Then he frowned for a moment. "Wilf," he asked quietly, "do you remember the night years ago when Father awarded you your first Order of the Imperial Comet?''

Brim nodded. ''Aye, Your Majesty,'' he swore earnestly. ''It's a night I'll never forget so long as I live.''

''Turns out, Father found it hard to forget, too,'' Onrad said. ''I talked with him about it the next morning. He wanted to do something for Carescria; seems he'd promised you he'd try to make things better there.''

''Yes,'' Brim agreed, closing his eyes for a moment while his mind whirled backward in time to a wartime night in Avalon when he'd been decorated by Greyffin IV.

''You may or may not know it, my friend,'' Onrad said, looking Brim directly in the eye, ''but those new Carescrian starship factories turning out Starfury 1Cs and other warships are a direct result of that evening.''

Speechless, Brim could only shake his head in wonderment.

''Thought you'd like to know that,'' Onrad said softly, putting his hand on Brim's shoulder again. ''Keep up the good work, then. We won't have much of a chance of ceremonies until we've won the war.''

Brim nodded as he struggled to recover his senses. ''Until we win the war, Your Majesty,'' he said.

''Meanwhile,'' Onrad said, ''keep your ears and eyes open. You'll be in the thick of things once the zukeed Leaguers get around to having a go at us. When I need to know what's going on in Defense Command, I'll be around to see things through your eyes.''

''I shall be ready, Your Majesty,'' Brim said.

''Good.'' Onrad turned to leave but stopped in his tracks. ''Oh, Brim,'' he said, frowning over his shoulder.

''Yes, Your Majesty?'' Brim answered.

''Try to keep yourself and your friend Barbousse out of trouble for a while. All right?''

''Absolutely not, Your Majesty,'' Brim said with a smile.

Onrad grinned. ''In that case,'' he said, ''I'll start making plans for the victory celebration.''

* * *

Eve Cartier never did reappear that evening; Brim was not particularly surprised by her disappearance, but somehow felt a tinge of disappointment. There was something special about the Carescrian beauty, although he couldn't somehow define just what that was. And it wasn't that he wanted to take her to bed, although he had to admit that he certainly would like to do that, too. Eve Cartier was an extremely attractive woman, in many different ways. And not the least of them was her love of the home he had utterly forsaken.

Eventually, Onrad departed. Soon after, Brim and Moulding called up a staff skimmer, said their own good-byes, and started for the boarding lobby. They left Aram in the company of a perfectly stunning flighted woman from the A'zurnian Embassy. The two were so deep in conversation that the young Squadron Leader failed to even notice Brim's new decoration, and the Carescrian felt rather guilty breaking in to say he was leaving.

"Daresay we won't see him for a while," Moulding commented as he and Brim walked along the brow.

Brim chuckled. "Aram won't need to be back until tomorrow morning's inspection," he said, "early, of course. There's a shuttle he can catch that ought to leave the two of them plenty of time for fun. But he'd better be on time, though, or I'll leave feathers all over the satellite. And I mean it."

"Tough words, Wilf," Moulding commented with a raised eyebrow.

"Tough war coming up, as I see it," Brim replied thoughtfully. "We're not dealing with a bunch of hardened Imperial veterans like we did in Fluvanna. The gang we landed from Gimmas this morning is little more than a bunch of talented amateurs."

"A willing bunch, though," Moulding said defensively.

"Oh, they're willing enough," Brim agreed. "Universe knows they're all of that. But if we—you, Aram, and I—don't keep the pressure on them now, while the Leaguers aren't aiming their best punches directly at our chins, it'll be even harder on them when the blows do begin to fall. Universe, Toby, remember what it was like for us the first time we ran into the Leaguers, and we'd been fighting The Torond for more than a month."

"I remember," Moulding replied thoughtfully, "all too well. We certainly are not leading the ships full of veterans that we were in Fluvanna." He gave a sad little chuckle. "I hadn't wanted to say anything, Wilf," he sighed, "because you couldn't do anything more than I could about it, except work the poor sods harder. And I was already doing that." He looked down at the pavement for a moment. "I still *am,*" he muttered.

Brim nodded as they flagged down a staff skimmer. "I know you are," he said. "And by doing it, you're also driving yourself. Doesn't take a medic to see how desperately tired you've become yourself."

"Speak for yourself, Wilf," Moulding said with a sage nod. "You didn't get those bloodshot eyes from too much rest, either." He laughed grimly. "If any of us are still around at the end of this next big scrap, then all the torment—for both the driver and the driven—will seem quite worthwhile, I should think. Especially if we win."

"*When* we win," Brim corrected. "Those Starfury drivers of yours are doing xaxtdamned well. They'll come through in the pinch. I know it."

"All right, 'when we win.'" Moulding laughed, punching the Carescrian on his forearm. "I'd almost forgot I was talking to Wilf Brim."

Brim grinned and punched his old friend back. "Keep up the good work, Toby," he said. "Don't give 'em even a moment of free time to think about what might happen. The more practice they get, the better they'll do when they've got real Leaguers to fight."

"They'll be ready," Moulding assured him.

Brim nodded and smiled. But inside, he wasn't so certain of anything. The only true test of a warrior's skill was actual war, and they hadn't had much of that—yet.

* * *

Brim got his own first taste of action the third morning after arriving over Avalon. He had taken Starfury R6595 on a lone-wolf mission to help calibrate one of the highly secret BKAEW tracking systems lofted to the five-hundred-c'lenyt level earlier in the year. The highly classified satellites—hardly more than four armored control rooms centered in a huge antenna system—were rumored to use KA'PPA instantaneous-communication waves for tracking starships at distances measured in hundreds of light-years, where mere light-speed-limited wavelengths were clearly impractical.

From the orbit of Avalon, he was instructed to set a course of 145:19, which would bring the ship to Galactic coordinates HK*452/-68:435, approximately thirty-five hundred c'lenyts off the occupied Effer'wyckean planet of Ellivuaeb. From there, he would slow through LightSpeed, change course, and fly as far as the Thias-Remo star system KA'PPAing his position in relation to several asteroid clusters along the way. Then, he and his crew could come home. At face value, it sounded like an easy run, in and out before breakfast—*if* they were lucky. However, the area literally swarmed with Leaguer starship bases, and in reality, their only chance of coming through without a donnybrook was to move as rapidly as possible, thereby minimizing the likelihood of interception by what would simply have to be vastly superior Leaguer forces. . . .

Starfury R6595 cleared FleetPort 30 while the capital below was still in its dark period and passed into Hyperspeed shortly afterward. Looking aft, Brim could see the muted blaze of his Drive plume curving gently to port as he put the helm over and picked up his course for Effer'wyck. Forward through the Hyperscreens, the 'Wyckean Void extended to the Effer'wyckean coastal stars, while a tiny galaxy of glowing data flowed constantly across his readout panels. Not a hint of stray gravity marred their course as they hurtled through the majestic emptiness of interstellar space. A beautiful flight, in anybody's estimation.

They crossed the hundred or so light-years in no time at all.

Ellivuaeb was large in the Hyperscreens when Brim's KA'PPA display suddenly chimed and filled with the old-fashioned language symbols transmitted by the system, "R6595 FROM KGL-32, ORBIT HYPOSPEED IN PLACE, PLEASE."

Brim nodded, slowing through LightSpeed and circling while they calibrated their instruments. It was very comfortable at the helm of a Starfury, and soon he began to feel drowsy as he repetitiously went on flying the same closed course again and again. The KA'PPA brought that to a quick end, however, as it began to chime and abruptly changed its display. "R6595 FROM KGL-32, IMMEDIATELY KA'PPA YOUR MEAN DISTANCE FROM ELLIVUAEB."

Brim frowned and turned to nod at the Navigating Officer. Something must be up; it was certainly not yet time for his broadcasts in the clear. "Send it," he said.

Only a few cycles passed before the KA'PPA display chimed in response. "R6595 FROM KGL-32, STEER 090:15 IMMEDIATELY."

Instantly, Brim came alert. *If* BKAEW really did work, a suspicious starship could be somewhere about, just outside the range of T6595's own proximity indicators. Perhaps the operators wanted to identify him on their readouts. He put the helm hard over and skidded onto the new course. Then he looked around him, rolled left and right a few times to check on blind spots. Everything *looked* empty enough. He was below LightSpeed, so both he and any possible attackers would be leaving no Drive plume to track.

"LOOK OUT, R6595, AT A YELLOW-GREEN APEX," the KA'PPA chimed, "YOU ARE BEING SHADOWED BY ANOTHER STARSHIP."

Immediately, Brim turned his head in that direction and glimpsed a small, brilliant dot, slipping behind an asteroid shoal. It was too far away to identify, but if it were a Leaguer ship, he meant to keep a discreet eye on it. Turning onto his original course to make the other Helmsman commit himself, he called for action stations and gave permission to enable the ship's disruptors.

Within three cycles, the dot had become a chevron, one of the Gorn-Hoff 262E killer ships, most likely. The Leaguer cycled through a half-dozen banks, setting up his attack, clearly of the opinion that Brim and his Starfury had not yet detected him.

In a matter of moments, the Starfury was ready for battle. It was Brim's first action since he led a squadron of Starfuries at the great battle of Zonga'ar—and something in his warrior's psyche had been missing the rush of adrenaline that always preceded battle. He steeled himself and listened as the small bridge came alive with muted voices and running feet, switching extra gravity boost to the generators while summoning 115 percent from the power chambers. *All right, Leaguer,* he thought with a smile, *let's see you try it!*

"Here he comes," someone warned quietly from the rear of the bridge.

Brim looked up as the Leaguer angled into a gentle spiral, clearly designed to bring him in on R6595's tail. He was only a short distance away, relying on darkness to mask his movements and running slow to make certain of his kill.

"Hang on," Brim shouted, then punched the thrust dampers all the way forward, throwing the Starfury into a very deep turn away from the planet. Now, he could keep his eyes on the Leaguer and still maneuver.

Taken by surprise, the enemy gunners opened fired, but they were much too late, and the huge bursts of energy glowed harmlessly far astern of their intended target.

Brim leveled out and continued his right turn. The Gorn-Hoff tried to turn inside, but his steering engines had insufficient energy at that speed, and he flipped into a spin, caught in the planet's gravity. Once again, Mark Valerian's superb design had triumphed, and for a moment, Brim could see the League markings—big crimson daggers outlined in white—on the pale blue undersurface of the enemy craft.

The Gorn-Hoff came out of its spin almost immediately, but

Brim was already in position—and the Leaguer knew it, for he began hurling the big ship around in an effort to throw off Brim's gun layers. However, his stunting availed him nothing. Alford, at the fire-control console, opened fire at about fifteen hundred irals, filling space with a blinding welter of tremendous explosions.

Even at a disadvantage, however, the enemy Helmsman flew his 262 with a certain familiar style—Brim wondered for a moment if they had tangled previously, perhaps in Fluvanna. Shifting his ship about and constantly varying the line of sight, the Leaguer obviously knew that the Starfury turned and accelerated better, so Brim guessed his only hope would be to dive. He was right!

Brim rolled the Starfury onto its back and followed, taking advantage of his quarry's regular trajectory while Alford opened fire again. They went down toward Ellivuaeb at blinding speed. As soon as Brim was just off the Leaguer's tail, Alford's firing correction became relatively simple, but the Imperials had to hurry. The Leaguer was slowly pulling away, luring them down toward the surface where other powerful weapons systems waited.

At Alford's next salvo, three flashes appeared along the Leaguer's starboard side near the edge of the rear chevron. The Imperial gunner fired again, this time hitting first on a level with the gravity generators and then working his way toward the bridge. For a fraction of a click, the ship seemed to hesitate in the middle of its dive.

The Drive doors suddenly popped open, only to disappear in a cloud of raw energy guttering out of the exhaust tubes. Then a more violent explosion at the base of the chevron and a thin black trail mingled with the energy gushing from his perforated energy chambers.

It was the end. A tongue of radiation fire appeared from the Gorn-Hoff's belly as the hullmetal began to un-collapse. It lengthened, licked at the trailing edge, and dispersed in incandescent shreds.

By this time, the two ships had plunged into the dark side of the planet. The Gorn-Hoff, however, was finished. Brim climbed up again in spirals, watching him. The enemy ship was nothing but a vague outline now, fluttering helplessly downward, shaken at regular intervals. An explosion. A black trail. A white trail. An explosion. A black trail. A white trail. Soon, it was no more than a ball of flames streaking toward the surface like a meteor that ultimately scattered into a shower of flaming debris and extinguished harmlessly before it hit the surface.

No lifeglobes had ejected; some sixty-odd Leaguers had smoked their last TimeWeed.

The KA'PPA chimed. "R6595 FROM KGL-32, LONG TRANSMISSION, PLEASE. DID YOU GET THAT LEAGUER?"

Brim answered immediately. "KGL-32 FROM R6595 ANSWERING AND TRANSMITTING FOR FIX. GOT HIM ALL RIGHT. ONE . . . TWO . . . THREE . . . FOUR."

Afterward, the BKAEW Controller ordered them back to port. The spot was going to get unhealthy in a *very* short time.

Brim agreed wholeheartedly; it was time to head for home. Immediately, he set course for Avalon.

The next few days were momentous ones both for Brim and the Empire itself. Nergol Triannic, the League Emperor, moved headquarters all the way from his capital on Tarrott to the little town of Pechte on the Effer'wyckean agri-planet of Nemel. The move had a chilling effect in the Imperial Admiralty, for it revealed—as no other action could—the Leaguer's confidence that Effer'wyck was all but subdued.

Had he planned for effect—and there were many who suspected the Tyrant actually did make his move for that reason—Triannic's action could not have come at a worse time for the Effer'wyckean government. From the very beginning, Effer'wyckeans had mounted a great hue and cry for aid for the Empire—and to a large extent, that aid had been forthcoming, even after the miracle-debacle of Aunkayr. Their pleas had a special effect upon Emperor Onrad, whose ties with the beleaguered province were both political and personal. Grand Baron Reynard, the dominion's titular leader, was Onrad's second cousin, twice removed, and the two had been close friends since early childhood.

Now, however, Baxter Calhoun was developing second thoughts about aid for Effer'wyck—serious ones. It was one thing to help a friendly neighbor defend against his enemies, but quite another when that neighbor appeared as if he would shortly lose everything he had been given. Especially now that "everything" would come in very handy when the same enemy attacked Avalon! Brim was present at the conference when Calhoun rose and shocked a small confab of wing leaders by saying, "If the enemy developed a heavy space attack on us this very afternoon, I could na' guarantee superiority around the Triad for more than two Standard Days. An' tha's the truth."

In the end, Onrad demanded that Calhoun allocate four more squadrons of Defiants to the flagging Effer'wyckean campaign, and the Carescrian Admiral at last had to give in. Afterward, however, Calhoun prudently allotted the ships and crews with the proviso that they must operate from bases on one of the Triad's five planets.

Still the Empire waited. Intelligence from Sodeskayan spy masters indicated that the League High Command had been seriously considering an invasion of Avalon since before the turn of the Standard Year. After their recent victories, only the disastrous whipping they received at Zonga'ar had made the opportunistic Triannic hesitant. That and the fact he'd won so quickly that his Generals found themselves well ahead of their ability to plan. Too, he retained hopes that the CIGA movement he surreptitiously funded over the years would effect Imperial capitulation before he had to fire a disruptor. So the war continued, but only in and around the cringing dominion of Effer'wyck. The rest of civilization watched—waiting for what would happen next.

Two days following Brim's arrival at FleetPort 30, the watchers were rewarded—this time with an act of cowardice and treachery that shocked even the most cynical among them. At approximately Night:4:76, Standard Imperial Time, Grand Baron Rogan LaKarn of The Torond declared war on Effer'wyck, stealing advantage from the apparently inevitable victory his League allies would soon obtain in that dominion. To Brim, perhaps the most offensive part of LaKarn's act was not its rank cowardice so much as its intrinsic cynicism in regard to The Torond's Grand Baroness Margot, who was also "Princess of the Effer'wyck Dominions." And although the mysterious noblewoman had been missing from public view since Brim's destruction of the Leaguer space fort at Zonga'ar, she was, after all, LaKarn's wife—if indeed she was still alive. . . .

With this move, the Effer'wyckean situation became extremely confused. Soon afterward, General Hagbut gave way to Onrad's prodding and landed Imperial troops of the First Protean Division on the Effer'wyckean planet of Breyst at the same time that elements of Imperial Fifty-first were being evacuated from planets circling the huge binary star at Havre. A day earlier, other units of the same Fifty-first retreated onto the barren planet of Va'lery when they found themselves cut off from a main Effer'wyckean division by advancing Leaguers. Now *they* were calling for evacuation, too. Early the next evening, Brim received a top-secret message from the Admiralty:

TNY 3346-1-A16E GROUP 445Y 216/52012
[TOP SECRET-IMPERIAL PALACE]
SORTIE ORDER

FROM:
BU FLEET OPERATIONS;
ADMIRALTY, AVALON

TO:
W. A. BRIM, CAPTAIN, I.F., FLEETPORT 30
<QWE7EF475512-FQ90-CJ13245JGQA-LJG>
SUBJECT: TRANSPORTATION ARRANGEMENTS

TOMORROW AT DAWN:2:31 YOU WILL TRANSPORT EMPEROR ONRAD V, TWO OTHERS, CLASSIFIED DESTINATION. H. MAJESTY PERSONALLY

CARRIES COORDINATES. INSURE STARSHIP FULLY ARMED. RETURN AT H. MAJESTY'S DISCRETION.

NOTE; YOU WILL SORTIE WITHOUT ESCORT.

FOR THE EMPEROR
A. T. ZAPT, MAJOR GENERAL, I.F.

[END TOP SECRET IMPERIAL PALACE]
TNY 3346-1-A16E

Scant metacycles later—following an all-night session of frenzied cleaning, polishing, and scrubbing—P7350 and her deservedly tired crew were ready as Brim could make them. He had just changed into a clean uniform when the Crown Prince and his guests arrived without fanfare aboard a small, nondescript Fleet shuttle. Puffing from an all-out run halfway around the rim of the big, artificial satellite, Brim met them at the boarding hatch.

"Morning, Brim," the Emperor said with a smile. "Shame to get you up so early, but I've scheduled a number of meetings at the other end, and I want to get them all finished in a single day."

Brim laughed inwardly. "Oh, you didn't get us up, Your Majesty," he said with a smile. "We're ready to lift ship anytime you are."

"Somehow, I had no doubts about that," Onrad said with a wink. "And by the way, I think you'll find that you've already met both your other passengers."

It was true. Brim recognized the next one out immediately. "Lord Jaiswal," he said, moving to help the small man steer a large grip-all through the hatch.

"Hello, Brim," Jaiswal said in a deep voice, straightening himself with a great smile. "Our paths haven't crossed since the Dytasburg Conference, have they?" Wearing the white satin coveralls, gray cape, and black velvet cap that seemed to be his personal trademark, the squat, muscular official had a massive, frowning brow, sharp nose, pointed mustache, and the cold eyes of a professional assassin. A wealthy man by dint of many activities—some reportedly legal—Jaiswal was patriotic nearly to the point of obsession and considered by many CIGAs as one of their most dangerous enemies in Avalon. Along with Brim's Carescrian mentor Baxter Calhoun, he had personally funded construction of the first Starfury, K5054, and during the years that followed exhibited a certain flair—perhaps genius was a better description—for directing production. Shortly after naming him Lord Jaiswal, Onrad V also appointed him Minister of Starship Production, and immediately, the smallish Jaiswal bent to his new set of tasks as if the whole Empire depended upon his efforts—which, in large measure, was true. . . .

The third passenger to back out of the shuttle was a huge Sodeskayan.

"Nik?" Brim demanded, narrowing his eyes in amazement.

"Wilfooshka!" the Bear exclaimed, turning to lift Brim from his feet.

"Nik Ursis," Brim stammered. "What in the name of Voot are *you* doing here?"

"After Zonga'ar, how can they win war without us?" Ursis answered in mock seriousness. He stood at least a quarter again as tall as Brim with dark reddish-brown fur, a long, urbane muzzle that terminated in a huge, wet nose, and small gray eyes of enormous intensity. Like his colleague Borodov, he wore elegant fang gems at either side of his grin. Also like his old friend Borodov, he cut a dashing figure in his country's distinctive *papakha*, soft leather boots, and maroon Fleet Cloak. A highly respected theoretical physicist and Drive engineer in peacetime, Ursis served as Dean of the famous Dytasburg Academy on the G.F.S.S. planet of Zhiv'ot. However, he was also a warrior without peer, and like many of his Sodeskayan contemporaries, he had a natural proclivity for what they termed, simply, "The Hunt."

"Brim" Onrad chuckled, "you've got more friends and

acquaintances than Horgroath has moons. Everywhere you go, it seems like old home week for xaxt's sake.''

''I've noticed that, Your Majesty.'' Brim laughed. ''Probably I'm getting old—it takes a long time to run into so many people.''

Onrad took a long look at Brim in feigned judgment. ''Good thing the Leaguers haven't caught wind of this so-called aging of yours.'' He laughed, then checked his timepiece. ''We'd better be on our way, then,'' he said. ''We've a raft of important meetings and only a few metacycles to get through them.''

''By the way, Your Majesty,'' Brim interjected quietly, ''the Navigator doesn't know where those meetings are to be held yet.''

''Oh.'' Onrad pursed his lips. ''That's right, Brim,'' he said, ''after you lift off, set course for Gimmas. I'll give him the real coordinates once we're into space.''

Brim paused a moment, then shrugged inwardly. It *was* Onrad's trip, after all. Actually, it was Onrad's *ship* as well—Emperors owned everything so far as the Fleet was concerned. Including, at least for this trip, destinations. ''This way, Your Majesty,'' he said, and led the way into the corridor.

They arrived at P7350 after a short walk—passing a number of astonished faces—and boarded the ship through a full honor guard Barbousse had thoughtfully assembled at the head of the tube. Only a few irals into the boarding lobby, however, Onrad began to peer around and sniff the air. ''What's in xaxt's name is that I smell?'' he demanded. ''If I didn't know better, I'd swear someone spilled a whole bucket of metal polish somewhere.''

Opposite Brim—and behind the Emperor—a number of faces suddenly went to deep red, and it was obvious that the honor guard, all of whom had been a part of the spiff detail, were having serious difficulty stifling bellows of laughter, especially Barbousse, who had driven them like galley slaves.

''Um, yes, Your Majesty,'' Brim replied, having his own difficulties with nascent laughter. ''We, er, try to keep the ship as clean as possible.''

"Glad to hear that," Onrad said, breaking into his own grin. "And never get the idea that I don't appreciate the spiff work you've done on my behalf. It bloody well shows you've pride in your ship. Spirit, that's what it is. And it's going to take all the spirit you can muster when you start meeting the Leaguers in force. Right, Brim? Ursis?"

"Aye, Your Majesty," Brim replied.

"Like dark ice caves and howling snow, as they say," Ursis agreed.

Onrad rolled his eyes. "As they say," he repeated helplessly. "Now, Brim, how do you find the bridge in this partially gutted bucket of bolts?"

"I'll take you there straightaway, Your Majesty," Brim replied. "Chief," he said, turning to Barbousse, "show Lord Jaiswal to the jump seat you rigged in the attack station. Nik, they'll find you a place in the Drive chambers." With that, he nodded to Onrad and started off for the bridge companionway.

P7350 was climbing out past flight level 800 before Onrad tapped Brim on the shoulder from his jump seat immediately behind the helm. "I'd imagine you're anxious to learn where we're going now, aren't you?" he chuckled.

Brim turned as the last orbiting buoy faded in the gloom. "Oh, no, Your Majesty," he said with a grin. "It's Falco, the Navigator, who's *really* curious."

"Smart Carescrian zukeed," Onrad chuckled. "I assume Valerian left the Nav station up here in this abbreviated bridge."

"The console directly behind your seat on the left, Your Majesty," Brim said. "Lieutenant Falco."

"Falco," he heard Onrad say a moment later, "they gave me these two disks—said you'd know what to do with 'em."

"Aye, Your Majesty," Falco replied, "I'll take care of them." Moments later, Brim's course-director panels came alive with a flood of colored directional vectors, all registering OFF COURSE warnings of one sort or another. *Effer'wyck!* he grumped to himself. He should have known. Onrad would have to see how bad things were with his own eyes, no matter what the risks. All the security made sense, now, too. League forces would be little more than a few light-years distant from the conferences. Putting the helm over, he carefully but quickly set course for Luculent.

"Bloody embarrassing to keep everything from you people so long," Onrad continued from his jump seat. "It was the only way I could talk that staff of mine into letting me make this trip at all. Damned fools see spies and assassins around every corner."

"Beggin' the Emperor's pardon," Brim answered, "but I can't say as I blame them at all. You'd be quite a prize for the Leaguers to capture and parade about in front of their cameras. A disaster of that magnitude might just win them a whole war."

Onrad sighed. "I know, Brim," he said quietly. "It's one of the penalties one pays for being Emperor. One of the big ones."

Brim got a straight-in approach to the Effer'wyckean capital of Luculent the first time he asked for it. Clearly, someone on the surface knew who was aboard his Starfury, but all the same, it was evident that traffic—at least civilian traffic—in and out of space was nearly nonexistent. Probably, he surmised, everyone who had someplace off-planet to go—and a way to get there—was already long en route. But even so, the city's great network of avenues below looked characteristically busy as he overflew lofty old Legend Tower, asserting its own meaningless construction at the very center of town. An afternoon of intermittent rain was waning on this part of the planet; to port, he could see great slabs of light among the showers. Farther out, the immense Effer'wyckean National Museum of Galactic Art gleamed soddenly, dominating a tiny forest completely surrounded by the ancient crystalline building. Off to the left rose the glistening towers of the grand Norchelite cé Effer'wyck (one of the great examples of Gradgroat cathedral architecture) begun nearly a thousand years in the past.

He recalled prowling the narrow streets nearby with Margot shortly after the first war, she disguised as one of the city's many prostitutes against discovery by her husband's secret police. They'd stopped at every third pastry shop for flaky, gooey, buttery sweets, eating them as they walked, getting sticky-faced as two children and licking their fingers. Afterward, in a little top-floor flat with a large window overlooking the city's famous lake, they made love again and again until they felt there was nothing more they needed to invent before they died. And then they went off for more pastries.

Almost a normal afternoon below in Luculent. But as he turned into final, Brim could see the great boulevards were not just busy, they were *swarming* with people. He bit his lip. The citizens were evacuating the city—in chaos. The great metropolis was vomiting out an almost pitiful collection of conveyances; shining, high-speed skimmers, ancient goods carriers covered with a half century of dust. There were lorries, carry-alls, delivery vans, even construction carts. Had he seen a wheeled vehicle in the snarled traffic, if would not have astonished him at all. Every box that could hover and provide traction had been dug up and was now laden with treasures that had once spelled home to these panicked city-dwellers.

As he lined up on the ruby landing vector, he ground his teeth in compassion for the pitiable clutter of gravity machines below—they carried the people too insignificant to get off the planet. Most of them wouldn't even get very far out of town. Without spare parts, without mechanics, without energy resources, they formed long caravans of doom. How long would the older vehicles run before they failed? Braking, stopping, starting, turning in the midst of an inextricable jam. And the survivors would make no more than ten c'lenyts a day through the maze of disabled wrecks.

A lifetime of Helmsmanship forced Brim's mind back to the business of landfall. And if the city's roads had been jammed with refugees, Lake Doering that fronted the terminal district was uncharacteristically empty, for it led only to outer space, and those who could leave that way had already gone. He'd never seen the lake that way. Luculent was one of the largest, most cosmopolitan, and busiest cities in the known Universe, in many ways a rival of Avalon herself. Yet today, its once-teeming space harbor looked as it must appear during the national holidays. The pretentious old Dortmond Imperial Terminal itself was nearly deserted as he taxied up to one of the general-navigation gravity pools. It lent an unnatural character to everything in sight.

Once P7350 was moored—and special guards dressed in mufti were deployed around the ship—Onrad, Ursis, and Jaiswal were whisked away aboard a great, darkened limousine skimmer. "Take in the city if you can," the Emperor confided to Brim just before his departure. "It may be the last chance you get for a long time, and the Effer'wyckean Secret Police will know where to find you when it's time to go home."

Brim smiled thanks and saluted wordlessly. But he did not take advantage of Onrad's kind offer, nor did he pass word to the others that the alternative was available. He and his crew were paid to chauffeur—and, if necessary, protect—the Emperor, not to enjoy the surroundings, tantalizing as they might be. He did take a few moments out to buy one of the country's fabled timepieces in a duty-free shop of the terminal block. At the going prices, he even had his name engraved on it. Aside from that, he remained within walking distance of the ship.

CHAPTER 4

GravAnchors and Identities

Toward midday, local time, Onrad and Jaiswal sent word that they would require nearly the whole day in Efferwyck learning the situation firsthand. Ursis, however, returned during the late afternoon and immediately joined Brim on the bridge.

"Nik," the Carescrian exclaimed, looking up from a display filled with administrative minutiae, "why didn't you tell me you were coming?"

"Secret mission," Ursis said as he tossed his Fleet Cloak over a darkened navigational display. "Anastas Alexi has told you about the position I've taken with the Intelligence Services?"

"He told me of it," Brim said with a smile, "not about it."

This time, it was the Bear's turn to smile. "Everything about it is secret," he said. "Right now, everybody thinks I'm still somewhere in Gromcow."

"Pretty damned secret if you can't tell your friends," Brim complained in feigned petulance.

The Bear laughed. "I only got in last night, Wilfooshka," he said, rolling his eyes. "I haven't even checked in with the Embassy."

"What are you going to be doing?" Brim asked.

"Liaison work," Ursis replied. "I'll be back and forth all the time, so we'll have ample time to share a few goblets of Logish Meem, friend Brim."

"I'll hope so," Brim replied, then he frowned. "What's it like out there?" he asked.

The Bear shook his head gravely. "Worse than I imagined," he said, settling heavily into Onrad's jump seat. "'Wycks have panicked. Utterly panicked. Today, Wilf, I talked to people at all levels and ranks, many from front-line planets—wherever those happen to be at any given moment. Big Cheeses in High Command try to make Onrad believe they still have control, but they don't. Nobody has control, except maybe Leaguers. Xaxtdamned CIGAs have so weakened whole government that military has no effective leadership above battalion level. Little armies, little squadrons—fragments—all try to fight same enemy, but no real coordination from High Command." He squeezed his eyes shut for a moment. "I have talked to many brave men out there, fighting Leaguers tooth and claw. But alone—in small, uncoordinated groups—they haven't chance of icicle in collapsium furnace."

Brim pursed his lips. "And it's our turn next in Avalon," he said to no one in particular. "I wonder how we'll fare in that furnace."

"Depends," Ursis said quietly.

Brim looked up and frowned. "On what, Nik?"

The Bear smiled kindly and put a hirsute, six-fingered hand on each of Brim's shoulders. "On things you already know about, Wilfooshka," he said. "Training, spirit, bravery, commitment to dominion, equipment. Nothing new." He frowned and shrugged. "'Wycks have it all, except perhaps spirit—and they even had that in beginning. But without coordination, then all 'usual' things break themselves individually against coordinated opposition. You understand."

Brim nodded. "Yeah, Nik," he said, "I understand."

"So, friend Brim," Ursis continued, leaning back in the seat, "when Leaguers finally come after Avalon, as they will, if everything else is in place—spirit, bravery, equipment, and the like—immediate future of our old Empire will probably depend on your countryman Baxter Calhoun, whom Onrad has determined will lead Defense Command.'' For a moment he peered critically at the claws extending from his long, slim fingers, then he nodded to himself. ''With help of BKAEW, he will most likely prevail against confusion.''

''Yeah,'' Brim agreed quietly. ''I have already seen a little of what BKAEW can do.''

Ursis grinned. ''So I have heard. Voof! For first time in . . . what, five, six hundred Standard Years, starships can be sensed and positioned before they slow below LightSpeed. Newest BKAEW sets—as you already know—can 'see' all way across 'Wyckean Void and beyond. It may well become most critical technology in coming war. At least, is how we Bears see things. And believe me, furless friend, we watch, because no matter how things turn out in Avalon, Sodeskaya is Triannic's next target.''

''Makes sense,'' Brim said. ''But BKAEW's pretty new stuff. I've only seen a couple of stations.''

Ursis laughed. ''You haven't been here all that long, Wilfooshka. BKAEW is well past experimental stage. Each of your five planets has at least three of those crazy-looking satellites.''

''I didn't know that,'' Brim said. ''But then I haven't been especially looking for them, either.''

Ursis laughed. ''But I'll bet you *have* noticed how much more accurate your vector controllers have been during past month or so?''

Brim frowned. He had, come to think of it. ''I guess I hadn't been doing much questioning lately,'' he admitted, nodding toward the display cluttered with day reports, manning tables, ship availability projections, budget authorizations. He laughed unhappily. ''This exalted position of mine requires I spend as much time tending to admin garbage as I do trying to kill Leaguers.''

Ursis laughed. ''When one is busy just keeping head

attached to shoulders—as you are—is quite easy to neglect other things,'' he said, then raised both his eyebrows and an index finger. ''*There,* my Imperial friend,'' he said with a chuckle, ''a Sodeskayan aphorism even humans can understand.''

''Amazing,'' Brim said in mock astonishment. ''Next thing, you Bears'll be smoking deodorized Hogge'Poa in those Zempa pipes of yours.''

''Fat chance of that!'' Ursis chuckled. ''Not so long as lady Bears think Hogge'Poa smells sexy.''

''Lost cause, eh?''

''Believe it, friend Brim. Believe it. . . .''

When Onrad and Jaiswal finally did return to the ship, Brim had little trouble guessing the outcome of their talks.

Striding directly from their limousine with no outward sign of emotion, both men quickly acknowledged Barbousse's honor guard, then hurried into the ship's tiny boarding lobby. ''Let's get out of here, Brim,'' Onrad said, his lips pressed into a white slit in his face. ''I cannot much longer stand this ichor of defeat. . . .''

Later, once they were into deep space and safely on the way back to Avalon, Onrad gently tapped Brim on the shoulder. ''I suppose Ursis has already told you about the conferences,'' he said.

Brim put the ship on autohelm and turned in his recliner. ''He did, Your Majesty,'' he said, ''at least the conferences he attended.''

''Bad?'' Onrad asked.

''In his eyes, Your Majesty,'' Brim replied.

''In mine, too,'' Onrad said grimly, ''*and* in Jaiswal's. The defense back there in Effer'wyck is now in tatters. Oh, they'll fight on as long as they can. Especially if we send more reinforcements—which we will almost certainly have to do if we hope to put the Empire back together after the war. But they can't last anymore than a few more days, and we shall have to be on our guard every moment or they'll try to take us with them. Nations that go down fighting rise again,'' he asserted with a fierce look in his eyes, "but those that surrender tamely are finished. . . ."

The Emperor's short-range predictions were all too accurate. Within two Standard Days, the Effer'wyckean capital of Luculent was bloodlessly occupied by the League with parades and celebrations of great pomp and ceremony. Galactic media everywhere suddenly filled with views of Triannic and his henchmen marching along the Luculent's wide Boulevard of Heroes.

At last came the great blow. Even while the last Imperial troops were reembarking for Avalon, Effer'wyckean Prime Minister Holleran-Millard KA'PPAed to the Universe from the little planet Darendyl in the Forbean provinces, "It is with a broken heart," he began, "that I tell you today that fighting must cease. . . ."

Three short days later, on the twenty-sixth (the 1,250th anniversary of the Empire's victory at the battle of Ool'retaw), an Effer'wyckean puppet government signed armistice with the League, and the Empire began final preparations for the invasion that must certainly follow on the heels of Triannic's latest conquest.

That night, as Leaguers proudly toured the Effer'wyckean capital, Onrad appeared throughout the Triad's media, broadcasting simultaneously to all five of the Home Planets and by KA'PPA to the far reaches of the Empire. Brim joined most of the off-duty officers of FleetPort 30 in the satellite's big wardroom where a huge global display had been wheeled in from one of the situation rooms.

During most of the day, the media had been rife with a succession of pundits reviewing the Effer'wyckean situation in minute detail, and by the time Onrad was due in the big globe, the room was both crowded and strangely quiet—a far cry from its usual high-spirited atmosphere. When the Emperor's image appeared in the center of the globe, a murmur of palpable admiration swept the officers. Brim had never seen the man so wrought up, and doubted that many of the others had either.

After brief statements of introduction, the burly Emperor

adjusted his spectacles and launched into the topic that everyone knew was coming. ''The Battle of Effer'wyck is over . . .'' he stated in a voice that was uncharacteristically hesitant—almost slurred. ''I expect the Battle of Avalon is about to begin.'' Everyone in the wardroom was now listening in absolute silence, hanging on his every word. ''Very soon,'' he continued, glowering from the full-sized display as if he were talking personally to each of his viewers, ''the whole fury and might of the enemy must be turned on us. Triannic knows he will have to break us on these five planets or lose the war.'' His words grew louder and more assured as he approached his emphatic conclusion. ''Let us therefore brace to our duties,'' he growled, thrusting his chin forward as if in defiance, ''and bear ourselves in such a manner that if this hoary old Empire and its dominions last for a thousand Standard Years or more, living beings throughout the Universe will say that *this* was the finest moment of all!''

A stunned hush extended the silence for perhaps three clicks more, then the wardroom suddenly erupted in an emotional paroxysm of shouting and acclamation that continued until everyone was literally breathless. Brim, however, stood aside during the initial rush for the bar, watching reflectively and remembering other such nights filled with wild bravado by people who had little conception of what *really* lay in store when they encountered the outrageous, barbarous visage of battle. He closed his eyes for a moment while a thousand visions—each more horrible and bloody than its predecessor—paraded before his eyes. Hellish noise . . . blinding light . . . concussion. Fright so palpable you could reach out and touch it. Screams filling your battle helmet that couldn't be turned off. Death. Death. More death! Grinding his teeth, he waited until there was room at the bar, then using Captain's privilege, he carried two whole bottles of Logish Meem back to his cabin and drank himself senseless.

Next morning, at the weekly Squadron Leaders' briefing, a badly hung-over Wilf Brim learned from Imperial staff planners that Triannic's promised invasion—which his jackbooted Controllers had code-named Operation Death's Head—might be only a matter of weeks, perhaps days, away. Hundreds of thousands of Avalonian civilians on all five planets had already been put to work under General Hagbut in what was euphemistically called the "Home Guard," making defensive preparations—while CIGAs demonstrated stridently against them. A number of fights had broken out between the workers and their noisy opposition, slowing the defensive preparations and causing general upheaval. But as General Drummond, Commander of the Home Fleet, noted in his midmorning address, CIGA membership *did* appear to be evaporating by the day.

His observation was the only completely positive note in a generally troubled gathering, for within Imperial military circles, it was recognized that the Emperor's ability to resist invasion was riding at absolute nadir. Even the irrepressible Hagbut admitted in secret session during the afternoon that his ill-trained and ill-armed Home Guard could do no more than delay Triannic's victory march in Avalon by perhaps three Standard Weeks—if that.

Within a week, the Triad began to feel the full might of Admiral Hoth Orgoth's Military Space Arm. It was almost a relief to Brim when the first actual blows fell, and for the remainder of the forty-day Standard Month—while Triannic gloated during visits to the sites of his conquests—Brim flew constant patrols with each of his two squadrons in the vicinity of Avalon.

As the month of Heptad began, the Imperial situation was only slightly improved from the beginning of the previous month. However, definite progress *was* being made, and each passing day made it a little more difficult for the Leaguers to launch a successful invasion. On the First, the number of Imperial killer ships totaled 607, an increase of 189.

Unfortunately, they were nearly alone in their defense of Avalon against what many Sodeskayans estimated to be in the neighborhood of thirty-five hundred League warships. Almost half of these consisted of GH 262s and 270s, the latter a larger and somewhat clumsier version of the 262. These killer ships were to protect little more than a thousand long-range attack ships, and approximately three hundred Zachtwager precision attack craft. ("Zachtwager" was short for the Vertrucht word *Zachtwagerheizenforst*, or simply "precision shooter.") According to Ursis, many important Leaguers felt that the ratio of attack craft to killer ships was much too high (approximately one to one), but Triannic continued to concentrate on building attack ships.

During the following week, invasion evidence continued to accumulate as Leaguer forces practiced landing operations on Memel, another Effer'wyckean planet. At the same time, fat Admiral Hoth Orgoth's star fleets pressed their attacks on intra-Triad shipping to the utmost—causing a noticeable strain on the Imperial Defense Fleet that now found itself flying more than three hundred sorties a day. . . .

Leaguers everywhere! Yellow bellies, crimson dagger insignias, and chevron-profiled starships swarming like great insects around a convoy of light-limited space barges and interplanetary packets. Great eruptions of energy flashed in the darkness like new stars. Space was crisscrossed with a veritable rainbow of disruptor beams. On patrol today in newly acquired Starfury D7436, Brim instinctively blinked as he dived close by a disabled Gorn-Hoff trailing black ribbons of smoke on its way toward destruction below—no point in wasting energy, the zukeed was already finished. Swallowing hard to clear a bitter taste from his mouth, he pulled out violently and took off after another Leaguer. Moments later, Gordon, the Gunnery Officer, pressed his triggers and the whole Universe seemed to explode as fourteen big disruptors salvoed with a preposterous roar, shaking the spaceframe and dimming the Hyperscreens.

Missed!

Clearly surprised, the Leaguer fell away. Off to starboard,

Moulding fired on him and missed too—but now a gray Gorn-Hoff, its turrets ablaze with disruptor fire, was after *him*.

"Look out, Toby!" Brim broadcast on the short-range Helmsman network. "Break starboard!" Quickly he skidded the Starfury around, but too late. The Gorn-Hoff was already out of range. Inside his battlesuit, Brim was drenched in sweat.

In front of him, two Gorn-Hoffs were converging to attack an ancient interplanetary packet—so old that its bridge was still decorated in the burnished gold of the Guild. Brim glanced in the rearview screen. Moulding was still there, flying as if the two ships were attached by cables.

From the rear of the bridge, Brim could hear Gordon calling off firing parameters. Outside on the decks, the turrets were swinging just left of center. Once again, R6595 shuddered from the hammerblows of its own disruptors. Three flashes, a belch of radiation fire, and an angry trail unfurled in the Leaguer's wake.

Just then, Brim spied a roiling sheet of radiation fire just where Moulding's Starfury ought to have been at that moment. His heart skipped a beat—but in that same moment it was Moulding's triumphant voice that shouted in the Helmsman's network.

"Did you see that, Wilf? I got the bloody zukeed!"

Out of the corner of his eye, Brim could see Moulding's Starfury keeping station two hundred irals off his starboard pontoon. What a relief! He opened his mouth to congratulate his friend when . . . suddenly a thunderclap. A burning slap through the faceplate of his helmet. His eardrums felt as if they had just been pierced by a shriek of air exiting through a hole just melted through his forward Hyperscreen.

Another!

This blast carried away his whole forward Hyperscreen assembly in a rush of painful brilliance and concussion. He broke frantically; the Leaguer was so close that the flash of his big disruptors was blinding without the Hyperscreens for protection. But half his own turrets whirled as they opened return fire, and the Gorn-Hoff was forced to break away.

In the first moments after the explosion, Brim lost all notion of what was going on. For ten cycles at least, he blindly followed Moulding's instructions over the Helmsman's network. When he finally picked up a thread of sensibility again, R6595 was halfway back to Avalon. His head was swimming and there was a warm trickle from his nostrils. Blood? He could vaguely hear someone—the BKAEW director or Moulding?—in his helmet phones, but the COMM system was obviously damaged, and he couldn't make out what was being said. Miraculously, a check throughout the ship revealed only superficial casualties and major damage apparently limited to the bridge area. Nevertheless, Brim decided to put down at the nearest FleetPort rather than chance a really serious mishap due to battle damage that might have gone undetected. "Nesbitt, you still alive after all that?" he asked.

"More or less, Captain," the Navigator reported in a shaken voice. "What's on your mind?"

"Getting this bus into some solid, friendly berth," Brim replied. "Soon as possible and with minimum maneuvering."

"Aye, sir," Nesbitt responded. "Sounds like a great idea to me."

Moments later Brim's nav panel reconfigured with a new course. "Ariel, eh?" he muttered.

"At our present sidereal, Captain," Nesbitt replied, "FleetPort 19 seems to be the most direct route to a friendly base."

"We'll take it," Brim said, then switched a global display to the systems officer. "Thompson," he ordered, "keep an extra close watch on the steering-engine controls. I'll want to know immediately when anything shows out of tolerance. Understand?"

"Uh . . . *understand*, Captain," Thompson replied in a nervous voice.

Brim nodded and returned to his controls with a grimace. So much for green crews. He hated to think what would happen when they took some real damage. Then he shrugged. This was an easy initiation. They were bloodied now, so to speak, and wouldn't have to face their "first time" again. Maybe it was all for the best.

Maybe. . . .

* * *

"All hands secure from deep-space quarters," squawked the blower, "man your berthing stations, special mooring details. All hands secure from deep-space quarters; man your berthing stations, special mooring details. . . ."

FleetPort 19 appeared identical to FleetPort 30, except for the name emblazoned in old-fashioned characters below its upper antenna field. And of course its planet Ariel orbited farther out from the Triad than did Avalon. At present, only a few ships were moored about the periphery, indicating that some of its squadrons had yet to return from their sorties. Brim began his approach as soon as the controller assigned him a berth. He shook his head; if it wasn't the smallest berth on the periphery, it was certainly in the running for such a distinction—between two heavy cruisers nearly a third again as large as his Starfury.

For a moment his mind's eye remembered his days in the Carescrian ore barges when all that mattered was unloading quickly, and if you banged into a neighbor in your haste (or perhaps "accidentally" disabled a competitor that way), so be it. He chuckled grimly. What an introduction to the Fleet! At the Academy, he quickly learned that so much as a single collision—anywhere—could ruin a Helmsman's entire career. And the rule was still in effect. Imperial Helmsmanship standards tolerated only perfection. Nothing, absolutely nothing, would substitute.

With the generators at dead slow he came abreast of the berth. The two heavy cruisers and their great, frowning bridges on either side made it look half as large as he knew it was. And framed by jagged shards of the blasted Hyperscreens, the scene to port would have assumed on a character of impending danger had it not been for the superb docking systems winking at him for his shadows.

Reversing the starboard gravity generators, he applied gentle power to those in the port pontoon and . . .

Wait!

Instead of coming to a halt and twisting her stern to port, the ship was swinging her *head* to port and picking up speed—in a tight curve *away* from the berth! Instantly, he fed more reverse to the starboard generators, but nothing happened. Meanwhile, the damaged Starfury had continued all the way around her curve and was now heading toward the center of the station—picking up speed every moment.

Instinctively, Brim put all four generators into reverse and poured on the power while alarms beamed from the satellite jangled in his helmet.

Still nothing! Except that the ship was no longer curving. Instead, it now seemed intent on pinioning the nearest of the two cruisers beside his intended berth—dead center. The reverse actuators had failed!

"Stand by for collision bow on," the blower howled. "Stand by for collision bow on. All hands close airtight doors forward of frame thirty-four. All hands close airtight doors forward of frame thirty-four."

Grinding his teeth, Brim put the helm over hard to starboard and threw half power to both port generators while someone behind him in the bridge crew began mumbling Gradygroat litanies.

Litanies or no litanies, prayer wasn't going to be enough!

"Collision alarm, bow on! Collision alarm, bow on!"

In desperation, Brim literally stood on the right gravity brake actuator. That did it! With a grinding roar that could be heard as if it were in the next compartment, both starboard gravity generators jammed themselves into full power reverse, sending the ship into a violent cartwheel that nearly ripped the right pontoon and trouser from the main hull. Every weld in the spaceframe groaned and creaked while hullmetal on the main deck actually wrinkled before his very eyes. A cataract of stars flashed diagonally across the broken Hyperscreens and the voice circuits filled with startled shouts and screams of panic as they again headed precipitiously on a collision course for the main station.

"Belay the noise, you xaxtdamned jellyfish!" Brim shouted angrily above the raucous clamor. Coming off the brake and the power at the same time, he leaned into the helm, skidded the ship slightly to port, and passed over the boreal antenna field with nearly ten irals to spare. Then, with a little maneuvering room, he banked carefully into a vector to both cancel his orbital speed and permit gravity to bring him to a halt. Finally, rolling the ship onto its back, he headed up and over, again matching the satellite's orbital speed and using his gravity-brake circuits to activate the reverse. Only when he had regained stable control of the ship did he notice that the bridge—indeed the whole voice circuit network—had gone completely silent.

"N-nice m-m-maneuvering, Captain," the FleetPort 19 Controller stammered as Brim approached at no more than a crawl.

"Thanks," Brim said through his teeth. Inside his battlesuit, he was drenched in sweat and vexed as a wet crascon—both with himself for letting the ship get away from him and with the unseasoned crew for openly displaying their fear. Grinding his teeth until he got control of his temper, he called Barbousse at a gunnery console aft, "Chief, I'll need both GravAnchors immediately. You handle 'em, and put a good man at the aft docking cupola."

"Aye, Cap'm," Barbousse answered as if this were the normal manner of mooring. "We'll be makin' the Atalantan mooring?"

"That's it, Chief," Brim affirmed. "Drop 'em at my command." The "Atalantan" maneuver was old-fashioned ship handling—and difficult—but absolutely essential in space when working room was scarce and automatic facilities were missing. This time, the missing facility was the very ability to maneuver!

He concentrated. GravAnchors were little more than small, powerful tractor units with optical cleats for mooring beams. Once activated, their only purpose was to automatically maintain a point in space by exerting thrust in the opposite direction from any force applied to them. He'd situate both out from the satellite to secure the starship's bow while he used the stern mooring beams to draw the ship backward into her berth. Easier said than done—but achievable nonetheless.

Rapidly calculating, he worked the parameters in his head. The forward mooring projectors had a maximum range of little more than four hundred irals, so he picked three hundred as a workable scope and allowed for a good thirty-three percent margin of error.

Now, with 300 irals maximum between the anchor and the bow, a 664-iral ship, and her stern close in to the satellite when he was finished, he ought to drop the anchors about 1400 irals out. Narrowing his eyes, he made a small correction to starboard, but since he was eye-balling everything anyhow, "close" was as good as he was going to get.

Approaching with the satellite off to port, he waited until the ship had coasted to about 150 irals short of a position abreast the berth. "Drop starboard, Chief," he ordered tensely. "And let the beam surge as we move away." That would hold moderate tension on the beam but let it slip enough to permit the ship to move.

"Starboard GravAnchor out with surge, Cap'm," Barbousse replied.

Immediately Brim put the helm over full while twisting the nose of the ship away from the satellite with generators and gravity brakes. In the corner of his eye, he could see a torrent of gravitons streaming from the GravAnchor as the mooring beam tried to drag it along. Things were a lot easier when you could predict what was going to happen!

While Barbousse eased out distance from the first GravAnchor, inertia continued to move the slowly twisting ship along its original path until about 150 irals past their berth, he ordered Barbousse to drop the second GravAnchor.

"Dropped with surge, Cap'm!"

Miraculously, the stern had come around well, and was now in almost perfect position for backing into the slip—were the reverse circuits working. "Send the stern beam over and heave 'round the warping head!" Brim ordered tensely. The rating at the stern cupola had only a single chance to project his mooring beam for capture by the optical bollard on the wall of the satellite. If she missed, the stern would come around and he'd lose control again—this time with GravAnchors to further complicate the situation! Heart in his mouth, he watched in the aft-view display as a thin green ray flashed to the reflecting mechanism, caught, flared up,and . . . held! Immediately it began to draw their stern into the narrow berth.

"Check the starboard bow beam, Chief . . . now!" he ordered.

"Check starboard . . ."

Then as the distance from the two anchors became equal: "Check port!"

"Check port, Cap'm."

They were in! Or at least aimed properly to go in. Now, it was only a matter of easing the bow beams and heaving on the stern to draw themselves into the berth. In the space of half a metacycle, the ship was safely moored, a repair crew was already swarming around the bridge, and Barbousse had sent out a launch to retrieve their GravAnchors.

All in a day's work. . . .

It was an exhausted and aching Wilf Brim who trudged out of the brow airlock and doffed his battle helmet for the first time since leaving FleetPort 30 Avalon a *number* of metacycles ago. The Triad was on the opposite side of Ariel and the station's transparent boarding tube was all in shadows as he made his way toward one of the main portals leading to the station's interior. A slim, graceful figure wearing a beguilingly open Fleet Cloak met him halfway across the tube.

" 'Twas a fine landin' you made, Wilf Brim," Eve Cartier said in the gentle voice he knew so well. "Weel done, sir." Her words seemed to cradle his exhaustion in a comforting veil, and she took his arm soothingly while she looked at him with a sparkle in her eyes. "Faith, it's also a ge'at black eye you've got, mon."

Brim tentatively touched his cheek. It *was* tender. "Canna' trust Carescrians," he chuckled, reverting to an accent he'd renounced (with a great deal of difficulty) more than twenty years ago. Surprisingly, it felt almost, well, *natural*. "You know that, noo, chield," he continued, letting the two decades slip into nothingness. "We're always gettin' into wee scrapes."

She smiled and squeezed his arm. "Weel, weel, Mr. Brim," she said. "Perhaps I've misjudged. I always thought you were ane o' those haughty Imperials."

"That's why you ne'er came back to see me at the *Benwell* reception, noo?" Brim asked roguishly. Her close proximity was making him forget all about the aches and pains he'd collected from being thrown about in his seat restraints. Slimness accentuated the wide-set swelling of her smallish breasts beneath an Imperial uniform that fit like a glove—all the way to her boot tips.

Her blush was visible even in the semidarkness. "That," she said with an embarrassed little smile, "is probably as good an answer as I'll come up wi' myself." She disengaged his arm as he held the airlock door for her. "I will say, tho'—just in case you're interested—that there's nothin' permanent between the man and myself."

In the main corridor, Brim felt his own cheeks flush, and he turned to look Cartier in the eyes. "It's none of my business, Eve," he said, "but, yeah, I . . . ah . . . am . . . ah . . . interested."

"I sort of hoped you might be," she said, looking at him from the corner of her eye. "An' it just so happens I'm available for supper once you've reported to the sick bay an' then checked on your ship."

Brim slowed his steps and frowned at the beautiful Carescrian as he was struck with a most compelling sense of pleasure. "In that case," he said, "the bastard Leaguer who shot up my Starfury did me a *big* favor."

"E'en countin' the black eye?" Cartier asked.

Brim grimaced. "Oh, yeah, I'd forgotten about that. You sure you want to be seen with me? I must look like some low-brow street brawler, and I've no clothes but this battlesuit."

"I've seen the kind o' brawlin' you do, Mr. Brim," she said with a smile, "an' I'll be *most* proud to ha' supper wi' you.

Besides, everybody weel want to meet the Helmsman who docked his Starfury wi' his GravAnchors.''

''I'd bet a year's credits you can do the same,'' Brim said, looking her in the eye.

''Oh,'' Cartier laughed, ''I've flown my share o' ore barges. It's but recently they trained Carescrians from the ground up, so to speak. We both started the hard way.'' Then she smiled and put her hands on his arm as they came abreast of an elevator bank. ''Now get on wi' you. Sickbay is up two levels—you'll see the signs. An' I'll send someone along wi' somethin' to wear.''

''Where will I meet you?'' Brim asked.

''I'll be in the wardroom when you're ready,'' she said, ''savin' us a table wi' a view.''

''With a view?'' Brim asked.

''But o' course,'' Cartier said., ''Fleetport 19's a number o' years older than FleetPort 30.'' Then the elevator doors slid open and she nodded toward the empty tube. ''On you way, Mr. Brim. You'll see for yourself soon enough.''

Komenski, the Surgeon, required what seemed like at least five Standard Years before her ministrations were finished, and Brim ended up with a bandage around his forehead and an eye patch to hold a H-Plasm compress in place for the evening. ''You must have been thrown around pretty violently,'' she said, adjusting her glasses. ''You're a mass of bruises from head to foot.''

Naked as a newborn and feeling every one of those aches, Brim nodded. ''Accurate diagnosis, Doctor,'' he said, agnozingly sitting up on the examination table. ''Damn Leaguer really took a dislike to us.''

''Probably you won't die from it, though,'' Komenski mused, ''in spite of his intentions.''

Brim winched as he tried to move his shoulders, wondering idly what there was about surgeons that he could sit naked in front of one—a female, no less—and carry on a conversation as if he were fully dressed. "The way I feel right now, I may regret that more than he."

"Or she," Komenski amended.

"Too true," Brim allowed.

"Speaking of which," she said, pointing to a fresh uniform and Fleet Cloak hanging on the wall along with a jump suit. She turned to wash her hands. "An orderly dropped the jump suit off while I had you in the healing machine. But a little while later a perfectly huge Chief Petty Officer—a *Master* Chief at that—delivered the uniform. One of your crewman, I suppose. Said he always packed one of your uniforms—just in case."

Brim smiled and shook his head in awe. "Barbousse," he mumbled.

"Bless you," the Surgeon said.

"And you, Doctor," Brim chuckled, beginning to don the uniform in spite of his aches and pains. It had been a long time since he'd dined with a truly beautiful woman—especially a beautiful *Carescrian* woman who made him think of lavender mists . . . green rolling hills strewn with mossy boulders and ancient roads that lost themselves mysteriously in the everlasting cold and drizzle . . . proud, ruddy faces in spite of hardship. Another Universe, almost. Carescria. For all its poverty and benighted existence, it was her home. And his, too, even as much as he'd tried to forget. . . .

"You were certainly far away, Captain," Komenski observed, breaking into Brim's reverie.

"Yes," Brim agreed. "A long way."

"A good place, I hope," she said with a quizzical frown.

"I don't know," Brim said, staring off into an infinity of thought while he pulled on his boots. "I didn't used to think so, but now. . . ." He shrugged and shook his head. "I simply don't know. . . ."

FleetPort 19's wardroom was a page of Ariel's pre-war past, more like *Benwell*'s richly appointed wardroom than the stark utilitarianism of FleetPort 30's interior spaces. Low ceilings with authentic-looking wooden beams, darkly paneled walls, carved wood-and-leather furniture glowing with years of careful polishing all gave the room an aura of the exclusive supper clubs Brim associated with the very wealthy. Bustling waiters dressed in well-tailored uniforms, the subtle odors of good food and spicy camarge cigarettes, an indistinct hum of urbane conversation, and the musical jangling of expensive crystal completed his illusion—and made it nearly impossible to believe that a war was going on in the same sky only a few light-years distant.

Seated in a darkened alcove beside a blast-shuttered window that once would have looked out over the gentle curve of Ariel's far-off horizon, Eve Cartier was absolutely stunning. It took her a few moments to recognize him at the entrance, but once their eyes met, she smiled and beckoned to him. Magically, she had again transformed a regulation fleet uniform into as seductive an outfit as he could remember. It took a real woman to get such an effect from everyday Fleet vestments. "What was all that aboot only havin' a battlesuit to wear?" she asked with a surprised little smile, smoothing her long, black hair.

"Faith, I told only the truth," Brim said, slipping easily back onto his Carescrian accent. "'Twas Barbousse who packed m' extra uniform. I knew nothin' aboot it."

She relaxed in her chair and crossed her long legs, for a moment exposing a length of frantically white thigh. Then she smoothed her skirt. "Won't you sit, my handsomely dressed Captain?" she asked.

Brim grinned. "I thought you'd never ask," he said, taking the chair beside her. "And thanks for the loan of the jump suit."

"The battlesuit would hae been fine," she replied.

"Not with you looking the way you do," he said. "You've somehow managed to turn a commonplace uniform into something rather splendid."

She laughed. "How long has it been since you've seen a woman, Captain?" she said in mock seriousness.

"Hey," Brim laughed defensively, "I'll brook no questioning of tastes here. *I'm* the one at this table with special hardware for judging female appearance."

"Weel, thank you, then," she said. Color rose slightly in her cheeks, but Brim could tell she was quite accustomed to being called beautiful. She simply was.

"So what do you recommend in a Logish Meem here?" he asked.

"I fear I don't know what to recommend," she said, drawing her lower lip between her teeth. "Unlike you, Captain, I've spent most o' my life as a Carescrian, w' just plain meem—an' *that* on very special occasions." She laughed a little sadly. "I only tried m' first Logish Meem a few short years ago."

Brim nodded. "Yeah," he said. "I went through the same thing twenty years ago, myself. And it's always embarrassing. Everybody else had been doing the 'right thing' all their lives—an if you didn't know what that was, you were a xaxtdamned fool."

"It *war* tougher then, warn't it, Wilf?" she asked suddenly.

Brim nodded. "In some ways," he said. "I was the first Carescrian in the Helmsman's Academy, and if you think people are prejudiced now, you should have been around then." He closed his eyes for a moment, remembering the indifferent cruelty his wealthy, often-titled classmates visited on him. Only a disastrously rising casualty list among Helmsmen had opened the Academy to lower-class cadets—at the price of surprisingly vile reactions from the gentry who had exclusively populated Imperial military schools for more than a thousand Standard Years. He shook his head as he returned to the present. "On second thought, you *shouldn't* have been around then."

"I know it's a different story today, Wilf," she said. "You took the heat for all of us."

"Oh, I took heat," Brim agreed, signaling a rating who hurried over to their table and bowed.

"Captain Brim," he said, "it is an honor to serve the man who retired the Mitchell Trophy. What can I bring for you and the Commander?"

Brim considered for a moment. "Thank you, Yeoman," he

said presently. "And I think I remember a Medoc with the Logish appellation, vintage 51019. Is that correct?"

The rating's eyebrows rose. "It is, Captain," he said. "Logish Medoc, oh-nineteen. An excellent choice. But how did you know we had any? That is rare treasure."

"My Chief Petty Officer Barbousse," Brim replied with a smile. "He knows that I favor Logish Medoc from the late teens, and evidently checked out your cellar before I got here. I found *this* pinned to my uniform." He showed both the waiter and Cartier.

Logish Medoc, 51019, partial case.
Logish Soma-Medoc, 51012, two cases.
Logish Monor-Savill, 51017, one case.

"The Monor-Savill oh-seventeen is excellent also, Captain," the rating murmured.

"We'll start with a bottle of the Medoc," Brim said.

"Aye, sir," the rating said with another bow and disappeared into the dimness.

Cartier smiled. "I take it at least *some* of the heat is gone," she said. "Certainly where Logish Meem is concerned."

"Yeah," Brim agreed with a grin. "Oh, I've learned the art of ordering Logish Meem—and a few other so-called 'social graces,' Eve. But the heat is never gone completely. It returns—often in the xaxtdamndest times and places." He shrugged. "Like everything else, one way or another, it all depends on people."

"Yes," she said presently, "people." For a moment she peered at him as if she could place herself within his soul. Then she relaxed. "There's no menu, in spite of the surroundings, Wilf Brim."

Brim laughed. "I'd hope not," he said. "Because if there were, we'd most certainly be somewhere on the surface in a private club—and absent without leave."

"A pretty serious offense, in anybody's book," Cartier said as the rating delivered their meem in a gloriously dusty bottle.

"Go ahead and open it," Brim ordered. "Commander Cartier will put it to the proof."

"Aye, Captain Brim," the man said, touching a narrow band ringing the bottle's narrow neck. It sparked a few times, then fizzled. "Well sealed, Captain," the man observed with raised eyebrows. "Shall I try again?"

"By all means," Brim said, savoring the rich purple color of the meem inside.

The rating carefully place a small wire around the scorched groove produced by the fizzled opener. Moments later, this blazed up and decapitated the bottle in a small cloud of sparks.

"You said the lady will taste, Captain?"

Brim nodded. "Eve?" he said.

"But, Wilf," Cartier protested, "I do na' know onything aboot meem—especially Logish Meem."

"You'll know if you like it, I'd wager," Brim replied.

"Weel, yes," she allowed. "No question aboot that."

"If you don't like it, we'll order something else for you," Brim prompted. "See what you think."

Cartier took a careful sip from a tiny silver goblet the rating had partially filled. Then her eyes grew wide. "Great Universe, Wilf," she said. "'Tis marvelous!"

Brim grinned. "So are you, Eve," he chuckled, then turned to the rating. "Mister," he said, "you may pour for both of us."

"An' perhaps bring us some supper, so I do na end up on the floor from this," Cartier laughed. Then settling back in her chair, she grasped the stem of her goblet delicately and raised it. "Here's to the heat, Wilf Brim," she said. "You take it an' I take it, but the mair we use up of it, the less there'll be for those who follow us from Carescria."

"To the heat," Brim said, hardly believing he was saying the words—especially sober as a judge. "And to those who follow us," he added. *Witches*, he thought to himself as he enjoyed his first sip of the grand old Logish Meem. Eve Cartier could weave a spell with the best of them. . . .

* * *

After a long, relaxed supper of conversation about the war, excellently prepared fish from one of the local lakes, and most of the Medoc, Cartier extracted two slim camarge cigarettes fro somewhere inside her cape. "Ha' one?" she asked, leaning over a cleared dessert plate.

"Thanks, but I'll enjoy yours," Brim said. He meant it. He'd always loved the spiced smoke of the tiny cigarettes, but had a healthy regard for the daily runs that allowed him to eat nearly all he wanted without developing too much of a paunch.

Her camarge lit on the first puff, and she settled back to inhale deeply, suddenly staring at him so intently that she might be preparing to sketch his face. At length, she sat forward in her seat and looked him directly in the eye. "Wilf Brim, my handsome countryman," she began, "who in the name of Voot are you, anyway?"

Taken aback, Brim cocked his head and smiled. "Who am I?" he asked.

"Yes," Cartier replied. "That's what I want to know."

"Well . . . how about 'Wilf Brim'?"

"No," Cartier laughed. "*Who* are you, na *what* are you. An Imperial? A Carescrian? A Commander or a Helmsman? Did Margot Effer'wyck sell you out to the aristocracy? Who are you, Wilf Brim—or do you e'en know?"

Completely unprepared for her questions, Brim leaned away from her and crossed his arms, his mind whirling to grasp the questions she'd fired at him. "I—I d don't know," he stammered after what seemed to be an eternity of largely disconnected thoughts. The crazy thing was that he'd given the answer truthfully, not simply to deflect the pressure she had suddenly placed on him. He *didn't* know.

"Hmm," Cartier mused. "You are a truthful ane, aren't you?"

Brim could only nod his head; her questions had landed like a sack of bricks. And he couldn't answer them because she was correct. He had no idea who he was, because after all these years, he could identify with no one but himself.

"I wondered if that might na' be the case, Wilf Brim," she

said, placing a comforting hand on his arm. ''Nobody could give up his own dawnin' as thoroughly as you have without throwin' away a ge'at deal mair into the bargain. Mair, perhaps, then he'd e'en planned.''

After a long, thoughtful silence, Brim thrust out his chin, just a little irritated by the unexpected questions—especially since he couldn't answer them. ''All right,'' he conceded, ''I probably *have* thrown a lot of personal baggage away. What's so wrong with that? What's wrong with being my own man? I've always been damned independent, and it's let me remain that way.''

''Wilf,'' she protested, putting a hand to her mouth. ''I did na' mean to imply that anything was—or is—*wrong*. Voot knows you've done weel for yourself. I just wondered who you felt you were.''

Brim shrugged mentally. It *was* nice to have such a lovely person concerned about him. ''What else were you wondering about, Eve?'' he asked, letting a smile break through in spite of everything. Cartier, he imagined, could bring a smile to the visage of a stone asteroid.

She blushed. ''Oh, nothin' important, Wilf Brim,'' she said, but her eyes told more truth than her words.

''I don't believe you,'' Brim chuckled. ''And you aren't a very good liar.''

''Are you certain you want to know what I think, Wilf?'' she asked. ''It might not make you happy.''

Brim frowned again, and a strange feeling began in the pit of his stomach. ''Tell me,'' he said theatrically, in an attempt to defuse a situation that was rapidly going out of control. ''I'm ready for anything.''

''All right, Wilf Brim,'' she said after a small hesitation. ''But I think I'm going to forever regret bringin' the whole thing to the surface in the first place.''

''Friends,'' Brim said seriously, ''never regret what they say to each other, especially when they're telling the truth.''

''Weel,'' she said at length, peering at him as if she could see all the way to his soul, ''in my eyes, you're a lot more than simply independent. You're *lonely*, Wilf Brim,'' she said. ''You're probably the loneliest man I think I have ever met.''

''Lonely?'' Brim asked with astonishment. ''Eve. Great Universe! How could I be lonely? Why, most of the time, I've got so much company I'd give my right arm for a few moments with myself.''

''Wilf,'' she said with a sad little smile, ''that's not what I meant.'' But before she could go on, their rating appeared beside the table and bowed.

''My apologies for the interruption,'' he said, ''but a Chief Barbousse is outside with an urgent message for Captain Brim.''

Somehow thankful for the interruption, Brim took Cartier's hand for a moment. ''Looks as if we'll have to continue this, Eve,'' he said. ''I think Duty's just called again.''

She smiled. ''It ha' a way of doing that, Wilf,'' she replied, ''especially in a war.''

Then, in spite of his recent discomfiture, Brim heard himself saying, ''Let's meet for supper again, Eve. Soon.''

''I'd love that, Wilf,'' she replied, looking him directly in the eye, smoothing her long, straight hair, ''. . . soon.''

''Until then,'' he said, pushing back from the table. As he stood, she settled back in her chair and crossed her legs again.

''Be careful, Wilf,'' she said.

''You, too. . . .'' Then he turned and made his way through the lavish old wardroom to where Barbousse waited in an anteroom with a dispatch case under his arm.

''Top secret from the Admiralty, Cap'm.''

Within the metacycle, the two men were in a fast packet, bound for Avalon and another of the interminable staff meetings. Strangely, all the way in, Brim found he couldn't put Eve Cartier's words from his mind. Lonely? How could he be lonely in the midst of such chaos? *And how had something so normally inconsequential become significant in the first place?*

On the surface, Brim found himself with a group of Wing Commanders providing ''front-line'' information to high-level staff meetings. In answer to growing demands in the High Command for more merchant-fleet protection, Calhoun was warning that the escort burden might become unbearable if the Leaguers also increased attacks on ground targets—or the FleetPort satellites.

The meetings broke up with no clear consensus (Brim disagreed). But throughout the remainder of that single week, 15 Imperial starships and most of their 12 crews were lost, for a total of more than 450 casualties. Nevertheless, if the constant struggle *was* beginning to wear the defending starship crews, Brim at least found himself thankful that many of his newer arrivals were receiving invaluable first tastes of space combat while the Leaguers' main intent was killing merchant ships and not defenders.

That same week, meem rationing began on the five Avalonian planets. Brim was pleased to learn that many bartenders actually blamed the CIGAs for this affront to civilized existence. It was little things like that, he observed with a chuckle, that eventually made people angry enough to win wars. . . .

CHAPTER 5

One Last Torpedo

On the morning of Heptad third, Brim was aloft in Starfury D1923 with Moulding on his wing, orbiting five hundred c'lenyts off Melia, the planet of Commerce. Their job—along with thirty other Starfuries positioned along an arc stretching nearly half a light-year—was to protect a large supply convoy of HypoLight spaceships going from Melia to Proteus.

The Triad was just disappearing behind the planet when the two Imperials completed another spinward leg of their assigned patrol area. At the surface, the planet's whole boreal hemisphere soaked beneath a heavy layer of cloud that flashed malignantly here and there with wicked-looking bursts of lightning. Thousands of irals above, a flight of Defiants appeared to skid across the planet's multicolored disk making for FleetPort 28 in synchronous orbit above the opposite hemisphere.

As Moulding kept station on the outside, Brim eased into a right turn, grimacing wryly behind the mask of his battlesuit. It *was* difficult, he considered soberly—*damn* difficult—to continually let the Leaguers bring the war to him. Sometimes, he wished he commanded normal Starfuries with their large crew and intragalactic range. Now, *there* were ships that could take the war to the enemy! This new kind of remote-controlled, defensive patrolling at the beck and call of some distant BKAEW technician was sometimes repugnant to him—and to a lot of the other Helmsmen who dearly wanted to wade in and show the Leaguer bastards what a real fight was all about.

He shook his head and scanned the starry darkness around him. Eventually, he thought. Eventually, they'd be on the offensive again. And this time, no Treaty of Garak would save the Tyrant to begin still another round of killing. . . .

With effort, he forced his mind back to reality. Plenty of time to plan the future once he'd helped win it away from the Leaguers. But for the duration, whole fleets of zukeed bastards were still out there waiting. He could feel their presence—and *their* plans for after the war were totally unlike his own. At all . . .

While he searched the darkness around him, out on the tips of his Starfury's pontoons, tiny antennas sensed incoming radiation from another ship. They relayed their captured data to the Starfury's APW-11 proximity warning system, and presently, a yellow area began to blink on Brim's threats panel, slowly at first, then with increasing frequency as the stranger approached. "We've got company," he said calmly into the short-range COMM system as he extended his turn into a full circle.

"I've noticed," Moulding replied. "They should be coming from spinward."

"Hang on a moment, Toby," Brim interrupted tensely, "I think I can see them." Out ahead, two distant graviton plumes were perfectly silhouetted against the dark undercast. "Orange-Yellow and crossing. . . . Just above the horizon. . . ."

"Daresay," Moulding answered. "I see the bastards, too—sneaking in for a little innocent mayhem, one supposes."

Brim narrowed his eyes and sounded action stations while his ship raced silently and undetected through the utter darkness of space. But as airtight doors slammed and the bridge filled with excited voices, the thrill he normally felt at the beginning of combat was—well—missing, somehow. He felt tired; seemed like he'd been tired for weeks. He shrugged mentally. Like millions of Imperials before him, he had a job to do for his

Empire—and this one was a long way from over. Taking a deep breath, he resignedly pushed his thrust dampers to the stop and curved in toward the two unsuspecting Leaguers. A steep bank and a hard pull brought him in at their Orange-Yellow and closing rapidly.

Scant heartbeats later, he was above and behind two GH 262-Es, in perfect position to attack. No time for philosophy now—only actions and reflexes. He ordered the disruptors energized and gave Goreman, the Gunnery Officer, permission to fire when he was ready.

It didn't take long at all. At only medium range, their initial salvo of disruptor fire sparkled all around the starboard "wing" of the rearmost Gorn-Hoff, instantly silencing its two aft-firing turrets. In the corner of his eye, Brim saw the surprised leader frantically peel off and claw upward toward free space. Goreman quickly boosted off another short burst. This time, the Gorn-Hoff shot out a long, thin streamer of gravitons, followed by a dazzling plume of radiation fire. Suddenly, the chevron-shaped killer ship flipped onto its back and spiraled toward the stormy undercast, burning furiously.

"My compliments," Moulding radioed. "That puts paid to one Leaguer this morning."

"Thanks . . ." Brim answered. "Too bad his zukeed friend over there at Purple-Blue doesn't share your enthusiasm." Off to the port, the second Gorn-Hoff was streaking out of the darkness back toward their flight level. While he watched, the enemy starship rolled into a vertical bank, then hurtled around to come at them from behind.

Instinctively, he pivoted his Starfury to counter the threat, its spaceframe creaking and groaning with the strain. But the surprised Helmsman of the Gorn-Hoff overshot, and Brim rolled immediately onto his tail. A moment later, Goreman got off a long burst that flickered just behind the Gorn-Hoff's armored bridge—again with no apparent effect.

Brim lined up for a second shot, but this time, the Leaguer countered with a tremendous fusillade from its rear turrets that sparkled and hammered at the Starfury's armor. Then its

Helmsman rolled and dived out of the way, streaking vertically for the surface in an attempt to throw off Brim's aiming devices against the ground clutter. The Carescrian followed, heedless of danger as he was during the days when he piloted ore barges. Soon, the Starfury's hullmetal skin was glowing cherry-white from atmospheric heating, and the temperature on the bridge had began to climb precipitously. No starship was designed to survive in these temperatures; the deep cold of outer space was their natural element, and normal landfalls were made gradually, to keep reentry heat within manageable ranges. Grinding his teeth, Brim turned down his battlesuit temperature and continued the dive. This chase would go to the ship with the best streamlining—and he was betting everything on his Starfury. Mitchell Trophy racers, on which Mark Valerian had based his designs, had been beautifully shaped to get them in and out of the atmosphere as rapidly as possible. That early design decision was going to count in the next few moments, or he would know the reason why.

And even as he made his prediction, the Leaguer—now glowing incandescently—suddenly pulled out and headed directly for one of the nearby storm cells. Enemy or no, the Helmsman had guts, at least in Brim's estimation. Temperatures on *that* flight bridge must long ago have reached the melting point of some metals. With a nod of grudging appreciation, he followed around in a wide curve toward the roiling, flickering clouds.

Moments later—only a few thousand irals above the surface—Brim found himself bumping violently through swirling turbulence, rain, and hailstones, but he held his course grimly while the proximity indicator guided him along the Leaguer's path. Goreman didn't *need* to see the Gorn-Hoff; the forward heat scanners were all that was necessary to aim. He began firing off short bursts into the murk as Brim veered through the sky, tracking the Leaguer as if its Helmsman were flying both starships. Presently, the two ships erupted back into the evening sky, Brim's eyes adjusting only in time to see the Gorn-Hoff send out a stream of gravitons and reverse course back into the cloud—just as if it were in the midst of some primitive fight between two old atmospheric flyers.

Once more, Brim careened after him into the roiling mists, jolting violently in a thousand directions as he coursed through the frantic blackness. Lightning crashed explosively near his starboard pontoon. Battling desperately to approximate the enemy Helmsman's course, he ground his teeth in feverish concentration on his instruments. A moment later, the proximity indicator's yellow eye blinked again. Reflexively Goreman fired a blind, fan-shaped salvo into the gloom—then they were once more in clear air. Ahead, the Gorn-Hoff was now trailing a thread of white vapor—that stopped abruptly as it turned again, this time so tightly that the two starships abruptly switched position.

Now, the deadly Gorn-Hoff was in the tail position, and it was Brim's turn for trouble. Shimmering bolts of energy flashed past his Hyperscreens. The unfamiliar thunder of disruptors blasted his ears. *And Moulding was nowhere in sight!* He must have become separated in the cloud.

Heart in his throat, Brim simultaneously jammed the gravs wide open, hauled the helm hard right, and slammed the steering engine to starboard. R6595 rolled precipitously onto its back in the *beginning* of a split-S maneuver—but instead of arcing over into a dive, Brim held the inverted starship on course, alternately kicking his helm and swerving violently from side to side.

The enemy pilot also whipped his Gorn-Hoff inverted—but in the excitement of the chase, he actually *completed* his maneuver and continued through into another power dive.

One long heartbeat later, Brim completed his *own* split-S—now carefully calculated to bring him out of its diving half loop at a point in space directly behind his opponent's tail, where his disruptors could do the most damage. Within moments, the Starfury was in position, and Goreman fired from no more than 150 irals.

This time, bits and pieces flew from the fleeing Gorn-Hoff. It slowed and a large panel fell into down position. Somehow the Leaguer Helmsman managed to keep his ship in the air. . . .

From years of habit, Brim moved in close to finish the job. The Gorn-Hoff was still weaving desperately, but not so nimbly as before. In the background, he could hear Goreman preparing his disruptors. . . .

Suddenly, he shook his head angrily. "Enough death," he whispered, grimacing to himself. "Don't shoot!" he ordered. That Gorn-Hoff was going nowhere. It would soon either land, or disintegrate in the air. Either way, it and its crew were out of the war.

Instead, he coasted alongside the stricken starship. It surprised him that he had no feeling at all for the Leaguers—neither hate *nor* compassion. His emotions were numb. Glancing across into the bridge, he saw one of Triannic's elite Controllers in a black battlesuit at the controls. From a transparent helmet, the Leaguer gazed warily back, waiting. His hair was so blond, it appeared almost white.

Brim raised a fist with his thumb down in the universal sign of "Get out of the sky."

The Gorn-Hoff's Helmsman clearly understood. He hesitated for only a moment, saluted across the few hundred irals that separated the two starships, then gingerly swung off toward the surface.

With a casual glance backward, Brim lifted his Starfury's nose into a gentle climb and took up a heading back to his assigned station. The Leaguers were on their own now.

Only clicks later his proximity alarms went off again, followed almost immediately by the thunder of disruptor fire. As Goreman whirled his turrets sternward, R6595 shuddered convulsively, and Brim was nearly knocked senseless against his seat restraints when a near miss shattered the overhead Hyperscreens in a stunning explosion and filled the bridge with whirling crystal shards. Heart pounding in his throat, he rolled instinctively right and glanced aft. There was the Gorn-Hoff, its control panel still hanging in the slipstream, its disruptors pounding away at him as if their combat had never ended.

Brim saw red. "Get the bastard!" he growled deep in his throat, then horsed the Starfury around in a tight turn that the Gorn-Hoff's riddled spaceframe could never again possibly match. As Goreman fired, Brim closed to within a few hundred irals of the Leaguer's swept-back hull. With icy precision, he skidded slightly to one side while the Starfury's powerful disruptors fired a long, deafening salvo at the bridge area from so close it was impossible to miss. The shattered Gorn-Hoff faltered in midflight as if smashed by some giant hammer, and debris bounced noisily against the Starfury's Hyperscreens. Suddenly, the Gorn-Hoff nosed over and hurdled down toward the undercast. Brim followed in hot pursuit, wind thundering through the shattered overhead Hyperscreens as R6595 plunged completely through the clouds, matching the Gorn-Hoff's headlong dive as if the two starships were now physically attached.

Perilously low, the enemy Helmsman suddenly pulled up into a turn—but this time, his crippled Gorn-Hoff could no longer gain altitude. Grinding his teeth, Brim closed in with relentless determination. Goreman launched off salvo after salvo until suddenly brilliant red and yellow flames vomited back over the Gorn-Hoff's "wings," highlighting the red daggers painted at the tips.

Now trailing thick clouds of black oily smoke, the Leaguer faltered once more, stalled vertically, then cartwheeled, spinning lazily to port like a blazing leaf. Incredibly, it leveled off at the last possible moment loosing a small flurry of lifeglobes in its wake before it skimmed shakily along a rocky hillside, then sank to the ground at high speed, blossoming at last into a giant puffball of lurid flame and starship parts.

Brim circled the rising column of smoke while the fire—and his anger—burned themselves out together. As the lifeglobes bounced to the surface, he thought about the other Helmsman: singularly brave and capable, but programmed to a totally different set of moral rules. And he'd known that. He shook his head angrily. What a fool he had been! After years of dealing with Leaguers, he, an Imperial, had allowed himself to deal with those rules on Imperial terms—and he had prevailed. But only *just*. A scant few clicks more and. . . . He shivered. Never again would he risk a ship and crew by showing mercy to Leaguers. People like that didn't want mercy because they didn't really understand what it was.

After long moments of contemplation, he called in Search and Rescue crews—the prisoners would have valuable information—climbed back through the overcast into bright morning sunlight, and once more set course for his assigned station. Moulding would be waiting, and he was anxious to claim both Gorn-Hoff prizes for the ship. One glance at his KA'PPA display told him that similar battles were taking place all around the Triad. True to Sodeskayan predictions, the war had abruptly become very serious in the neighborhood of Avalon.

For the next two Standard Weeks, the Imperials guarded their five planets 'round the clock while Nergol Triannic's Generals drilled the huge army of jack-booted Controllers, land crawlers, and siege engines they had assembled on the nearby planets of occupied Effer'wyck. Yet despite all conjecture—Imperial as well as Leaguer—they only *drilled*. The promised invasion failed to come. Moreover, intelligence data from Sodeskaya quoted the League Emperor as stating that his decision as to whether the operation should take place during the Standard Month of Nonad or be delayed until next Pentad would be made after his Attack Forces had carried out more powerful forays against the Avalonian Home Planets. If these had caused ''significant damage,'' he would invade.

Ursis's critique from Sodeskaya: Triannic had become a frustrated Emperor—to his own considerable distress. The present inactivity of his huge land forces was a constant drain on his resources that could not continue indefinitely. And for once, he had apparently lost his usual vision about how to bring his actions to a conclusion.

It was also fairly clear he had diminished confidence in Admiral Hoth Orgoth's claims that all-out war from space could provide the answer. Three of his most trusted advisers had recently told him in secret that such an offensive could take as much as two Standard Years. His strategic program for the present, then, was to continue unrestricted space warfare against Avalon in preparation for possible land operations and conceivably begin an actual invasion during the Standard Month of Nonad—if conditions and preparation were all satisfactory. Otherwise, he would probably postpone the invasion until the following year.

It was good news for the hard-pressed Imperials. At least the *immediate* threat of invasion had become more remote. But they were a long way from declaring their beloved Triad secure, and they knew it.

Meanwhile, fighting around the five planets grew more intense daily until in mid-month a terrific series of raids commenced during which the Leaguers suddenly abandoned their attacks on Imperial shipping and commenced picking targets seemingly at random among the five planets themselves—while carefully avoiding Avalon City proper.

These raids cost the Leaguers dearly, for attacks against ground targets necessitated flying a great deal closer to the Imperial FleetPort systems. Indeed, on the first day of the revised strategy, thirty-eight of the attacking starships were confirmed destroyed and forty-six claimed damaged. At the same time, however, thirty-two Imperial killer ships were also destroyed—serious losses of twenty-three full crews listed as missing or dead plus nearly half the crew members of a Defiant and two more Starfuries. Brim's starships suffered their own damage during the day-long mayhem, and as the second morning began in orbit over Avalon, so many of them were under repair that he found himself "grounded."

No sooner had he reported in as down for at least a day than a directive arrived from the Admiralty ordering him to the surface immediately to attend one of Onrad's War Cabinet meetings in place of Gallsworthy, while the latter participated in a shipping conference on Helios. Aram, whose Defiant was also laid up, accompanied him.

"No rest for the weary, I suppose, Cap'm," Barbousse said

as the three strode briskly across the transparent mooring tube to the shuttle.

Brim laughed and looked out through the transparent walls at the curve of the planet, just taking shape as a slim arc of light hundreds of c'lenyts to lightward. Flashes of disruptor fire punctuated nearby space, indicating that the Leaguers' new offensive continued without letup. "Probably more true for you, Chief, than me," he said, winking at Aram. "At least we get to do something a little bit different—while you shovel mountains of admin trivia."

The ruddy-feathered A'zurnian nodded emphatically. "I think I'd rather face a whole squadron of Leaguers," he said in feigned gravity.

Barbousse chuckled. "Don't you fret about me, gentlemen," he said. "I've got a mob of ratin's to do the real borin' stuff. But it does bring an idea to mind, beggin' the Cap'm's pardon."

"What's that, Chief?" Brim asked.

"Well sirs," the big rating said, "when we finally do win the war, I think it might be a fittin' punishment to make those bigwig Leaguer brassheads gather up all the admin stuff they've caused an' put it in some sort of orderly filin' system. Now talk about a livin' death. . . ."

Aram broke into gales of featherly laughter while Brim guffawed and slapped the big man on his broad back. "Chief," he said, "we'll take *that* one up with the Admiralty this afternoon. Who knows, with a threat like that, they might simply give the whole thing up and go back home. I know *I* would."

"Meanwhile, Cap'm," Barbousse said, returning to his accustomed seriousness as they reached the entrance to the brow, "I'll have everythin' ready for your signature when you get back." He saluted. "Careful down there, if you will, sir," he said. "No tellin' what them CIGAs are liable to do now that things aren't goin' their way anymore."

"I'll keep an eye out, Chief," Brim promised, returning the

salute, then motioning his grip-all into trail mode, he followed Aram into the brow.

True to Barbousse's premonition, CIGAs were out in force along Brim's route from Lake Mersin to the Admiralty, today protesting Attack Commands' fifth successful assault on the League's invasion buildup in Effer'wyck. The Imperial raiders had damaged a critical cable bridge (seriously hindering assembly of invasion landing craft) and destroyed a large number of attack ships on the ground.

Placards carried by the League sympathizers bore shopworn messages blaming Imperial "aggression" for causing the present hostilities, and the carriers themselves appeared to be just as confident of their cause as ever. But a closer look revealed that their ranks were noticeably thinner than only a month previously—and a nearby counterdemonstration loomed like an ominous storm nearly ready to break over their heads. Clearly, some sort of tide was beginning to turn. Brim hoped there was still time. . . .

At the Admiralty, the two officers sat quietly in the cabinet meeting while Hagbut continued to predict an invasion. As the General and other high-ranking members of the Imperial government debated the state of affairs, a wall-sized situation board behind him showed BKAEW-based reports beginning to arrive indicating large raids were again building up over Effer'wyck.

Aram shook his head wearily as more and more Leaguers headed their way. "I feel guilty sitting here," he whispered to Brim, "while our people are out there risking their necks."

Brim nodded. "I know," he whispered back. "I feel that way every time you people go off without me. But we can't fight *every* battle."

"I'm so bloody tired," Aram said wryly, "it feels as if I've damn well tried."

"Yeah," Brim agreed with a grin, "I know what that feels like, too. . . ."

At the conclusion of the Cabinet meeting—during which Brim and Aram were asked to testify on three separate occasions—

General Harry Drummond, Commander of the Home Fleet, met them in the lobby of the auditorium. "Mornin', gents," he said in the sham accent he used years ago when he and Brim first met during the Mitchell Trophy races. "Cap'm Brim, sir," he asked, " 'ave you learned yet to pronounce m' name?"

" 'Iggins, General," Brim chuckled. " 'Ow's that?"

"Brim," the General said, extending his hand warmly, "you may just amount to something yet."

"I try," Brim said, shaking the man's hand.

"True enough," the General said with a huge grin, "you are one of the most trying persons I've encountered yet."

While Brim groaned, Drummond extended his hand to Aram. "And you must be Aram of Nahshon," he said.

Aram laughed and shook the General's hand. "One of these days, General," he laughed, "I may die these ruddy feathers blue."

Drummond raised an eyebrow. "Then you'll *really* stand out in a crowd," he said.

"You've got that right, General," Aram said with a grin, "but at least nobody'll *know* me."

"A point well taken, young man," Drummond chuckled. "I'll have to keep my eye on you." Then he turned to Brim. "Wilf," he said, "we need to discuss one of those 'need-to-know' things. Are you free for a metacycle or so?"

"Of course, General," Brim replied. "Aram, meet you in the wardroom?"

"When you're ready, Captain," the A'zurnian said. "General, I'm proud to have met you."

Drummond paused and smiled seriously for a moment. "I'm rather proud to have finally met *you* in person, Aram. Not too many of us get to go after a battleship with just a destroyer." Hatless, he saluted, then, motioning Brim to follow, he led the way along a high-ceilinged marble corridor to a bank of lifts guarded by two armed sentries. There he produced his personal ID card and nodded toward the Carescrian. "I've arranged Blue clearance for Captain Brim," he said. "Code nineteen, four fifty-seven A."

"Nineteen four fifty-seven A," the guard repeated, consulting a small logic scriber, he ticked off an entry, checked Brim's ID, and opened the lift.

Somehow, Brim felt little surprise when the car began to *descend* at high speed, boring its way through what seemed like thousands of irals of earth before it came to a gentle stop deep beneath the Admiralty.

"*Abysmal* place," Drummond quipped as the doors opened to another set of armed guards.

Brim groaned again. "Low-down description if I ever heard one, General," he whispered as the guards checked their IDs once more.

Drummond grinned, punching Brim lightly on the forearm. "I admit it, Wilf," he said, striding across the small lobby to a door with no latching mechanism. "But I'll make up for it in here." He touched his ID to the center of the panel and the massive door slid aside. Inside was a sparsely furnished living room occupied by a single, un-armed Sergeant. "How's our guest?" Drummond asked.

The Sergeant jumped to attention. He was a huge man, almost as large as Barbousse, and looked as if he could take care of himself in any situation, with or without weapons. "Alive, General," he said, smiling grimly, "but certainly not by my wishes."

"Nor by mine," Drummond growled. "But he's valuable, so we'll keep him awhile longer. Besides, I think the Captain here will want to meet him for at least two reasons."

"Yes, sir, General," the Sergeant said, "I'll wake him." He strode to the inner door.

Brim frowned. "Somebody I'll want to meet, General?"

Drummond smiled and raised a finger. "Let's see if you remember him," he said. "You described him quite well in your report."

"My . . . ?"

Before Brim could finish, the Sergeant opened the door. "All right, Von Oster," he said. "Someone to see you."

Moments later, a tall, blond man appeared at the door

dressed in a bright yellow jump suit. Brim had seen prisoners of war before—that explained the yellow uniform; the man was clearly a captured Leaguer. But where had they met? Fluvanna? He'd certainly attended his share of parties and masques at the Fluvannian Palace prior to the outbreak of open hostilities. Perhaps even during the years he raced for the Mitchell Trophy. He'd certainly met enough Leaguers in those days. . . . Then it came to him. "Melia!" he exclaimed, nodding to the Leaguer. "*Rogvor Melia nagvor gorbost sagar. Vorgost?*" he asked in perfect Vertrucht.

"*Dovinc nagvor Melia,*" the Leaguer answered angrily. "And you need not speak in the Father Tongue, Imperial. I am capable of conversation in your own bastard Avalonian."

"I'd forgotten you spoke their language, Wilf," Drummond said, "Where did you pick up that particular talent?"

Brim smiled. "In Carescria," he said. "We ore-barge Helmsmen dealt with Leaguers all the time before the war. Triannic was one of our biggest customers."

"A lot of us remember that," Drummond said. "A little before Praefect Dorner's time," he said, nodding toward the Leaguer. "I assume you two recognize each other."

"Says he was shot down over Melia on the nineteenth," Brim replied. "I got two Gorn-Hoffs that day, and. . . ." He pursued his lips and stared at the Leaguer. "The second Helmsman had blond hair like that."

"Foolish Imperial," Dorner spit with contempt. "If that was you, your cowardice nearly did you in. I all but had you."

Brim ground his teeth. "Cowardice?" he demanded. "Dorner, I gave you a chance to save your life and the lives of your crew. And you tried to shoot me."

"Well of course," the Leaguer said as if he were talking to a retarded child. "Isn't that what this is all about. Killing?" He laughed. "If you had any backbone at all, you'd be a rather good warrior, er. . . I didn't catch your name."

"Brim," the Carescrian said.

At that, the Leaguer narrowed his eyes. "Did you say *Brim*?" he asked with a new look on his face.

"That's right, Dorner," Brim said.

The Leaguer stared for a moment as if he were surprised. "Wilf Brim of the Mitchell Trophy?" he asked.

"I raced," Brim replied.

"So," the Leaguer said, "I believe, then, that you know my Commander well." He laughed sardonically. "From the asinine questions your Imperial colleagues have asked me, I already extrapolate that my crewmen have talked too much. Therefore, it will come as no surprise to your General Drummond when I tell you that my Commander is none other than Provost Kirsh Valentin. I assume you have heard of him; he has mentioned you on occasion."

"Me?" Brim asked. "Why?"

"He also is a fool," Dorner said with a cruel smile. "He holds you up as both the bravest and most dangerous of Imperials. But I know you for the coward you really are. You do not have the, how do you say, 'guts' to win a war."

"I had the guts to spare your life, Leaguer."

Dorner laughed. "Those kind of . . . guts . . . will reward you with defeat," he said. Then he frowned. "Perhaps there is something alike between you and the Provost," he said. "He has lost much of his former respect because of his views on the war. Some of us are suspicious that he does not think we should be in this war at all."

This time, it was Brim's turn to laugh. "I can't imagine old Kirsh speaking out against war," he said. "If anybody were ever a first-class warrior, it's him."

"Perhaps," the Leaguer said, "but that is not how the, er, 'skuttlebutt' goes." He laughed. "And now, gentlemen," he said, "you have had your little gloat, and I shall provide no more new information—at least not unless I am drugged."

"The only drug you'll get is the minimum TimeWeed you need to stay alive, Leaguer," Drummond said through clenched teeth. "You have given us more information than you know. We figured Brim's presence would make you talk, and it did."

"But you learned nothing new," the Leaguer gloated.

"On the contrary," Drummond said with a little smile. "You

see, Von Oster, you were the only survivor; the rest of your crew died on impact in their defective lifeglobes.'' With that, he turned to the Sergeant. ''He's ready for camp, now, Nelson. See he's on his way without further delay.''

''I'll take care of it, General,'' the big man said.

Nodding, Drummond led the way from the room.

Later, on his way to meet Aram in the Admiralty's Great Wardroom, Brim noticed the Emperor striding toward him across the great lobby with a small flotilla of escorting bodyguards racing in his wake. ''I say, Brim!'' he called out. ''Wait.''

Brim stopped in his tracks and saluted, even though it was indoors. ''Your Highness,'' he said by way of greeting.

Once more, Onrad was outfitted in full Fleet uniform. ''Understand they shot you up a trifle,'' he said, returning Brim's salute with a little frown, then offering his hand.

Brim nodded. ''A trifle,'' he said, grinning while he gripped the Emperor's large, soft hand.

''Anyone killed?''

''No, Your Majesty. We were awfully lucky.''

''Brim,'' Onrad chuckled, ''you're *always* lucky, especially when there's fighting concerned.''

''You've got *that* right, Your Majesty,'' Brim replied, thinking how often he'd nearly lost his life only to find himself saved in the barest nick of time by some ridiculous stroke of luck. ''Now, if I can just find out how to *avoid* some of that fighting. . . .''

Onrad laughed. ''When you've discovered how to do that, you can give me lessons!'' he said. ''Meanwhile, I've decided to use some of your luck myself, today.''

''I'll gladly share whatever I can, Your Highness,'' Brim laughed. ''What can I do for you?''

Onrad checked his timepiece. ''Turns out,'' he said, ''I'm to meet an old friend of yours in about a metacycle. Oodam Kav Navee Beyazh, the Fluvannian Ambassador. We're scheduled to inspect one of those new BKAEW satellites.'' He frowned.

"Poor devil," he mused. "Things aren't going well in Fluvanna right now. The Leaguers want that dominion in the worst kind of way, but with our own situation here in Avalon, we have barely the resources to aid even those planets of theirs that produce Drive crystal seeds, much less their capital." He shook his head. "That leaves Magor open to attack anytime, and there's nothing anybody can do about it except fight with what little they have and suffer. It's a bad situation."

Brim swallowed hard. Raddisma and his unborn child were in the thick of it, then. And there was absolutely nothing he could do for them. He couldn't even acknowledge. . . .

"So," Onrad continued, "I thought I'd take him with me out to the BKAEW site and show him that we've got some tricks up our sleeves, too. Won't win the war by itself, but every little bit helps."

"Aye, Your Highness," Brim agreed absently. He hadn't been aware the war was going that badly in the out-of-the-way dominion half a galaxy away. Since Raddisma was the Fluvannian Nabob's favorite consort, they corresponded very infrequently by necessity.

"And," Onrad continued, "when I saw you in the lobby just now, I thought, what the xaxt, without a Starfury to fly, he doesn't have much else to do—especially since Chief Barbousse handles all the admin garbage." He laughed at his own joke. "Besides that, you and the Ambassador seem to have become fast friends, so we'll both cheer him up. What do you say, Brim?"

Chuckling silently to himself—who turns down his Emperor just because he's tired?—Brim smiled gamely. "I'd love to, Your Majesty," he said. "I'll have Aram go back without. . . ."

"Aram?" Onrad asked. "You mean that young A'zurnian you put in charge of your Defiants?"

"Aye, Your Majesty," Brim answered. "Aram of Nahshon. His ship was shot up yesterday, too."

"Well, Bully!" Onrad exclaimed. "Unfortunate that he got shot up, and all that, but a fine opportunity to cement relations between the two dominions. Bring him along, too. Nime," he said to a shapely aide, "have a staff skimmer take Captain Brim and his A'zurnian friend out to my shuttle. Brim, we'll meet you in about two metacycles." With that, he started off across the lobby.

"Aye, Your Majesty," Brim chuckled to the receding Imperial party.

"Where would you like to meet that skimmer, Captain Brim?" Nime asked, a small note recorder in her hand. She now had a smile on her face that let Brim know she understood how he felt—and a whole lot more.

"How about the front steps?"

"You'll have it," she said. "Front steps, at"—she checked her timepiece—"Brightness, two, and fifteen. All right? I'll have battlesuits for both of you waiting at the shuttle."

"Thanks, Nime," Brim said ruefully, checking his new Effer'wyckean timepiece against hers. "I can hardly wait."

Nime laughed. "I can tell you're simply dying to climb into a battlesuit, Captain. I'm sure you have very little chance to wear one otherwise."

"Yeah," Brim replied, shrugging gamely. "Just one of life's little pleasures, as they say." He winked. "Brightness, two, and fifteen," he said and started off across the lobby to find Aram. By the time he messaged Barbousse and took care of a thousand details he had planned to handle in person, it was going to be a *long* day indeed.

Dressed in borrowed—if elegant—Imperial battlesuits, the two Helmsmen boarded the shuttle just moments before Onrad and his party arrived. From his window in the passenger compartment, he watched five huge limousine skimmers pull past with small, self-important flags fluttering from either side of their burnished prows. Only cycles later, Ambassador Beyazh dodged his head under the low hatchway and burst into the cabin. Erect, fierce, and patriarchal in every feature, he could well be mistaken for some heroic statue come to life. He wore a white shirt with lace ruffles at the neck and cuffs, an expensive-looking gray business suit, and a crimson fez around which was tied a white turban. Great, dense eyebrows, glowering, deep-set eyes, and an ebony mustache with stilettolike ends twisted nearly vertical provided a unique visage for this entirely unique individual. Nodding to Aram, he seized Brim's hand and grinned. "How excellent to see you again, Captain," he exclaimed. "So few months have passed since I saw you off to Gimmas Haefdon, yet how terribly much has come to pass." Turning to the A'zurnian, he nodded. "You must be Aram of Nahshon. The Emperor has told me of your bravery."

"The Emperor exaggerates," Aram replied, coloring to an even deeper shade of red than he was accustomed.

"So does Aram," Brim added, "the opposite way."

Beyazh winked at Aram. "Keep up the good work, young man," he said. "And know that you are appreciated in every corner of the Empire." As Onrad entered the cabin and took a seat behind the Helmsmen, the ambassador turned to Brim. "As usual, Onrad speaks highly of your exploits, also," he said.

Brim chuckled grimly. "We're all in this thing up to the neck," he said, "mostly trying to stay alive."

"Sounds all too familiar," Beyazh said, settling into a seat across the aisle.

"How *are* things at home, Mr. Ambassador?" Brim asked, not daring to ask about Raddisma or her pregnancy—which by now must have become quite visible.

"Not good," Beyazh answered. "I wish I could say otherwise, but I cannot. The thrice-damned Leaguers appear over Magor five or six times a day, blasting and burning at will. Our shelters are filled with people who have lost their homes. And for some reason, their accuracy has improved at least tenfold, even when they fire at nearly LightSpeed. Sometimes I think that they have some new kind of aiming system."

Brim bit his lip. Poor Raddisma. . . . "Ah, how is Nabob Mustafa holding up?" he asked.

"Good of you to ask, Captain," Beyazh said. "So far, His Majesty seems to be weathering the storm well enough." He chuckled. "Why, the old rake has even fathered a child on Raddisma, his Chief Consort. You remember her, don't you?"

"Er, yes," Brim said, feeling his cheeks burn in spite of all his efforts to remain calm. "She's doing, ah, well also, one h-hopes."

"So far as I can see," Beyazh replied with a gruff chuckle. "She's the size of a house, yet she is *still* one of the most beautiful women I have seen anywhere in the galaxy. Mustafa keeps her hidden in the deepest shelters during the raids. The old boy seems quite proud of his accomplishment." He laughed. "You'd think he'd done the whole thing by himself."

Brim swallowed hard. "Y-yes," he agreed, feeling his face flush even more, "he's c-certainly had some help in that department."

Even as he spoke, the Helmsmen sounded an alert and the Imperial launch was quickly on its way to Early Warning Station 19, orbiting nearly a thousand c'lenyts above the planet Avalon.

Compared to the huge FleetPort satellites that based whole squadrons of starships and their crews, the BKAEW station was not much more than a dust mote in space. Consisting of four small globes joined into a four-sided structure by connecting tubes, the little satellite was dwarfed by a huge parabolic antenna formed of Queldon mesh and pierced by a complex array of directional KA'PPA emitters, the latter developed in secret during a crash project at the distinguished Allied Radiation Center research laboratories on Proteus, the science planet. Brim had noticed the little orbiter a number of times on his way to and from patrol, but had never had occasion to pass closely enough to observe details.

After a silky-smooth docking at the globe directly behind the large parabolic antenna—Onrad's Helmsmen *had* to be good, Brim considered—they entered the structure through a long, transparent tube that served as both vestibule and brow. In the background, Proteus's disk was divided nearly in half by light and darkness, and to port the Triad blazed forth at full radiance.

In the golden brilliance, Brim could see that each of the station's four globes was equipped with a single boarding tube that could accommodate two small space vehicles. Three other moored shuttles were visible, while a tiny HSTS (Hyperspeed Torpedo Scout) occupied the second set of mooring optics on their own tube. Four figures in battlesuits stood at rigid attention on the deck of the deadly scout ship, which consisted of little more than a Drive crystal surrounded by five 533-mmi torpedo tubes, all contained within a stiletto-shaped hull whose mostly transparent nose of Hyperscreen crystal housed its crew of four. A brace of forward firing, superfocused 225-mmi disruptors protruded from winglets on either side of the bow, completing an armament package all out of proportion to the ship's actual size. Onrad and Beyazh stopped for a moment to return the salute through the transparent walls, then Onrad himself led the way inside, with the station master—a near-sighted wisp of a Commander named Ismay who was clearly more comfortable in the sheltered confines of a lab—following as if *he* were the one who had arrived for a tour.

"That's Onrad," Brim whispered with a grin. "Just as if he'd been here a hundred times before."

"Emperors *always* know where they're going," Aram whispered back. "Don't they?"

Brim rolled his eyes toward the top of the tube. "I shall forever hope they do," he said in mock reverence.

"So shall I," Aram chuckled. He clearly meant it.

Inside, the BKAEW station seemed cramped, as it should with walls as thickly armored as the bridge of a heavy cruiser. Brim and Aram were the last ones into the scanning chamber and just in time to hear one of the operators inform Onrad that forty Leaguer attack ships had just slowed out of HyperSpace and were approaching from nightward. As wild patterns of multicolored data flowed over the large master display, Brim watched the ship's progress and visualized unflappable controllers in distant filter centers calling up Starfuries and Defiants to meet them. Within cycles, strong forces of Imperial defenders began to appear at the edges of the display and converge on the incoming Leaguers. Brim watched Onrad monitoring the developing battle with intent concentration. After a few more clicks, he began to shake his head in rapt, clearly emotional silence while his eyes actually filled with tears.

"Are you feeling all right, Your Highness?" Ismay asked.

With obvious effort, the Emperor nodded. "Yes, Ismay. I'm all right. Just please don't speak for a moment. I have seldom been so moved in all my life." After that, he watched in silence, listening to the whispered undertones of the operators as they worked their displays. Finally, after watching the battle for what must have been at least five cycles, he sighed and shook his head. "*Never,*" he rumbled to Ismay, "in any field of mortal conflict—has so much been owed to so few by so many."

The words burned in Brim's mind. Onrad had *personally* been out there in the heat of battle—he'd seen trusted friends blasted into particles and die screaming for air in ripped-open battlesuits. And because of it, he was one of the few Emperors in history who could actually *feel* what things were all about. Intrinsically, he understood the effects his pronouncements would have. Brim had always trusted that the man would be a fine Emperor; it was times like this he felt he knew *why*. . . .

Scant moments later, a whole squadron of GA 87B Zachtwagers took advantage of the confused situation to attack the BKAEW site itself, and Brim instantly discovered one of the most terrifying aspects of duty aboard the new early-warning stations. The station occupants got to actually watch the plot as League warships zeroed in on their particular satellite. And there was no way to shoot back!

"Great Universe, Onrad," Beyazh gasped in apparent fascination, "what a party! There's the whole bloody League Fleet out there, except for Hoth Orgoth himself, and I wouldn't be surprised to hear his voice on the COMM channels!"

But despite the Ambassador's bravery—or was it ignorance? —tension began to mount in the crowded control room as it became evident that the station itself was to be the target.

"I think it would be a good idea," Ismay warned calmly, "if everyone donned his helmet. Now!"

No stranger to the hazards of war in space, Brim had gotten into his clicks before the man's warning, and was activating its seals when the first attack arrived in the form of a direct hit on one of the two power globes. The whole structure juddered violently, pulsing local gravity and knocking everyone from his feet. Brim ground his teeth in surprise. How in xaxt had the Leaguers managed a direct hit with the first salvo. They'd hardly slowed below LightSpeed, yet their shooting was . . . magnificent—no other word would do. Less than a click later, a second disruptor salvo smashed home with terrific concussion, shutting down all the displays in blinding flashes of light. And so far as he could discern, the Leaguers had fired no more than a dozen salvos. For two direct hits! Yet they'd passed at such velocity that their targeting systems couldn't have had a chance to take effect. . . .

A third, more distant hit smashed home with a terrible creaking and groaning as if one of the spheres had been torn away completely. The local gravity pulsed violently, then faded, throwing the occupants of the chamber around like rag dolls, caroming off the walls and cabinets in a horrible confusion of arms, legs, and smashed furniture. The voice circuits filled with a cacophony of screaming fright and pain. And in the midst of this utter chaos, still another hit ripped a great crack in the armored shell of the control room, decompressing the chamber with an atmospheric explosion that carried whole consoles—with their operators—into the blackness of space itself. Brim found himself plastered against a curved surface beside a light fixture that once must have been the ceiling of the scanning chamber. Beside him, Emperor Onrad shook his head inside his battlesuit with a bloody bruise on his forehead. By the dim glow of a battle lantern, he could see Aram's wings spasmodically fluttering inside his special battlesuit jacket, clearly stunned though just as clearly alive. But where was . . . ?

"Beyazh!" he yelled over the voice circuits. "Where the xaxt are you?"

"Over here," the Ambassador answered, his words cut off by someone vomiting noisily in her helmet. Brim whirled to see an arm waving feebly from beside the crumpled remains of a display console—only irals from the great ragged fissure, through which the little HSTS could be seen bobbing at the end of a single mooring beam that had somehow managed to remain powered. Its four crewmen, protected only by their battlesuits, could never have survived the blasts, but the ship appeared to be undamaged. Turning quickly to the Emperor, he peered into the faceplate to see a brow wrinkled with absolute rage. "You all right, Your Majesty?"

"I am thraggling well NOT all right," the big man bellowed angrily. "I am bloody incensed!" He turned to Brim as still another hit landed somewhere in the structure and shook the floor, silently now that there was no air to carry sound. "I want to get those bastards!"

Brim chuckled in spite of the desperate circumstances. That was Onrad. No thought of escape or safety—he wanted to fight back!

Suddenly the Emperor glanced outside and fastened his attention on the HSTS. His brow wrinkled in thought. "Brim," he demanded, nodding toward the little ship. "Suppose you'd be willing to go after those bastards if we could?"

Another hit smashed home. "You bet I would," Brim growled. "But what'll we use to . . . ?"

Onrad nodded toward the HSTS. "How about putting a torpedo up their bloody arses," he whispered with a smile. "Xaxtdamn better than sitting here for Leaguer target practice. Brim! D'you suppose that little ship still flies?"

Brim considered only a moment. "We won't know unless we try, Your Majesty," he said.

"Did you ever fly one?" Onrad demanded.

"At the Sherrington plant, Your Majesty," Brim replied with a nod. "A number of times."

"For Voot's sake, Brim," Onrad bellowed, sending the confused babble on the voice circuits into absolute silence, "drop the thraggling 'Your Majesty' for a while. If that little ship'll fly, you're in charge. Got that?"

"I'll try, Your . . . er . . . All right. We go. Aram!" he yelled. "You hear all that?"

"Aye, Captain," the A'zurnian replied weakly. "I'm ready."

"Good," Brim said. "You're in the right seat. Oodam. What shape are you in?"

"Mad as a soaked Rothcat," the Ambassador roared. "Let's get the bastards. In my day, I was a damn fine torpedoman."

"I'll take the disruptor," Onrad rumbled. "I'm a xaxt of a shot."

Brim glanced around the ruined chamber. There was nothing any of them could do here. And the Leaguers seemed to have temporarily broken off their attack. "Let's get started then," he yelled, "before the bastards have another go at us." Pulling himself hand over hand in the lack of gravity, he started for the new exit the Leaguers had provided.

Outside, the little station was a shambles. One of the globes was utterly gone; the only clues to its previous existence were the jagged ends of three connecting tubes. Another globe blazed with the hellish, coruscating light of a radiation fire. The monster antenna system was crooked off at a hopeless angle, and it was only too obvious that no warnings would come from Station Ventnor for a long time to come.

Pulling their way along handholds set into the walls of the brow, the four could see their Imperial shuttle had also been wrecked as well. The HSTS had survived by good fortune alone, miraculously sheltered by the brow itself from the blast that had shattered the scanning chamber wall. In relation to Brim, it was floating stern outward and upside down, anchored by a single emergency mooring beam that must have activated when the station's power failed. And although there was considerable flash melting over its port bow area from the blast, the little ship appeared to be in a relatively good condition. Her unfortunate crew, however, was nowhere to be seen.

Brim turned to Aram as they reached the end of the brow. "How does it look to you?" he asked, taking his emergency lifeline from its packet on his battlesuit. He activated its anchor end, watched it self-test successfully, and slammed it smartly against the side of the tube.

After a long pause, the A'zurnian laughed grimly and attached his own emergency lifeline. "Well, right now, anything looks better than playing target for a bunch of thraggling Leaguers."

Brim nodded, wondering how long they had before the Leaguers returned to finish their job. "I'll check it out, then," he said. "Your Maj . . . er, Onrad. Oodam, wait here with Aram while I go have a look. No sense trapping us all out there if it's got damage we can't see from here."

"Right," Onrad agreed.

With that, Brim pushed off across nothingness toward the HSTS, landing feetfirst between the dorsal torpedo tubes beside the open bridge hatch. From his new vantage point, the space station was now directly overhead with his three companions appearing to protrude horizontally from the curved wall. It was precisely the reason why a local "up" was always established in relation to any large space object. People simply worked better that way. Ignoring a momentary feeling of vertigo, he forced his orientation to the ship itself and started down the ladder, feeling local gravity take hold as his boots reached the third rung. After that, things became a lot easier. He motioned to Aram to follow and continued into the little starship as its automatic proximity alert sent alarms to his helmet.

"Unidentified targets approaching at high speed; ETA in four point five one cycles," the voice warned. "Unidentified targets approaching at high speed; ETA in four point five one cycles."

They needed to be on their way quickly!

On the cramped little control bridge, Brim immediately ran a systems verification: everything shipshape except for some mooring elements damaged by the Leaguer blasts. Then, popping his torso out of the hatch, he motioned the other three to board. "On the double!" he shouted into the voice circuit. "We've got more visitors."

By the time they scrambled aboard, he had connected power to the main bus and was watching the remainder of the readout panel come alive with flowing patterns of color. "Looks like she'll fly," he said as Aram thumped breathlessly into the systems seat beside him.

The A'zurnian ran his own sequence from the systems console. "She'll fly," he acknowledged tensely, "but the gravs took some damage. They're down to the last redundant control elements."

Onrad chuckled over the voice circuits. "Not to worry," he said. "You're safe as long as you stick with me. Emperors never get killed in combat. Besides," he added, winking from his faceplate, "I'm a crack shot with these disruptors which"—he paused momentarily—"have just completed all their diagnostics."

"Target ETA in one point five one cycles."

The deck trembled under their feet as Brim spun up both gravs at the same time—ignoring vociferous complaints from the power system. "Sounds good to me," he said presently. "Oodam, how about the torpedoes?"

"All five check out with no problems, Wilf."

"Target ETA in point five cycles."

"Everyone set?" Brim queried. He called up ENERGIZE on the control panel and directed it to PROPULSION just as the proximity alarm sent a shrill screech into each of their helmets.

"Go!" replied three voices in unison.

The gravs caught immediately; Brim swiped the lone mooring beam into oblivion and eased the little starship away from the ruined brow. As the distance increased, a number of figures in battlesuits appeared at the crack in the side of the globe waving their arms in the universal sign of "Good Hunting!" then dodged back behind the shelter of the wrecked sphere's wall.

With proximity alarms shrill in his ears, Brim simply mashed the thrust damper to maximum output and pivoted the nose up and around its pitch axis, skidding to within a few irals of the wrecked station before the little starship reversed course and shot off directly into the face of the Leaguers. Not a moment later, the station disappeared behind them in three brilliant discharges of energy followed by the blurred images of three Zachtwager attack ships. Three *more* direct hits in no more than a dozen shots, yet the Leaguers passed with such speed they couldn't possibly have taken time to fire after slowing from LightSpeed. How the xaxt had they done *that*?

Cranking the HSTS around a second time, he took off in pursuit, heedless of the enemy's sudden—devastating—prowess with their disruptors. "Let's get the bastards!" he yelled with blood lust coursing into his veins. "Oodam, I'll need torpedo tubes one and two."

Two small icons as an overhead panel turned from red to green. "Done," Beyazh declared.

Pushing the HSTS to maximum acceleration, Brim planned to overhaul the Leaguers as they circled in for a second attack, firing across the tangent of their curve, but instead the two Zachtwagers continued to accelerate in a straight line toward the 'Wyckean Void, and opening their Drive doors, sped quickly into Hyperspace. "Gorksroar!" he cursed, but his voice was drowned out by the proximity alarm with another indication of targets approaching from aft and clearly heading toward the damaged BKAEW station. Hauling the little ship around in a semicircle, he lined up on the Leaguers' predicted path. "All right, Oodam," he said into the voice circuits, "there's two more of the zukeeds. Do you have 'em?"

The Ambassador hesitated for only a moment. "Got 'em," he declared. "Coming on the target display now. Two more Zachtwagers. And from the way they're moving, they've just come out of HyperSpace. Hold 'er steady for a moment. I'll have to really lead the bastards. . . ."

After what seemed like ten million Standard Years, a brilliant flash just above Brim's console dimmed the Hyperscreens for a moment. A second followed close on its heels. As the view cleared, Brim could see the torpedoes streaking out into the darkness at the head of glowing trails of gravitons that vanished quickly as they appeared. Only after a few moments did he glimpse the Zachtwagers streaking in from starboard, no more than glowing motes against the starry sky, flying straight and level with the calm assurance that no Imperial starships were in the area.

Abruptly the closest Zachtwager burst into a roiling puffball of radiation flame. At the same time, its partner skidded to starboard, throwing a tremendous wave of gravitons forward as its gravity generators were reversed, slowing—but not stopping—the angular ship along its flight path. Then, in the blinking of an eye, the graviton plume reappeared at its stern, and the Leaguer began to accelerate once more, this time at an oblique angle away from the station.

''Great Helmsmanship!'' Brim exclaimed. ''He dodged it!''

''After the bastard!'' Onrad bellowed in frustration. ''We're s'posed to *kill* Leaguers, Brim, not admire 'em.''

''Right!'' Brim said, sending full military power to the gravs. He put the helm over hard and followed the Leaguers out across the 'Wyckean Void toward Effer'wyck. ''Beyazh! Ready tubes three and four,'' he yelled.

''Ready, Wilf,'' the Fluvannian said tensely as two more icons blended from red to green.

Now, he had to gain enough on the Leaguer ship for Beyazh to make an angle shot. Torpedoes were notoriously inaccurate and short of range when fired directly into a graviton exhaust. Fortunately, in spite of the HSTS's limited performance below LightSpeed, GA 87s were even more limited. Named Zachtwagers or ''precision shooters'' by developers at Gantheisser, GA 87s were awkward-looking, angular starships that mounted three enormous forward-firing 483-mmi single-shot disruptors as main armament and a pair of movable 30-mmi disruptors firing aft. The ships were used mostly for ground attack. Sent in prototype form to Fluvanna for evaluation during the League's pre-war attempt to capture the important little dominion, the GA 87 found little opposition from the poorly equipped local forces (except the rare Starfuries of the IVG, when they invariably suffered disastrously). As a result, the type's performance was seriously overrated and few changes were made to the design before they were placed into mass production. Even during the early wartime campaigns, GA 87s proved able to blast their way through brief campaigns against Korbu, Gannat, and A'zurn with relative ease. This furthered their reputation to an extent far in excess of actual abilities. However, against high-performance starships like Starfuries and Defiants, GA 87s quickly showed themselves to be slow and poorly armed, proving easy targets for the powerful killer ships currently operating with the Imperial Fleet's Defense Command.

Only moments after Brim and his improbable crew gave chase, the Leaguers opened up with their rear-firing 30-mmi. DR81 disruptors. Onrad quickly joined in with ranging shots from the HSTS's big 225-mmi. disruptor. But when the Hyperscreens cleared, the Leaguers were surrounded by the glowing halo of Gandom's v_e effect and heading for HyperSpace with all the thrust their Drive crystals could provide.

"We've got 'em now," Brim said, keying open the Drive exhaust. At the same time, he switched main-bus power to the little ship's Drive crystal. With a deep rumble that vibrated every component of the HSTS's stout little hull, the crystal came alive and the starscape outside began wobbling and shimmering as normal photon light blended to an angry red kaleidoscope that brought space itself to a wilderness of shifting, multicolored sparks, the Daya-Peraf transition. Brim shut off the laboring gravity generator—it wouldn't be needed until they had returned to HypoLight speeds—and watched while the Hyperscreen panels synchronized with the Drive. Then, vision cleared ahead, returning to the full majesty of galactic space—and the Zachtwager now trailed by a whirling green wake, its Hyperspace shock wave bleeding off mass and negative time in accordance with the complex system of Travis Physics that ruled flight above LightSpeed. As he had planned, he was now on a parallel path with the Leaguers, offset about six points to port.

After glancing aft to check his own Drive plume, the Carescrian trimmed ship for maximum velocity and sent more power to the crystal. They were soon overtaking the Leaguers at a much higher rate of change, and the GA 87 began laying down a deadly barrage of energy from its rear-firing disruptors. Onrad put a stop to the latter with a quick barrage of disruptor fire that must have resulted in considerable damage despite the extreme range.

"How's that for a worthless figurehead?" Onrad crowed.

"A xaxt of a shot!" Beyazh said, his voice filled with awe. "Those zukeeds are a long way off."

"See, Wilf?" Aram quipped. "I always said Emperors must be worth something," eliciting a howl of mock protest from Onrad.

"I'll never question you again," Brim chuckled grimly, then ground his teeth. Ahead, the peripheral stars of Effer'wyck were already beginning to define themselves as brighter entities against the general glow of the galactic center. He turned in his seat to face Beyazh. "Oodam," he said, "let's finish the Leaguer off quickly and head back. We're getting a long way from Avalon."

"Less than a cycle from now, and counting," Beyazh assured him.

Brim nodded and returned to his controls. Each click passed like a Standard Year of trouble, and at a velocity of nearly 26M LightSpeed, they were penetrating enemy-controlled space at an alarming rate. If the Leaguers had anything at all like BKAEW—and he was certain they did—alarms would soon be going of all along the Effer'wyckean frontier.

"They're in range. . . ." Beyazh said tensely. "Hold 'er steady."

The fleeing Gantheisser was now a quarter-on silhouette, little more than six c'lenyts distant.

"Steady. . . ."

Brim was so intent on his controls that when the tubes actually fired, he nearly started out of his Helmsman's console. Especially when Beyazh had excitedly keyed the torpedoes *before* he yelled . . .

"Fire!"

"Thanks a thraggling bunch, Mr. Ambassador," Onrad grumped shakily.

"Yeah," Aram added. "You kind of got the drill backward, didn't you?"

"Sorry," Beyazh whispered sheepishly. "But look," he exclaimed, pointing through the forward Hyperscreens, "in spite of my poor procedure, I have indeed scored another hit!"

The fleeing Gantheisser was suddenly enshrouded by a scintillating halo of purplish light with a bright red core than grew rapidly, changing shape and color until like a gigantic puffball, it caved in on itself and collapsed to a few sparkling shards.

And before the last remnant of the Leaguer ship winked out among the stars, Brim had reversed course and was heading back toward Avalon with the Drive crystal still at top speed.

"Scratch one more Gantheisser!" Onrad said happily. "Now this is a xaxt of a lot better than playing target, wouldn't you say, gentlemen?"

"Damn straight!" Beyazh exclaimed.

"Brim," Onrad ordered. "We'll enjoy a bit of the most Logish Meem I can find in the palace when we get this little bucket of bolts back to Avalon! Damned if I haven't *dreamed* of somehow getting into this war. . . ."

"Oh, Gorksroar!" Brim whispered between his teeth.

"Gorksroar?" Onrad demanded. "What Gorksroar?"

At that moment, the proximity alarm went off again.

"*That* Gorksroar," Brim replied grimly, pointing up and aft where two big GH 262-Es were driving in at high speed for a kill in such close formation their "wings" overlapped port to starboard. The yellow tips of their chevron-shaped starships marked them as a couple of veteran warriors for certain.

"Voot's vermin-filled beard," Onrad growled. "I should have thraggling known. . . ."

"Beyazh," Brim yelled, hauling in the little ship's helm. "Get that last torpedo ready. NOW!"

Moments later, the last torpedo icon changed to green. "Now," Brim warned, holding up his hand, "we're not going to fire this one. Instead, we're going to jettison it."

"Jettison?" Beyazh exclaimed. "An armed torpedo?"

"Yeah," Brim said through clenched teeth; the Leaguers were catching up fast, "but set the fuse for proximity—at about five hundred irals."

"A space mine!" the Fluvannian whispered. "Of course."

"If they'll just hold off firing a few more clicks," Brim grunted, his eyes glued to the aft view display. The bastards had to be *just* where he wanted them. "Ready . . ." he warned. A whir behind the aft bulkhead told him that the number five torpedo-loading hatch was open. The Leaguers were nearly on top of him doubtlessly arguing about who would get to fire first. He darned not wait another moment. . . . "Let 'er go!" he bellowed, then shoved the thrust dampers into MILITARY OVERLOAD and cranked the little starship around in the tightest turn he could manage without bending the hull. . . .

CHAPTER 6

Starship Thieves!

No sooner had the ejector mechanism cycled than space itself erupted in a blinding inferno of raw energy as both Gorn-Hoffs fired ranging shots—at precisely the wrong time for the HSTS, which had come through only half of Brim's intended escape maneuver. The little ship's hull took tremendous blast waves along its whole spine, which thwanged audibly like a child's elastic band. The local gravity pulsed and every loose object in the cabin took on a life of its own, caroming off the walls as if they were old-fashioned projectiles. The next instant, their whole Universe seemed to go mad in a cataclysmic explosion of light and silent concussion that spiked their Drive into silence. The starboard Hyperscreens shattered in a great confusion of flying crystal shards while Brim braced himself, waiting for the final instant of pain that would reduce him to atoms. . . .

It never came.

Panting in his suit as if he had run a hundred c'lenyts, he looked around the cabin—as his companions looked at him in obvious surprise.

"By all that's holy to the Gradygroats," Onrad whispered timidly. "D' you suppose we're dead?"

"N-no, Your Majesty," Aram quipped in a shaky voice. "I

don't think so. Otherwise, we wouldn't be watching that." He pointed out through the remaining Hyperscreens.

"By Voot's great, greasy beard," Oodam whispered in a reverent voice, "we g-got the bastards." Outside, both Gorn-Hoffs had barged past them on momentum alone and were now diminishing in the distance whipping and looping through aimless circles, completely out of control. Each had apparently lost a "wing," one starboard and one port. Space around them was filling with lifeglobes. "You put that torpedo right between 'em, didn't you?" he said.

"I tried," Brim said weakly, just now getting his breathing under control.

"Voot . . ."

The HSTS itself was now rapidly losing velocity, coasting down toward the great constant of LightSpeed, to which all HyperLight vehicles must return without Drive power to keep them going.

"Now what?" Aram asked.

"I was afraid somebody was going to ask that," Brim whispered, " 'cause we sure can't stay here. This place is gonna be full of rescue vessels in a matter of cycles—and none of 'em will be speaking Avalonian."

"Got a point there," Onrad said. "But lifeglobes're out for me. I can't be captured alive."

Brim nodded. He understood. "Can you restart the Drive?" he asked Aram.

The A'zurnian bent to his systems console. Miraculously, *it* still appeared to be operational. "Drive's dead," he said presently. "The crystal itself checks out, but there's no way I can route power to it. The control system probably fused out during the energy surge when the torpedo got those two Leaguers."

Brim nodded; he'd been afraid of that, too. "What about the grav?" he asked. "Can you start *that*?"

"Yeah," Aram said after some moments of consideration. "But we won't have much control."

"Right now," Brim said, "we only need enough control to

get the xaxt out of here. After that, we can worry about finer maneuvering.''

''But how are we going to get below LightSpeed?'' Aram asked. ''We need the Drive for braking, don't we?''

''The Fullstop,'' Brim said, pointing to a red button beneath a clear plastic plate at the lower right of the readout panel. ''It has its own paths to the Drive.''

''Holy Voot, I didn't think of that,'' Aram said. Every vehicle that operated in space had one—by intergalactic law. Otherwise, disabled ships could drift forever. Typically, the devices stored enough energy to bring ships to a full stop from whatever speed they were making at the time of failure.

''Hit it, then,'' Brim commanded. ''Those two Gorn-Hoffs are probably drifting at close to 30M LightSpeed. That'll put a lot of distance between us.''

''Everybody strapped down?'' Aram asked, sliding the plate from atop the red button.

''My restraints are powered,'' Onrad said, nodding toward his armrest control panel.

''So're mine,'' Brim answered.

''Mine, too,'' Beyazh said.

''Wilf?''

''Yeah. *Go!*''

Aram mashed the red button and their Drive activated immediately—at full power, shaking the already weakened spaceframe like a leaf in a windstorm. Brim was thrown painfully against his restraints while loose items in the littered cockpit once more took on a life of their own. The remaining Hyperscreens burst pulverized from their frames, and outside, the view of the Universe went crazy again—this time in all improbable colors of the rainbow as the ship quickly slowed toward HypoSpeed. Slowly, the rainbow fused to crimson—then, haltingly, orange-outlined silhouettes began to appear out of the chaos. One moved, then another.

''We've made it!'' Onrad shouted.

''Looks like,'' Brim said tensely as the wrecked cabin

defined itself around him. Finally, normal vision returned. "Aram," he demanded. "What about those systems?"

"Fullstop's empty," the A'zurnian chuckled.

"*And?*"

"Grav looks workable, Wilf. But everything about this little tub is shaky now. Best we get her down somewhere—and soon."

"Er . . . when we're down . . ." Onrad began.

"When we're down . . . ?" Brim prompted.

"Same as the lifeglobe thing," the Emperor said quietly. "I can't be captured. The last thing before that happens, one of you shoots me. Understand? You've all got side arms."

Brim winced, then nodded. So did the others.

"Swear it!" Onrad snapped. "Don't think of me, xaxtdammit think of the Empire!"

"I swear . . ." Brim said presently.

"So do I," promised Beyazh in a tight voice.

"And I," whispered Aram.

"Let's get this thing on the surface, then," Onrad said.

Brim called up a HoloMap of the area on his navigation display. Manipulating the image, he homed in on the nearest Effer'wyckean frontier stars, then searched for ones with human-habitable planets. Moments later, most of the pinpoints of light dimmed considerably. Three, however, increased in brightness. One orbited a star directly on the 'Wyckean Void. When he "touched" it with a logic pointer, a dialog box appeared at its side.

Effer'wyck:
Frontier, Zone HN31.6 (G.V)
Star FTR8459/33.45499 (type-1)
Planet 3: Bra've (local appellation)
Habitable, anatomy types 2, 9, 9A, 13-21, some 25s (see Note CH-234)
Rotation period: 31 Standard Metacycles
Remote population centers: none dominant

Heavily forested in temperate band
History: greatest growth during mid 4800 century when population reached est. 645,000. Since then, gradual urban drift plus declining birthrate.

- General agriculture
- Ancient ruins: lost civilization

NOTE: Suspected advanced base for League Squadron 88.4 "*Angrieff*": 44+ GA 87 starships.

"Not a lot of choice," Onrad grumbled.

"It's closest, so it's *the* choice," Brim said firmly. "Turn up your battlesuit cooling units. With no Hyperscreens, it's going to be a little hot in here during reentry, regardless of how much I ride the gravity brakes. . . ." With that, he put the helm over and set course for the little planet its inhabitants called Bra've.

The little Effer'wyckean planet had long since ceased to reveal its curvature. The sky was still nearly black, a deep bluish purple, but it was no longer possible to see the stars as they appeared in outer space. The little Type-1 luminary star—never officially named according to Imperial records—had already outshone all its galactic siblings. Below, forests, rivers, and occasional cleared areas or fields were now visible in the dusk of late evening, including a large cold front that flickered with lightning and gave them a bump as they passed between some of its higher storm clouds.

Brim worked the controls delicately, attempting to get everything he could out of the ship's little gravity generator before it failed—which it would clearly do some time in the *near* future. Judging by the sounds coming from behind the rear cabin bulkhead, one, or more likely both, spin rotors on the primary thrust unit (which were also used in *braking* during landfall operations) had lost magnetic bearing units, and were now thumping and hammering dreadfully each time he changed the power setting. Inside, the cramped flight bridge looked as if it were victim of some disastrous fire, courtesy of their reentry heat, which Brim had—only *just*—managed to keep within the parameters of Imperial battlesuit cooling units. Raging flames that blasted through the empty Hyperscreen frames had been enough to melt and char nearly every item of organic origin. "A xaxt of a way to treat an Emperor, by Voot!" Onrad had chuckled at the height of the inferno. He'd been joshing, of course, but Brim agreed with him anyway. It was a xaxt of a way to treat a Carescrian, too.

"Hey, look at that!" Aram exclaimed, his voice scratchy on the voice circuit because much of the insulation had been burned from its exposed connectors. "Down there, about a c'lenyt off to starboard."

Brim forced his attention from the ship for a moment to a majestic hill rising green from the darker colors of the forest. Crowning its summit was a tiny village surrounded by an ancient stone wall and lighted by the fading twilight. It dominated the surrounding countryside like some great tanwahr's eyrie. As they glided closer, they could see the outline of a Gradygroat abbey that looked as if it had been built at least five centuries before the galaxy formed. Beyond, not more than another ten or fifteen c'lenyts, a small lake reflected the night sky from what appeared to be a heavily forested valley. Lowering the nose judiciously, he pulled back on the gravs to hush their passage, then took a deep breath. "I'm going to put us down on that lake ahead," he said while the grav renewed its frantic thumping.

"Sounds like the decision wasn't all yours," Aram chuckled grimly.

"The ship did have a *big* vote in it," Brim admitted.

At that moment, the grav gave a last, convulsive shudder and went quiet.

"I think it's changed its vote," Aram observed in the abrupt silence.

"WON-der-ful," Brim grumbled. "Just thraggling WON-der-ful." He ground his teeth. Without its grav, the HSTS could still outglide a brick, but not by much. He could pretty well estimate their point of impact by momentum alone—but it was *dark* down there—except for lightning flashes from the storm they'd passed.

"Oh, great!" Beyazh swore. "Look off to starboard. If that isn't a Leaguer base, I'll eat my helmet. The lights are just now coming on."

"Don't ruin your teeth, friend," Onrad said quietly. "Nobody'll take your bet. Those are Zachtwagers parked along the taxiways."

Brim had only a moment's glance to confirm their verdict—that was all he needed to get the essential message. "So much for *sneaking* onto this bloody planet," he groused. "Everybody within a hundred c'lenyts must have heard the gravs go."

"They didn't have to," Beyazh said. "We've clearly set off every proximity alarm on the base by now."

"*If* they hadn't got enough warning already from those two Gorn-Hoffs we gonged," Aram added.

"Pull your straps tight as you can make 'em, everybody," Brim cautioned, snugging down his own recliner belts until they hurt. "And set your battlesuits for minimum freedom," he added with a twinge of envy. He couldn't protect himself the same way. He had to keep his own suit flexible so he could fly the ship.

"Got you," Onrad said stolidly.

The others only grunted.

All that remained now was the steering engine. Brim would use that at the moment of impact in a final, desperate effort to soften their crash. And the forest itself—for they were heading rapidly into a lofty stand of gigantic trees. Just before impact, he switched on the landing lights and desperately picked two stout oaklike dicotyledons that looked as if they were just *slightly* farther apart than the width of their hull. If he could steer between them, the stout-looking disruptor winglets on either side would be ripped from their mountings, taking a lot of energy with them before the main hull hit anything more solid than brush. "Here it comes!" he warned and snapped off the lights.

After that, things happened much too quickly for anything but raw reflexes. The trees flashed past in a blur against the last vestiges of twilight, then in one terrible moment of concussion and noise, the whole Universe seemed to go wild in blinding sparks as the disruptor mountings tore free against the trees. Brim stood on the starboard rudder and for the slightest fraction of a moment he heard the steering engine whine. The ship skidded sideways in a cloud of broken branches and debris from the forest floor, sheering off trees as if it were some sort of forestry harvester. In the final moment, all he could see directly in their path was the biggest, thickest tree his benumbed mind could recall. He fumbled for the freedom control on his battlesuit, swiped it toward MINIMUM at the same moment that unbelievable concussion brought a personal galaxy of bright flashes to his closed eyes . . . followed by soothing darkness that swept all other sensation in its merciful path. . . .

Onrad's voice seemed to be coming from somewhere a long distance away. . . . "I think the poor bastard's still alive. . . ."

"Your Majesty?" Brim groaned.

"Wilf . . . ?"

"Yeah."

Stretched out uncomfortably on his back, the Carescrian could just pick out three figures bending over him in the darkness. His helmet was open and the cool, damp smell of the forest was strong in his nostrils. Distant lightning flashed fitfully, its distance-muffled thunder arriving only after a long delay. Yeah, he thought. The forest. . . . He'd survived the crash after all.

"Thraggling miracle you're still with us," Beyazh said. "You must have stiffened your battlesuit at the last possible click, otherwise you'd be smashed to jelly."

"Anything feel broken, Wilf?" Aram asked.

Brim spent a few moments moving various parts of his body. Everything felt *sore*, but . . . "I think I'm all right," he said tentatively.

"Can you get up?" Onrad asked.

"That's what I'm going to try next," Brim said, rolling over onto his stomach. Carefully, he drew his knees beneath him. So far, so good. Next he pushed his trunk and head erect to a kneeling position and turned his head this way and that. What remained of the HSTS lay in a dark, crumpled heap some twenty irals distant against the darker bulk of the giant tree.

"How's everything feel?" Beyazh asked.

"Like somebody once said," Brim quipped as he pushed himself arduously to his feet. "'A little pain never hurt anybody.' But I *have* just redefined the term 'sore.'"

"And?" Onrad demanded as lightning flashed through the trees again.

Brim limped a few highly experimental steps while the muted thunder came again. "I *think* I'm all right," he said in real amazement.

"Thank Voot for that," Onrad swore. "We've got to get moving. These woods will be alive with Leaguers at dawn."

"All right," Brim agreed tentatively, "but to *where*?"

"Well," Onrad said grimly, "I've been thinking about finding our way to that hilltop village we saw back there."

"There's also a Leaguer base in the same general direction," Aram reminded him over more thunder.

"I know," Onrad said. "But you're going to take care of both problems for us."

"Me?" Aram asked, then groaned with the same breath. "Of course!" he snorted. "I've been spending so much time in space that I hardly think of flying by myself anymore."

"How about that singed wing of yours?" Brim asked.

Aram shrugged. "It's flyable," he said, unsealing the wing covers of his battlesuit. "I practice every time I get on the surface where there's a bit of room." He looked up momentarily as lightning flickered in the sky, then began to unlimber his great wings like an athlete readying himself for competition.

"Takes care of that," Brim laughed. "But after we find the village—then what?"

"Your guess is as good as mine," Onrad admitted. "But where there's a village, there are bound to be Effer'wyckeans. And I can't believe they have any love for the Leaguers who are sacking their country."

"Got a point there," Beyazh agreed thoughtfully. "There's got to be more help there than out in the middle of the woods."

"What do you think, Aram?" Onrad asked, his face lighted momentarily by lightning.

"I'm ready to go anywhere," the A'zurnian said while a freshening breeze noisily rustled the high treetops, "just so long as we get going."

"Wilf?"

"Sounds good to me," Brim said. "I certainly can't think of a better plan, although I think that storm's definitely headed our way. Do you fly in the rain, Aram?"

"Haven't melted yet," the A'zurnian quipped.

"It's settled, then," Onrad said. "Now, what about weapons? We got anything but our side arms?"

"Yeah," Aram quipped, "as we say in A'zurn, 'You can get more with a kind word and a blaster than you can get from a kind word alone.'"

"True," Beyazh chuckled. "Well," he said, pointing to a long, badly dented metal box. "I dragged this out of the wreck while you were working on Brim. It *says* it's a survival kit, but I'm xaxtdamned if I can get it open."

"Probably jammed," Onrad offered after having a go at the lid himself.

"I'll take care of that," Brim said, making his way cautiously into the wreckage. A few clicks later, he returned with a stout metal rod about three irals in length. "Found me a 'Carescrian persuader.'" he chuckled darkly, and made for the box. Moments after a rending screech of metal against metal, the box lay open. "Always was good at precision tools," he said proudly.

"So I see," Onrad laughed. "Or rather *don't* see."

"It is sort of dark here," Beyazh agreed.

"Not anymore," Brim said, feeling through the contents blindly. "I'll bet this is. . . ."

"A flashlight," Onrad exclaimed as a dull glow illuminated the box's interior.

"And thoughtfully preset at minimum intensity," Brim said admiringly. "We really didn't need a bright flash of light right now, although that lightning must be messing up their orbiting light sensors in a big way." He quickly inventoried the contents: a week's rations (ANATOMY TYPES 2, 9, 9A, 13-19), four rapid-firing BL-58 blast pikes with sixteen energy cartridges, a case of thirty-six proton grenades, eight rapid-cure battlesuit patches, a first-aid kit (831-B RADIATION, ANATOMY TYPES 2, 9, 13-19), four backpacks with climbing gear, and a second flashlight. "Not bad for emergencies," he observed with a grin and passed out the blast pikes. Wiping the last clean of preservative gel, he slotted a power cartridge in place and ran a self-test sequence on the powerful weapon's tiny status panel. Moments later, a READY indicator glowed softly beside the safety switch.

"This pike's looking good," Onrad said over a loud roll of thunder.

"Mine, too," Aram said.

"Bad power cartridge here," Beyazh grumbled, heaving the finned cylinder into the wreck.

Brim tossed him another. That did the trick.

"Aram," Beyazh asked, "how much can you carry when you fly?"

"I'm pretty well out of shape," Aram admitted. "Probably I could carry a blast pike with this battlesuit on, but someone'll have to carry my backpack while I'm up."

"You won't be carrying anything on these missions, my feathery friend," Brim said. "The proximity sensors those Leaguers will be using scan for synthetic materials and metals. In a forest like this, they'll be specially set to ignore birds and the like. Even *big* ones."

"You've got a point, Wilf," Aram said. "I guess while I'm up, then, somebody will have to carry *all* my stuff."

"No problem, there," Onrad said.

"All right," the A'zurnian said, looking up through the trees. "Since we're in sort of a clearing here, I think I'll have my first look right now.'' Presently, he was out of his battlesuit, his reddish feathers black in the near darkness.

''You going to have any trouble finding us from up there?'' Brim asked.

''I was thinking of that,'' Aram answered. ''Probably the best way is for you to use the flashlight. In the dark I've always been able to return pretty close to where I took off, but forests like this begin to look the same from about five hundred irals on down.''

''That light'll also show any orbiting Leaguers where we are,'' Beyazh warned.

''I'm pretty sure our storm will take care of that,'' Brim said.

''Right,'' Aram agreed. ''Besides, you won't flash it until you hear me calling. I'll simply fly a grid pattern in the general area until I hear one of you yelling or I see the flashlight blip. How's that?''

''Sounds good to me,'' Onrad said. ''May Lady Fortune smile on you.''

''By Voot's beard, may she thraggling crawl in bed with you!'' Beyazh swore.

''I think I like that even better,'' Aram returned with a chuckle. Then slowly his great wings began to beat the air. Moments later, he rose majestically into his own natural element.

Brim felt shivers race along his back as the A'zurnian became a dark shape among the stars and then disappeared completely. Now *that*, he thought with a smile, was flying!

No more than a quarter metacycle later, they heard singing coming from above the trees.

''There *once* was a flyer from Zeight,'' the voice went. ''Who traveled much faster than *light*. . . . He left one day in a *relative* way. . . . And came back the *previous* night. . . .''

''Hey, *Aram*,'' Brim shouted into the night sky. ''Over this way!''

''Which way?'' asked the voice after a rumble of thunder.

''*Over here!*''

''Say again!'' This time, Aram's voice was closer.

"*Over here!*"

"Yeah," Aram said. "Blip the light—at GLOW. I think I'm right above you."

Brim set the flashlight at GLOW and blipped it once.

"That's enough," Aram warned. "I'm comin' in."

Immediately, Brim watched an area of sky become even darker, and moments later Aram was down.

"How'd it go?"

"Piece of cake," Aram said. "Aside from the wind—which is definitely getting worse as the storm approaches. But we have to get going right away. I spotted three search groups coming through the woods in our general direction. They must be starsailors, 'cause they're making enough noise for two battle groups of soldiers." He paused for a moment. "Listen," he said. "At least until dawn, I'm going to take my helmet up with me and stay there while you three walk. The helmet's so small it'll look like static on their proximity alarms, and we can stay in touch with the secure voice circuits. Besides that, I'll be able to track you without the flashlight and I can keep you on the most direct route possible."

"We've got nearly ten metacycles before it gets light," Brim said, looking at his timepiece. "Can you stay up that long?"

"Depends on the storm," Aram said, looking up as lightning flashed through the trees. "If I get tired, I'll let you know. Anybody have problems with that?"

"None here," Brim said after a moment. "It's clearly our best chance."

"All right," Onrad said, "let's split up the rest of this gear and get moving."

Within half a metacycle, they were on their way, Brim and his two nonflighted cohorts marching and stumbling single file through the forest at the direction of a large "bird" flying over head. Bringing up the rear, Brim found himself chuckling in spite of the desperate circumstances. *Here we go again,* he thought to himself. Funny how things went in a war. It hadn't been *that* long ago he'd been afraid he might be bored with his job as Group Leader. . . .

* * *

"So how you doing up there?" Brim asked into the helmet microphone of his battlesuit. Aram had been aloft for nearly a metacycle, now, and from the rush of the wind, the storm was about to break.

"It's a little bumpy up here," Aram answered, "but I'm fine aside from that." He chuckled. "You're the poor sods who have to carry backpacks. How's it going with you?"

"If it weren't for the honor of the thing, I'd rather be in a starship myself," Brim quipped.

"Yeah," Aram agreed. "I know what you mean."

"Where are you, anyway?" Brim asked.

"About two c'lenyts from you—over the Leaguer base."

"Anything going on there?"

Aram laughed. "Until the rain started, it looked like an anthill somebody poked with a stick," he said. "Now, they're pretty much settling down."

"Probably waiting till morning to come looking for us," Brim suggested.

"That's my take," Aram assented. "And . . . wait a moment," he said. "*Here's* something interesting."

"What?" Brim demanded.

"Hang on . . ." the A'zurnian said.

A much longer, louder rolling sort of thunder came from the direction of the base: clearly the sound of a starship landing on a Becton tube. The first drops were filtering through the trees and the wind smelled strong with rain. Nearly a quarter metacycle passed before Aram came back on the line.

"One of those little Gorn-Hoff 219s just landed," he reported excitedly. "You know, the executive starships their High Command uses for the VIPs."

"Yeah," Brim said. "Two Helmsmen, twin spin-gravs on pylons aft, eight or so passenger seats. Plush."

"You've got it."

"And . . . ?"

"*Big* brass," Aram replied as lightning flooded the forest with momentary brilliance. Rain was now falling steadily, and the wind had become a constant moaning in the treetops. "The base people sent a *limousine* skimmer to meet it. Soon as the 219 rolled to a hover, a couple of black-suited Controllers got out, and the ship moved back out to the ready area at the launch end of the Becton tube. It's sitting there right now with the hatches open and the crew loafing around outside."

"So?" Onrad asked. "What do you have in mind?"

"So that 219 would sure be a sporty way to get back to Avalon," Aram said. "I'll bet it's even ready to take off."

"You mean *steal* it?" Onrad demanded.

"Absolutely," Aram replied.

"Damn," Onrad chuckled thoughtfully. "A Leaguer executive transport. Now *that* appeals to my sense of comfort. And, oh, wouldn't it just *provoke* the miserable bastards!"

"Maybe it's a trap," Beyazh suggested cautiously.

"I doubt it," Onrad said after a pause. "They don't even know we're alive, much less anywhere near their base. Aram. How far away are we from the ship?"

"The 219?" Aram asked.

"No, the thraggling *Benwell*," Onrad snapped.

"Er . . . sorry," Aram said in an embarrassed voice. "You're less than half a c'lenyt away."

"Good," the Emperor said. "Brim, do you think you could get that bucket of bolts started? I know you read Vertrucht."

"It's damn well worth a try," Brim answered. "I'd rather take my chances with that Gorn-Hoff than a village full of frightened Effer'wyckeans."

"Yeah. Me, too," Beyazh said. "But it's really up to you, Your Majesty. You're the one most at risk tonight."

"I say, let's go for it," Onrad said without a pause. "I'll damn well spend the night in Avalon if I have my choice."

"Next stop, then, *Avalon*," Aram declared. "Turn approximately one hundred points to your right and start moving as fast as you possibly can."

"Got you," Onrad said, looking up through the drenching rain. Without another word, he started through the sodden undergrowth with Beyazh and Brim in his wake.

* * *

After nearly half a metacycle of rough going, the A'zurnian ordered them to halt in a clearing.

"What's up?" Brim asked.

"I'm coming in for my battlesuit and a knapsack with some of those grenades," Aram said. "It's the next part of my plan." Moments later, he appeared overhead., "I'll also need the flashlight again to get all the way down."

"You've got it," Brim said, opening his visor and slitting his eyes against the rain as he looked up to blip the light.

Presently, the A'zurnian splashed to the ground. "You're no more than five hundred irals from the field boundary," he explained a little breathlessly.

"You getting tired?" Brim asked, handing him the battlesuit.

"No more than from a long, fast walk for you," Aram said, "against the wind. Don't forget, at home, this is my *normal* mode of getting around." He struggled into the battlesuit as best he could in the heavy rain. "Now," he continued, "here're my thoughts. First, there's a mesh barrier about sixteen irals high surrounding the base. I couldn't see it from the HSTS, but it's there and the support posts carry powerful lights. I assume the mesh itself is lethal."

"Good assumption," Beyazh interrupted. "I've seen those fences before. They'll kill at about two irals' distance."

"No surprise there," Aram said. "I'll get back to that in a moment. Right now, I need to tell you about my plan. First, I'll want everyone at a point just short of the cleared area surrounding the fence—directly opposite the 219 we're going to, er, 'borrow.' Got that?"

"So far, so good," Brim said.

"All right. I'll take some of these proton grenades and fly to the opposite end of the base where they have a lot of temporary buildings and hangars. They took the bigwigs there in the limousine skimmer. My guess is there're stored flammables in some of those shacks—stuff that grenades could set to burning in short order."

"That'll get their attention," Onrad said.

"Right you are, Your Majesty," the A'zurnian continued. "At least that's what I hope for. That'll give you three the opportunity to cut an opening in the fence with your blast pikes, then make a run for the 219."

"And take care of the crew," Onrad said.

"And get it running," Brim added, knowing whose job *that* would be.

"While you're off doing the easy stuff," Aram quipped, "I'll continue to drop grenades here and there to keep the Leaguers occupied."

"And once we've got it ready to take off, you'll fly back and the four of us will take off. Is that it?" Onrad asked.

"That's my plan," Aram said, placing his helmet back on his head. "But we'll all have to *hustle*. It's getting tough to fly up there, and the battlesuit's going to make it worse."

"How many of these grenades can you carry?" Brim asked, handing over one of the fist-sized ovals.

Aram bounced it a few times in his hand while thunder split the night like a disruptor salvo. "With the battlesuit and the knapsack, probably a dozen or so," he said presently. "Zaxt—maybe one more for good fortune, too."

"You sure?" Onrad asked. "You've been up there a long time."

"Thirteen," Aram repeated firmly.

"Thirteen it is," Brim said, testing the grenades carefully, then placing them in an empty knapsack. When he was finished, he handed it to Aram who clutched it by one of its straps in his left hand. "See you in the 219, my friend," he said.

Aram gripped Brim's shoulder. "You get that Leaguer bucket of bolts started, Wilf. I'll be there—count on it." Then, with a drumming of wings, he was gone, crabbing almost sideways as the wind carried him along.

The three waited only a moment for their first guidance.

"Turn about three points to your right, and *go*!" Aram ordered in a voice tight with strain.

"Got you," Brim answered, grinding his teeth. The young

A'zurnian was fast reaching the end of his energy rope. Evidently, Onrad had heard the same bad news, because he was fairly running in the darkness. It was going to be a near thing!

Lights began to shine through the undergrowth after only a few moments. "Looks like we're there, Aram," Brim reported. "What do you see?"

"You're there," Aram assured him. He was breathing with effort now. "There's a patrol of sentries heading your way on the outside path, but I can't wait any longer. I've got to drop a couple of these grenades."

"Start dropping 'em," Onrad ordered. "We'll take care of the sentries." Then he turned to his two companions. "Ready?" he asked, unslinging his blast pike.

"Ready," Brim assured him, bringing his own weapon to hand.

Beyazh only nodded. He'd been carrying his at the ready for the last quarter metacycle.

After that, it seemed an eternity passed until a pealing discharge boomed out of the distance. "Let's go for it!" Onrad thundered, and took off through the last of the trees like a land crawler, Brim and Beyazh at his heels. They stopped just short of the clearing, and Brim poked his head through the underbrush.

"Gorksroar," he swore, dodging back into the cover. "Hold everything!" he whispered. "Those zukeed sentries are no more'n a couple irals away." Three gray-suited Leaguers had stopped to poor through the fence at a rising cloud of smoke and flame coming from one of the hangars.

"What about the 219?" Oodam asked in a hushed voice.

"It's right where Aram said it would be," Brim answered. "Crew and all, less than a thousand irals inside the fence. But we've got to do something about those guards before we worry about anything else." He thought for a moment. "Let me try it alone. The less noise we make, the better."

"Go for it," Onrad whispered.

Thumbing off the safety, Brim waited until a second grenade rent the downpour, then burst into the clear. Before the startled

Leaguers could turn to face him, he cut the first two down with a high-energy blast that burned them completely in half.

The third Leaguer, clearly faster than his unfortunate comrades, threw himself to the ground while he swung his own pike to the ready.

Brim likewise dived for the ground, but before he could aim his BL-58, the Leaguer leaped to his feet with a sideways motion—directly into the killing radius of the fence. With a blinding flash and a loud, sputtering hiss, he was instantly reduced to clouds of greasy blue smoke and steam, attracting the attention of the 219's Helmsmen who had been standing in the downpour while they watched the mysterious explosions with obviously growing concern.

"Get the *fence,* xaxtdamnit. *Now!*" Brim yelled as the third grenade detonated somewhere in the midst of the Zachtwager parking area. With that, he began to spray the deadly barrier with his blast pike. The mesh resisted momentarily, until, under attack from three powerful beams of energy, it shredded in a blinding flash of loosed energy, sparked noisily for a moment on either side of the smoke-filled rift, then returned to silence, while the 219's crew gawked in bewildered amazement. By now, sirens were filling the air, and every light in the base was burning.

When the fourth grenade explosion momentarily recaptured the attention of the two Leaguer Helmsmen, Brim and his two comrades took off through the fence at a dead run. The two bewildered Leaguers spun around once more and did a fast double take at the three figures in Imperial battlesuits splashing through the downpour at them with large-blast pikes. Desperately groping for their side arms, both made for the shelter of the 219, but a volley from Onrad's blast pike cut one of them down before he'd covered ten irals. The second dived for the ground and scampered through a puddle toward the ship on his hands and knees.

It gave Brim the few clicks he needed.

The Leaguer scrambled into the hatch, but as he tried to pull the circular door shut behind him, Brim arrived and desperately shoved the barrel of his blast pike over the dripping sill. The door stopped with a jarring crunch, and Brim heard the Leaguer shout with fright and anger. He looked up through the rain into the crack just in time to sight down the trembling barrel of a powerful Zspandu-50 blaster held by a glaring, mustached Helmsman in gray uniform. The next thing he sensed was the loud crack of a discharge—followed by a muffled splash as the Zspandu tumbled onto the ground in front of his eyes.

"Got the bastard," Oodam said matter-of-factly, swinging the door open again. "Bet he had *your* wind up."

"N-nonsense," Brim said over a rolling volley of thunder. "I'll get fresh underwear soon as we get back to Avalon. . . ."

The next explosion wasn't a grenade. Even in the midst of his wild sprint, Brim could see it came from the Zachtwager parking area: source of a glowing cloud of reddish smoke or steam and tumbling debris that billowed swiftly into the morning sky. The whole base had become a chaos of sirens, rain, explosions, lightning flames, and confusion. He heard the fifth grenade go off just as he pulled himself into the 219. A headless Leaguer leaked blood across two luxurious seats upholstered in priceless ophet leather. Fighting back his gorge, he threw the body over a stack of wooden crates strapped to the deck at the rear of the passenger compartment, then ran forward to the little ship's flight bridge and flung himself into the Helmsman's station.

By flashlight, the instrument panels *looked* normal enough. Of course, they ought to, having clearly been designed for use by five-point people (anatomy types 2, 9, 9A). Before him, a queer-looking crystal about the size of his fist was secured at its base to the glare panel and attached to a temporary-looking box on its right by a number of bright-colored cables. Clearly, some experimental device, but at the moment, not very interesting.

"The *master switch,* dammit," he mumbled to himself. *Where is it?*

Outside, lightning revealed a number of soldiers splashing toward the hole blown in the barrier. He'd expected the broken mesh to report its damage to Security, but the damn Leaguers were out to fix it a lot faster than he'd dreamed! Aft, in the cabin, he could see Onrad and Beyazh guarding the hatch with their blast pikes, the remainder of the grenades piled neatly in the aisle. They'd thrown the other Leaguer's body from the hatch.

Just then, another grenade went off outside—a lot closer than the others. He'd lost count, by now, but the A'zurnian must be getting to the bottom of his knapsack.

He willed himself calm by scanning the panels again for the master switch. Between the two consoles, he located the generator temperature gauges, and below them what must be an energy bypass actuator. Next to it was the graviton cutout control, and the cooling-flap levers with their indicators. Temperature gauges, regulators, boost controllers. All there. . . . The grenade explosion was followed immediately by a clap of thunder he could almost feel. He'd found the Hypospeed propulsion cluster, all right. And the Drive cluster was clearly below that. But where was the xaxtdamned master switch? Everything on the thraggling starship was worthless unless he could find it. He jumped as lightning blasted the early-morning twilight.

Wait! There right in front of his nose among the controls! A big red switch marked ZOMORT, "starter." He snapped his fingers in annoyance. It wasn't with the systems stuff at all. Damn Leaguers! He pushed it in, and every panel in the flight bridge began to glow. *Universe!*

Now to start the xaxtdamned thing. He scanned the panels for a power regulator; he knew there had to be one of those *somewhere*. . . . Shaking his head, he gave up. It would simply *have* to be in the right position. Once again, he concentrated on the Hypospeed cluster: the gravs. First things first. His eyes stopped for a moment at a large green slide mechanism, but he had no idea what *that* was for, and decided to leave it right where it was.

Unfortunately, things weren't quite that easy. He knew that GA 87s flew below LightSpeed on spin-gravs, but what type were they? The Leaguers installed *both* interchangeably, but each had a different starting sequence. "ZN-type," spin-gravs required hitting the START circuit for a few clicks *before* keying energy boost. Otherwise, the plasma field could be drowned and the whole starting sequence would have to be repeated—after waiting for the revolutions to reach zero.

On the other hand, "YZ" types required the starter and ENERGY BOOST to be applied simultaneously. And if BOOST were keyed more than a few moments before—or after—START, short-circuiting could actually damage the interrupter mechanism. Unhappily, no one had yet invented a workable coupler.

Taking a deep breath, he knew he'd have to guess. Somewhere on board the ship was a set of manuals he needed. But he had no time to search for it anymore. Wiping steam condensed on the Hyperscreens, he glanced outside where more sentries were splashing along the fence, accompanied by a small skimmer that mounted a large roll of mesh and numerous tool boxes. So far, they hadn't noticed the bodies near the hatch—or considered them important enough to interrupt their fence mending.

Then he looked aft toward the port spin-grav at the end of its stubby "wing" pylon. Its teardrop housing had two rows of cooling doors just below the interruptor assembly. He'd seen both ZN and YZ types with them, but the latter were much more likely to need extra cooling because of the energy required by simultaneous use of both systems.

"Wilf!" Aram's haggard voice came over the battlesuit circuits. "I'm down to my last two grenades," he gasped. "How're you comin' with the ship?"

"I'm ready to try a start sequence," Brim replied. "You all right?"

"A lot better now the knapsack's empty," he said, "but this damn battlesuit feels like it's made of lead and the wind's just plain bad."

"Can you last awhile more?"

"A little while. But *hurry*."

"Right, then. Drop those eggs as far away from us as you can, then keep your altitude till I call. If I can't make this bucket of bolts fly, make for the village on your own. No sense in all of us being caught."

"Got you," Aram answered, but Brim hardly heard; he was back with the controls. There was no time to lose!

First, he started the auxiliary power unit and watched the instruments begin to register. Next, he toggled the energy-change switch and gated the power impeller. Two green indicators marked VLADAM-A and VLADAM-E showed he'd successfully set the plasma. He nodded. Now for the gravs themselves.

Outside, he could hear shouting, now. He switched on the clearview and watched the Hyperscreens clear. A lot of gray-clad soldiers were running toward the hole in the fence. Nearly all of them glanced curiously toward the 219, but continued doggedly on their way.

Brim muttered silent thanks for the Leaguers' propensity to follow orders absolutely, then grimly switched the starter to TOVO, or "port." Scanning the rest of the instruments for a moment—none *seemed* out of tolerance—he cracked the thrust damper, then hit ZOMORT and ROTH-TA (energy boost) at the same time. Instantly, the spin-grav whined, its interruptor strobing brightly. "One . . . two . . . three . . ." he counted as the strobing increased linearly. At "ten," he mashed the ENABLE button—the spin-grav fired, caught for a moment, but sputtered and died as he delicately worked the thrust damper.

"Gorksroar!" Now, he had to start all over again.

"What happened?" Onrad demanded from the passenger compartment as lightning crackled somewhere downfield—accompanied by an earsplitting crack of thunder.

"Don't know," Brim admitted furiously. "Probably too little on the thrust damper." Keeping himself *just* under control, he reset everything, retoggled the energy-change switch, and once more gated the power impeller. The indicators marked VLADAM-A and VLADAM-E returned to green, and he cracked the thrust damper a second time.

With sweat running along his ribs, this time, he pushed the damper a hair farther. Too much, and he'd really bollix things up. The shouting was getting much louder outside, and a number of black-uniformed Controllers had gathered in a circle around the ship. Far down the field, he could see the limousine skimmer pull onto the perimeter road in clouds of spray! He squeezed his eyes shut while he contemplated shooting Onrad!

Heart in his mouth, he hit ZOMORT and ROTH-TA. Obediently, the spin-grav whined, its interruptor strobing. "One . . . two . . . three . . ." he counted. At "ten," he mashed the ENABLE button again. Once more the spin-grav fired, caught almost instantly, but *again* started to sputter and die, shaking the whole spaceframe no matter how he worked the thrust damper.

Then it came to him. The green slide. That was the thraggling power regulator! With a shaking hand, he nudged it toward the middle of its track and . . . the failing grav deepened in timbre and rapidly smoothed out into steady thunder.

"Aram!" he shouted as he started the second spin-grav.

No response. . . .

"Aram! Can you hear me?"

"Yeah, Wilf. She started?"

"Just now. Get your feathery ass down here right away."

Brim never had a chance to hear his answer, for at the moment, a tremendous hubbub began outside the cabin. He glanced to his left just in time to see at least twenty Controllers rush the 219's hatch through ankle-deep water, side arms at the ready. The jackbooted Leaguers immediately fell back under a withering barrage of fire from Onrad and Beyazh, who had finally shown themselves at the door. Moments later, the few survivors were in full retreat, splashing pell-mell for whatever shelter they could find while they shouted wildly at another squad of gray-clad soldiers who were clearly still on the way to deal with trouble that might come through the damaged fence. And *they* were armed with blast pikes, enough of them to seriously damage the 219!

The still-disciplined soldiers immediately unslung their pikes, and began advancing in a unit behind an extremely capable-looking noncom with a look on his face that nearly froze Brim's blood.

"*Com'on,* Aram!" Brim yelled into the voice circuit. "Time's a'wastin'!"

As he spoke, a tremendous explosion tore the very center out of the advancing Leaguer formation, breaking the soldiers' discipline and sending the few survivors off in every direction.

Heartbeats later, a form dropped to the ground and leaped through the hatch. "All right," Aram yelled breathlessly, "let's get the xaxt out of here!"

Working the steering engine with his feet, Brim pushed the thrust dampers forward and the little ship began to move toward the entry port of the Becton tube. As Onrad slammed the hatch, everything outside seemed to be erupting in little waterspouts speckled with dirt clods and debris as the Leaguers called up heavier disruptors—at the same moment the limousine skimmer pulled directly into Brim's path. Two officers jumped out, completely ignoring the storm and arrogantly began to fire their side arms at the Hyperscreens. Brim didn't mind running *them* over, but he didn't want to hit anything quite as solid as their limousine, so he bumped the steering engine to port.

Too much!

"Oh, GORKSROAR!" he bellowed as the 219 careened all the way around in a circle and headed for the limousine again—this time one of the brass hats splashed off in a *most* undignified manner. The other however—blond, square-jawed, and strikingly handsome in a somehow familiar manner—peered for a moment at the 219, stepped cautiously aside, then pocketed his blaster with a great, swashbuckling grin. Next he waved his sodden cap, grinning as if he had suddenly recognized an old acquaintance—which clearly he had. Brim recognized *him* at the same instant.

"*Kirsh Valentin,*" he whispered more to himself than anyone else—his long-time adversary through *two* wars and a number of years deceitfully labeled "peace." The blasted Leaguer could do nothing to influence the situation either way—and seemed to be enjoying himself immensely as his long-time rival made a fool of himself at the helm of a small starship!

Almost blinded with sweat, Brim returned the grin in spite of himself and waved back, only *nudging* the steering engine. He got past the limousine this time with merely a loud scrape as the ship's ventral safety cladding removed most of its passenger compartment.

Then, abruptly, they were at the portal. Carefully prodding the thrust dampers forward, Brim switched to local gravity and nudged the ship onto the glowing tube. "Hang on back there!" he bellowed, standing on the gravity brakes and shoving the thrust dampers all the way to their forward stops.

As thunder filled the control bridge, a dripping Aram slipped into the co-Helmsman's seat and buckled in. "Think she'll fly?" he quipped as rainwater ran from his feathers and collected in puddles on the cabin floor.

"We're going to find out right *now*!" Brim answered grimly, and glanced back at the still-grinning Valentin, who had just raised his hand in a casual salute. In spite of a sodden uniform, the Leaguer's smile was infectious. Brim returned it again—and the salute—then released the brakes. Instantly, the little ship surged forward through the sheeting rain, staggering along the Becton tube until Brim hauled back on the unfamiliar controls—a bit too soon! The ship lifted only for a moment, then sank uneasily back to the tube. "Fly xaxtdamnit!" he urged. "FLY!"

This time, the 219 lifted again, still too early for comfort, but Brim's innate skill as a Helmsman kept it airborne—amid howls of protest from the flight warning system. He could almost feel Valentin's scornful laughter on the back of his neck. Moments later, however, the little ship began to steady as it bumped and clawed its way blindly into the storm. Soon, they were accelerating toward LightSpeed. "Aram, you got the Drive figured out yet?" he demanded.

The A'zurnian hesitated only a moment. "What's a *Czambell*?" he asked.

"A Drive crystal," Brim translated.

"Then, I've got it figured out," Aram whooped. Presently, a

deep growl began to build beneath their feet. "Avalon, here we come!" he chortled happily.

"Yeah, Avalon," Brim repeated. Now, it might actually be true. Their 219 could outspeed any of the clumsy Zachtwagers back at the base, and with a little luck, they'd be well into the Void before the Leaguers could call in anything faster. Unfortunately, the bigger trick would be figuring how they would get anywhere near the Triad in a ship with the red daggers of the League painted boldly on either side of its hull. He felt for his new Effer'wyckean timepiece to clock their passage and . . . "It's thraggling *gone*," he exclaimed angrily, checking all the pockets of his borrowed battlesuit.

"What's gone?" Aram asked, looking up in surprise. "Is there something wrong with the ship?"

Brim shook his head in exasperation. "No," he grumped, "there's nothing wrong with the xaxtdamned ship. I've just lost my new timepiece back there, the one I bought in Luculent just before Effer'wyck threw in the towel. Gorksroar!"

"You thinking of going back after it?" Aram joked.

"No," Brim said, throwing a bogus punch across the little flight bridge. "But if someone ever finds it, they'll know I've been there. I even had my name engraved on it." He thumped the armrest. "Damnation," he pouted. "I'd hate to think of some thraggling Leaguer enjoying my timepiece. I never owned one that good before."

Aram frowned. "Probably won't matter much if people know *you* were there."

"Yeah," Brim agreed, shaking his head in disgust. "Let's just hope Onrad didn't drop his, too. . . ."

Just to be on the safe side, Brim set a roundabout course for home: an old smuggler's trick he'd learned from Baxter Calhoun. The enemy base had begun broadcasting demands for a general interception before he could even accelerate into HyperSpace. But as soon as the little 219 passed above LightSpeed, he made a sharp turn—directly into the path of a fierce gravity tide—then fought his way through raging streams of gravitons parallel to the Effer'wyckean frontier, dodging in and out of spacecoast stars for nearly half a metacycle before he actually set course for home. The ruse clearly worked (as others had over the centuries, according to Calhoun), for KA'PPA communication was abruptly flooded by calls from every Leaguer warship in the area—all heading at their best speed for positions along a line of flight leading directly from the base to the Triad.

"The bastards are really after us, aren't they?" Aram remarked after watching the static-filled KA'PPA display for a few moments. "I've never seen 'em make so much of a fuss."

"You're right," Brim agreed. "It's like they've forgotten about everything else. Just look at the KA'PPA—Your Majesty, you need to see this—they've even recalled a couple of raids that just got started for Avalon."

Onrad stepped to the flight bridge. "Where's the KA'PPA on this Leaguer garbage scow anyway?" he demanded.

"Right here, Your Majesty," Brim said. "Right below this big crystal 'thing.'"

The Emperor frowned and stared at the crystal. "I'm no Helmsman, but I've never seen anything that looks like that. What d' you suppose it is?"

Brim laughed and turned in his seat. "Got no idea, Your Majesty," he said, "and I've never seen anything like it, either. I think it's only a temporary mount, though. And the ship handles fine without it, so. . . ."

Onrad nodded and turned his attention to the KA'PPA, which if anything was even more active with messages now. "By Voot," he swore, "they're raising a lot of fuss about losing one little transport. D' you think they know I'm on board?"

Brim shrugged. "How could they know?"

"Couldn't be any of the survivors at the BKAEW satellite," Onrad said with a frown. "That place is so classified, nobody who's even a slight risk gets in." He shook his head. "It's got to be coincidence."

"Thraggling WON-der-ful," Brim grumped as KA'PPA traffic requesting help with the search *continued* to build. As the little 219 sped homeward, they even received an angry rebuke from a passing GH 262 because they hadn't joined in on the search for the *Weg'wysershmook* ship. He frowned for a moment. "*Weg'wysershmook?*" That was a word in Vertrucht he hadn't often heard. Its derivation had something to do with glass or mineral crystals, though. But then, he only had a good working knowledge of the Leaguer language; he was far from being an expert in technical terms. Chuckling grimly, he KA'PPAed back (in perfect Vertrucht) that his ship was flying a secret mission and that *they* would find themselves in serious trouble if they attempted further communication.

KA'PPA transmissions from the Gorn-Hoff ceased immediately.

Brim's chuckling ended not more than a quarter metacycle later, however, when the 219's proximity alarm wailed and the little ship was suddenly blasted off course by a tremendous explosion that ripped the very fabric of space not more than a thousand irals to port. A ranging shot, clearly. Brim swung in his set just in time to see four Imperial Starfuries turn onto his tail—at such a reckless speed that they were on top of him before he could make the slightest move. Pitching heavily in an area of gravity turbulence, the sleek, deadly ships outclassed the 219 in everything, especially size and in speed. There seemed little hope of escape.

"I *used* to think they were rather attractive starships," Aram quipped grimly, swiveling in his recliner.

"Yeah," Brim answered. "Surprising how your mind can change about things. Get on the KA'PPA and see if you can. . . ."

Space went wild as all four Starfuries opened up at the same time, battering the little ship in a zigzag path with tremendous explosions to port and starboard.

Self-preservation instincts took over Brim's reflexes. Defying everything he knew about spaceframe safety, he kicked the steering engine hard to starboard, pulled the helm right back, then sideways in one seamless movement. The violence of the maneuver took him by surprise, too. Even the Hyperscreens blacked out in confusion and the whole ship groaned in strident protest. As the others shouted in consternation, Brim was flung violently against his restraints, grunting in pain while his shoulders and pelvis were nearly crushed by the straps.

But it saved them. . . .

When the screens cleared, Brim found he'd put the little ship on its back in relation to the Starfuries, which—surprised at his unexpected movement—passed by in a great rush of gravitons. Again, entirely by instinct, he pulled the helm and straightened out, running the powerful Leaguer Drive at military overload directly into the teeth of the graviton stream. Somehow, the little Gorn-Hoff managed to stay in one piece.

Saved for the moment, he thought—but for what? There was nowhere to hide, and the Starfuries would be back on him in a moment.

"DON'T SHOOT. WE'RE IMPERIALS," Aram KA'PPAed.

"What's going on?" Onrad demanded in a dazed voice. "Those're Starfuries out there."

"Couple of loyal subjects, Your Majesty," Brim said as the KA'PPA display remained blank, "merely doing their duty for the Empire."

"You mean . . . ?"

Brim ground his teeth, trying to stabilize the little 219 as best he could—his attitude indicators had been confused since the first disruptor shot. "The bastards are thraggling playing with us!" he explained. "We're just a couple of Leaguers to them."

"They *must* know we're unarmed," Oodam complained in an outraged voice.

Brim tried all the controls. Everything seemed to answer. Normal Drive crystal temperature—the bastards hadn't hit anything vital. "Armed or unarmed," he replied at length, "smoking us to space dust counts toward somebody's score."

"Universe," Onrad whispered.

"Here they come again!" Aram warned as a great flash of light and energy concussion blasted them sideways.

Brim skidded toward the blast, just as a second explosion erupted in the position they'd occupied only moments before.

"Poor shooting," he growled to no one in particular. "Must be a couple of rookies."

"EMERGENCY! EMERGENCY!" Aram KA'PPAed amid Brim's violent maneuvering and the murderous near misses. "WILF BRIM IN GORN-HOFF 219 WITH FLUVANNIAN AMBASSADOR AND SPECIAL PASSENGER UNDER ATTACK BY STARFURIES. PLEASE ASSIST. PLEASE ASSIST."

Abruptly, the shooting stopped—but not because of the messages. Peering out the Hyperscreens in surprise, Brim watched a brace of Gorn-Hoff 262s streak in from HyperSpace behind two of the Starfuries, one of which exploded in a huge, roiling ball of radiation flame. There were no lifeglobes—the cold-hearted Imperials had paid the price for negligence. The remaining three Starfuries immediately dismissed their smaller prey and turned to meet the Leaguers, their disruptors flashing brightly in the blackness.

Brim needed no urging. Putting the helm over once again, he drove off across the void in a straight line for Avalon.

"EMERGENCY! EMERGENCY!" Aram KA'PPAed again. "WILF BRIM IN GORN-HOFF 219 WITH FLUVANNIAN AMBASSADOR AND SPECIAL PASSENGER RETURNING TO AVALON. PLEASE ASSIST NOW. PLEASE ASSIST NOW."

Moments later, the KA'PPA came alive—only now, the language it displayed was Vertrucht. "GLAD TO ASSIST, MY OLD ADVERSARY," it read. "I LOOK FORWARD TO GREETING YOU—AND YOUR 'SPECIAL PASSENGER' IN EFFER'WYCK. YOU WILL, OF COURSE, CEASE KA'PPA BROADCASTING." It was signed simply, "VALENTIN."

CHAPTER 7

Eve Cartier

Brim hardly needed to glance out the side Hyperscreen when his proximity alarm screamed again and a large starship hove into sight just off the port side. It was one of the Leaguers' new GH 270-A attack craft, and every one of its disruptors seemed to be pointing at his very forehead! He laughed in spite of himself. How Valentin had pulled that off, he'd never know! But then, if the wily Leaguer were nothing else, he was resourceful. He pursed his lips and considered for a moment. "We probably ought to try broadcasting another KA'PPA message anyway," he shouted to Onrad. "It's the only weapon we've got—and you can bet that zukeed Leaguer is dying to learn who our 'special passenger' is, so he xaxtdamned well won't be shooting to kill. How do you feel about that, Your Majesty?"

The Emperor thought about that for only a moment, then laughed. "It's all right with me, Brim," he laughed. "I've got nothing to lose. Oodam? How about you?"

"Why not?" Oodam grumbled.

"Aram?" Brim asked.

"I'm game, too," the A'zurnian replied. "What do you want to send?"

"Something short," Brim mused, "Like, 'WILF BRIM AND SPECIAL PASSENGER ABOARD CAPTURED GH 219. UNDER ATTACK. HELP.' Put it out all in a burst," he ordered, "then hang on to anything you can grab, all of you. And set your suits for MINIMUM FREEDOM again. They'll want to make certain we don't do that again. Understand?"

"Understand," Aram said, starting to key in the message.

"In the back there," Brim prompted. "You hear that."

"Yeah," Onrad grunted. "We heard. We're set."

"Ready? Aram?"

"Ready, Wilf. . . ."

"Send it," Brim said through tight lips, ready to fight the controls through the punishing barrage he knew would follow their message: *near* misses, calculated to destroy the 219's ability to communicate—or do much else, for that matter. He took a deep breath, crossed his arms over this faceplate, and braced himself for the worst.

And braced. . . . And *braced*. . . .

"Great thundering Universe!" rumbled Onrad's surprised voice from the passenger compartment. "Will y' look at *that*!"

Brim cautiously opened his eyes, expecting any moment to be blinded by the flash of a disruptor. It didn't happen. Next, he carefully scanned the Hyperscreens and . . . Voot's greasy, vermin-infested beard! *Now* there were *five* large starships driving through space behind him. The four newcomers were Starfuries, and all fifty-six of their mighty disruptors were trained on Valentin and his Gorn-Hoff.

Unfortunately, the latter's disruptors were *still* pointed at his own personal forehead! A standoff if he'd ever heard of one! Rolling his eyes in absolute disbelief, he glanced down at the KA'PPA display, which was now displaying a question—in Avalonian. "QUESTION FOR WILF BRIM: WHAT LOGISH MEEM DID SISTER EVE ENJOY RECENTLY DINING WITH A FELLOW CARESCRIAN?" It was signed, "E. CARTIER, LT. COMMANDER, I.F."

"Eve!" Brim gasped over the voice circuits.

"Huh?"

"Er, nothing, Your Majesty," he replied, turning in his seat. "But it seems as if the ball has passed back to our Empire."

"So it would seem," Onrad whispered while he peered out the Hyperscreen port beside him. It was the first time Brim had ever heard an Emperor flabbergasted.

Come to think about it, he was a bit flummoxed himself. In short order, he had to somehow remember what meem he had ordered the night he'd had supper with the beautiful Carescrian. Dammit, where was Barbousse when he needed him? *He'd* know; it was *he* who had researched the spirits in the first place. Soma-Medoc, was it? The FleetPort 19 wardroom had a lot more of that than . . . Wait! There had also been a case of Manor-Savill as well. But they'd both been from the *early* teens. What was the other . . . "Logish Medoc fifty one oh nineteen!" he bellowed abruptly.

Startled, Aram raised an eyebrow. "Sir?" he asked.

"Never mind," Brim replied bemusedly, reaching in front of the A'zurnian to enter the characters himself. "LOGISH MEDOC 51019." "Send that," he ordered. Then, he waited. . . .

" 'HERE'S TO THE HEAT, WILF BRIM,' " appeared a moment later. "HOW ARE YOUR PASSENGERS?"

Brim took a deep breath. That was *one* problem out of the way.

At the same moment, Onrad appeared with Oodam on the flight deck. "Tell her your passengers are healthy and damn well ready to go home, Aram," he ordered.

"Aye, Your Majesty," Aram replied.

Moments later, another message appeared in the KA'PPA display—this time in Vertrucht. "SO, BRIM," it read, "IT SEEMS THAT I SHALL HAVE TO FORGO YOUR COMPANY IN TRADE FOR MY LIFE. WHAT A PITY. I SHOULD LIKED TO HAVE MET YOUR 'PASSENGER.' ANOTHER PRINCESS, PERHAPS?"

Brim grinned and reached in front of Aram again. "YOU WON'T LEARN ANYTHING FROM ME, VALENTIN," he sent in Vertrucht. "I NEVER KISS AND TELL. IT'S THE SECRET OF MY—CONSIDERABLE—SUCCESS."

"UNTIL OUR PATHS CROSS AGAIN, IMPERIAL SCUM."

"I'LL LOOK FORWARD TO IT, LEAGUER CLOWN." Brim sent as the Gorn-Hoff put its helm over and curved gracefully off to starboard—with its disruptors continuing to track Brim's forehead until it disappeared into the distance.

"SHALL I SEND SOMEONE OFF TO BLAST HIM?" appeared in the KA'PPA window.

Onrad shook his head. "Tell her 'no,' Aram," he said. "That Leaguer crony of Brim's never fired on us—as did our *own* ships."

Immediately, the four Starfuries moved into formation around them—and were joined within the next quarter metacycle by fully three additional *squadrons* of the powerful interceptors, forming a nearly impenetrable shield around the little Leaguer starship.

Brim actually enjoyed the remainder of his return to Avalon. It was easier flying a strange starship when he didn't have to worry about people from *both* sides blowing him to kingdom come.

With the planet Avalon a huge disk in Brim's forward Hyperscreens, Defense Command KA'PPAed a sparse order slowing the powerful formation out of Hyperspeed, but withholding landfall clearance for any of the starships. Moments later the 219's Hyperscreens stopped translating and became transparent to normal photons, Brim received a LightSpeed-limited radio message—without video—from General Harry Drummond himself. "Brim," the General grumbled through an unmistakable chuckle, "you have the *xaxtDAMNDEST* talent for trouble I've ever encountered. How DO you do it?"

"Er. . . ." Brim answered, "I'm not entirely to blame this time, General. It's the company I keep."

Drummond laughed. "By the Universe, now *that's* an excuse I'll accept! You certainly have been traveling with fast, and often troublesome, associates."

"Aye, sir," Brim replied in as innocent a voice as he could muster.

"Well, my Carescrian friend," Drummond continued, "tell

you what. Because I believe in your innate goodness—as well as that of your A'zurnian comrade in outrage—I have decided to remove the two bad influences you have with you. How does that sound?''

Brim looked at Aram and rolled his eyes to the top Hyperscreens. ''Does that sound wonderful to you?'' he asked.

''Just thraggling WUN-der-ful,'' the A'zurnian answered—with his microphone shut off.

''We both think that sounds wonderful, General. We appreciate your efforts on our behalf.''

''Good,'' Drummond said, suddenly serious. ''In approximately five cycles, you will sight I.F.S. *Oddeon* in a parking orbit. She was on final for landfall on Lake Mersin when we first picked up your initial KA'PPAs; she's been standing by ever since, just in case the message was genuine, which—thank the Universe—it was. When the storm abates a bit more, you'll immediately moor to *Oddeon*'s boarding pipe and transfer your two passengers—who, we *strongly* suggest, should board the battleship with their battlesuits faceplates darkened. After all, the hatches won't match, so their battlesuits will have to be sealed anyway.''

''Sounds like a plan to me, General,'' Brim said. ''I'll take care of the mooring, but perhaps you should pass on the suggestions yourself.''

Drummond thought about that for a moment. ''Yeah,'' he grumbled. ''Probably that's not a bad idea. What sort of shape's the key passenger in?''

Brim thought for a moment about that. ''Healthy as a racing zorquine, General. Not even winded.''

''No, I mean, how does the, er, passenger feel about the possible consequences that might have resulted from the, er, 'mission'? You'd think a certain amount of shame would surface.'' He paused for a moment. ''And to tell the truth, *you* ought to feel a bit ashamed for letting such an important passenger *get* in such trouble.''

Brim decided to ignore the General's second comment, even though he *was* feeling a bit irresponsible concerning the episode. He considered his words carefully. "I think you'll find the passenger is pretty well satisfied with, er, his or her own actions, General," he said, speaking privately into his microphone. "At the time, there were exceptionally compelling grounds for the 'mission,' and during subsequent actions, I personally saw some real bravery—not bravado, mind you—along with the kind of leadership we all have expected. With the greatest respect, General, you probably won't want to, er, *dwell* on feelings of shame the passenger *ought* to have."

The radio was silent for a moment, then Drummond laughed softly. "Well spoken, Brim," he said. "I sincerely appreciate the words."

"Thank you, General," Brim said, stifling a great sigh of relief. "Would you like me to put the passenger on, now?"

"Absolutely," Drummond said, "*after* you disable the transmit, please. We won't need answers."

"Aye, sir," Brim said with a grin, then switched off the master transmitter and turned in his seat. "General Drummond for you, Your Majesty," he announced. "I'm afraid we won't be able to send your answers. . . ."

No more than half a metacycle later, Brim watched Onrad and Beyazh making their way safely through the battleship's transparent boarding tube and breathed a sigh of relief. He winked at Aram. "Let's take this little tub and head for home," he said.

The A'zurnian grinned. "Nobody *has* claimed it yet, have they?"

Brim nodded. "Eventually, it'll go to the labs on Proteus for evaluation," he said. "But they'll have to come get it from FleetPort 30, 'cause I'm not flying it any farther than that."

"Besides, it *does* have rather bizarre markings, wouldn't you say?" Aram quipped.

"Yeah. Really. . . ."

"Imperial Gorn-Hoff 319-JE from *Oddeon*," the battleship radioed. "You may seal ship and cast off at your convenience."

"Thank you, *Oddeon*," Brim replied. He turned to Aram.

"*Nodzoff* means 'locked,' and *Sadzoff* means 'sealed,' my friend."

"I'm on my way, Wilf," the A'zurnian said, heading aft into the passenger compartment. Moments later, he returned to his seat. "The hatch is now *nodzoffed* and *sadzoffed*," he reported with a grin.

Brim nodded. "You always were a quick study, Aram," he chuckled. Then he keyed the radio. "Gorn-Hoff 319-JE to *Oddeon*," he sent, looking up at the battleship's imposing superstructure and awesome disruptors in terraces of superfiring turrets, "casting off." He canceled the mooring beams that had secured the little ship to its giant counterpart and nudged the steering engine to port.

"We're free," Aram warranted, peering out the starboard Hyperscreen.

"Gorn-Hoff 319-JE to *Oddeon*," Brim warned, "we are clear of your boarding pipe. May stars light all thy paths," he added, passing the age-old Imperial salute to the great old battleship.

"And thy paths, Star Travelers," came his answer. Above him, on the battleship's great, towering bridge, someone waved. Then with a massive stateliness, the colossal starship began to move forward, totally unaffected by heavy gravity chop from the Triad. Moments later, the big ship banked ponderously, then turned toward the completion of its interrupted landfall, still escorted by the three squadrons of Starfuries.

Just as Brim was getting the little 219 under way again, Eve Carescrian's voice filled his helmet speakers. "Imperial P8350 to Imperial Gorn-Hoff," she said.

"Imperial Gorn-Hoff 319-JE," Brim acknowledged with a frown.

"Captain Brim," she said formally, "should I assume you will be in Avalon day after tomorrow for the Squadron Commanders' meeting at the Admiralty?"

Brim snapped his fingers. Somehow, her voice—and the mention of something so workaday as a meeting at the Admiralty—

brought him back to reality. "Er, yes," he replied. "Ah . . . perhaps we could . . . meet afterward?"

"I shall count on that, Captain," she answered. "Imperial P8350 out."

"Imperial Gorn-Hoff," Brim acknowledged. And even the amused look on Aram's face couldn't erase the happy grin her message brought to his own.

The war hadn't paused at all in Brim's short absence. On his return to a badly mauled FleetPort 30 (where at least twenty large blue pressure patches covered jagged holes blown in the satellite's skin), Barbousse stolidly ignored the damage and announced with pride that Home Fleet's Attack Command had launched another highly successful strike on the League's invasion buildup in Effer'wyck. Leave it to Barbousse to ferret out the good news!

But later, in his office with Moulding, he learned that the Leaguers had been all too busy themselves. Early raids by large formations of Kreissel 111s the previous day resulted in heavy damage at the great commercial starship docks on the planet Melia while other groups—mostly Zachtwagers—continued the campaign against BKAEW satellites. The Rontnev BKAEW satellite had been so badly damaged it was rendered unusable, causing a considerable gap in Defense Command's warning chain. Later in the morning, Defense Command's starbases had again been targeted. The Hawkinge starbase orbiting polar Avalon was badly damaged during a savage attack by Trodler 215s and Gantheisser GA 87B Zachtwagers.

Throughout a lengthy midmorning respite, repairs had been made to the damaged BKAEW sites, but the next round of assaults began about midday, with more than forty attack craft, and it became clear then that the Leaguers were now specially targeting Defense Command. Defending squadrons—including Brim's 11 Group—had already been scrambled, and destroyed twelve raiders. But enough of the Leaguers got through that FleetPort 30 itself had taken the grievous damage Brim saw (with ten casualties) when he landed. And it was only one of the many other Defense Command bases damaged in the raids. FleetPort 13 (orbiting Proteus) was so badly damaged that it could only accommodate two squadrons instead of its usual three. Then, no more than a metacycle later, two full groups of GA 87s attacked FleetPort 24 over Ariel, rendering a nearby BKAEW inoperative. But this time, before they could re-form for the flight home, one of the Leaguer groups found itself intercepted by two of Aram's Defiant squadrons, which promptly shot down twelve out of the twenty-eight attackers. Elsewhere, other Leaguer attack groups had been similarly savage.

"Sounds pretty wild to me," Brim commented in self-defense. He was rapidly reaching information overflow.

"Yes, right-ho," Moulding agreed with a grim smile. "Except 'wild' isn't nearly strong enough, Wilf." He shook his head. "The word is you and Aram came through a bit of bother yourselves while you were gone on your mysterious trip, but among the chaps here at FleetPort 30, the pace is also beginning to tell. . . ."

Old-timers, he explained—survivors of perhaps a month at the most—were fast wearing to a frazzle, and bothered by empty places that kept appearing in the mess. New faces would appear out of the training bases, become familiar for a few days, then disappear with hardly a trace. Not only that, but word of the mortality rate was spreading below, on the surface. Replacement crews were now reporting for duty frightened out of their wits, but somehow their morale held. "They may be a bunch of mollycoddles, those new crews," Moulding said proudly, "but for all that, they came through tough as hullmetal when it comes to fighting for the old Empire."

"I'd hoped that might be the case," Brim mused quietly. "Makes me wonder where—and how—Amherst and his pack ever recruited so many CIGAs."

Moulding shook his head. "I'm dashed if I know," he said thoughtfully. "But I imagine many of the swine who *did* are having second thoughts right now. I've only begun to tell you how the Leaguers acquitted themselves yesterday."

Brim sat back in his chair. "There's more?" he asked.

"Oh, I'm only now getting to the *interesting* parts," Moulding said. That very afternoon, he explained, squadrons from FleetPort 30 intercepted a third main thrust against Avalon as it moved toward Prendergast Point, the great commercial harbor area 320 c'lenyts to the Austral of Avalon. Both Starfuries and Defiants made a good intercept, causing the attackers to fire blindly to complete their mission. "But this time," Moulding said with revulsion, "the bloody murderers blasted the outskirts of Avalon City itself. I personally think they did it by accident, but. . . ." He paused for a moment. "Mark my words, Wilf," he continued presently, "those Leaguers quite altered the pattern of the war in that raid. So far they'd been damned careful not to damage the Imperial capital itself—most probably so they wouldn't bring down the same thing on their own capital. But all that's going to change now or I'll eat my battlesuit."

Brim nodded. From what he knew of Onrad, the Leaguers' blunder would certainly precipitate some sort of immediate retaliation. However, it would be nothing in comparison to what the Emperor would wreak on the Leaguers' capital should initiative in the war someday pass to the Empire. "You're right there, Toby," he said. "Whoever made that decision sealed the fate of Tarrott." He rose from his chair and paced for a moment. Tired as he was, he couldn't fight off a certain sense of excitement. "Could anything else have happened while I was gone?" he demanded.

"Oh, absolutely, old sport," Moulding said. "Whatever else you were doing, you missed quite a bit of excitement."

Brim laughed. "Believe me, Toby, I didn't lack for 'excitement.' "

"Yes," Moulding agreed, "knowing you, I shouldn't doubt that a bit. Unfortunately, I suspect you'll have mixed thoughts about how the day ended."

"*Mixed* thoughts?" Brim asked him with a chuckle.

Moulding nodded. "If you're anything like me."

"Go ahead," Brim said with an abrupt sense of foreboding.

"Well," Moulding began, "the Leaguers' random firing on

Avalon that morning caused extensive damage—and loss of life—no more than a c'lenyt from a hall where some five hundred CIGAs were holding a rally. They'd given it a lot of advance hype and publicity—and chosen for their theme something like 'How Our Empire Forced the League into War.' "

Brim grimaced. "Cowards and traitors, the whole lot," he growled through his teeth. "How in xaxt did they attract an audience of five hundred with total Gorksroar like that? I mean . . . all they have to do is look up in the thraggling sky!"

Moulding looked at Brim with a dour smile. "Actually, Wilf," he said, "numbers were their downfall."

"Numbers of people attending?"

"Regrettably so," Moulding said with a frown. "In addition to the five hundred fellow CIGAs, they also attracted an angry mob of local residents—more than a thousand strong. People whose homes were burning even while the CIGAs were cheering on their attackers."

"Universe," Brim whispered. "I take it the residents got out of control."

"Somewhat," Moulding answered. "They stormed the hall, ripped off all the doors, and beat five CIGAs to death before the police could restore order."

"Mother of Voot," Brim swore darkly, shaking his head in disgust. "If indeed Triannic's ultimate goal is to destroy the Empire," he said, "he's off to a good start turning the citizens into bloody savages. . . ."

Early next day, Brim read in the morning's Top Secret Intelligence Bulletin that seventy-one Leaguer starships had been destroyed the previous day. In comparison, Defense Command now had 689 serviceable machines, compared to 631 three days previously. Jaiswal's efforts were clearly beginning to pay dividends. A negative rate of attrition, he considered with a smile, in spite of Admiral Orgoth's best efforts to eradicate the Imperial Fleet. Not bad for a gaggle of amateurs! Hanna Notrom, League Minister for Public Consensus, would have her hands full making something good out of that for her controlled media. Ursis had already reported that the Imperials' spirited defense was severely shaking Orgoth's confidence. And now, if the Sodeskayans' intelligence reports were accurate—as *always*—a number of his crews were now in disgrace for firing on Avalon City itself. The responsible Leaguer captains had been dragged from their ships upon landing and summarily transported to Tarrott for punishment. That, he considered as he donned his battlesuit for a morning patrol, ought to *really* boost the morale of Leaguer flight crews!

Later that morning in the FleetPort 30 wardroom, Brim and most of his off-duty officers watched Emperor Onrad broadcast one of his "heart-to-heart chats" to all five planets circling the Triad. The already-imposing man appeared to have actually increased in stature since his highly secret adventure in Effer'wyck. Brim smiled. He deserved it—even if he was a damned fool to get caught up in such an incredibly dangerous lark. Besides, he thought, *nobody* could make a speech like the new Emperor. Nobody.

". . . The gratitude of every home in our Triad," Onrad was declaring with a steely mien, "in our Empire, and indeed throughout the whole civilized galaxy—*except* in the abodes of the guilty—goes out to our brave Imperial starsailors, who, undaunted by odds, unwearied in their constant challenge and baneful danger, are even now turning the tide of galactic war by their prowess and by their devotion. . . . Never," he concluded, "in the field of mortal conflict was so much owed by so many to so few. . . ."

"Wonder who he's been talking to who claims he's 'unwearied'?" Moulding quipped in an aside.

"Don't know," Brim replied—recalling with a smile the Emperor's emotional words just before the attack on the BKAEW station. "But all that 'owing' business probably refers to the mess bills your boys are running up in the wardroom. I understand those things are reported to the Admiralty on a regular basis. . . ."

* * *

In space, a marked lull in the battle began to evince itself that very afternoon by a virtual absence of Leaguer starships anywhere in the vicinity of Avalon, except for a series of extra vicious attacks on Proteus, the science planet. Mysteriously, these seemed to be concentrated around the huge intelligence complex near the austral pole. In Brim's eyes, at least, the lull was primarily caused by severe gravity storms that had begun to move through the area, but the attack on the intelligence labs mystified him. Intelligence operations were not usually the stuff of which really important targets were made. . . .

That afternoon, however, still another reason for the lull came to light when Barbousse personally shunted a handful of dispatches to Brim's display on the flight bridge as Starfury R6595 waited for the next attack in one of the ready-alert slips. "Um, thought you might want to read this right away, Cap'm," the big rating called from a weapons console.

"Thanks, Chief," Brim said, looking up from his instruments with a frown. Normally, Barbousse had little time for Brim's personal mail, watchfully delegating such mundane tasks to his own subordinates. "Anything special I ought to see?" the Carescrian asked.

"Um . . . well, Cap'm," the big rating started, "you might just want to look at the new TSIB there on the top of the list."

Brim turned to ask a question, but Barbousse was on his way out of the bridge. Settling himself back in his seat, he brought his correspondence list to the display. Sure enough, its first entry was the midday Top Secret Intelligence Bulletin. With mounting concern, he OPEN'ed the document and nearly gasped when he read its first entry:

1. FLUVANNA UNDER SIEGE
In a surprise move early today, the Imperial Fleet of The Torond (ostensibly led by Grand Duke Rogan LaKarn but under close supervision by League military 'advisers') and powerful units of the League's Military Space Arm mounted an all-out attack against selected targets among the planets of Fluvanna and

> laid siege to its capital city, Magor, on the planet Ordu. According to Sodeskayan sources, most of the Leaguer units were "borrowed" from large forces in Effer'wyck deployed against the Imperial Triad, and will almost certainly result in a lull in the raids over Avalon.
>
> Nearly the entire Fluvannian Fleet and all units of the Imperial Fleet (stationed at Varnholm Hall outside Ordu) are engaged. . . .

Brim's heart turned cold. Fears for Raddisma and their unborn daughter palpably gripped his chest. And in those moments, he knew he wasn't alone in his worries. Barbousse himself had formed a romantic attachment there during their tour with the IVG. That's what had so upset the normally unflappable starsailor! Unfortunately, there was nothing either of them could do to help. In fact, until they were off alert, they couldn't even send for new information.

Metacycles later, when Brim did return to his office, he immediately put through a call to friends at the Admiralty. From them he learned to his dismay that because of the present threat to the Triad itself, a decision had been made to abandon the Fluvannian capital and concentrate all remaining forces in defense of the three Drive-crystal-producing planets: Voso Gannit, Voso Gola, and Voso Truvalu. Recalling Onrad's feelings on the subject, he'd suspected that would be the policy. But what would now be the fate of Fluvanna's Nabob and his court? Were they to be simply abandoned? His Admiralty contacts didn't know, and a whole series of desperate calls to the Public Information Section of the Foreign Office went unanswered. He had no special influence in that hotbed of arrogant intellectuals (many of them CIGAs). After a formal inspection of FleetPort 30's engineering bays (of which he could remember virtually nothing), he shared the bad news with Barbousse and then retired to a night of tossing and turning in his bed.

The following day was even stormier than its predecessor, and after most BKAEW sites reported only occasional Leaguer starships anywhere near the Triad, Brim found himself spending most of his time pacing the floor and trying to get news about Fluvanna—mostly to no avail. Even Barbousse—a man at times *feloniously* resourceful—came up with no more than scuttlebutt.

"It's either more secret than anythin' I've ever seen," he explained to Brim, "or—beggin' the Cap'm's pardon—those silly clowns in the Admiralty still haven't figured out what to do." He shook his head and looked Brim in the eye. "Cap'm," he said uneasily, "I've got . . . well . . . *sentimental* attachments myself in Fluvanna. If you'll remember, I . . . er, sort of . . . formed an association with a Fluvannian lady. Chief Petty Officer Tutti—Chief Consort Raddisma's private chauffeur. I want you to know, sir, that I'm doin' *everythin'* I can to get some word of what's happenin' out there."

Brim smiled and put his hand on the big man's arm. "So it's pretty safe to assume that you've known about the baby," he said.

Barbousse turned scarlet and he looked down at his boots. "Both baby an' mother were doin' fine as of the end of last week," he asserted. "This thing that LaKarn and the Leaguers are doin' has caught everybody off guard. I'd never have let either of the ladies get into this kind of trouble."

"Thanks," Brim said lamely. "I don't know what else to say."

"No thanks necessary, Cap'm," Barbousse said. "We've taken care of each other over the years. It's been a good arrangement."

"The best," Brim said with real feeling—at the same moment that an orderly put his head around the corner.

"Captain Brim," he said. "Sorry to interrupt, sir, but I have a top-secret dispatch for you personally, direct from the Imperial Palace."

"A *personal* message?" Brim asked with a raised eyebrow.

"Aye, sir."

"I'll be outside if you need me, Cap'm," Barbousse said, passing the message to Brim and ushering the orderly out the door before him.

Sitting at his desk, Brim lightly touched his right index finger to the plastic envelope's Imperial Seal, then withdrew it. In a few moments, the seal completed its processing, recognized his fingerprint, and vaporized in a cloud of odorless smoke. Inside the envelope was a single sheet of light blue plastic, engraved in gold with the Imperial Seal of the Emperor.

The Imperial Palace
30 Octad/52011

My Dear Captain Brim

With this letter, We take pleasure informing you of Our decision to evacuate the Fluvannian Nabob, Mustafa IX Eyren, The Magnificent, and His Principal Consort, Raddisma, to the Fleet base at Atalanta, Gimmas Haefdon. Certain of their chief servants, and others from the Court at Magor, Ordu, will accompany them during this period of invasion danger in that city. Because you won many friends there during your tenure as a member of Our Imperial Volunteer Group, We thought you would wish to know.

Accept, Captain, the assurances of Our highest consideration, etc., etc.

Onrad V, Vice Admiral, I.F.,
Grand Galactic Emperor,
Prince of the Reggio Star Cluster,
and Rightful Protector of the Heavens.

As Brim read the words, a wave of relief seemed to wash over him like cooling water in a desert. "We thought you would want to know," he repeated to himself, over and over until . . . "Barbousse!" he shouted. "You still out there?"

Barbousse poked his head inside the office. "Aye, Cap'm," he said with a very serious mien. "I . . . er . . . just got a message, m'self. . . ."

"It can wait," Brim said, holding up a hand. "This can't! Come in and shut the door."

"Aye, Cap'm," Barbousse said with an interested look on his face. He softly pulled the door shut behind him.

"Sit down," Brim said, indicating the single guest chair he permitted in his office.

Barbousse sat.

"Chief," Brim began, "you'll have to trust me with this one, but I've got good news."

"Aye, sir?"

"Both Chief Tutti and Raddisma are safe. I can't tell you anything more than that, but it's true. All right?"

Barbousse smiled and allowed himself to relax in his seat for a moment. "Aye, sir," he said, looking Brim directly in the eye. "An' I'll always appreciate your telling' me that. Believe that."

Brim nodded. "Thank the Universe," he whispered more to himself than his long-time shipmate. Then he shook his head and came to a more rational mien. "I'm sorry for interrupting. What was *your* message?"

Barbousse's face colored. "Well, beggin' the Cap'm's pardon, an' all that, er, my message pretty well said the same thing, 'cept it came by word of mouth from an"—he pursed his lips and shrugged—"er, one o' m' *sources*, Cap'm. But just in case your, er, *source* didn't mention it, Consort Raddisma an' Chief Tutti are both goin' to Atalanta. The Emperor's evacuatin' them along wi' members of the court, there."

Brim felt his face go red. "Thank you, Chief," he said. "And speaking of appreciating. . . ."

"You won't mention this to anybody, will you, Cap'm?" Barbousse interrupted. "That comes from one of m' *best* sources."

"Chief," Brim said, smiling in spite of his embarrassment. "My lips are sealed."

"So're mine," Barbousse said. "Always."

Later, reflecting on why the Emperor had bothered to tell *him* about the decision to evacuate the Nabob and his court from Magor, Brim came up with a thousand answers—and *no* answers. Finally, with typical Carescrian pragmatism, he decided never to question gifts, in whatever form they came. The following morning, he departed for the surface to attend the Squadron Commanders' meeting at the Admiralty. The miraculous lull in the fighting made it seem almost as if he were going on leave.

Somehow, the day's endless harangues about augmenting base safety, managing "personnel," producing Officer Effectiveness Reports in a "timely fashion" (whatever *that* meant), maintaining vigilant security, and other such administrative minutiae failed to keep Brim's interest. He sat quietly in the rear of this meeting room or that auditorium as the day passed, collecting endless handouts and attempting to look interested in the appointed subject while he alternately speculated about having a daughter and watched Eve Cartier trying not to notice how much he was staring at her.

After what seemed like ten Standard Centuries, the agenda crawled painfully to its end. He lied to Moulding and Aram, telling them they should go out on the town without him because he had yet another briefing to attend. Then he stalled around until most of the other officers had filed out of the large Weathersby Auditorium, after which he waited until Vice Admiral (the Hon.) Keith Hunt finished with whatever he was telling Eve. Finally, he sauntered—casually, he hoped—out the door, meeting her "quite by accident" in the huge domed lobby of the Admiralty. "Eve!" he exclaimed in feigned surprise. "I didn't know you were here today."

Cartier smiled demurely. "Faith, Captain Brim," she said, smoothing her hair. "An' who else wad stand in for me, now?"

"No one could e'en—*even* try, so far as I'm concerned," Brim answered, resolving this time to resist a lapse into the

Carescrian speech patterns of his youth. "Especially now that the meetings are over."

"Hoot Mon but they were lang, weren't they?" she asked, ignoring his obvious "correction."

"I think we're supposed to get something special from meetings that are especially long and boring," Brim said, "but I've never been smart enough to understand what that is."

"Thank the Universe they're not all luik that," she said, then they both stood for a *long* moment in silence.

"I, ah . . ." Brim stumbled, straightening the collar of his Fleet Cloak, "h-hoped you might have the evening free."

" 'Tis the very idea I tried to get across the other day on the radio," she said, "hopin' that you might hae the same evenin' free."

"Looks like wishes do come true sometimes," Brim said.

Cartier laughed. "If that's so, then perhaps we'll win this war very quickly and stop the bloody killin', for that's certainly *my* wish."

"Sounds good to me," Brim said, "but I don't suppose I'll hold my breath."

"Nor I," Cartier replied, glancing sideways to see her reflection in a mirror.

"Maybe this evening we can make the war go away for a while."

"I guess I've been countin' on that, Wilf Brim," she said.

"What sounds good to you?" he asked.

"I don't know," Cartier said with a little smile. Then she laughed. "Compared to you, my guid Captain, I'm but a simple country maid from Carescria." Then she blushed. "Probably at my age we ought to forget aboot the 'maiden' part—but the rest is true."

Brim smiled and gently put his hand on her forearm. "There wasn't anything 'simple' about the Helmsman of a Starfury who came up with a way to save my life the other day," he said.

"*An*' your passengers," she added. "Very important people, eh?"

Brim felt himself blush.

"Do na' worry," she said, placing her own hand over his. "I won't ask now. But after the war, Wilf Brim," she continued with a grin, "I'm going to want to know who they were. Got that?"

"Got that," Brim chuckled.

She narrowed her eyes for a moment. "Can you at least tell me wha' in the name of Voot you were doin' flyin' around in that wee Gorn-Hoff 219? I mean, you're noted for bein' a bit unconventional, Wilf Brim, but. . . ."

"Well," Brim said with a frown, "would you believe I was taking it off to a Gradygroat monastery for use as a hymnal delivery vehicle?"

"That's wha' you're going to tell me noo?" she asked with an expression of feigned amazement.

"It's as good an explanation as any I can give right now," Brim said, feeling his cheeks burn a second time.

Cartier squeezed his hand, then let go. "If tha' is your story, I'll believe it," she said with a grin. "But after the war, you'd better come clean aboot that, too."

Brim held his hands palm upward. "Eve," he protested. "Me? Come clean? Whatever can you mean?"

"If there's onything you *haven't* learned to do, Wilf Brim," Cartier said with a grin, "it's luik innocent. Besides, your reputation for trouble precedes you like some ge'at starship travelin' at LightSpeed."

"What can I say?"

"Hmm. Probably nothing. But perhaps you might take me somewhere for a guid supper." She paused a moment. "No," she added with a frown, "I should like to go somewhere for an *excellent* supper—with all the sophisticated trimmin's I've heard aboot in Avalon. I'll e'en buy."

"We'll see about the tab," Brim said with a smile and thought for a moment. "Now, there's an elegant little place a few streets off Huntington Gate that . . ." he continued, but Cartier interrupted.

"I've nae wish to hear aboot the place, Wilf Brim," she said. "I want to *go* there."

"And so do I," Brim said, indicating the Admiralty's elaborately etched Dommian crystal doors, through which the last gleams from the Triad were now streaming. "We can e'en—*even*—find transportation outside."

"Weel done, sir," Cartier said in a satisfied voice, again glancing at herself in one of the great Admiralty mirrors. "I'll go preen for a few moments while you see to the reservations. . . ."

Only cycles later, they were seated in the roomy back seat of an immaculate Avalonian taxi, careening through the wild traffic of Locorno Square on their way to Gin Tobin Lane, a narrow street two short blocks off Huntington Gate. Brim smiled to himself as they sped past the usual CIGA demonstration—*noticeably* smaller than usual. It promised to be an interesting evening.

The Staff & Star was nearly impossible to spot from even so narrow a street as Gin Tobin Lane. It was first necessary to enter a little cobblestone alleyway that looked more like a private sidewalk than a public thoroughfare. But if one followed that special pavement for no more than 150 irals along a sharp right curve (around a stately Trompian-era mansion that had been a camarge tobacco shop since long before Brim was a cadet), he would come to the entrance to what long ago must have served as a sizable mews-cum servants quarters. Protected from Avalon's often-rainy climate by an elegant lavender canopy, its spectacularly carved stone doorway depicted a whole panoply of beasts and birds peculiar to Avalon's literature from pre-starflight epochs. During peacetime, it was something that only the most fortunate tourists ever got to see.

The great, paneled door opened just as they stepped beneath the canopy, and a billow of warm, yeasty redolence replaced the cool damp of Avalon's early autumn. Before them in the tiny forecourt stood an elegantly bewigged maître d' attired in a style borrowed from perhaps ten centuries in the past. He wore a long, highly ornamented frock coat buttoned only at the waist that extended all the way to his knees. Beneath, he had a black cravat-bow over a double ruffed shirt and satin knee breeches, long white silk stockings, and high-tongued, buckled shoes with low red heels. "Captain Brim, Commander Cartier," he said, bowing deeply from the waist, "it is a genuine honor to serve both of you this evening. Your table is waiting."

"May I take your arm?" Cartier whispered.

Brim felt himself blush. He'd been stuffy because of their uniforms, and he knew it. "I should be honored," he said, suddenly aware all over again of how fundamentally beautiful this middle-aged Carescrian woman really was. He shook his head. A Carescrian. Just like himself. . . .

Inside, The Staff & Star did credit to its historic reputation. Brim had never discovered (nor did he particularly *want* to know) if the decorations were original or reproductions. The interior looked precisely as it had the evening a cadet-smitten young debutante first escorted him to supper there (only to break off their relationship when her wealthy parents discovered he was a Carescrian). Over the years, he had enjoyed the grand, old restaurant's fare as often as he could, and was determined that Eve Cartier would cherish the atmosphere as much as he did so long ago.

The main dining room was lighted only by candles in baroque sconces and chandeliers that provided *just* enough illumination—neither too little for gazing upon elegant companions nor too much to incite the interest of neighboring tables. Great ruby-red draperies hung from tall, narrow windows that marched like ancient soldiers along one long wall; high mirrors, darkened by sheer age, adorned the others. And between them, elaborately framed representations of ancient, seagoing ships—not one of them depicted by a modern hologram—hung from the ancient plaster. The high ceiling was supported by elegantly gilded beams framing trompe l'oeil paintings of chimerical flighted beings that were almost lost in the hazy darkness. And the atmosphere was an altogether agreeable chaos of odors, from the delicious aroma of cooking food to the mysteriously foreign scents of camarge tobacco and the Bears' famous (or perhaps infamous) Hogge'Poa.

"'Tis beautiful, Wilf," Cartier whispered as they followed the maître d' across deep carpeting to an intimately sized table located a comfortable distance from a quintet of musicians (also dressed in frock coats and pantaloons) who coaxed gloriously non-intrusive harmonies from graceful stringed instruments.

As she took her seat, Brim became acutely aware of the comfort her hand provided while it rested gently on his arm. Few women he'd encountered had been able to make him feel so . . . well, "*kindred*" was a word that came to his mind. But it didn't quite fit, because for a long time he'd had decidedly unsisterly dreams concerning his beautiful countrywoman. After the traditional Avalonian napkin ceremony, an ancient Meem Steward bowed and presented him with the restaurant's large meem list.

"Noo that is wha' I ca' a meem list," Cartier remarked softly.

"Would you like to look it over?" Brim asked, offering the huge book across the table.

Cartier smiled and shook her head. "I hae seen quite a few o' them since my assignment to Avalon. I should much rather you choose somethin' for us. Luik you did at FleetPort 30 that evenin'."

Brim peered over the top of the book into her brownish eyes and smiled. "And what if tonight I have evil intentions when I order?" he asked.

She laughed. "You ne'er know, Wilf Brim," she said, relaxing in her chair and crossing her long legs. "Perhaps I e'en *share* some o' those intentions. We shall ha' to see how the evenin' turns out."

And, at least to Brim's way of thinking, the evening rapidly became one of the most pleasant he could remember. They seemed to share a boundless set of interests and took time with their order, pausing to sip—and savor—the grand old Logish Meem Brim had selected after considerable study of the list. By the time they were ready for the main course, it seemed to

Brim as if meeting the beautiful Carescrian was one of the most fortunate occurrences of his life. They even talked about Margot Effer'wyck, for Cartier was naturally curious about the woman she had risked crew, ship, and life to search for after Brim's battle at Zonga'ar.

"She really did try to save you, didn't she," Cartier said, pausing to look Brim directly in the eye. "She maun love you very much to compromise her chield that way."

Brim frowned and returned her gaze. "I don't think I'll ever know if she loves me," he said presently. "Once, a long time ago, I believe she did. Now, it's anybody's guess. From what I gather, TimeWeed leaves little in one's brain but ardent yearnings for itself. But I think vestiges of our love clearly remain." He felt himself blush. "We met a few evenings in Fluvanna," he said. "And the old spark was there—or at least seemed to be, even though, to be truthful, something *was* missing."

"But did na' later she . . . er . . . try to hae you killed in an ambush?" Cartier asked.

"Yes," Brim admitted, "she did." He shook his head. "At least it certainly seemed to be the case. Yet, why did she later save my life at Zonga'ar at the risk of her own?"

Cartier smiled. " 'Tis not my place to answer such questions," she said. "I don't know how the minds of Princesses work."

"I understand," Brim said with a grin, somehow anxious to drop the subject. "As you told me earlier, you're only a poor Carescrian maiden."

"I hae dropped the 'maiden' business," Cartier said, cocking her head to one side and smiling. "A maiden my age would na' be a very interestin' person."

"You've been married?" Brim asked.

"Once," she said with a faraway look in her eye. Then she winked and smiled with a feigned look of iniquity. "But I didn't wait for *him* to come along."

"Eve Cartier, I'm shocked," Brim chuckled as the Meem Steward emptied the bottle into their goblets.

"Another bottle?" the man asked.

Brim looked across the table at Cartier and raised his eyebrows.

She glanced demurely at the ceiling and thought for a moment. "Nae, Wilf," she said presently, "I've had quite enough, thank you."

"You didn't like it?" he asked.

"Oh, on the contrary," she said, closing her eyes dreamily, "I *luved* it."

"Then?"

"I've had eneugh for tonight," she said quietly. "But if you'd like another, don't let me stop you."

Brim considered that. He'd chosen an especially rich, full-bodied Logish Meem to go with the braised game and berries they'd both ordered. Ultimately, however, he shook his head and thanked the busy Steward who bowed and quickly disappeared among the tables.

"If you change your mind . . ." he said.

"I do na' think I shall," she replied, smoothing her hair. "I ha' enjoyed the meem, but I hope there's mair to this evenin' than just a meal an' drinkin', Mr. Wilf Brim. I've spent the best part o' the last twa' weeks at the helm of a starship tryin' to kill people—and damn nearly gettin' killed myself a number of times. The fact is that I'm tired, my handsome countryman, an' I don't want onythin' to interfere wi' what' I think you hae on your mind."

Brim raised an eyebrow. "Universe, Eve," he said with no little concern. "Have I been staring at you *that* much?"

She smiled. "Eneugh," she said.

"I'm terribly sorry," Brim said—and meant it.

"Oh, please don't be sorry, Wilf," she insisted, placing her hand on his. "I luve to be stared at that way. Every woman does at the right time and place."

"Then I'll continue," Brim said softly.

"See that you do," she replied.

He did.

* * *

After a light dessert of fruit and cheese, she puffed one of her tiny camarge cigarettes to life and inhale deeply with her eyes half closed. Then twisting in her chair while she settled back, she crossed her legs once more and exposed a considerable stretch of thigh. "'Tis been a wonderful evenin', so far, Wilf Brim," she said, looking him directly in the eye.

"Indeed it has," Brim agreed with a smile, then waited. They sat in silence for a long moment. Clearly, the next step—whatever it was going to be—was up to him. "Er...where do you plan to stay this evening?" he asked tentatively.

She smiled. "I hae nowhere to stay, Wilf Brim," she answered, her eyes still glued to his. "Whar' are you stayin'?"

Brim leaned forward in his chair. "Nowhere yet," he said, his heart in his mouth. "Er... would you like me to find a place we could share?"

"Wilf Brim," she said, slowly stroking her wrist with two fingers, "was that a suggestion that we share a bed?"

He grinned. "More than just share a bed I hope, Eve," he said softly.

Smiling, she reached across the table and took his hand. "Wilf, you've been mentally taking my clothes off all day, haen't you?"

"Yeah," Brim admitted, "I guess I have."

"Then find us a private place where you don't hae to pretend," she replied with a little smile. "I luve it when a man undresses me. After that, weel, we'll explore. All right?"

Brim nodded, his mind working furiously. Where? Then it came to him. Baxter Calhoun was part owner of a lovely little pension just off Vereker Square, and he had offered its use to Brim on a number of occasions. "I need to make a call from the lobby," he said. "You'll wait?"

"I see nobody else here who's offerin' to take my clothes off for me," she said. "I'll wait."

"Just sit still and don't tell anyone that's what you're looking for," Brim whispered in her ear. "Otherwise, I'll have to fight every man in the place...."

Moments later, he was in the lobby, ringing up the personal HoloPhone of his old mentor and shipmate, Rear Admiral Baxter Calhoun, Commander of the Imperial Defense Command, at his headquarters in Old Royce Abbey, a converted Gradygroat monastery in the outskirts of Avalon. . . .

CHAPTER 8

If...

"Admiral Calhoun's Residence," drawled the pretentious voice at the other end of the connection.

The HoloScreen before Brim was blank, as he expected. "My name is Brim and I want to speak to the Admiral," he said.

"*Who* are *you*?" the lofty voice inquired. "And what is your business?"

"My name is Brim," he repeated, "as in Wilf Brim. I know the Admiral's in because I spoke to him this afternoon during the officers' meetings."

"And your business, Mr. Brim?"

"*Captain* Brim, Imperial Fleet."

"Your *business* Captain?" the voice repeated, clearly unimpressed by a mere Captain.

Brim fought his tempter to a draw, then laughed to himself. The man was only doing his job—and a damned good one at that. "Listen, mister," he said, "my business concerns Baxter Calhoun and myself. Just go tell him that Wilf Brim needs the Vereker Square apartment—tonight. Got that?"

"The Vereker Square apartment?" the voice said with an immediate change in inflection. "One moment, please."

As he waited, Brim could imagine a very efficient servant scanning a list of personal contacts on an information outlet. "Ah, yes," the voice said presently, this time in almost friendly inflection. "Captain Brim, Imperial Fleet, lately of the IVG. Very good, Captain. I shall connect you with the Admiral directly."

Moments later, the display came on and filled with Calhoun's ruggedly handsome visage. He was comfortably dressed in an ancient-looking athletic suit and grinning from ear to ear. In the background, someone who was a dead ringer for one of Avalon's most celebrated actresses reclined on a plush sofa. She was mostly dressed. "Weel, m'boy," the powerful Carescrian exclaimed. "What's this aboot usin' the Vereker Square apartment, noo? Sounds like an important tryst to me."

Brim grinned. "It is that, Cal," he said simply.

Calhoun narrowed his eyes for a moment. "'Tis a guid thing, too, young Brim," he said. "You've waited *much* too lang findin' yourself someone to take your mind from your work. Quite a few o' us hae been afraid you'd eventually go to pieces."

"I think this lady will take my mind off the war for a few metacycles," Brim said, feeling his cheeks burn.

"Guid!" Calhoun said energetically. "I shall na' keep you, then, but you maun know that I'm pleased for you—an' a wee relieved, too." He looked off to his left. "Barnat," he ordered, "the apartment on Vereker Square. Is it ready?"

"I have already informed the lock of Captain Brim's identity card," his voice said calmly.

Calhoun looked back into the display. "'Tis done, young Brim," he said. "The apartment's yours anytime you need it—subject, of course, to prior availability. Just ring up Barnat." He grinned again. "Noo go recharge yourself. Universe knows you need it." He then threw the perfect parody of an Imperial salute—and the display went abruptly dark.

"Sorry I took so long," Brim said, returning to Cartier and their table. "I hope you haven't changed your mind."

She smiled shyly. "Not on your life, Wilf Brim," she said. "Who knows how long I might have to search for someone who's willin' to help me."

"Don't bother—I'm your man," he promised, helping her from her chair. They picked up their Fleet Cloaks in the lobby, then walked arm-in-arm to the curb where a cab was waiting. They started to board when Cartier shook her head and suggested they walk. "'Tis only a short way to Vereker Square," she whispered, putting her nose gently against his. "'An' part of a very beautiful night ha' already passed much too speedily. If we walk, perhaps we can stretch our pleasure . . ."

In spite of the walk, long pauses they made in the shadows fanned their desire to a point that was almost unbearable. By the time they reached the apartment, they were both quite ready for making love. No sooner were they inside the door than Cartier slipped out of her Fleet Cloak and stepped to the middle of the floor. There, she turned and faced him with lowered eyes and a little smile. "Now, Mr. Wilf Brim," she said in her gentle voice, "I should be very honored if you would take off my clothes. A lang time, noo, I've been wonderin' if you'll like what you see, an' I'm anxious for m' answer . . ."

Afterward, their first coupling happened almost too quickly—two people desperate to thrust away the horror of war if only for a few short moments. At first Brim struggled to pace himself to the slower tempo of her sex, but by the time they stumbled into bed, Cartier had been almost as frantic as he. They made love fiercely—almost violently—before they both exploded in a blinding, thrusting frenzy of passion. Afterward, she lay rigid in his arms, literally soaking the bedclothes and wracked by tremors that shook her whole body. A long time passed before she subsided in quiet sobbing.

"Are you . . . all right?" he asked when he was able to force his own breathing under control.

"Y-yes," she whispered, her face wet against his chest. But almost immediately, her body was again wracked by violent tremors. After what seemed like a long time, he felt them ease. "Eve?" he whispered.

"Sweet mother of Voot," she whispered after a long time, tightening her leg over his waist as if she were holding on to a life jacket. "I g-guess I wanted you a lot mair than I realized."

Brim felt damp hair against his cheek and savored the erotic scents of her body—he could never remember her wearing any kind of artificial perfume. He had needed her pretty badly himself!

After a long, comfortable silence, she turned her head toward him and opened her eyes a little. "Do Princesses make as much noise as I did?" she asked softly.

"I don't remember," Brim whispered tactfully. "I tend to be awfully noisy myself when it's that good."

"Mmm," she murmured, burrowing her nose into his chest. "It was guid for you, too, then?"

"Yeah, It was *very* guid," he whispered. In a few moments, Cartier's breathing came long and regular, and little by little he felt her body relax. Carefully reaching toward the nightstand, he waved the room into darkness, then drew the bedclothes over them both . . .

Twice during the night, they awoke with *most* compelling needs that they compulsively satisfied—though each time they came together their exertions took on considerably more character. Brim found his shy Carescrian lover to be astonishingly inventive, and wound up with great admiration for her former lovers. "Some 'simple country maiden' you are," he whispered, attempting to catch his breath after one of her more astonishing efforts. "Where in the Universe did you learn to do that?"

" 'Tis none of your business." She laughed, rolling her hips slowly while she straddled his waist. She was absolutely gorgeous—in the very prime of her life. He wondered why it was that middle-aged men chased young girls when there were real women like this who could even carry on a witty conversation! Small, pale-nippled breasts hung full-bellied and ripe against an almost painfully slim chest, and her slight belly met the thick, black thatch of her crotch in a glorious swelling of smooth, soft flesh. As he'd slowly disrobed her, he'd been literally dazzled by the sight of her long, slim legs and gently pouting buttocks.

Then afterward . . . What she didn't know about making love wasn't worth consideration; there seemed to be nothing she didn't enjoy . . .

When morning came, they found they had slept till well past dawn—a rarity for squadron officers during this war, at least.

"I feel so rested, I can na' believe it," she said, stretching luxuriously on the stained bed sheets. "Especially wi' the wee sleep I've managed."

Brim laughed dreamily. "Should I perhaps apologize for your loss of sleep?" he asked.

Following a great yawn, she hunched her shoulders with obvious pleasure and grinned from ear to ear. "Na' when you've made me feel so wonderful," she said.

"Most happy to assist in any way," Brim said in his most flowery voice. "Besides, my most seductive Carescrian beauty," he added, "you have made me feel pretty wonderful yourself."

"Your 'Carescrian beauty'" Cartier mused, peering at the ceiling for a moment. "That's what you just said, isn't it?"

"You are a beautiful woman, Eve," he replied earnestly. "Perhaps the most beautiful woman I have ever met."

"I thank you for that, Wilf Brim," she said soberly. "You have indeed made me feel beautiful tonight. But you also called me *Carescrian*." she said. "Does that perhaps make me different to you?"

Brim thought about that for a moment. "Funny," he said presently. "I wonder if it does. I have seldom felt so close to anybody as I do right now. But then, it might also be a reaction to the kind of intense passion you seem to be able to arouse in me. I don't think I have ever been so worked up in my life—and that is no exaggeration."

"Do you think it might also be that we share so much in the way of our essentials?" she asked.

"Because we're both from Carescria?" he asked.

"Weel, my good lover," she said, "in its own way, Carescria

gave us beginnings that are rather exceptional.'' She looked him in the eyes. ''Have you given any thought to who you are since last we talked on it?''

Brim crossed his legs and sat beside her on the bed, ''I was wondering when you'd get to that,'' he said, more seriously than he'd intended.

''Were you noo?'' she asked with raised eyebrows. ''I knew I maun regret tellin' you wha' I was thinkin' at the time,'' she said.

''Nothing to regret,''Brim said, shaking his head. ''It made me give some real consideration to myself.''

''About who you are?''

He smiled. ''Some,'' he said. ''But more about my being independent—and lonesome.''

''They all go hand-in-hand, the way I see them,'' she said. ''Tell me first aboot who you are, then. I want to know.''

''All right,'' he agreed. ''But it isn't going to answer your question—it's only brought about more questions for me.''

''And?''

''And crazy—or stupid—as it may sound, I guess since I joined the Fleet, I've gone through life pretty well defining myself as who I'm *not*.''

''Then, who are you *not*. Wilf Brim?'' she asked.

''Well,'' he said, ''first and foremost, I'm *not* a Carescrian.''

''Oh? So you really *do* deny Carescria, Wilf Brim?'' she asked.

''Er, yes . . .'' Brim started, shrugging uncomfortably. ''Yes, I do. I certainly brought nothing out of there but the clothes on my back.''

''Hmm,'' she said with a smile. ''An' here I thought you learned to fly starships at the asteroid mines luik I did.'' She giggled for a moment. ''I learned a lot mare than *that* there, too.'' she added.

This time, it was Brim's turn to grin. ''I thought so!'' he said, placing his hand gently on her stomach. ''I learned a lot about life there, too. But I never knew you could do what you did in *gravity*.''

"Noo you do," she said with a little smile.

"Yeah," he said. "I guess we both took a few things with us when we left home, didn't we?"

"Mair than you luik to admit, Wilf," she said. "An' you just called it 'home'—as you should."

"But I'm an Imperial," he protested.

"Ane way or anither, we're all of us Imperials," she said. "There's a lot good aboot the old Empire, much as we complain. But ask yourself this, Wilf, are you *as much* an Imperial as your good friend Toby Moulding, for example?"

He had to think about that for a few moments, but at last he nodded. "I think I am," he replied, frowning—the woman might be beautiful, but could ask the damndest questions.

"In truth, you are," she said. Then, opening her legs slightly, she took his hand and placed it on the tangled dampness of her crotch. "But would you say the Emperor thinks so?" she asked.

Somewhat nettled by her implications, Brim withdrew his hand. "I think so," he said. 'I'm damned certain Toby Moulding doesn't have *two* Imperial Comets.

"Hoot, mon," she said, gently touching her fingertips on his forearm. "I'm not talking onythin' like medals an' awards. I'm not even talkin' friendship. Pshaw, Wilf, the whole fleet gossips aboot the friendship that exists between you and the Emperor. It's real."

"Then? . . ."

"Does the Emperor think o' you as his *Imperial* friend or his *Carescrian* friend," she said.

He thought about that, trying to remember how Onrad usually addressed him. "I suppose he still thinks of me as a Carescrian," he admitted, "in spite of everything I do to discourage it."

"What do you mean by 'in spite of'?" she asked.

"Like losing my accent—which was *damned* hard—and, well, you know, I'm an Imperial. *Not* a Carescrian. What the xaxt's wrong with me?"

"In my eyes, 'tis that very *negation* of Carescria you ha'

wrong wi' you, Wilf," she said. "Look what havin' something in common did for both o' us when we war' doin' somehtin' basic like makin' love. You're missin' that throughout your life. You're denyin' your home."

"My home's anywhere I happen to be," he said. "Right here, for example."

She looked around the room with mock appreciation. "Nice place you've got, Brim," she said with an outrageous look.

"Thanks," he said, rolling his eyes toward the ceiling.

"It was just a way to make you see that somethin' like what you're tryin' doesn't really work."

"Tell me about 'doesn't work,' " he growled, finally losing his temper completely. "It's all right for you to love Carescria and keep your damned sexy accent and even brag about the place. Xaxt, Baxter Calhoun heads up all of Defense Command, and Starfuries from the new Carescrian plants are what's saving Avalon from the Leaguers. People *love* Carescrians these days! Why, we're almost as popular as Sodeskayan Bears who have been saving the Empire's bacon for centuries. But when *I* started out nearly twenty years ago, it was a xaxtdamn different story, let me tell you. You don't have any idea what I went through just to be the first Carescrian graduate from the Helmsman's Academy, I had to put up with Gorksroar from people who *still* can't fly a starship as well as I did my first day as a cadet."

"An' who do you blame for all this, Wilf Brim?" she asked earnestly. "Tell me?"

"I blame the Xaxtdamn . . ." He stopped in midsentence, staring her in the face. "Sweet Mother of the Universe," he whispered, as if he couldn't believe his own words, "I blame *Carescria*." He shook his head again and again and again. "That's what you've been trying to tell me, isn't it?" he said dazedly.

" 'Tis helped make you a lonely man, Wilf Brim," she said, sitting up to take his hands gently in hers. "But, 'tis also like you, for I've ne'er once heard you blame the people who actually made you suffer. You haen't, you know."

Brim shrugged. "No sense blaming them," he said. "They couldn't help how they felt. In those days, that was simply 'the *way*.'"

"'Twas probably tha' very attitude tha' gave you power to change as much of the auld system as you did all by yourself," she said. "But now—perhaps 'tis time to change *Wilf Brim* a bit. Do you suppose you might? I think you'd be much happier."

Brim blinked and looked at the beautiful—wise—woman sitting naked before him on the bed. "With some help from you, Eve," he said seriously. "I actually think I could."

"Wilf Brim, you'll find me *very* available," she said. "E'en if I didna' find you a most excellent lover and friend, wi'out the sacrifices you made then, I'd ne'er ha' gotten where I am today."

"That's not true," Brim said, feeling his face begin to flush. "Even without me, the last war killed so many of the aristocrats that they had to recruit from the 'lower classes,' as they used to call us."

"Many still do call us tha'," she laughed. "But 'tis endin', Wilf. I can tell—an' you broke the ice for us all."

"Surely you give friend Calhoun a bit of credit for your rapid commissioning," he said.

"O' course I do," she said. "But I've often heard the Governor tell aboot how you 'took the heat,' e'en for him."

Brim opened his mouth to speak, but she placed a finger on his lips. Lying back on the bed, she drew up her knees and placed his hand between her legs again. "Sh-h-h," she whispered. "Eneugh talk for this time. We've just time for a quick go before we maun catch our shuttles. Can you do it once mair, my *most* Imperial lover?"

Brim gently bathed his fingers in her warm moistness and almost immediately experienced a familiar sensation in his loins.

"Ooo," she exclaimed, lifting her head slightly to peer into his lap. "I guess you can, can't you?"

He did. . . .

* * *

Somehow, they both arrived back at their bases on time—but later, neither could explain how that happened.

The Leaguers' inactivity around Asterious ended abruptly at midday on Octad thirty second as the gravity storms of the past few days began to move out toward the galactic rim. Minor feints by Leaguer ships caused several Defense Command squadrons to be sent out, but nothing major developed, at first. Then, shortly after midday, BKAEW stations reported two massive buildups—Orgoth's normal strategy—and all of Brim's ships were scrambled. While they were out on patrol, however, a number of GA 88A formations reached FleetPort 30 almost unimpeded. And although the starbase suffered extensive damage from nearly flawless Leaguer marksmanship, Brim received communiqués assuring him that work crews had already begun space wharf repairs, even while the raid was still under way. This in spite of N-ray mains that had been repeatedly broken by enemy disruptors. Between battles, the Carescrian paused to wonder why FleetPort 30 in particular was so specially honored, but had little time to ponder arcana like the frenetic workings of Leaguer minds.

For almost two Standard motacycles, Leaguer attacks kept the Imperial defenders at battle stations. Eleven Group starships flew nearly one hundred sorties alone, but most were fruitless. Once slowed below LightSpeed, the Leaguers turned either way along the planetary orbits, patrolling this way and that in an obvious attempt to lure out Imperial killer ships. Then fifty some heavy cruisers again attacked the starbases themselves. On the heels of this assault, another large raid took place.

Abruptly, still another huge raid was unleashed on Melia, again concentrating on all the known Intelligence laboratories. Speeding in to the defense, Brim could see an impressive barrage from orbital forts erupt over the planet before he even spotted the raiders. His squadron has been placed where it could do little for the present, so he watched helplessly while the Leaguers unleashed terrible destruction on the sprawling complexes below. And from snatches of KAPPA traffic below, he could tell they were operating with all their new found accuracy. How had they improved themselves so?

As the day continued, more civilian targets were attacked—everywhere—including Avalon itself, in spite of the defender's best efforts. On one of a seemingly endless succession of patrols, Brim watched in an aft-view display as a long line of Starfuries followed him down and swept around at terrific speed to strike right into the heart of a huge Leaguer formation. But with only two squadrons, his wing was hopelessly outnumbered, and the majority of raiders got through. Even in the heat of battle, Brim found himself amazed by the accuracy by which the Leaguers were firing their huge, single-shot bombardment disruptors. If something weren't done to combat this extraordinary improvement, the Empire was going to find itself in real trouble, no matter how many Leaguers Defense Command managed to destroy.

Finally, the raiders left off and he led his squadrons home to FleetPort 30 with the daunting realization that Imperial forces were probably stretched well beyond the breaking point—on many fronts.

Gravity storms soon returned to Asterious, but feints and small raids nevertheless kept Defense Command under considerable pressure. A total of thirty-eight Leaguer ships had been destroyed the previous day, but twenty-two Imperial ships were also lost, and the number of serviceable starships in Defense Command dropped from 740 to 727. Considering the intensity of the fighting, however, remarkably few Imperial casualties had been incurred. Only two full crews were lost, although seven remained on the missing list. Defense Command was clearly holding its own, even though the new Leaguer accuracy caused considerable apprehension—coupled with renewed attacks on civilian targets that made it difficult for the defenders to fire from above for fear of blasting the very targets they were bound to protect.

In late afternoon, the gravity storms began to clear and a

Leaguer force estimated at two hundred plus starships was reported to be heading for Avalon City. In moments, all available starships in Brim's area were scrambled. The report, however, was inaccurate, and within a metacycle, the large force of attack ships and escorts turned up actually speeding toward the science planet and its nearby BKAEW orbiters. Similar attacks continued for most of the day with the usual Leaguer accuracy, but Orgoth's raiders paid a heavy price for the damage they inflicted, losing twenty attack craft compared to sixteen Imperial killer ships. And only one Imperial crew was lost; none were reported missing.

As the day ground to an end, Brim was heartened to hear the Imperial Attack Command had taken retaliatory steps at last—for the first time, a number of Imperial battleships and heavy cruisers had been dispatched to attack Tarrott, itself. However, the news was tempered by reports from Fluvanna, where an increasingly bloody battle for Magor continued unabated. As the tired crews of Defense Command crawled into their bunks for a few moments' critically needed rest, the whole Universe around them seemed to have fallen into a whirling paroxysm of war.

Roused after only a short respite, Brim found himself summoned to Avalon for a surprise command meeting. His muzzle-headed attempts to leave for the surface resulted in his missing the shuttle, and for long moments, he wearily sat in at the empty boarding port fighting back an irrational rage borne of intense frustration. Grinding his teeth, he forced himself back under control and with an effort focused his mind on the desperate need to remain level-headed. He had a war to wage, and ending up in the psychiatric bay—as were so many these days—was no way to win it.

Pulling himself to his feet, he started for his office so he could arrange for other transportation, when out of the corner of his eye he spotted the little Gorn-Hoff 219 moored lonesomely off in one protected corner of docking portal 44. From its placement at the brow, it was probably invisible from nearly anywhere else in the station—and certainly from space itself. He supposed in the madness of the past few days, the speedy little transport had simply been forgotten. He'd ordered someone to paint Imperial Comets over the League's crimson daggers. But aside from that, the 219 looked as if hadn't been touched since he and Aram docked it.

It *also* looked like a quick ride to the Admiralty...

Grabbing a HoloPhone at the door, he called Operations. "Carnaby," he shouted, watching in the HoloScreen as a young operator roused herself from a stolen sleep, slumped at her console.

"A-aye, sir." she stammered with a frightened look in her eyes. "I was just studyin' the...er...regulations 'ere, Captain."

Biting his lip, Brim turned a blind eye to the infraction of the Watchkeeper's Ordinance. The poor moppet had to be dead tired; he'd seen her on at least five patch crews in the last two days. "Good girl," he said, attempting to speak with the utmost gravity. "Be sure you pay particular attention to the parts about sleeping at a duty station. Those are *serious* violations."

"T-thank you, Captain," she said, blushing to a deep crimson.

"Carnaby," he said without further comment, "I want you to call up and schedule a parking place for me at the Fleet Base on Lake Mersin immediately. Can you do that?"

"I can, sir," she said, eager to please. "Immediately. When do you want it, please?"

Brim nearly fell victim of the grin that had been working its way to his face. "In about a metacycle," he said, finally abandoning all attempts to appear solemn. "It'll take me about that long to get there."

"Aye, sir," she said, placing her hand on one of the alarm systems. "An' shall I call up one of the Starfuries on alert status?"

Brim grimaced. "No," he said hurriedly, "don't do that. Just tell the people below to expect a captured Gorn-Hoff—the 219 we seem to have permanently acquired as the base hack.

It's got hull number''—he stood on tiptoe to read the little starship's hull number—''319-JE.''

''Right, sir,'' Carnaby answered, ''Imperial Gorn-Hoff 319-JE. Will you need a gravity pool, then, or will she fit on a grav pad?''

''A grav pad will be fine,'' Brim chuckled. With that, he strode across the wide deck of the mooring tube and into the brow. An ''Imperial'' Gorn-Hoff, no less. Even Valentin would get a kick out of that!

This time, he started both spin-gravs in short order and was about to cast off for the surface when for no apparent reason the mysterious crystal mounted on his readout panel began to flash excitedly. He frowned, scanning the panels for some ancilliary information. Now what?

Abruptly, alarms sounded in the COMM channel, and the sector Controller's emotionless voice filled the headphones of his battlesuit, ''610 Squadron, lift off and patrol base; you will receive further instructions in the air. 610 Squadron lift off quickly as possible, please. This is an emergency!''

Brim reached to switch off the 219, when the Controller broadcast again. ''Large enemy attack formation approaching FleetPort 30. All personnel not engaged in active duty take cover immediately.'' There was no time to get to his Starfury; it was on the far side of the big satellite. He was out of options—it was either head for the surface or helplessly play target again as he had done with Onrad a few days previously. Reclosing the helmet of his battlesuit, he turned in his seat and backed the little starship away from the brow. Starfuries were speeding away in all directions like insects whose hive is threatened. As he swung the nose out into space, he glanced up and saw the Leaguers—about a dozen GA 87B Zachtwagers—gleaming in the brilliant light of the Triad and coming straight on. Instinctively, he shrugged up his shoulders and ducked his head. Out of the corner of his eye, he saw three more Starfuries head spaceward in close formation—just as the Leaguers opened fire with their great single-shot disruptors.

One moment the Starfuries were racing along in close formation; the next, they were catapulted apart by a tremendous explosion—the Leaguers and their astonishing precision. How did they do it? They sure didn't have a xaxtdamned crystal strobing in the middle of their Hyperscreens like this little Gorn-Hoff did or they wouldn't have been able to hit a thing!

Or would they?

At that moment it hit him! The crystal. It was part of the aiming system Ursis was working on. It explained a lot of things that had happened since he'd helped steal the little Gorn-Hoff. The Leaguers who had been hunting for a "*Weg'wysershmook* crystal" ship . . . Valentin's desperate attempt to recapture him . . . the attempt to destroy a whole Intelligence complex (where logic dictated a captured ship would be stored). Before him in his captured transport was the key to their whole new aiming system!

He curved off and flew recklessly through the battle to test his theory. Wherever his crystal flashed, he slowed and circled the location at a circumspect distance until a Leaguer ship showed up—as invariably one would—and fired its big, single-shot disruptors as it flew through. He had it!

Suddenly an approaching Gorn-Hoff veered toward *him*, ignoring the point in space where the crystal flashed. He'd been spotted! He jinked, only to find another Leaguer curving in on him. Then another—and still *another.*

Putting the helm over hard, he headed for the surface at full acceleration as space erupted in a bedlam of monstrous explosions, each bouncing the 219 in a different direction until its sturdy spaceframe creaked in protest. Thank Voot their "unassisted" marksmanship was no better than ever! Reentry flames coursed along the little starship's flanks and every protrusion on the hull glowed with white heat, while cabin temperature began to rise ominously. For an eternity of clicks the tumult of confused disruptor fire continued, then fell away aft, as the Leaguers were engaged by avenging Starfuries, then he began to draw back on his power settings as the surface rapidly came up to meet him.

Some ten thousand irals above the cloud tops, he wrestled the now-incandescent starship out of its headlong plunge and peered around him. He was alone in the sky. And even though his battlesuit was putting out full refrigeration, he was sweating profusely in the heat. He checked the readouts and. . . The *crystal*. It was dark again.

He ground his teeth in anger as he listened to a status report on FleetPort 30. The mooring tube had a few more gaping holes that hadn't been specified by the original design charts and four men had been killed in a maintenance launch. But Barbousse estimated the base would be in full operation before the afternoon was over, so the Leaguers had very little to show for ten cycles or so of their confoundedly accurate shooting. Sad as it was to lose lives, the raid was further proof that try as they might, the Leaguers would never completely wipe out the Empire's system of FleetPort satellites. Shaking his head, he canceled the gravity pad he'd ordered, left word with Calhoun's office that he would be late for the meeting, and set course for the Intelligence laboratories on Proteus at top speed. His little Gorn-Hoff was about to cost Nik Ursis a whole case of Logish Meem.

Metacycles later, after cadging a ride back to Avalon and further mooching a staff skimmer to the admiralty, he noted a number of large HoloPosters on media kiosks exuberantly recounting the space battles around Asterious—and the losses inflicted on the Leaguers' vaunted Deep Space Fleet. Shops displayed stylish civilian battlesuits for both men and women, and street-corner displays demonstrated "How to Lie Down When the City Is Attacked," advising citizens they should be flat on their stomachs, battlesuit visors down, mouths slightly open, and gloves covering the all-important neck interface. Near the palace, a nascent CIGA demonstration protesting the raid on Tarrott aborted nearly as soon as it began when angry crowds broke through obviously reluctant police barriers, scattering bruised and pummeled protesters throughout one of the large parks nearby.

Brim slipped into the meeting nearly two metacycles late, taking a seat beside Eve Cartier that just *happened* to be empty on the aisle toward the end of the rear of the assembly hall. He was in time to learn that the previous day's Imperial raid against Tarrott had been a complete success, with all attack ships returning safely to their bases. Moreover, the Leaguers had been stunned as their city erupted in the same great explosions they had wreaked on Avalon—during his early days of overconfidence, Admiral Hoth Orgoth had promised that Tarrott would never be attacked. The League media had immediately erupted with banner denouncements of the "Cowardly Imperial Attack," and editorial caterwauling against "Imperial air pirates over Tarrott!" But the Leaguers' protestations served only one purpose in Avalon—they cleared the way for even more raids in the future.

Additionally, the League had lost 41 starships that same day—and the number of operational Imperial killer ships remained level at 728. Clearly, from the Leager point of view, Imperial forces must appear to be a long way from capitulation. But Blue Capes like Brim who spent their lives on the front lines knew better. The granitelike Imperial facade was beginning to crack from overwork, stress, and fatigue.

Brim and Cartier dined exhaustedly after the meeting and afterward spent the night in the apartment on Vereker Square. But before they could make love, they fell contentedly asleep in each other's arms, and dozed so soundly—and so late—that Cartier had to make a mad dash for the shuttle carrying most of her underclothes in her kit bag. Grinning, Brim wondered if he could have spent the same kind of night with someone he didn't feel so close to. Maybe—just maybe—he thought, there was more to this acceptance of his own origins than he initially estimated.

Attacks began early, with Brim, himself, reporting back to FleetPort 19 just under the wire—but more rested than he could remember. On patrol that afternoon, he mused that the strain on Defense Command was probably reaching some sort of a peak.

In each of the past three weeks, the Imperials had flown more than four thousand sorties—and the previous week, nearly *five* thousand, a record. This compared with an average of one thousand per week not more than a month and a half previously. The latest Leaguer tactic of flying large numbers of small raids was wearing on men and machines both. But the fact that the valiant crews of Defense Command had not cracked—nor had retreated into self-pity—showed that the once-unseasoned Imperial defenders had ultimately evolved into a fighting force at least as good as—and often far better than—their so-called "professional" adversaries from the League.

During the next day, Attack Command launched another successful raid on the League capital of Tarrott before regional gravity became turbulent again, causing a welcome, two-day lull in the fighting.

According to Brim's TSIB, Laga'ard Testetta, Foreign Minister of the Torond—home following talks with Hanna Notrom—had informed Grand Baron LaKarn that "doubts now seem to hang over the Leaguer offensive against Avalon." Similarly, Zoguard Grobermann, League Minister of State, officially blamed the prolonged delay both on hazardous gravity storms and League forces diverted to assist The Torond in Fluvanna. Even Triannic was reported to have growled that at least two more weeks of calm gravity were necessary before he could hope to neutralize the Imperial Home Fleet.

If the Leaguers' invasion of Avalon had been temporarily postponed, however, their intent to destroy much of it continued unabated as soon as the regional gravity moderated. FleetPort 30 was attacked early on the third morning and damaged in spite of heavy losses inflicted on the enemy. Brim's Starfury was also hit during a dogfight during that same attack and just made it back to the base before the Drive power failed completely. Raids continued throughout the day, and a second attack on the FleetPort caught him without a ship to fight in.

Repairing in disgust to the tracking room, he quietly took a seat at the back of the low-ceilinged chamber and watched a group of Leaguer attack ships emerge out of Hyperspace, then speed directly for Proteus, the science-colony planet. Suddenly, a dozen or so swung off course and headed directly for FleetPort 30, arriving within firing distance while the clutter from the previous raid was still being cleared. Starfuries immediately closed in and engaged the small squadron, but not in time to avert a second savage attack.

With alarms clanging stridently in his ears, Brim donned the helmet to his battlesuit—lately, he seemed to be living in it—then sprinted for Defense Central where Barbousse already would have taken command. But he was no more than halfway there when the deck buckled violently, throwing him from his feet as heavy disruptor fire again tore into the satellite. At either end of the corridor, airtight doors slid closed automatically, trapping him halfway through the big satellite's dormitory section. Before he could get up, the atmosphere filled with smoke—which cleared with a mighty roar as somewhere the damaged hull vented to open space. Simultaneously, the lights went out, replaced instantly by the dim glow of battle lanterns. Sealing his visor, he struggled to his feet and began to stumble blindly toward a wall phone when another savage blast took out the satellite's local gravity and launched him sideways through a cabin doorway where a wet and virtually naked woman struggled blindly to don a battlesuit—she'd obviously been showering when the raid began and had only heard the alarms when it was much too late. Heaving and gasping silently for air, she collapsed as he pulled himself to her side. Grabbing her battlesuit helmet, he jammed it over her staring, grimacing head and turned up the air—only clicks before a pitcher of liquid exploded beside her bunk and boiled in the vacuum of space.

Moments later, she ceased her wild struggles and her terror-goggled eyes clouded over. Abruptly, he recognized her as one of the BKAEW operators, and wondered how many more of the satellite's occupants had just died similar deaths. Taking a deep breath, he pulled the helmet from her head, then gently closed her eyelids and finished pulling on her suit—a difficult task now that gases from boiling body fluids had swelled her body at least a third again in volume like some grotesque balloon. When finally he stood, he reverently thanked Lady Fortune that the poor woman never regained consciousness while her blood was boiling. He'd seen that once: it was simply too horrible to contemplate.

After the attack subsided he activated the suit's voice communications system; his helmet immediately filled with groans and screams of those who survived. "Barbousse!" he demanded over the noise. "Barbousse! Can you hear me? Are you all right?"

"I hear you, Cap'm," said Barbousse's voice. "I'm safe. Where are you?"

Shaking his head in wonderment of yet *another* last-moment miracle, Brim gave Barbousse general instructions on where he could be found, *after,* he demanded, rescue crews first took care of the wounded. Then he sat back under a battle lantern and pondered on how he—Wilf Brim, Carescrian—had managed to stay alive for so long through so much trouble. He came up with no rational answers as he stared at the floating, bloated corpse for nearly two metacycles before Barbousse and a rescue team cut through the twisted wreckage to release him.

All told, more than sixty hits had scored on the satellite, each placed with an accuracy that Brim *still* found hard to believe. And even though he was certain he now knew part of how they were achieving it, the knowledge wasn't doing anybody much good until someone devised a way to counter it—or better still, to use it to the Empire's own best advantage. The Leaguers damaged workshops, repair hangars, stores, dormitories—even offices—ripping up service bays, severing service mains, and generally reducing the big satellite to a shambles. Sixty-five people had been killed or seriously injured—among them five flight crews. They'd finally destroyed the dock where he'd inadvertently concealed the Gorn-Hoff 219. But for all that, they didn't get what they were after. The little ship had been safely underground on Proteus for days.

At day's end, Defense Command crews had flown a record 1054 sorties—the previous record had stood only six Standard Days. Moreover, before the last watch was finished, 109 additional attack ships raided targets on Melia and Helios, in addition to smaller raids elsewhere. League losses totaled thirty-six starships to the Empire's twenty-five, but Brim and the other doughty Imperials were clearly approaching the limits of their strength and endurance as they struggled to sustain their part of Avalon's defense amid the twisted wreckage of FleetPort 30.

On the last day of Octad, Leaguer raids against Imperial starbases continued uninterrupted, with at least eight hundred starships of all types taking part. FleetPort 30 took even more punishment, but miraculously, the big satellite continued in operation, although none of the remaining Starfuries or Defiants based there remained completely serviceable. Brim often flew with reduced armament and propulsion, doing the best he could with what he had. From his all-too-infrequent rendezvous with an equally fatigued Eve Cartier, he knew that things were at least as bad in FleetPort 19—and, by inference, throughout Defense Command in general. His only comfort was the knowledge that the Leaguer crews were taking the same kind of punishment themselves.

One evening, a traveling company—brave souls all—put on a popular Laserta musicale in FleetPort 30's patched-up assembly hall. Brim and some 250 off-duty personnel formed a wildly appreciative audience. During one of the more popular ballads, raid alarms began to howl throughout the satellite. The troupe paused while audience and actors alike donned battlesuits, then the show went on, as if Hoth Orgoth and his Deep Space Fleet were just as unreal and innocuous as the clowns.

Less than a metacycle after the musicale, Brim found himself at the helm of a cobbled-together Starfury that was recently deemed more or less spaceworthy. Damage in the Drive crystal area made it incapable of faster-than-light flight, but it could still put up a good fight below the speed of light. He was just getting under way when yet another attack slammed into the base, this one much larger than the last. In a welter of explosions, the Starfury to his left was flung 'round like a cartwheel, then continued out of control like a huge child's top until its starframe crumpled and all three hulls disintegrated in a roiling burst of energy. Nearby, a second Starfury whirled aimlessly, both pontoons broken off. Grinding his teeth and expecting to be the Leaguers' next victim, he fed the emergency energy to the ship's big gravs and got away—temporarily. Directly ahead were echelons of League attack ships, and his disruptor crews opened fire on two GA 88s in succession, but the Leaguers had already completed their attack and were racing off into Hyperspace, where Brim could not follow. Abandoning them to other crews, he returned to the damaged base in high dudgeon, where not even Barbousse could find words to claim his angry frustration.

During another series of the raging gravity storms indigenous to the galactic center, Brim was called to Avalon to make a situation report. At first, he angrily refused to leave the battle, but Calhoun insisted. So grudgingly he caught a shuttle for the surface. Within the metacycles, he landed on Lake Mersin—in the midst of a vicious raid. Sprinting off the brow toward a shelter, he paused to look toward the sound of a starship diving at high speed. Moments later, it broke through the high haze, heading straight for the lake. Its turrets were all askew, and for a moment he took it for a GA 87B. It was turning very slowly, in a lazy sort of spin, and as its full silhouette appeared, he recognized it as a Starfury. At about five hundred irals, the turrets swung a little, and then just before it reached the surface, its gravs seemed to blow up and disintegrate. The doomed starship disappeared into the lake as a cascade of individual waterspouts, leaving only a puff of colored smoke to mark the common grave of forty-odd Blue Capes, and even that was gone long before Brim reached the shelter . . .

Finally, the Leaguers departed. Brim's staff skimmer picked its way through rubble-strewn streets to the meeting, where briefers confirmed what he'd known all along: that Imperial starbases everywhere were suffering terrific damage. Before the meeting ended, however, all reported that they were back to nearly full operation—except his own, which was capable of reduced operations only by superhuman effort. Conditions at all the damaged starbases were miserable, especially at FleetPort 19. In answer to anxious questions by Calhoun and his staff officers, Brim expressed his thoughts that if Imperials like himself seemed stressed, the Leaguers must be equally so—perhaps even more. According to the reports he'd heard earlier in the meeting, the last two days had cost Hoth Orgoth seventy-seven starships. And while his fellow Imperials had themselves lost sixty-five, a much higher percentage of their crews had survived to fight again (although a number of Leaguers survived as Imperial prisoners).

Wearily trudging along an Admiralty corridor after the meeting, Brim noticed few CIGA buttons and discovered that Amherst's once-lavish office had quietly been converted to a much-needed main-floor snack bar.

In the lobby, he was just about to reserve an after-supper skimmer-pool lift to the shuttle when he heard the musical lift of a familiar voice.

"Skipper, Hey, Skipper. *Captain Brim*!"

Tired almost beyond caring he turned—then in spite of his fatigue, he broke out in what felt like an ear-to-ear grin. He'd almost forgotten how. "Tissaurd!" he hooted to the diminutive officer. "What in Voot's name are you doing in the middle of *this* snakepit?" he demanded. "I thought bender people simply went invisible and stayed clear of trouble like we've got here."

Turning a few heads in the great domed lobby, she planted a long kiss on his lips before she stood back, grabbed his forearms, and shook her head. "Wilf Brim," she said, ignoring his banter, "you look absolutely terrible."

Brim stolidly maintained his grin—he didn't want to lose the sudden rush of pleasure he'd felt when he first saw her. "I'm all right, Nadia," he chuckled. "It's just that time has allowed you to forget how ugly I normally am."

"And how full of Gorksroar you are, Brim," she growled, looking up into his face. "You're killing yourself, pure and simple. You should see your eyes—maybe you shouldn't at that. There's more red in 'em than there is white."

"I'm not the only one who looks like that," he said. "Every Defense Command starsailor is the same way—at least the ones who are still alive."

"From the looks of you, Skipper..." she started. Then, biting her lip, she stopped in the middle of her sentence.

"'From the looks of me,' what?" Brim demanded.

"Nothing," she said firmly. "How long's it been since you relaxed with a woman?" she asked. "Naked, I mean."

He laughed. "The last time I tried something like that, we both fell asleep before we could get anything going. Since then... well, the Leaguers have kept everyone pretty busy."

"What are you doing tonight?" she asked.

"I'd planned to catch supper somewhere, then head back to FleetPort 30 in time to catch the Dawn Watch patrol. Only the toughest Leaguers fly when there's bad regional gravity."

"So you're not due back right away, are you?"

He made a sham leer from her chest to her legs. "Well," he said pointedly. "I *ought* to get back and...

She shook her head phlegmatically. "We won't make those kind of plans for tonight, Skipper," she said. "When you and I finally get it on in bed, you're going to do a lot more than sleep," she laughed. "What I'm talking about tonight is making sure you get a decent supper—with all your clothes on, or at least part of 'em."

Brim sighed theatrically. "Seems as if every time we get together, something *always* gets in the way," he said.

"Yeah," she chuckled. "It does seem that way." Then she smiled. "Well," she added with an impudent look, "if you're up to it, you can have a little after-dinner feel."

"First let's see if I last through supper," he said with a tired laugh. Actually, the thought of a few metacycles shared with the personable—and very attractive—middle-aged woman was, well, *stimulating*. He had greatly enjoyed their tour of duty together, and somehow the promise of an evening filled with spicy conversation seemed to be pumping energy into him from Voot knew where. "All right," he agreed. "You tell me where."

Her choice was the quiet, wood-paneled bar of a grand old hotel. Brim found himself immediately comfortable, and even alert, or relatively so. A single musician sat at the console of a massive looking instrument coaxing melodies from out of its depths that made him feel relaxed without being sleepy. "This is wonderful, Number One," he said. "My sincere compliments."

She grinned. "They have great rooms upstairs, too," she said.

"Somehow, I *thought* you might have seen one or two of them."

"Well," she joshed with a smile, "if I had to wait for you to take me up there, I might forget how to do it. And I *don't* mean climb stairs."

"Little danger in your forgetting *that*, I'd bet," Brim said.

"True," she admitted. "It's like riding a kid's gyrocycle, I guess."

"Only more fun."

"Yeah. Lots more . . ."

They shared a moderately expensive bottle of Logish Meem while they dined comfortably on fruits, chutney, cheeses, and yeasty, hard-crusted bread. Like all starsailors who once were shipmates, they shared a special kind of friendship forged in long watches, fierce gravity storms, and a deep, enigmatic love of space itself. Their conversation was reflective, often touching on old acquaintances and their fates. Had he heard any more concerning the fate of Margot Effer'wyck? Had some lucky woman finally stolen Toby Moulding's heart, or was there yet a chance for small, graying Commanders? Was Utrillo Barbousse still running everything?

"And who are you sleeping with these days, Wilf?" she demanded. "I don't mean that in a *literal* sense, either." She made a shy grin. "Has that leggy Carescrian woman—Eve Cartier, that's it—beaten me to bed with you?"

"None of your damned business," Brim replied defensively, but an inadvertent grin and burning cheeks gave him away.

"Aha!" Tissaurd gloated. "You don't have to tell me, I know." She smiled. "Wish I had long legs like that to wrap around a man."

"I'm certain you make up for it in other ways," Brim chuckled.

"Trust me," she said with a smile. Then she frowned. "Cartier's a real Carescrian, isn't she?" she said. "Understand she even used to fly one of Calhoun's, er, *privateers* I think he calls them."

"She did," Brim said. "That's where I met her. But what's this 'real Carescrian' business?"

Now it was Tissaurd who frowned. "I don't know," she said. "Just words that came to mind." Cocking her head, she peered at him as if she were seeing something in him for the first time. Then she raised her eyebrows. "Maybe I do know," she said. "She's not like you. She's *proud* to be a Carescrian; I've never known you to even mention it."

"Well," he said, "I've been working on that."

"Oh?" she replied.

"Yes, xaxtdammit," he said. "I'm beginning to feel all right about being a Carescrian. But I'm also—probably foremost—an Imperial. One who just happens to come from Carescria, that's all. Believe me, the two of us have talked about this a couple of times."

Tissaurd reached across the table and took his hand. "I'm glad to hear that, my future lover," she said. "I've never questioned your 'Imperiality,' if such a word exists. I can't think of anybody who does—except somebody like Puvis Amherst. For xaxt's sake, with *two* Imperial Comets to wear and connections all the way to the throne, you are *unquestionably* an Imperial, Wilf Brim. But there is still one big difference between the two of you—that has nothing to do with what you've got between your respective legs."

"And *that* is?"

"Eve Cartier is finally *proud* her home is Carescria."

"Who says I've got an exclusive on this 'no-home' business?" Brim demanded. "I can't remember you *ever* talking about your home."

She laughed softly and touched his arm. "It's because I've never left my home, Wilf Brim," she said.

"I don't understand," he replied. "I thought you were born in the Lampson Provinces."

"I was" she said with a little grin.

"Then why is it I never hear you talk about them?"

"Because we left there before I was a year old," she explained—then frowned. "Wilf Brim," she said after a moment. "I don't think you spent much time with the personnel records when we served together or you'd know I'm a Fleet brat—both my mother and father were Blue Capes. The *Fleet*'s my home, and I'm proud of it. You, on the other hand, act as if you have no home at all."

"That's damn near the same way Eve talks."

"Hmm. The more I hear about that woman, the more I like her—in spite of her damned long legs."

"I suppose that next you're going to tell me that I'm lonely," he said.

"No," she said. "I'll simply remind you that I said those words a year ago when we were off somewhere in space aboard old *Starfury.*"

Brim nodded. "I guess I do remember that," he said.

"The more you ignore who you are, the more you're going to insulate yourself," she said. "You know, Carescria's pretty well thought of these days."

"When I started in the service, it was the other way 'round, believe you me," he said.

"Oh, I know all that," she said. "But years of war and people like you, Calhoun, and that damned long-legged Cartier have gone a long way toward changing that attitude forever."

"It's not been that easy to forget," he said, realizing immediately that he was being forced down the very same road he'd traveled recently with Eve Cartier. "You weren't there at the Helmsman's Academy when I was. You didn't have to put up with a whole Fleet full of Puvis Amhersts who treated you like dirt no matter how well you did.'' He ground his teeth. ''It wasn't easy to be a Carescrian those days, and now it's hard to forget.''

''But denying Carescria, you direct the anger I just heard against the *Carescrians* themselves—not the people who made trouble for you.''

''I know,'' he said. ''She told me that, too.''

''Did she *also* tell you it's that same anger that makes you lonely?'' she asked.

''No,'' he admitted. ''She didn't. But then, who's to say you're right? Maybe anger hasn't anything to do with it.''

'' 'It,' '' she said, snatching at his word. ''Then you admit that you're a lonely man, do you?''

Flustered, Brim shook his head and prudently decided to sidestep the whole thing. ''No,'' he said. ''I admit to nothing except that I'll soon be too heavy-lidded to get myself back to the shuttle station.'' He grinned. ''How about a lift to the Fleet base on Lake Mersin in that finagled skimmer of yours?''

''All right, Skipper,'' Tissaurd said in resignation, ''I'll drop it for now. Hang on till I pay the bill and . . . stop off in the loo.''

''I'll be the one snoozing in the lobby,'' Brim said, this time only half in jest. He had a rather deadly war waiting for him, and desperately needed at least a few metacycles sleep to ready himself for it.

It was late when they pulled up in a parking lot, some distance from a portable gravity pad where the Night Watch shuttle tested its mooring in the damp autumn breeze coming off Lake Mersin. Most of the other small craft had long since departed. As she set the gravity brake, she smiled at him and opened the door. ''I'll walk you to your ship,'' she said. ''I wouldn't want you to fall asleep in the lot here.''

Brim smiled. ''I'm sorry I wasn't better company on the ride out here,'' he said. ''I'm simply worn out—physically and mentally.''

"You're always good company, my ex-Skipper," she said, taking his hand and starting across the concrete apron. "Sometimes, you don't always *need* to talk."

"Thanks," he said simply. He appreciated her, too.

Halfway across, she paused for a moment to look around, then drew him into the shadow of a large tool crib. "About that dessert, Captain Brim," she said with an impish little smile. "Still interested?"

He frowned. "Dessert?" he asked, then he closed his eyes and smiled. "Oh, You mean? . . ."

Looking directly into his eyes, Tissaurd opened her Fleet cloak. Beneath, she wore only crimson briefs.

"Good grief," Brim muttered. He had often fantasized about the diminutive officer, who had once—jokingly?—revealed her bosom to him in a dim, crowded bar. But his imagination had done her little justice. She was absolutely gorgeous. Her prominent breasts stood out like those of a woman half her age, tipped with the tiny, dark brown nipples that had never really faded from his mind's eye. She had a chunky torso, and though her legs were certainly short compared to Eve Cartier's, they were perfectly proportioned to the rest of her—at least what he could see of them above her high-heeled boots.

Pushing aside the Fleet Cloak, he embraced her nakedness and—for the first time—kissed her as a woman. Instantly, an overpowering thrill pierced him to his very soul. Even her breath tasted of passion as she thrust her tongue again and again into his open mouth. "Nadia," he whispered after a time. "You are magnificent."

"So are you, Wilf Brim," she gasped, pushing him to an arm's length. "And I definitely *do* want to keep you alive, so we are going to have to end this very quickly."

Brim nodded. Roused as he was, he knew fatigue would catch up with him all too soon.

"You haven't touched me, yet," she said, glancing down at her crimson briefs.

"Will you take those off for me?" he asked.

Without a word, she bent down and slid them to her ankles,

stepping daintily out of each leg hole. Then she stood, waiting while she held her cloak open to reveal a great triangle of dark thatch. "Now, my sexy Carescrian," she said. "So you don't forget that we have a date in bed someday . . ."

Dumbfounded, he stooped while she took his hand and, crouching slightly, slid it to her crotch where his fingers were immersed in a veritable puddle of thick, warm liquid.

She gasped for a moment as he explored more deeply, then once more covered his mouth with hers, gently probing with her tongue while her breathing became more and more strenuous. Abruptly, she stiffened and pushed him away. "No more!" she panted, drawing her legs together and rolling her pelvis almost violently. "Not until you are really in me."

Heart thundering in his ears, Brim ground his teeth while he fought his own near eruption to a standstill. "Sweet, Holy Mother of the Universe," he whispered in weak-kneed awe of the passion the tiny woman had managed to stoke within him.

After a while, she drew her Fleet Cloak closed and smiled again. "Just remember next time, Wilf Brim," she gulped, "that I prefer to take a *lot* longer getting this wet. Passion is like a fine old Logish Meem—to be *savored*, not downed in a single gulp."

"I'll remember," Brim said.

"I trust you will, Skipper," she said. Then she turned and pecked him on the cheek. "Now, just to be certain that we eventually *do* get to have our fun, I'm going to suggest that from here you walk *directly* to the shuttle." As she pushed him forward, she whispered, "one of these days, Skipper . . ."

He blew her a kiss as he started across the tarmac. "One of these days, Number One," he whispered back.

If he lived that long . . .

CHAPTER 9

Hope

Brim never did remember how he managed to find his way once he reached FleetPort 30. But early in the Dawn Watch, he was jarringly awakened in his own bunk by wailing sirens and groggily donned his battlesuit while he ran for the boarding tube. By working the clock around, 610's mechanics and engineers had kept their promise to muster eight more-or-less flyable Starfuries, including one for him—battered old R6495. He arrived at the ship just after Barbousse. The remainder of the tired starsailors dragged themselves aboard within the next few moments, and they had the ship well away from the satellite before the day's first raids began. Brim was still gulping down his first searing cup of cvceese' while he maneuvered into position for his day's first intercept.

They met their first Leaguers some eighteen thousand c'lenyts away from the Triad—thirty yellow-nosed Gorn-Hoff 262-Es running well below LightSpeed at about the same altitude. As the Leaguers curved around to meet them, Brim ordered his ships into line astern, then turned for an intercept. He dropped the nose of his Starfury and could almost feel the first Leaguer Helmsman pushing forward on his own controls to bring more disruptors to bear. In the next moment, he hauled back hard and led his seven battered veterans over the Leaguers in a steep, climbing turn to the left. Goreman loosed a salvo at the leading Gorn-Hoff, which immediately did a half roll—directly into the kill zone of Makira Cristobol's D7192, flying just off Brim's port side. Her gunners must have fired at full deflection, but they did it well. In the corner of his eye, Brim saw the big Gorn-Hoff give off a crimson jet of radiation fire, then it flicked out of sight.

After only a few cycles of furious action, the Leaguers turned and made off at a dead run toward Effer'wyck. Shortly afterward, however, reports began to flood in that FleetPort 30 was under attack again. By that time, Brim and his squadrons were too far away to assist in the satellite's defense, so all he could do was to listen helplessly as the damage reports came in.

When he finally led his ragged little squadron home, he could see the damage a long way off. Temporary blue pressure patches glared everywhere among the large areas of gray residue from radiation fires. The Boreal antenna field was now reduced to blackened stumps mounted on skeletal remains of what used to be the new communications room. Fully a third of the docking tube had been destroyed. The great satellite had acquired a tattered look, and it was immediately clear to see that only a single squadron could continue operations from its reduced facilities.

Brim made the decision to stay on with Moulding, and directed Arnm to take his Defiants on spinward where he could double up at nearby FleetPort 41. Then he ordered every remaining man and woman to the job of repairing the base, and before the end of Twilight Watch, there was not a single opening to be seen in the structurally sound parts of the satellite. Pressurization tests were under way by early morning while several unexploded torpedoes were marked off, and the patched boarding corridors were given a coat of bright yellow paint. Thus it was that by evening there was little to show for the Leaguers' accurate shooting. The rapid mending represented even more proof that the Leaguers were heading toward ultimate failure in their efforts to wipe out the FleetPort orbital bases. *If,* the dog-tired Imperial defenders could hold out long enough for that failure to occur.

Next day, however, the TSIB contained a chilling report: for the first time in nearly three weeks, Defense Command had lost more ships than the Leaguers—fourteen to fifteen. Moreover, the number of operational Imperial starships had also declined: from 701 to 690 in a single day. Five crews had been lost completely and another eleven nearly decimated. Even more alarmingly, signs of the terrific strain on the crews were beginning to show up in accidents and deaths from faulty judgment brought about by total exhaustion. That afternoon, flying one of the base hacks, even Brim had a serious near miss when he almost collided with a freighter during a takeoff run from Lake Mersin. Clearly, both men and machines were rapidly approaching their physical limits.

But in the very face of looming disaster, Brim's overall assessment of the war remained optimistic—especially concerning Leaguer starship crews. They were now exhibiting a much greater tendency to turn tail when attacked, in great contrast to their earlier performances, when they pressed the war with utmost determination. Clearly, morale was beginning to sag in Effer'wyck. He thought about what he'd heard concerning Kirsh Valentin, his old adversary—and arguably one of finest warriors in the enemy camp. If someone of *his* caliber was disillusioned about the war, what could the situation be among lesser individuals?

During the Evening Watch, Onrad stormed through on one of his whirlwind inspection and confidence-building tours. Before he piped off, he took Brim aside in his office where he told of a worrisome report from Calhoun warning that the Imperial Fleet might run out of crews if the League continued its attacks. "What's your take?" he asked, perching on the corner of Brim's desk and frowning. "I want to check this information with somebody who's actively involved in the fighting."

Brim frowned. "Well, Your Majesty," he mused, looking bleakly at his boots, "Voot knows we have no complaints about the replacement situation. We get new ships and crews as fast as we lose them. But if something doesn't give pretty soon, you could run out of *veterans*. It's brutal out there."

Onrad pursed his lips and nodded. "I can see that, Brim," he replied. "In the years I've known you, I have never seen you look so utterly tired—not even back at old Gimmas Haefdon during the last war." He stared off into another time and place, clearly finding it difficult to choose the right words. "People in the streets below see you Blue Capes through a thick pane of romance." he said with a grimace. "But by the very Universe, it must be hideous fighting for your very life every cycle of every day."

"I plan to survive," Brim said, mustering up the most confident look he could manage.

"You'd better, Brim," the Emperor replied. "I'm personally counting on your survival—along with many of your colleagues." He paced the floor for a moment. "In spite of Calhoun's worries—which I appreciate," he added forcefully, "we have every right to be damned well satisfied with our present results. I'm tempted to ask the old rascal why the enemy should continue attacks on this heavy scale if it doesn't represent something like his maximum effort—while our Fleet gets stronger with every passing day." He pointed a stubby finger at Brim. "And don't forget, my Carescrian friend, this little talk isn't intended as morale-boosting propaganda. I'm saying these words in the seclusion of your office—not on some public broadcast. I really believe them..."

Later, however, soon after Onrad departed for FleetPort 11, Brim found time to read a special intelligence bulletin warning that the Sodeskayans now predicted still another change in League tactics. And the latest reconnaissance starships were reporting that even more League attack ships had arrived at forward bases in Effer'wyck. With all *that* good news, he found it quite difficult to take much comfort in the Emperor's optimistic words—especially since nothing had arrived from Ursis concerning the captured crystals. If Defense Command didn't stop the Leaguers' attacks soon, there wouldn't be much Empire left to defend.

All through the next Dawn and Morning Watches, Leaguer media broadcasts showed fat Admiral Hoth Orgoth grandly touring the occupied City of Courts in Effer'wyck during a top-level conference with his Wing Commanders. Brim watched from what remained of the FleetPort 30 wardroom. Newscasters could only speculate about precisely what was being discussed at the highly publicized conference, but Brim was somehow certain it had to do with the change in strategy the Sodeskayans were predicting.

Throughout the three days that followed, League raiders continued their savage attacks on Imperial Fleet Starbases, and late on 5 Nonad, Triannic himself made an unusual speech from the great stadium that had been built for the Mitchell Trophy races a few years back. Brim expected it would be another round of chest thumping, but no sooner had the tyrant mounted the podium (before at least half a million cheering Leaguers) than he loudly began to inveigh against the Imperial counterraids that Onrad had personally ordered on the Leaguer capital. They were occurring with ever-increasing frequency and must have resulted in serious pressure on his minion, Hoth Orgoth, who had bragged publicly—on a number of occasions—that enemy starships would never fly above the city.

The seventh of Nonad began with nearly 170 Leaguer starships aiming for FleetPort 30 and bases nearby, but Starfuries and Defiants put up such a fight that little damage was done at all. Mysteriously, the Leaguers appeared unwilling to press their attacks with anything that approached their former determination. It seemed strange to Brim that such consummate warriors would slack off before they accomplished any of their stated objectives—especially that of crippling FleetPort satellites. More logically, he surmised, they were probably flying cover while they practiced other, more depredating activities to come, although he was hard-pressed to fathom what *they* might be.

That night—Avalon's night—the city was deliberately fired on (among a number of other targets throughout the Triad). Sixty-eight heavy attack ships with a huge escort raided the great space harbor, inflicting major destruction over a wide area. Afterward, as Brim exhaustedly warped his Starfury into a repair dock—he had taken five hits during a furious dogfight with five Gorn-Hoff 262s—he could see huge fires blazing on the dark surface below, but compared to previous raids, the attack had been almost inconsequential, and once more carried out in a lackluster fashion. When the last Leaguers had faded from the BKAEW displays, he climbed into his bunk with strange premonitions, unable to shake his morning conviction that these strange raids were not at all the best efforts of a superb war machine like Triannic's. For his money, the Leaguers were merely keeping up the pretense of war while they prepared something they felt would be a *lot* more virulent.

According to the next morning's TSIB, fighting the previous day cost twenty-three Imperial starships, but at the same time the Leaguers lost thirty-five. And Defense Command now had a total of 694 operational starships, 2 more than they started with the previous day. As Onrad perceived early on, the Imperials were operating in superb fashion, in spite of their chronic stress and fatigue.

However—at least for Brim—the good news was completely overshadowed by communiqués reporting the fall of Ordu. He ground his teeth as he imagined arrogant troopers from The Torond parading along the ancient streets. And after the parades . . . He shuddered to think about that and thanked the very universe that Raddisma and his child were safe in Atalanta—or at least as safe as they might be *anywhere* during the kind of war the Leaguers were spreading throughout the galaxy . . . .

During the next few metacycles, Leaguer activity near Avalon dwindled and soon ceased completely. After the BKAEW had been completely clear for more than two metacycles, all Imperial killer ships were ordered back to their FleetPorts. Again, Brim found himself in a quandary as to the Leaguers' intentions. It didn't take a Drive scientist to figure out that if they kept blasting at the FleetPorts long enough, they'd eventually put Defense Command out of business—for no other reason than there would be no more bases from which to operate. And with the fall of Fluvanna's capital, whole fleets of Leaguer ships could soon be added to the effort; even their slowest attack cruisers required no more than eight or nine days for the trip from Ordu.

Across the 'Wyckean Void in Effer'wyck, however, it turned out that nothing had stopped at all—except the actual raids. Imperial reconnaissance ships were soon reporting that Occupied Effer'wyck had become a literal beehive of activity—more than 600 attack ships and nearly 650 escort killer ships were being prepared at a furious pace all over the prostrate dominion.

In the midday TSIB, Sodeskayan Intelligence Command was quoted as having intercepted numerous Leaguer operational orders issued to Effer'wyckean squadrons. Many of these began, "In the evening of the twelfth day of Nonad, the League Space Arm will conduct a major strike against target Loge." The Bears were not certain what "Loge" stood for, but their guess was *Avalon*.

The Imperials agreed. So did Brim. *That* was what Orgoth was practicing for. . . .

During the late afternoon that day, Nergol Triannic and Rogan LaKarn tied up all KA'PPA channels for half a metacycle to announce their "joint" victory in Fluvanna. But more importantly, at the same time as the broadcasts—by design or by chance, Brim wondered—initial waves of some 150 Leaguer ships arrived over Avalon City, catching many of the defending squadrons unprepared. Soon afterward, another 150 starships arrived on their heels, circling slowly—almost majestically—'round and 'round the great metropolis in perfect formation. Then, in a series of devastating waves, they attacked.

On the surface, tremendous explosions erupted everywhere while more League formations approached. They came arrogantly in parallel lines, about two or three c'lenyts apart, with Trodler and Kreissel battleships escorted by GH 270As flying close behind them. Thundering above the city center, they banked, then flew back over the space harbor on Lake Mersin. Moments later, murderous disruptor fire landed on the vast gravity pool areas and among crowded houses in the streets beyond. And unlike their rather deceitful performance in many of the more recent raids, the Leaguers were now pressing for their targets with their old determination. Moreover, the prodigious marksmanship the crystals afforded them was having a devastating effect below. As he chased one Trodler TR 215 nearly all the way to the surface, Brim could see that whole suburbs appeared to be burning. By early evening, a vast white cloud of smoke—easily visible from orbit—covered the sprawling space-dock area, tinged black at the edge with flames licking at its base. While the planet's light/dark terminator slowly worked its way to spinward, the smoke turned into a heavy overcast, lighted from below by the raging fires.

Just after darkness at half a million irals altitude, Brim was climbing back from a low-level dogfight (during which both he and Goreman had lost a GH 262 against the ground clutter) when he found a squadron of Defiants flying in sections of stepped-up threes, but with no rear guard. He joined in—and moments later learned the truth of the old warning "beware of a fight 'gainst the light." He was making sweeps from side to side and peering earnestly into the rearview display when from out of the blinding Triad—and dead astern—disruptor flashes began sparkling along his port pontoon.

While shouts of pain and surprise filled the voice circuits, he ground his teeth and curved sharply onto a spin, simultaneously ordering Norgate, the COMM operator, to KA'PPA warning to the Defiants. Having apparently lost his assailant, he called for a damage estimate and started to climb again. But even before Chief Kondrashen could call back with an evaluation, flames began to pour from the pontoon, and soon the control-bridge environmental system began to disgorge whiffets of rank-smelling smoke, as if entire logic systems had melted.

Ordering the lifeglobes activated, he warned the crew they might need to abandon ship, then started for FleetPort 48 where there was an extensive repair facility. Soon, however, he realized he wasn't going to make that either—he had the gravs running at full boost and was still losing altitude steadily. By the same token, whenever he attempted even a slight turn, something in the hull set up a frightening vibration that made a mockery of his navigation systems. The only choices remaining to him were to order the crew out in lifeglobes—a risky thing at low altitudes—or put the ship down on Lake Mersin, which he could just make out ahead, reflecting the light of the burning city. The radio was no longer any help. Like his KA'PPA, it was now useless, having degraded to a cacophony of cracking and whistlings. He bit his lip while he gathered himself for the miracle he would have to accomplish were he to set the ship down without losing more lives than he already had.

When he reduced power to the gravs, the vibration gradually diminished. He'd clearly caught additional bursts near the steering engine, although the damage-control teams had yet to report it. Outside, one of Avalon's four satellites had risen and seemed to be rolling over a suburban landscape submerged in clouds of smoke. Somehow, his mind turned to Eve Cartier—if she were even alive after the day's battles. How wonderful it would be to be comforted by that beautiful, gentle woman with whom he shared so much. He had a crazy, desperate urge to put his cheek to her nurturing breasts . . .

Dragging himself back to reality, he set course for the conflagrations along the Mersin waterfront, following the banks of the Grand Achtite Canal. For long moments, he concentrated on his readouts; they seemed to have gone haywire. His faithful allies—radio altimeter, attitude indicator, pressure, and temperature all mocked him with zero readings.

"Attention all hands! Attention all hands," he warned over the blower—almost as if someone else were saying the words.

"All hands prepare for crash landfall. Secure airtight doors and set battlesuits for minimum freedom. Repeat. Secure airtight doors and set battlesuits for minimum freedom."

The Grand Achtite Canal blazed with lurid reflections of the fires ahead as Larkin, the COMM officer, tried six different radio frequencies. He called the Mersin Fleet Base and even FleetPort 30—with no answer. Everything appeared to be burned out; no radio, no identification, no recognition lights. In moments, the city's anti-starship disruptors would open up on him—they'd be tracking him now, waiting for the last possible moment before firing. Anything as low as he was might as well be a friendly in trouble. If they only knew!

Then, with a great thumping, the gravs seemed to lose most of their remaining power—clearly a second massive control center failure. Now he wasn't going to make it to Lake Mersin by any stretch of the imagination. He would have to ditch in the canal!

Abruptly, the sky around him came alive with light as what must have been every disruptor in the area opened up at him. Universe! Couldn't the deaf bastards below recognize the sound of Admiralty gravs? He turned on his landing lights—miraculously, those worked—then wobbled over what appeared to be a military installation of some kind, waggling the Starfury's pontoons to show he was in difficulties and . . .

At last! The firing stopped and moments later a thousand canal side street lamps blazed into glorious brilliance. No more than a c'lenyt ahead was one of the canal's turning basins—almost as good as a vector on Lake Mersin.

Mechanically he started his approach—a quick one with forty-five degrees of lift modification. The Starfury responded sluggishly. He concentrated his whole being on bringing the mangled ship—and what remained of her plucky crew—to a safe landfall. Ordering all nonessential systems shut down immediately, he leveled off between the two rows of street lamps whizzing past the side Hyperscreens. At all costs, he had to remain calm—no matter how much adrenaline his tired body had pumped into his bloodstream. A lump in his throat threatened to stifle him . . . careful . . . mustn't let her slip off the gravity foot now! Ahead, the street lamps suddenly widened into the turning basin. Gingerly, he tried to set her down in the first few irals past the mouth. A tiny tow barge flashed under the starship's belly, and for one wild moment, Brim could see through the eyes of its crew as his huge starship thundered out of nowhere only irals above their mastheads.

"All hands," he warned over the blower—as if they didn't know what was coming. "All hands set battlesuits for minimum freedom and prepare for immediate crash landfall . . ."

Now or never! He rammed down the nose to lift the tail and with the steering engine deliberately stuck the ruined starboard pontoon in to take up some of the shock. Perhaps that would prevent him from turning over.

On impact, Brim's veteran Starfury smashed down with all its twenty-seven thousand milstons displacement. At first, there was a terrific shock. The huge machine bounced up, hurtling him painfully against his restraints and the side of his recliner. A great expanse of hullmetal tore off the bow and passed within daggers of the top Hyperscreens. The pontoon separated with a deafening, shrieking pandemonium. Instinctively, he crossed his arms in front of his faceplate. A second terrific scraping screech and the whole Universe outside disappeared behind towering walls of water. Then came a jolt of such violence that he broke through his restraints, thumbing his own battlesuit to MINIMUM FREEDOM even as he smashed headlong into the instrument panel. The Universe dissolved into a sheet of red pockmarked with glittering points of light.

Then silence. Sudden—stunning—silence that lasted as long as the initial shock. After that, the voice circuits again filled with cries of pain and terror. Through the cracked Hyperscreens, Brim could see that the Starfury had come to rest nose down and canted steeply to port. He pushed his way out of his recliner and carefully stood with one foot on the arm and the other on the deck, peering around in the dim light of the ship's emergency lighting system. Many of the bridge crew were already making their way aft toward the companionway hatch, but a number of still forms remained slumped at their consoles. Opening his visor for a moment, he could smell the ship burning somewhere, and a bright flickering light was already reflecting from the water—only a few irals below the port Hyperscreens. Not that there was much to burn on a Starfury, but as the collapsium-96 hullmetal "uncollapsed" in the presence of oxygen, the terrific heat generated tended to set everything around it ablaze, too. He shut his visor and began to follow the others aft toward the companionway over and around the consoles that only a few metacycles ago seemed to have been so cleverly placed. He stopped at a number of "occupied" consoles, but managed to rouse only one other soul, whom he pushed groggily before him.

Abruptly, the companionway hatch burst open, and at least ten figures in battlesuits burst into the ruined bridge in front of a white-hot brightness. Trapped by the fire! In the lurid flickering, he could see that the last one through the hatch was Barbousse—who immediately slammed it shut and dogged it tight.

"Cap'm Brim," he shouted—silencing the clamor that now filled the voice circuits, "is that you?"

"It is, Chief," Brim growled from his headset. "Looks like the companionway isn't an option anymore."

"Right you are, sir," Barbousse replied. "An' this bridge won't be in a couple o' cycles, either. Fire's really spreadin' back there—fast."

Brim turned, started retracing his path to the forward end of the bridge. "Gotta take out a Hyperscreen panel," he said, looking around for something—anything—to use as a truncheon. A globular display had come loose on impact and lay smashed against the forward bulkhead near his feet. Grasping its heavy metal base, he climbed back into his dizzily canted seat and began to smash against the quarter panel. Its thick crystal was cracked in a number of places, but it stubbornly resisted his blows. Again he hit it. And again. Abruptly, a lurid brilliance filled the bridge—the radiation fire had claimed the aft bulkhead. Desperately, he smashed at the Hyperscreen again. There were only a few moments until they all fried in their battlesuits.

"Cap'm," Barbousse said. "Can I try?"

Shaking from his efforts, Brim climbed out of the seat. "Give it a go, Chief," he panted.

"Aye, sir," Barbousse said. Raising the blast pike he'd been carrying, he effortlessly blasted the crystal from its frame in a midst of glittering shards. Then with the butt of the powerful weapon, he carefully smoothed off the jagged edges that remained in the frame. "A little noisy," he observed, ushering the survivors out and into the water, "but there's nothin' better than a blast pike for openin' Hyperscreens."

Brim had to chuckle in spite of himself. "You make quite a point there," he said, waiting until the big rating had exited before he took one last look around the bridge—the radiation fire was now only a few irals away. He scrambled out onto the deck and jumped into the flame-lit water. As his battlesuit bobbed him to the surface, he took one last look at the Starfury, towering over him—a smoking, crumpling skeleton that blazed gruesomely from stem to stern. Then he swam as quickly as possible to the slimy stone breakwater of the turning basin where eager hands reached out and dragged him onto dry land.

Around him, the great city of Avalon was also in flames. Acrid smoke assaulted his nostrils as soon as he opened his helmet while huge, pear-shaped bursts of flame rose up above the horizon of blazing goods houses that surrounded the turning basin. Thunderous, deafening explosions erupted from nearby disruptor hits and the heat on his face felt as though he were standing in an oven. He looked at the pitifully small gathering around him while debris pattered and clicked to the pavement around him.

"What're we going to do?" someone asked shakily on the voice circuits.

Someone else was sobbing in his helmet. "This is *awful,*" another groaned.

"Quit grumbling and feel thankful you've got battlesuits to wear," Brim growled. "The Chief and I are going to use ours to see if we can help people who don't have them. I suggest the rest of you split up into pairs and do the same. We'll meet back here . . ." He checked the cheap timepiece he'd purchased to replace the good one he'd lost in Effer'wyck. It was broken already. "At dawn," he finished. "Now get snapping. All of you! The Fleet isn't paying us to lollygag around watching fires. Got that?"

"Aye, Skipper . . ."

"Got that, Captain."

"See you at dawn, Captain."

In moments, they were gone. Grimly, Brim nodded to Barbousse. "All right, Chief," he said, "let's see what we can do." With that he began jogging along a street that was a better vision of Hell than the worst apparition that had ever slithered from the nightmares of a religious zealot. The final raider departed nearly sixteen metacycles after the attacks began, and for the remainder of his life, Brim's dreams were haunted by the images of that lurid night filled with horror . . .

As dawn came to Avalon City on that first anniversary of the Imperial declaration of war, the sky remained nearly dark with heavy layers of smoke. Everything still appeared to be blazing, and it seemed as if the valiant, all-night efforts of the Imperial fire brigades had amounted to nothing at all. As Brim and Barbousse wearily returned to the ship with singed and blackened battlesuits, they watched men, women, and children begin to emerge from their holes into the gray, smoke-filled morning. Nothing seemed to have escaped the Leaguers' fury.

They were the last to reach the crash site, though it was inarguably clear that the other members of the crew had likewise spent the night assisting the stricken city in any way they could. Three were missing, two of whom had seemingly disappeared from the face of the planet. The third was last seen entering a burning building moments before it collapsed. The ship itself had been reduced to a pile of twisted wreckage protruding awkwardly from the turning basin some two hundred irals from the seawall.

Brim led the battered little group on foot nearly ten c'lenyts to the Lake Mersin Fleet Base, where he immediately checked in with FleetPort 30 and set up return transportation for himself and his crew. The Leaguers would surely return—as soon as they possibly could. And after he saw what kind of damage they could cause, he was anxious to get back behind the helm of a Starfury again. He had a *number* of personal accounts to settle, and he wasn't at all selective about which Leaguers began to pay.

Unfortunately—at least in Brim's way of thinking—as soon as his whereabouts became known, Calhoun dispatched a staff skimmer to bring him to a special Admiralty conference for Emperor Onrad. But just as the driver pulled up to the debris-strewn entrance to the skimmer pool, one of the seemingly tireless reception aides shouted across the lobby, "Captain Brim—there's a call for you. Do you want to take it here?"

Brim nodded and signaled the driver to wait, then strode across the lobby to a bank of HoloPhones. "Switch it to this one, mister," she said, enabling the display and pressing the RECEIVE zone. Immediately, a tiny image of Eve Cartier appeared above the transceiver. She looked awful, as if she had been crying all night.

"Wilf?" she said through swollen eyes, "I'd heard you were down an' there were no survivors at the wreck." As she spoke, her eyes filled with tears and she buried her nose in a large handkerchief. "Thank the Universe you're all right," she said muzzily. "I thought you were . . . dead."

Brim bit his lip, touched to his very heart that someone cared that much about him. "I've got a lang habit o' living, Eve," he said quietly with his old Carescrian burr. "'Tis made me quite indisposed toward death."

She blew her nose and took the handkerchief from her face. "Stay that way, my very special Carescrian friend. I'm afraid I've become exceptionally attached to you lately."

"And I to you, Eve," he admitted. "The terrible thing is that we can't let ourselves feel that way. Our only chance of survivin' this war is to consider ourselves already dead. Either that or stop fightin' an' try to hide out somewhere safe till it's over."

She nodded an wiped her eyes again. "The coward's way out," she whispered. "Neither o' us could live that way either—that would be *worse* than death."

"Then don't—for Voot's sake—don't get attached to me." he said earnestly. "Not in the middle of this madness, anyhow. Otherwise, *you're* liable to end up dead." He shut his eyes for a moment, silently grinding his teeth. "And," he added presently, "though I'm not attached to you either, by the Universe if I'm still alive when this war ends, I will be then." He smiled while she blew her nose again. "But in the meanwhile," he whispered behind his hand, "I'll be glad to take your clothes off for you—anytime you'd like."

This time, she smiled a little, too. "You'll do mare than just that, won't you?" she asked.

"Try me," he said.

"I will," she promised, "next time we're together. An' the next time after that, too. Whenever you want me. Just be careful, Wilf Brim."

Brim glanced up as the driver stepped into the lobby. "I'm coming," he called across the lobby. Then he looked at her in the display. "You be careful, too, my beautiful friend—and may Fortune smile on your every move."

"Smile, my foot," she whispered with a wicked little smile. "I want him right here between my legs."

"I'm not so sure Fortune's a male," Brim broke in. "But leave that part to me, anyway."

"Mmm," she said, blushing visibly. "Yes, you, er, certainly, ha' a certain talent in *that* department."

"Those great legs help a lot," Brim replied with a nod to the driver, who was now actively indicating the door with his head. "But I'm afraid I'm going to have to go now."

"Thanks for being there," she said softly.

"Thanks for calling, Eve," he replied.

She blew him a kiss and the display went dark.

It took the driver nearly two metacycles to pick his way

through the six c'lenyts of rubble-strewn streets to the Admiralty—normally a fifteen-cycle drive. Avalon would never be the same again. . . .

Before he was called on to speak at the meeting, Brim discovered that the huge raid had reawakened invasion jitters throughout the High Command and Onrad's War Cabinet. In Hagbut's view, the tremendous disruptor bombardment was merely a softening-up operation. Calhoun, on the other hand, was not at all certain that he agreed. In fact, his judgment was that with the new direction of the war, luck had at last smiled on the hard-pressed Empire.

"*Egad*, man!" Hagbut barked out, clearly horrified by the Fleet Commander's point of view. "Can you *see* what's going on out there? By Universe, those bloody Leaguers are now blindly slaughtering innocent civilians right and left—even *children*! Have you no feelings at all?"

Calhoun stood with a grim look on his handsome face, and ignoring the Emperor completely, glowered down at the bantam General—who inadvertently shrank back in his chair.

"Yes, General," he answered quietly. "I ha' seen outside. The methodical Leaguers ha' noo switched their attacks from my vital FleetPorts to the cities below," he said. "An' you needn't tell me aboot human sufferin'," he continued. "In the short run, it's clearly been increased a thousandfold. But the *important* point is not the short run—wars aren't won in the short run. That suffering is not in vain, for in the *long* run, Orgoth's switch to attackin' the cities means an end to any chance that Triannic's Deep Space Fleet can achieve space supremacy by shuttin' down our FleetPorts. *An'*," he added significantly, "that very supremacy is vital to any invasion plans the Leaguers might have. In other words, gentlemen," he said, looking over the two tables of men and women seated in the small, underground conference room, "today, we have begun winnin' the war!"

* * *

After the meeting, Onrad separated himself from the circle of high-ranking staff officers and ministers who normally surrounded him at the door and took Brim by the arm. "Valuable input, this morning, my Carescrian friend," he said, leading the way down a corridor, "although it's a damned shame you had to be shot down to get those insights. You lose many of the crew?"

"A little less than half, Your Majesty," Brim said. "And three of them were killed helping out in the city last night after we crashed."

Onrad nodded. "I heard about your orders after the crash," he said. "Those people of yours—they did a lot of good. So did you and Barbousse."

"Thank you, Your Majesty," Brim said.

"Once again it is I who must thank *you*, Brim," the Emperor said. "You and those people you ordered into the flames were seen by a lot of people. More than you—or they—can imagine. Most people were afraid to come out of their holes. But because of the risks you and your crew took, literally hundreds of people in that devastated area know that *somebody* official cares about them. That's *terrifically* important, for there were far too few municipal firefighters to go around last night. And a number of them were hurt or killed doing their duty, so we won't be able to muster even *that* many tonight."

"And there *will* be a raid tonight," Brim added.

"According to the latest BKAEW reports," Onrad said "the first waves are on the way even as we speak." By that time, they—and a hundred nervous-looking bodyguards, it seemed—had emerged from a tunnel onto one of the city streets nearby the Admiralty.

Everywhere around them there were red-eyed, filthy men and women clearing debris from the previous raid. They stopped in their tracks and stared as the Emperor peered at the destruction. Then, suddenly they began to cheer. "Long live the Emperor!" they cried as if they were embarrassed for him to see the devastation in which they stood. "Long live Onrad the Fifth!"

Brim struggled to keep his emotions under control. By the Universe, he thought as tears of pride burned his eyes, the Leaguers would never tame these people. *Never.*

Suddenly, at his side Onrad put his military cap on the end of his scepter and twirled it around in the air, bellowing, "Are we downhearted?"

The Avalonians replied with a rousing chorus of "No!" and "Never!"

Nor, Brim thought with a smile of pride, would the Leaguers ever tame the *Emperor,* either. By subjecting these people to such terror and havoc, Nergol Triannic had just made it *very* necessary to win the war he had started. For if eventually he lost, this raid had become the signature on death warrants for every city in the League—and those of its allies.

On the way back through the tunnel to Onrad's war cabinet room, the Emperor snapped his fingers. "Oh, yes, Wilf," he said as if he were simply passing the time of day, "that reminds me."

Brim wondered what "that" was, but amiably kept his silence, interested more in what the Emperor was reminded *of.*

"You remember that absolutely beautiful woman who serves as the Nabob's Principal Consort—Raddisma, or some such silly name?"

Did he *remember* . . . ? "Aye, Your Majesty," he replied, at pains to act as though he were only midly interested, "I remember her."

"Well," the Emperor continued, "of all things, it turns out that the old rascal's got her preggers—and she's just about at term. So I decided to move their government-in-exile here to Avalon." He grimaced and shook his head. "I hope that doesn't turn out to be a mistake." Then he shrugged and looked at Brim. "It's too late to worry about any of that—they're due sometime tomorrow. I think you met what's her name—Raddisma—during your days in the IVG. Saved her life or something like that. Anyway, I thought you might like to say hello when they arrive."

Brim felt his cheeks burn. "Er, I certainly would," he replied as they emerged once again into the Admiralty. "If I'm not flying," he added a little guiltily.

"Good," Onrad said. "I'll have Colonel Zapt leave you a

message at FleetPort 30 when they arrive.'' He grinned. ''You can then consider yourself summoned to an urgent staff meeting here at the palace by royal fiat. The meeting will be canceled by the time you arrive, but then—since you're already here—you'll be required to visit the Fluvannians. All right?''

''Thank you, Your Majesty,'' Brim replied.

At that, Onrad peered across the floor toward a small armada of very important-looking people bearing down at them. ''Time to play Emperor again,'' he said, rolling his eyes. ''It's how I earn my modest living.'' Then he winked. ''But the job's a lot safer than slugging it out toe to toe with a lot of bloody Leaguers, which is what *you're* going back to, my Carescrian friend. So I think I'll make the most of it. I'll be in touch.'' With that, he turned and strode off across the great marble floor.

On his way to the entrance, Brim thought about what the Emperor had called him—''my Carescrian friend.'' Only weeks ago, that would have rankled him. A lot. Now? Well . . . he had to admit that it didn't bother him a bit. Come to think of it, he rather liked the appellation. Emperors usually didn't have Carescrian friends. And this one did.

He smiled as he walked toward the transportation desk to find himself a ride to the FleetPort shuttle. Eve Cartier—and, in her own way, his old friend Nadia Tissaurd—had managed to have quite an effect on his life. He frowned. He'd never before let people tinker with his inner workings. Was it the Universe that was changing—or was it him?

Before he departed in the shuttle, Brim learned that the Leaguers had lost forty-one starships during their savage attacks on the city, compared with only twenty-eight lost by the defenders during that same time period. Good news, by all estimations—but it *did* rankle him that he had personally piloted one of those twenty-eight. He resolved there and then that he would make the Leaguers suffer greatly for *that* particular indignity.

* * *

Clearly encouraged by their own propaganda, the Leaguers launched a second day of massive raids against Avalon City shortly after dawn, causing considerable harm from the first shot onward. Without an available Starfury to skipper, Brim could only watch helplessly, waiting for either replacement ships to arrive or another Starfury to be released from the maintenance hangar.

Neither occurred before the unscheduled arrival of a large Sodeskayan starship . . .

Brim had been working most of the afternoon to whittle down a great stack of documents Barbousse earlier shunted to his "signature" queue. It meant understanding—on an individual basis—such war-winning items as "Budget Considerations for the Overuse of Gortam Sealant" in which he was to personally report on how he would reduce FleetPort 30's consumption of the expensive Drive-chamber sealant by at least twenty percent. Another required him to ponder "Unprofessional Sexual Practices in the Imperial Fleet," then produce a long, complex report for a highly vocal group somewhere halfway across the galaxy. He had just opened still another document requiring a report on "Wardroom Hygiene in the Storage and Preparation of Logish Meem Types," when the door burst open in a cloud of Zempa pipe smoke and Ursis burst excitedly into his office.

"Wilfooshka," he exclaimed with a great smile on his face, "we can now trash Leaguer starships in even more efficient ways than previously employed."

Brim grinned and switched off his workstation—he'd get to those details when he wasn't so busy trying to win a war. "Sounds like a great pastime to me, Nik," he said, shoving the chair in the direction of his old friend. "How're we going to bring this little trick off?"

"With Gorn-Hoff crystals," the Sodeskayan said, straddling his chair seat and leaning his elbows on its wooden back. "Little starship you brought home from Effer'wyck was real treasure chest—for us. No wonder Leaguers were so interested in its destruction."

"I take it the crystal on the instrument panel *did* have something to do with aiming disruptors," Brim said.

"You take it right, my furless friend," Ursis replied. "Crystals like that have everything to do with it, and are entirely responsible for their improved shooting. Bringing back that little ship may have been *very* important to whole outcome of war."

"Universe," Brim said. "And it sat around here for nearly a week while the Leaguers were looking for it everywhere."

"I know," Ursis said with an ironic grin. "But upon such small visitations from Lady Fortune sometimes turn the fates of whole empires."

"I'll settle for some help with this one battle," Brim said.

Ursis frowned. "May be not enough time for that," he said, "but we shall see."

Brim nodded. He understood. "So how do the damn things work?" he asked. "Do the Leaguers follow projected beams like I think they do?"

"You were right on the money with that guess," Ursis said. "Narrow *KA'PPA* beams, at that." He laughed. "Here we thought our BKAEW stations were only new applications of KA'PPA technology in Universe, but opposition had been hard at work, too—only on different tack."

"So how does it work?" Brim demanded.

Ursis smiled. "Simply," he said, "like most worthwhile scientific breakthroughs. As you guessed, crystals are heart of special KA'PPA receivers hooked into navigational and gunnery systems. Back in Effer'wyck, Leaguer controllers send three ultra-narrow KA'PPA beams that intersect on precise point at which disruptors preset to certain focus should fire at target. Nobody knows what kind of transmitters they use to project beams of such incredible accuracy, but they clearly work." He shook his head. "At any rate, a ship carrying the crystal need only intersect one of three beams, then follow it to the point where it intersects with other two. Then they fire disruptors—with deadly accuracy you have already seen."

"So that's it," Brim said. "Well, you said it was simple."

"Except for transmitters," Ursis said. "*Those* have our greatest laboratories baffled."

"Not good," Brim observed.

"For time being, not that bad, either," Ursis said.

"I don't understand."

"Well," Ursis continued, "actually, for present, all we need do is *receive* those signals—which we can do thanks to crystals you brought home with you from Effer'wyck."

"Crystals?" Brim asked. "I only brought one back, didn't I?"

"None of you looked inside crates strapped to deck in passenger cabin, did you?" Ursis asked.

"No." Brim replied. "We didn't."

"Each crate contained ten of those crystals," Ursis explained. "Right now, we have three hundred twenty of them—and a workable breadboard of how to hook them up."

"Voot's beard," Brim exclaimed. "We *did* hit the jackpot, didn't we?" Then he frowned. "But what's this about needing only to *receive* the signals. Don't we have to destroy the transmitters as well?"

"Absolutely not," Ursis said with a great smile. "At least not for the present. We want to *use* the system exactly the way it is—to *our* advantage."

"I'd hoped you were going to say something along those lines," Brim said with a grin. "Now, how do you propose we do it?"

The Bear held up a long, tapered index finger. "Simply, of course," he said. "That is why I am confident it will work."

"I'm all ears," Brim said.

For the next twenty cycles, Brim sat quietly while Ursis explained the plan he had developed to counter the Leaguers' new technological accomplishment. And aside from a fundamental dependence on the Leaguers' own crystal receivers, the Sodeskayan's scheme depended on old-fashioned exploding mines and space anchors as its basic elements. The two had been combined to produce a sort of self-propelled hybrid with enough raw explosive power to rip the belly out of a battlecruiser.

Nothing spectacular there; torpedoes had served the same function for more than a thousand years—and at HyperLight velocities. However, addition of a captured crystal and receiver logic provided the primitive-but-deadly hybrid package with ability to follow one of the Leaguers' narrow-focused BKAEW beams as well as accurately sense its intersection with the other two beams—where it would stop and wait for a collision with one of Admiral Hoth Orgoth's attackers. Cheaply manufactured and relatively easy to transport, "Loiterers," as the Sodeskayans had come to name the mines, could inflict terrific damage while assuming only a relatively easy passive role.

"That's *wonderful,*" Brim exclaimed when Ursis finished his explanation, and the Bear agreed. Eventually, the system would altogether deny the Leaguers of using their triangulation system—and utterly devastate their attack forces while *they* went through the process of discovering what was causing such heavy losses. It was the kind of solution Brim had come to admire—inflicting the maximum punishment on the enemy only when *he* attacked.

"One correction, Wilfooshka," the Bear said with a grimace. "Is *almost* wonderful."

"I don't understand," Brim said.

"Well," Ursis said, "we've certainly got plenty space mines and anchors. Everywhere."

"Then?"

"Crystals," Ursis said. "They require time to 'grow'." We won't have first shipment of completed 'Loiterers,' as we call them, for at least one week—and then only trickle at first before necessary thousands begin to fill supply pipeline."

"That week could spell real trouble," Brim said with a grimace. " I assume you're aware of yesterday's sixteen-metacycles-long raid as well as one going on down there even as we speak. In a week, there might be nothing to protect."

"I understand," Ursis replied thoughtfully. "I've been in touch—as have many Sodeskayans. In our way of looking at things, cities of Sodeskaya will be next to feel onslaught of Leaguers."

"Sorry, Nik," Brim said, putting a hand on the huge Bear's shoulder boards. "It's just that I was down there in the city for most of the night after we got shot up. We're going to be in deep trouble if we don't get something to counter that new accuracy of theirs."

"I did not mean to imply we have nothing," Ursis said. "Indeed, we *have* come up with effective way for you to fight this menace. Just not so effective as new Loiterers—but almost."

"What's that?" Brim asked.

The Bear smiled. "Has to do with three hundred or so crystals you brought home from Effer'wyck, my furless friend. Is looking like you saved day in many ways."

"Huh?" Brim asked. "Three hundred-odd cobbled-up space mines are going to be *swamped* in the kind of raids we're having now. How does *that* save the day?"

"How about if we mount them in certain Starfuries and Defiants—ones that will fly with Squadron Leaders and"—he added significantly—"Wing Commanders. Since your BKAEW satellites can predict with some accuracy *when* enemy raids are coming—and even general area of target—you ought to be able to do even more damage if you lead your squadrons to precisely *where* enemy ships will go to fire disruptors. I think you humans call it 'target practice,' don't you?"

Brim shook his head. "Of course!" he said. "Why didn't I think of that?"

"You have had your mind on other things lately," the Bear answered, "like trying to stave off invasion, save five occupied planets from destruction, and stay alive. Small things in themselves, but time-consuming nonetheless."

"Thanks, Nik," Brim said.

"Think nothing of it, friend Brim," Ursis said.

"Er, when do we get started with the installations?" Brim asked. "We'll need one for Toby Moulding and one for Aram, at least."

"And one for Wilf Brim," Ursis added.

"I *hoped* you'd say that," Brim sighed. "But when?"

"In starship docked outside is team of engineers who are ready to start installation whenever you give word."

"You mean they've been waiting while we talked?"

"Well, more or less, Wilf," Ursis said. "Is only mannerly thing to do. You *are* Base Commander, after all."

Brim shut his eyes. Sodeskayans! "Nik," he said softly as he could. "There's a Starfury I often use in the repair bay even as we speak. They can start on that one right now."

"Is good," Ursis said. "That must be one Chief Barbousse told us about when we arrived. Engineering team has been working on that one since we arrived."

"I thought you said they were waiting."

"Oh, but they were," Ursis protested. "By now, ship will have been opened up. When you give word, Voof! Installation begins . . . !"

Meanwhile, the first wave of raids that day accomplished little disruption to the Imperial war machine, although Avalonian civilians *did* continue to suffer. And the second blow showed signs of poor preparation—some attack ships arrived without killer cruisers and vice versa, with deadly consequences for the attackers. The third—and main—blow was launched with some 150 attack ships and killer escorts heading for Avalon. They were hit twice by Starfuries and Defiants on the way but managed to keep going until, nearing their target, they ran into a small squadron led by Brim in the first crystal-equipped Starfuries. At point, the slaughter began. On the instant the Leaguers in Effer'wyck switched on their target beams, Brim picked one up and quickly followed it to its intersection. Then he drew off half a c'lenyt to simply orbit the point with all fourteen disruptors aimed and energized. Moments later, a big Kreissel 111-K came flashing by and before it could even open fire, it virtually disappeared in a full Imperial broadside whose every disruptor was precisely on target!

With wild cheers echoing on the voice circuits—which he couldn't bring himself to stifle—Brim followed a second beam to its intersection, then called in another Starfury to wait while he sought out a third beam. Working rapidly, he managed to place another two Starfuries at intersections and arrived at still another just in time to pick off a *fifth* Leaguer in a great puffball of radiation fire and spinning starship parts, at which time the panicked survivors fired at anything on the ground they could hit and ran for home, spreading damage over a wide area. For the first time since his arrival in Avalon, Brim returned to FleetPort 30 that evening with a smile on his face. The Imperials had a chance now. Tomorrow, at least fifteen more squadron leaders would begin to operate with crystal beam receivers.

The ancient warship carrying Fluvanna's deposed Nabob, his Consort Raddisma, and much of their court, arrived over the city, making safe landfall only metacycles following the third raid. Someone very influential among the Imperial High Command had ordered an unusually large Imperial escort for the old vessel, and not a single attack had been made against the strong convoy.

After a headlong shuttle flight from FleetPort 30 to what remained of Grand Imperial Terminal on Lake Mersin, Brim arrived to meet his beautiful—*very* pregnant—one-time lover at the brow as she disembarked onto the main concourse. However, it was first necessary to wait until the "official" welcoming ceremonies were complete.

First off the ship was Mustafa, the Nabob, who was met by Prince Onrad, members of his War Cabinet, and Oodam Beyazh in an unsparing show of support for the deposed monarch. After speeches by both Emperors, the royal entourage was forced to detour around high piles of debris that seemed to be everywhere, and the moment they had been bundled into their limousine skimmers, brigades of dusty people restarted their noisy sweeping machines as they continued to keep the main thoroughfares clear. Endless throngs of travelers were still passing through the huge terminus with little regard for the war that was raging around them, and any sustained interruption of the basic flow would smother the Empire in certain economic defeat.

When finally Petty Officer Cosa Tutti assisted Raddisma off the end of the brow, it was the first time Brim's eyes had met the Consort's since their considerably fecund one-night liaison in Brim's cabin aboard I.F.S *Starfury* in Fluvanna. Even nearing the end of her term, Raddisma was beautiful—and regal as ever.

"Raddisma," Brim said, taking her hand, "you must be nearly dead after that long trip. How do you feel?"

She smiled wearily. "*Extremely* pregnant, Wilf Brim," she said with a tired little smile. "Our daughter seems *most* anxious to be born. A trait of impatience she most certainly has picked up from her father."

Brim grinned. "Certainly not!" he said with a feigned indignation.

Raddisma took his arm as they started slowly across the littered marble floor. "We shall see, Wilf Brim," she said. "It is only presentiment, of course, but I have a feeling she will be a great deal like you."

"She'd at least better *look* like her mother," Brim said. "If she misses having the kind of beauty she can get from you, she'll hate both of us—forever."

Raddisma stared at him. "Am I still beautiful, Wilf Brim?" she asked.

"Still the *most* beautiful," Brim said, looking into her glorious almond-shaped eyes.

"Even swollen as I am everywhere?"

"Perhaps even *more* beautiful," he said. Then surreptitiously he patted her distended stomach. "However," he added with a little grin, "you may have some competition in *here*."

"I shall never compete with my daughter, Wilf," she said. "Whatever attributes I possess I gladly bequeath to her." Then she looked into his eyes and her countenance grew dark. "Except the title of Consort," she said. "May she *never* be a whore. It's been a good life for me, I'll admit but, well . . ." She pursed her lips for a moment. "I didn't have quite the start in life I plan for her. Earning a living on my back—and other more athletic positions—placed me in a considerably better income bracket than the one to I was originally accustomed."

"I didn't know," Brim mumbled, searching for the right words to say.

"No," she replied quickly, her little smile returning, "I shouldn't think you've had much experience with whores."

"I meant, er..."

"I know what you meant, Wilf," she said, covering his lips with a perfumed finger.

"No," Brim protested, "I don't think you do."

"Oh?"

Brim placed his hand over hers as she held on to his arm. "What I meant was that I would never permit such a thing to happen to my daughter."

"*My* daughter," Raddisma said. "You contributed nothing but a few squirts of your semen." She grinned and blushed slightly. "You contributed them magnificently, I might add, but she is *my* daughter, as I indicated in my letter."

Brim opened his mouth to chime in, but she continued on without interruption. "Remember, my proud father-to-be," she said as they walked through the crowded, dusty terminal, "that Mustafa, the absolute Nabob of Fluvanna, has accepted her as the child of *his* seed. And that gives her *quite* a few advantages neither of us could give her—alone or together. Besides, as I made quite clear in my message, when I decided to *keep* those squirts of semen you provided, I also vowed to absolve you of any responsibility," She laughed a little. "You did, as I remember, ask me very seriously if you needed to take any precautions—and I deliberately told you that you did not."

"I appreciate that," Brim interjected. "But what if I *want* some responsibility? It just so happens that I kind of *like* the idea of having a daughter."

"You can have all the responsibility you want, Wilf Brim," she said, "as her favorite 'Uncle.'" She shook her head. "Just what kind of a father do you think you would be when you spend most of your time whizzing around the galaxy?"

"Well . . ."

"Well, *nothing,*" she said, wrinkling her nose and smiling happily. "You have no idea how delighted I am that you have a real interest in this"—she placed her hands on either side of her distended abdomen—"altogether *giant* child. But unless something happens to me—or to Fluvanna—please don't do anything that would affect her royal status. Maybe someday, a long time from now, we'll tell her—together. But not now. Besides. It would simply devastate Mustafa to know that someone else has shared my passion—and will again, as soon as my body is ready."

This time, it was Brim's turn to blush—he could feel his cheeks burn.

She smiled; she couldn't escape noticing. "Yes, my Carescrian lover," she whispered, "even now I can think of taking you between my legs again." By this time, they had come to the main entrance where a literal caravan of chauffeurs and limousine skimmers waited at the curb to escort Mustafa's court to their new residence in Avalon.

Brim took a deep breath. He'd never before met *anybody* like Raddisma—and didn't expect he ever would again. "Do you know where you will be staying?" he asked.

"Yes," she said with an amazed look. "Mustafa and I are to be housed in the Royal Palace itself. Can you imagine that? Everybody else is being put up at the Eubry House on the other side of town. This Prince Onrad of yours is a strange man." she added. "To my knowledge, no other refugee rulers—not even the deposed Grand Earl of Effer'wyck—stays at the Royal Palace."

"It's *you.*" Brim joshed. "As a man of true taste, he enjoys living under the same roof with one of the most beautiful women in the galaxy."

"Oh, *of course,*" she said with a smile. "And I'm the only one who looks like a large starship."

Brim shook his head. "When will I see you again?" he asked.

She laughed. "My daughter and I have a rather restricted

social schedule for the near future," she said. "But I shall be free at least to dine whenever you happen to be in town."

"I'll be back in a couple of days," Brim said, handing her into the first limousine. "I'll try to message you first."

Petty Officer Tutti winked as she followed her mistress through the door. "My regards to Chief Barbousse," she whispered.

"He'll be here tonight to receive them in person." Brim replied under his breath. "I will personally send him on a critical mission to the palace. It will then be up to him to decide what the mission is all about."

Watching the limousine pull away from the curb and merge into the traffic winding though the rubble-filled boulevard fronting the terminal, Brim shook his head, very much impressed by the Fluvannians' unique accommodations. At least twenty royal refugees from all over the galaxy were housed in much lesser circumstances all over the beleaguered city. Yet the helpless, deposed of Nabob of a small domain halfway across the galaxy and one of the Empire's best-known courtesans—pregnant, no less—were on their way to live in the Imperial Palace itself. Somehow, he could see the fine hand of Onrad in all of it—and Borodov: the old Sodeskayan knew about the baby. Nodding quietly to himself, he began to understand how fortunate he was, and resolved that he would somehow make the Emperor's largesse worthwhile.

As he rode the shuttle to FleetPort 30, hundreds of Imperial civilians lay dead and wounded in the tormented ruins below—but less than half the raiders had managed to actually reach the city with their weapons, and twenty-eight Leaguer starships had been destroyed in the attempt.

When the raids tapered off that night, reports showed that Defense Command had also continued to suffer. During the second day of raids on Avalon, nineteen Starfuries had been destroyed and Lord Jaiswal's struggle to keep up operational starship strength was becoming increasingly difficult: the total had dropped to 659, the lowest in nearly a month. Yet—at least so far as Brim was concerned—advantage had absolutely shifted to the Empire, for the League was no longer concentrating on military targets. Moreover, they were themselves experiencing mounting casualties without effecting commensurate damage to the Imperial war effort. Picking his way across the temporary repairs to a replacement Starfury that had arrived in his absence, he learned from Barbousse that she had been patched together from the wrecks of three fallen Starfuries. He shrugged. "She'll do," he said with a tired grin. "She'll do. . . ."

CHAPTER 10

Loiterers

For most of the next two Standard Days, fierce gravity storms enabled Defense Command to recover some of its expended strength. Leaguer activity was limited to reconnaissance and isolated ground attacks. No Imperial crews were lost, and only one starship (a reconnaissance-configured Defiant) was missing in an extra-violent storm off Effer'wyckean border stars.

In fact, the second morning of this unexpected respite appeared as if it might just pass without any Leaguer activity at all. At midday (Avalonian Standard Time), however, Nergol Triannic KA'PPAed a boastful personal message directly to the Imperial Palace that he would call off the continued bombardment of Avalon if Onrad would simply step down and turn the reins of government over to the representatives of the League.

Afterward, Ursis reported at a broadcast staff meeting that the Leaguers believed they had everything necessary in place for their invasion—except, as usual, control of space. Triannic had made his little oration at the request of his High Command—minus Hoth Orgoth. They wanted to see if their goal could be reached by substituting a little bluff for the large number of starships that it now appeared would be realistically necessary to tame the Empire's apparently indestructible Defense Command. Ursis added, however, that barring success in that forlorn endeavor, Triannic still maintained personal hopes that Orgoth's huge raids on Avalon might *also* play a decisive role in the war, possibly coercing the Empire to capitulate without the necessity of invasion.

For the first time, the Sodeskayan intelligence community openly called Triannic's thinking "confused."

Late in the day, some 150 attack ships made it through slackening storms to inflict heavy damage on all parts of Avalon City. At the same time, however, Imperial Attack Command launched another of its *own* raids against Tarrott, this time leveling the city's prized Great Civic Terminal and blowing both dams on Lake Tegler while Brim and a number of volunteers flew raids on concentrations of invasion forces in Effer'wyck. It was extremely dangerous to attack there because of the tremendous concentrations of enemy killer ships as well as the paucity of Imperial starships available for long-range escort duty. Nevertheless, not only did the Imperial raiders raise considerable havoc among the occupying Leaguers, they also came back totally unscathed, indicating that the enemy Generals were as much unprepared to counter punishment as they were to give it out. *That,* in Brim's way of thinking, boded well for the Empire's future.

On his return to FleetPort 30, he found a summons to provide more firsthand testimony at another round of Onrad's War Cabinet meetings in Avalon the next day. Feeling a little guilty about missing the battles that were sure to come on the morrow—especially with Ursis's new crystal system working so well—he messaged his availability, and turned in early. Actually, he looked forward to the opportunity to more completely know this beautiful woman who—on the spur of the moment, it seemed—had decided to be the mother of his first child. . . .

"Faint hope of our capitulation," Onrad broadcast to the people of Avalon in an official morning answer to the Tyrant's question of the previous day. "Faint *bloody* hope of that. The crux of this war has now arrived. We must regard the next week or so as a very important part of our history. It ranks with the days when the Vorgoth Horde was approaching Asterious or when Admiral Desterro stood between disaster and Ramoth's Grand Fleet at the Antar Triad. And as we did then, we shall again triumph. . . ."

After Brim's subsequent attendance at the War Cabinet—where he found himself consulted far more than he had expected—he and Raddisma waited for the all-clear to sound, then dined simply in an elegant little cafe only a few rubble-strewn blocks from the palace; it was clear that the baby would be born soon. As they talked, he found himself utterly charmed by this incredibly beautiful, straightforward woman, who freely revealed her innermost hopes for the future—and especially for the future of "her" daughter. Later, as Brim took his leave at the palace gates, he felt a deep, intense pride that she had somehow chosen *him* to father her daughter. They promised to meet again within the week—either at another restaurant or in one of Avalon's birthing hospitals.

As if desperate to achieve the superiority in space he had promised his Emperor, Hoth Orgoth ordered wave after wave of raiders against Avalon City the next day. His initial thrust of about 250 starships comprised four formations. The first turned back early; both the second and third turned tail, aborting their attacks early after vigorous interceptions while still in deep space. The fourth squadron managed to fight its way to the outskirts of Avalon and even fire disruptors on the city—but it suffered tremendous casualties at the hands of Starfury and Defiant squadrons "fortuitously" positioned at intersections of the BKAEW aiming beams. Brim was among the defenders who savaged the unfortunate group of Leaguers.

The large formation of Leaguers had been sighted early on by watchful BKAEW operators over the planet of Avalon. All flyable starships of 11 Group—eight Starfuries and twelve Defiants in five flights of four each—were soon aloft in the area. Brim immediately dispatched two flights of Defiants (those whose leaders were without receiver crystals) to intersect the Leaguers present course nearly halfway out across the 'Wyckean Void. He then led Moulding with four Starfuries, Aram with four Defiants, and his own flight of four Starfuries back over Avalon to the general area in which Sector Control predicted the Leaguers would attack.

He didn't wait long. Within cycles, he sighted large numbers of approaching Leaguers, under such heavy attack they could no longer be described as a formation. Moments later, his crystal came to life—as did the other two crystals allotted his wing. Positioning two Starfuries at that intersection, he quickly located a second beam and began to circle its intersection. Moments later a big Kreissel 111 hove into view and was immediately blasted into subatomics without firing its first shot. Before he could locate another beam, however, a small group of Kreissels with an escort of two Gorn-Hoff 270s flashed past his nose. He opened fire at a point-blank range, getting one of the 270s on fire. The other broke off immediately and headed for Effer'wyck.

In the suddenly crowded sky, he next picked up another beam but before he could follow it to its intersection he encountered still another Kreissel and attacked at a high deflection angle, blowing large chunks from the port side of its bridge until at least three League killer ships drove him away.

Now, with the Leaguers on his heels, he dived for the surface, his rear turrets blasting away at a stubborn Gorn-Hoff that didn't break off until they were no more than ten thousand irals from the surface. Making a steep, climbing turn to starboard, he zoomed vertically into the fight where his gunner got a number of shots at still another Gorn-Hoff from no more than six hundred irals' distance. As this unfortunate Leaguer dived steeply, apparently out of control, Brim spotted another Gorn-Hoff and closed to attack him from astern, all forward turrets firing short bursts from nine hundred to three hundred irals' range. This 270 dived and crashed to the ground in flames . . .

Brim returned to FleetPort 30 reporting two authenticated kills, and a number "damaged." Too tired for the usual victory celebrations, he headed directly for bed. Counting his tour in Fluvanna—he'd been fighting the war for nearly *two* solid years now—and it was beginning to tire him out. He could only thank Voot that the Leaguers appeared to be getting tired, too!

On the fifth morning of the Leaguers' onslaught against Avalon City proper, intense gravity storms returned to the area, all but shutting down operations on both sides. Brim's morning TSIB indicated that the previous day's fighting cost the Imperial defenders twenty-nine aircraft against the League's twenty-five. And even though a good proportion of the Imperial losses could be made up by midafternoon of the next day, operational starships had fallen by 12 to 679. One crew was reported lost and five were missing.

In spite of the tempestuous regional gravity, however, approximately forty-three Leaguer attack ships, most heavy cruisers, did make it through the storms that day—and indeed managed to inflict even more damage to Avalon. A further forty people were killed, and the strain in the city remained intense.

As Brim moored at FleetPort 30 after a sortie in which the ship he was flying shared destruction of a Kreissel 111 and damaged three Gorn-Hoff 262s, he learned that one of the audacious late-afternoon raiders had even blasted the Royal Palace, landing a number of disruptor hits in close proximity to where Onrad was at work in his office. His thoughts went immediately to Raddisma as Imperial media services made the most of the occasion, anxious to prove that the new Emperor was as much at risk as everyone else. But common logic told him that little danger could have come to either Onrad or Raddisma, and he dismissed the bald-faced propaganda with a smile of derision. Places like the palace were so well protected that literally *nothing* could harm its occupants so long as they remained inside.

Weren't they . . . ?

Somehow, "common logic" failed to ease his mind as he shut down the Starfury's helm, and when he wearily quit the bridge, he had still not shaken the forebodings of tragedy, especially since—for the first time since he could remember—no one was at the end of the brow to greet his victorious crew.

Had something gone wrong? Where *was* everybody? Before he reached the ship's boarding lobby, he found himself tearing along the corridor at a dead run— on a course for his office and a private HoloPhone from which he could place a call to Raddisma.

He never made it. . . .

On the far side of the boarding tube, Onrad himself waited with a grim face, a black eye, and a bandage covering his swollen forehead. Silently, the two made their way through a sea of raised eyebrows to Brim's office, where Onrad gently closed the door.

Brim's heart nearly stopped from dread as the Emperor began to speak. Somehow, he *knew* what was coming next.

"Wilf," Onrad said quietly, "for all my supposed talent at oratory, I simply don't know how to put this nicely." He grabbed Brim's hand and looked him straight in the face. "Emperors are supposed to have no friends—only interests. The fact that you have nevertheless *become* a friend, and a trusted one at that, makes this so difficult that I almost sent someone else to tell you," he continued, staring at the wall as if he couldn't stand his own words. "It was that bond of trust between us that brings me here this afternoon to tell you that Raddisma was killed in the raid that you must by now have learned damaged the palace late this afternoon. Neither of us were in the deep shelters, as we should have been."

Brim staggered backward until he caught his balance on the desk. "Sweet mother of the Universe," he gasped in utter despair. He had never experienced a wave of grief like this—not even when his sister died in his arms.

Onrad shook his head bitterly. "I shall always blame myself for her death," he continued in a voice high with strain, "both because she was here in Avalon at my personal request and because I had not moved the palace hospital farther underground."

From somewhere deep in his despair, Brim found compassion for the Galactic Emperor who had just prostrated himself because of a single death. "You can't blame yourself for doing the best you could for her," he said. Then, it began to dawn on him that the man was here to tell *him* about the tragedy—not Mustafa. He opened his mouth to speak but Onrad continued, his eyes fastened somewhere thousands of c'lenyts distant.

"Miraculously," the Emperor continued, "she did manage to deliver your daughter in the metacycle before her death. The little girl was still being prepared in the palace infirmary when the Leaguers' shots hit the wing where Raddisma was resting . . ."

"My daughter!" Brim exclaimed, the thought—and the words—about Mustafa blasted from his mind. "She is alive?" he asked.

Onrad put his great, strong hand on Brim's shoulder. "She is very much alive, Wilf," he said. "A beautiful young woman, even now. Raddisma would have been *very* proud—as will you."

Brim shook his head for a moment and peered at the Emperor. "Wait a moment, Your Highness—did you say, *my* daughter."

Onrad smiled, "Yes, Wilf," he said. "I've known her true parentage for a few months, now."

Brim closed his eyes again. "Somehow, I thought you had. *That's* why you brought Mustafa Eyren and his court to Avalon, isn't it?"

Onrad smiled, "Well," he said, "I'll admit that had a lot to do with it."

"Universe," Brim whispered. "How can I ever *begin* to express my gratitude . . . ?"

"For getting her killed?"

"For doing what you thought was best for her *and me*, Your Majesty." Brim stated firmly. "They might both have been killed in Atalanta. Hador Haelic's under attack, too, you know."

"Thanks," Onrad said simply. "You've been damned good about it." Reaching inside his cloak, he handed Brim a small, pink envelope. "Here," he said. "She left this with Petty Officer Tutti—who was fortunately with the baby when the blast came."

Brim ground his teeth as he looked blindly at the envelope—it was the old-fashioned kind of communication Raddisma favored; she had a deep respect for trappings from bygone ages. "I only hope to the Universe she didn't suffer much."

Onrad shook his head. "I was only two rooms away, Wilf," he said, pointing to the bandage on his forehead. "I got there moments later, and as I am a man, I can attest that the poor woman never felt a thing."

"What a horrible, *horrible* waste this war is," Brim said bitterly, unfolding the letter that was written in traditional ink on antique paper.

> Dear Wilf,
>
> Since you are reading this letter, I will have passed away for one reason or another without being able to say a personal farewell. Not what I intended at all. I believe that I loved you—or was certainly on my way to that comfortable state of repose. I also believe that I might have made you happy. Perhaps in another life.
>
> This letter is not about me. Rather, it is about our daughter who I shall also presuppose has survived; Tutti would not have otherwise delivered this letter. I shall now have to ask that you at least keep an eye on her until Mustafa Eyren finds her some sort of a home. With a new Chief Consort replacing me in his bed, the Nabob's interest in this female child will wane rapidly. Perhaps you can use your influence to

insure that she goes to a good future. I had such fine hopes for her!

Again, it is imperative that you understand you have no responsibility for this child other than what you choose to take for yourself. It is certainly no fault of hers that she was born, but then it is none of yours, either, since the decision to conceive was exclusively mine during one special night of complete ecstacy. I am truly sorry that I failed to survive long enough to carry out this responsibility on my own.

Thank you for whatever you are willing to do.

Love,

Raddisma

Brim's eyes filled with tears and he handed the letter to Onrad. "She was quite a lady, Your Majesty," he whispered. "I think you should share this."

Carefully placing his eyeglasses on the bridge of a swollen nose, Onrad took the letter and read it. Presently, he looked up. "One night?" he asked. "That's all you knew each other?"

"That's all," Brim said.

Onrad smiled. "Well, you must have made *quite* an impression, my friend," he said. "Since she moved in, she followed any news that reached the palace about you. And she kept a sizable journal of media pieces that mentioned your exploits," He pursed his lips for a moment, then peered at Brim in a conspiratorial way. "Hmm," he mused. "Old Mustafa's going to be problem here for a while, but—unless you have some good objections—I'm going to take the child into the palace household. Being born here on an Imperial planet, she'll have her choice of citizenship when she grows up. So we'll simply have to spoil her sufficiently that she makes the right choice when the time comes. Besides,'' he said with a smile, ''a little girl will considerably brighten up the palace—especially since we shall all be living some distance underground for a while. She'll have Petty Officer Tutti as her personal governess and her favorite 'Uncle' Wilf can visit her anytime he is in town. How about it, Admiral?'' he asked.

It took Brim a long time to force through the rush of emotion that captured his entire being. ''W-what in the Universe could I possibly say to such kindness, Your Majesty?'' he stammered, only half in control of himself.

''How about 'yes'?'' Onrad asked softly.

''Yes,'' Brim managed to choke. ''Please.''

''I'll take care of it immediately,'' Onrad said, then he blinked and held up an index finger. ''Oh, yes,'' he added, reaching inside his cloak once more. ''The doctor gave me this for you—it nearly slipped my mind.'' This time, he handed Brim a small plastic envelope embossed with Onrad's Imperial seal.

Brim opened it carefully and withdrew a small, personal-sized hologram. It pictured a tiny, wrinkled infant, clearly born only metacycles before.

''She's pretty as a *picture*, isn't she?'' Onrad said, looking over his shoulder. ''What're you going to name her?''

''N-*name?*''

''Yeah. She's got to have a name, you know.''

Brim grimaced. The furthest thing from his mind during the last year was finding a name for a baby girl. He looked at the hologram. His daughter had Raddisma's lovely almond eyes—and wore a pink ribbon around a shock of black, curly hair. By the very Universe, she *was* beautiful. He had closed his eyes for a moment, thinking of names, when it came to him, ''I've got it!'' he said.

''The name?''

Brim nodded.

Onrad waited a few moments, then smiled. ''Are you going to tell me what it is?'' he asked impatiently.

Brim smiled. "The only name she *could* have, Your Majesty. 'Hope.' "

This time, it was Onrad who closed his eyes for long moments, clearly too full of emotion to speak. Finally, he nodded and smiled. "It'll do," he said, a tear starting down his cheek. "It'll *damn well* do. . . ."

As the Triad's first rays warmed FleetPort 30, Barbousse wakened Brim with a special bulletin newly decoded from the Admiralty. According to Sodeskayan Intelligence sources, Hoth Orgoth's High Command in Occupied Effer'wyck had taken advantage of the gravity storms to organize what promised to be a colossal, maximum-effort raid. For two days running, "borrowed" attack ships had been arriving from bases throughout the League's conquered empire, and were now approaching numbers that could literally swamp the Imperial defenses, good as they had become. Clearly, the Leaguers were rapidly building up to some sort of climatic event.

Only metacycles later, the midday gravitological forecast from the Admiralty predicted that the turbulent gravity would soon begin to stabilize, bringing (relative) calm to the galactic center—and a renewed threat of invasion to Avalon. In midafternoon, Brim boarded a shuttle for Avalon to meet Calhoun at another War Cabinet meeting in Avalon. There, he was called for firsthand information only twice, but he *did* listen to Hagbut warn that a large number of transport craft the Leaguers had previously dispersed to remote sections of Effer'wyck were now being gathered at locations on habitable spacecoast planets from which an invasion might be launched. Afterward, Hagbut's staff presented a cogent-but-lengthy dissertation warning that these movements—in conjunction with the increased scale of attacks on Avalon City itself—indicated a Leaguer incursion was not only likely, but it was imminent.

And much as he disliked giving in to fear-mongering, Brim was very close to embracing the idea that an invasion very well *might* take place in the near future. He shivered as he caught a staff skimmer to the shuttle stop at Lake·Mersin Fleet Base.

From the reports he'd heard, the Imperial defenders were going to need a lot more than three hundred crystals jury-rigged into the odd Starfury or Defiant. If someone didn't deliver Ursis's self-propelled space mines soon, the good people of Avalon would be learning Vertrucht in the *very* near future.

The first Leaguer raids reached Avalon before Brim even made it to the shuttle base. Caught out on Vereker Boulevard when the explosions began, his driver pulled to the curb and ran for shelter. By now rather acclimated to being shot at by Leaguers, Brim simply got out and watched the unfolding battle with a sort of professional interest. Judging from the noise—and thundering salvos from Universe only knew how many disruptors—he estimated that at least a hundred Leaguer starships were attacking over a wide area, while bringing even more terror and death to the city. After a while, he climbed behind the controls of the staff skimmer himself and continued on toward the base. He could be hit equally well standing still or on the move, and the latter got him closer to the front of the shuttle boarding line, so he drove. But he came to an abrupt halt at the blazing wreck of a Gradgroat-Norchclite cathedral—it had clearly been hit within a metacycle. Pulling to the curb, he rushed inside—two great oaken doors had been blown across eight lanes of thoroughfare—where he encountered still another scene out of someone's private vision of Hell. Two blood-drenched women were calmly piecing bodies together and laying their ghastly creations in cartons placed in neat rows on the floor. Unable to confront the gruesome scene before him, he looked up into what must have once been a high, vaulted ceiling. Now, all that remained were shards of supports along the tops of the walls. A disruptor beam must have pierced the roof like an eggshell and burst among a group of women and children sheltering in the sanctuary. Fighting his gorge to a draw, he choked, "Can I . . . er . . . g-get help for you?"

One of the women shook her head and spoke without looking up from her terrible task. "No, thank you," she said in horror-dulled voice. "It's really not a *difficult* job. And actually, the stench is the worst part of it."

"Except, perhaps for all the missing parts," the other woman chimed in. She grimaced with effort as she pulled a rather hefty right leg from the large pile of scraps they'd collected between them, then placed it beside the frail left leg of a child. "If we're too lavish making one body almost whole," she said, "then others have gaps in them, you see. And we can't have that, can we?"

Next morning, as Brim sat in the splintered wreckage of FleetPort 30's wardroom, he nodded grimly reading a special dispatch from Military Intelligence. It quoted an intercepted Situation Report from Hanna Notrom, League Minister for Public Consensus, to the League's Military Attaché in a neutral country. In it, she boasted that fully six Imperial FleetPorts had been rendered useless, among them FleetPort 30, itself. . . .

Less than a metacycle later, he laughed balefully as he set out from that very satellite to face an early-morning raid of at least 150 Leaguers. The starship he was taking into combat was so patched up it would only just fly. But the Leaguers' aiming crystal still functioned atop his center readout panel, therefore he might do *some* damage. Glancing aft, he could see that the majority of Starfuries he led on the mission were in much the same condition as his own: heavily patched and not always flying a true course. On top of that, he could barely hold his own eyes open, and he knew that only the greenest replacements had cadged any real rest in the past three weeks. He took a deep breath and sipped a scalding mug of cvceese' to keep himself awake. Outside, local gravity was working up to a real space purger. If the flight he led was typical, then Imperial Defense Command itself had moved very close to "overwhelmed" status—while the Leaguers were still building up to their big raid. The only thing that kept him going at all was the almost certain knowledge that his opponents were experiencing the same fatigue as his own—along with a growing frustration at their inability to clear the skies of defending starships.

Even so, it was going to be a *close* thing, indeed.

* * *

Early on Nonad fifteenth—amid powerful waves of violent regional gravity that rocked the whole satellite—Brim tried to rest in his office while he read the TSIB. This morning's version contained a special summary bulletin. Late the previous day, Sodeskayan Intelligence had delivered top-secret transcripts of a high-level conference held in Tarrott the previous afternoon. In effect, Triannic had officially given Orgoth only until the seventeenth to sufficiently batter the Imperial Fleet so that an invasion could take palace. Otherwise, the Tyrant would postpone his invasion of Avalon and turn his energies to other conquests.

Two more days, Brim thought solemnly. Could Defence Command hold out? This day of relative ease—thanks only to blustering gravity—was benefiting both sides equally. But Fleet gravitologists predicted a rapid clearing during the Night Watch. And then "The Great Raid," as Eve Cartier had begun calling it, could begin—at the Leaguers' pleasure. He shook his head. At least a few shipments of mines had started to arrive at the FleetPort satellites. He presently had eighty some stashed away and at least a hundred were due on the morrow. All in all, perhaps two thousand or so would be available by the time the battle began. But they would have to be used wisely, or the slight advantage they gave the Imperial defenders would be quickly frittered away . . .

Two URGENT communiqués from Calhoun arrived shortly after midday. The first contained revised orders implementing a new Imperial strategy based on the Sodeskayan intelligence. The League's forthcoming all-out attack would be met with a single, desperate throw of the dice upon which would now rest the whole fate of the Empire. Calhoun had concluded that *this* was finally the time to throw all his defending forces against the League attack, including the last of his meager reserves.

Brim leaned back in his chair with his hands clasped behind his neck and thought about the momentous decision his fellow Carescrian had just made. It meant that if Triannic decided after the battle he could now invade, Imperial forces would have no resources to meet him. He nodded to himself. It was the right thing to do. If indeed it appeared to the Leaguers that the time was ripe for invasion, then Defense Command would have pretty well been beaten anyhow. He was ready. And, he supposed, so was nearly everyone else—on both sides of the war.

Taking a deep breath, he shook his head in resignation and called the second "urgent" communiqué to his display. Then he gasped aloud.

2134DSFGK-3FDG GROUP KLJ9W 375/52012
[TOP SECRET]
PERSONNEL ACTION MEMORANDUM, IMPERIAL FLEET,
PERSONAL COPY

FROM:
BU FLEET PERSONNEL;
ADMIRALTY, AVALON

TO:
W.A. BRIM, CAPTAIN, I.F., FLEETPORT 30
<893BVC-12-K2134MV/57320AS90DWQER07GW0>
SUBJECT:DUTY ASSIGNMENT
(1) AS OF THIS DATE, YOU ARE PROMOTED REAR ADMIRAL (LOWER HALF) (UNRESTRICTED LINE).
(2) YOU ARE IMMEDIATELY DETACHED PRESENT ASSIGNMENT SECTOR COMMANDER, FLEETPORT 30
(3) REPORT VICE ADM B. CALHOUN, COMMANDER, HOME FLEET,
DEFENSE COMMAND, AS COMMANDER, 13 GROUP.
(4) YOU WILL IMMEDIATELY RELOCATE PLACE OF RESIDENCE TO
FLEETPORT 19, ARIEL. RELOCATION ALLOWANCE DOES NOT APPLY.

FOR THE EMPEROR:

LUAN TERRIL, CAPTAIN, L.F.

[END OF TOP SECRET]
2134DSFGK-3FDG

Suddenly he remembered Onrad's words as they discussed his daughter's future: "How about it, Admiral?" the Emperor had asked. He'd *known*!

At that moment, Barbousse raced into the room. "Cap'm," he panted, nearly out of breath. "I've b-been *transferred*! An' I didn't even know."

Brim bit his lip. It was hard to believe a man with Barbousse's contacts had been surprised with a reassignment. "Where to, Chief?" he asked with a real frown of concern.

"Um . . . to FleetPort 19. I'm to report to—well, I don't know *who* I'm to report to. Rear Admiral Gamriel was killed a couple of weeks ago. *His* replacement, I guess. Cap'm Brim, can you *do* anythin' about it? I'll be glad to turn down the promotion if I can keep workin' for you."

"You mean you *want* to work for a Carescrian? One who regularly puts your life at risk?"

"Aye, sir," Barbousse said, visibly upset.

"And what's this about a promotion?"

"To Chief Warrant Officer, Cap'm. But all that's a bunch of Gorksroar anyway. No matter what they want to call me, I'm still a Chief and mighty proud of it . . ."

Brim shook his head. Notwithstanding a friendship that went back to the day he'd joined the Fleet, life would be *hard* without Barbousse. The fine hand of Onrad was in *this*, too. "Chief," he said with as serious a mien as he could muster, "*I* just got a reassignment, too."

Barbousse clapped a hand to his forehead. "Sweet sufferin' Universe," he swore. "What's happened to m' contacts?" He shook his head as if he were recovering from a physical blow. "Beggin' the Cap'm's pardon," he asked, "but, um . . . where to?"

"FleetPort 19," Brim said.

Barbousse did a perfect double take, then wrinkled his nose, closed his eyes, and nodded. "You got promoted, too, didn't you, er . . . Admiral?"

Brim nodded with a grin that was a lot more emotion than smile. "Congratulations, my good friend," he said, grasping the big man's hand. "There is nobody more deserving than you."

"Except *you*, Admiral." Barbousse stood back and saluted. "My most heartfelt congratulations to you, sir."

"That's my first flag salute," Brim said, returning the compliment solemnly. "How fitting it should come from you."

"Beggin' the Admiral's pardon—for the first time—but I think we make a fine team," Barbousse observed.

"We'd better," Brim said. "The Emperor's counting on us."

"Aye, sir," Barbousse said. "I was beginnin' to suspect he had somethin' to do w' this." He shook his head. "I mean, my contacts *never* get fooled like that."

"Think your contacts can find us a ride to FleetPort 19?" Brim asked. He presently had less than one Standard Day to organize for a battle that could decide the fate of the whole empires—and most assuredly his own neck.

"I'll have a shuttle waitin' in a few . . ." Barbousse started when Moulding suddenly burst through the door.

"Wilf!" he clamored. "What's happened to you? I've just been ordered to take over your job here at FleetPort 30?"

"It's a long story," Brim said with a tired smile.

"Um . . . I'll get transportation ready," Barbousse said, starting for the door.

"Oh, Chief!" Brim called. "Schedule a meeting for tonight—FleetPort 19's wardroom. Group and Squadron Commanders. Twilight and two."

"Aye, Admiral," Barbousse said, knuckling his forehead. "Twilight an' two." Then he turned to Moulding and grinned. "Oh, an' congratulations, Cap'm Moulding," he said.

"Thanks, Chief," Moulding said, then looked at Brim in

puzzlement. "How'd he know *that*?" he demanded, but Barbousse was already hot-footing down the hall.

"As I said," Brim muttered, offering his old friend the chair and desk he was now vacating, "It's a *long* story . . ."

At precisely Twilight:2:0, Barbousse stepped to a table that had been placed at one end of FleetPort 19's once-elegant wardroom, now a mass of pressure patches and splintered wood paneling. The Warrant Officer paused for a moment while the room quieted, then, taking a deep breath, he announced, "The Admiral!"

With a scraping of chairs, thirty-odd men and women who steered the efforts of 13 Group struggled to their feet and stood as straight as their various stages of fatigue permitted. It was not a time to demand smart military protocol, and Brim knew it as he strode through the door to the table. "Seats!" he said crisply.

After the second round of shuffling and scraping ended, he grimaced. "First," he said to the sea of haggard faces—even the magnificent Eve Cartier showed a bit of age tonight—"I appreciate what it has cost most of you to come here tonight. Metacycles of precious sleep, if nothing else. But I doubt if many of you are more tired than myself—for the self-same reasons." He paused for a moment, then nodded. "Well, Hoth Orgoth's little operation could very well come to an abrupt end as early as tomorrow."

That got their attention. The coughing and foot shuffling that had almost immediately formed a background for his talk stopped, and many of the slouching bodies straightened in their seats. Glazed eyes suddenly focused.

"That's right," he said. "For those of you who haven't had the pleasure of plowing through TSIBs three times a day, Triannic's given Admiral Orgoth only through tomorrow to put up or shut up."

Here and there around the room, Brim watched more of the nearly enervated eyes begin to come alive. Were the thoughts behind them of opportunity—or simply apprehension at yet another battle to be fought against ever-increasing odds?

"This time," he continued, nodding at Barbousse, "we've got a few nasty surprises for the zukeeds." He frowned as the big Warrant Officer activated a globular projector that displayed a three-dimensional, holographic representation of the new space mine prototype. A number of eyebrows instantly rose in curiosity. Toward the back of the room, Eve sat with the same kind of tired little smile she always had after they'd made love. Earlier that evening, his promotion had made her as happy as if she'd been promoted herself—now she trusted him to lead her in battle. He took a deep breath. *That* was responsibility! He paused to let people study the image as it turned slowly above the projector.

"It's what we call a 'Loiterer'," he began presently. "An outgrowth of the inconveniently secret technology that's permitted some of us to help you pick off a few extra Leaguers the last few days. And *this,*" he said, changing the view to an animated representation of the Leaguers' new BKAEW beam aiming system, "is how we're going to use them to break the back of Orgoth's big attack tomorrow . . ."

Dawn: 2:78, with the last details they could think of resolved—or at least as much resolved as possible—the collected Sector and Squadron Leaders from Group 13 rose and snapped to attention, then raced for the starships that would return them to their bases. Reconnaissance flights over a number of Effer'wyckean planets were already reporting the kind of activity that normally presaged a heavy raid on Avalon. Only *this* activity involved the greatest number of war machines that had ever been recorded. All along the Effer'wyckean frontier, habitable spacecoast planets were crowded with every kind of space barge known—packed with land crawlers, siege engines, and hordes of ground troops. All destined for the Triad and Avalon City.

As Eve Cartier took her leave, she quietly placed an ancient RuneStone from their native Carescria in his hand. "I weel know there's na magic, Wilf Brim," she whispered. "But this ha' alway' brought me guid fortune—an' m'forbearers, too. Today, m'blue-eyed lover, you'll need it mair than any of us . . ."

Reports from Moulding in FleetPort 30 indicated that day was dawning beautifully below in Avalon City. Over Ariel in the torn wreckage called FleetPort 13, Barbousse woke Brim to inform him that matching gravitational conditions had returned throughout the Triad; they both knew that the Leaguers would soon be active. The Carescrian arrived at his Starfury just as nearby BKAEW plotters picked up forty plus enemy starships assembling in the Eppeid area of Effer'wyck, then a force of twenty plus, followed by a second force of forty plus.

Now, the Leaguers moved toward Avalon without their usual feints and subsidiary attacks to lure Defense Command starships into space prematurely. Clearly—at least to Brim—they were acting in as much desperation as himself. Half a metacycle later, he personally led all of the sixteen squadrons his five sectors could muster in a "Big Wing" formation. In their wake flew a raffish gaggle of ten commandeered civilian cargo packets crewed by Imperial starsailors and loaded with some forty Loiterers each. The crews were ready to release their mines as soon as the Leaguers' aiming beams began to appear.

An estimated two hundred enemy starships appeared below LightSpeed just before midday. This was nearly ten clicks after Leaguers in Effer'wyck had designated their first targets with BKAEW beams—and at least three clicks after Loiterers had been sewn everywhere that intersections could be detected. Imperial squadrons tore into the Leaguers nearly ten thousand c'lenyts out into the 'Wyckean Void, for the first time outnumbering the enemy and shredding their formations. Within cycles, the sky above Avalon filled with dogfights.

As Brim directed his forces—mixing in with the actual fighting whenever he could—he knew that a second Leaguer attack at the same time would be deadly, because there were no reserves. Not with his squadrons nor with the other four

Imperial groups wheeling and turning in the emptiness above Avalon.

Driving towards first Kreissels and Zachtwagers, he watched the Leaguers rush in to fire their big, single-shot disruptors, only to suddenly disappear in bright puffballs of energy when they smashed into the new space mines. Wild cheering filled the voice circuits as ship after ship burst into flames over the still-smoldering city. "Belay the noise!" he bellowed, even while he slammed on the power to catch a fleeing Kreissel. No sooner had he lined up on the Leaguer from below and abeam than Lawrence, his Gunnery Officer, blew half its "wing" off in a deafening, all-disruptor salvo. On breaking away, however, he himself came under attack by Gorn-Hoff 262s from both above and astern. Evading these, he flicked off into a second attack on the surviving Leaguer attack ships, this time almost vertically from below, then dodged shots from three more Gorn-Hoffs that opened fire way too early—the enemy had rookies, too. He was just taking out after another Kreissel when the Leaguers swung around and headed their broken formations back toward Effer'wyck. Many had yet to fire a shot at the city below.

As the Imperial BKAEW screens cleared, round one clearly belonged to the Imperials. Brim, however, found his initial elation somewhat tempered by the fact that the number of rounds to be fought was entirely up to the Leaguers—who had a lot more resources to throw into their effort than had their Imperial opponents . . .

Rushing here and there to regroup the forces in his group (and discreetly check on the welfare of Eve Cartier), Brim discovered that two Starfuries and three Defiants were unaccountably missing from their squadrons. Almost mysteriously so—no one could remember hearing anything about them on the voice circuits. But there was little time to consider the matter in detail. The commandeered packets had scarcely finished gathering in their unexploded Loiterers when BKAEW sites began reporting that a second force of Leaguers was on its way. This time, the warning was shorter and the formations were much larger than their predecessors, with up to fifty attack ships in a group. One wave comprised three such formations, approaching in line astern with GA 110s between each.

This time, it was 13th Group's turn to wait close in over the city while the other four groups pushed out into the 'Wyckean Void for early interceptions. With seven Starfuries in his wake, Brim banked into a wide left turn, watching the little cluster of packet ships suddenly break up into individual units darting here and there to jettison their Loiterers like a swarm of insects—the Leaguers' targeting beams were on!

In the distance, pinpoints of brilliance began to blaze and wane in the starry darkness as the battle was joined. These grew closer, spreading to fill a sizable arc of the sky. He turned and winked at Barbousse who had taken over the main forward battery.

"All hands to battle stations," he announced over the blower. "All hands to battle stations." The short respite he'd granted the crew was over.

Now it seemed as if a solid mass of gravity plumes was coming at them—what appeared to be at least a million Leaguer starships, slowing below LightSpeed as their attack craft lined up for attacks on the helpless city below. Brim watched his main turrets swinging as range finders measured the swiftly narrowing distance. To better extend their firepower, he ordered his little eight-ship squadron into independent quads and for the second time that day, a bloodthirsty thrill of elation coursed through his body. He tightened the seat restraints as his muscles keyed to the oncoming challenge. Swinging the ship's head slightly up and to port, he made for the Leaguers, even while the killer ships separated from their charges and spread out to meet his oncoming challenge.

"Break starboard!" he called, jamming the thrust dampers all the way forward. "Diving!" Moments later, six massive Admiralty A876 gravity generators had spun up to maximum thrust and the big Starfury was hurtling down on the Leaguers like some avenging demon, with three others duplicating his every move in finger-four formation.

Lining up on the nearest Kreissel 111, he pulled slightly off to one side while Lawrence salvoed twice. The Leaguer's bridge lit up for a moment as if a great light had been ignited from within. Three or four puffs appeared in the slipstream. Then Brim had to break right countering two Gorn-Hoff escorts that rolled into a tight turn and brought themselves head-on to himself. Ruby aiming beams from their disruptors formed long, glittering tentacles snaking their way toward him, then curled down to pass close by under the pontoons. Space became a whirling confusion of brilliant flashes, hurtling starships, and tremendous explosions as disruptors on both sides hit home. In the corner of his eye, Brim saw three angular Zachtwagers dive in formation toward the city. Hauling the Starfury around, he started in pursuit until all three simultaneously disappeared in blasts of light that dimmed his Hyperscreens. Clearly, they were victims of Loiterers.

As was another *Starfury* beginning its run-in toward a brace of Kreissels. . . .

"Sweet mother of the Universe," Brim swore as he caught the graceful starship literally dissolving in the self-same distinctive blue-green detonation of a Loiterer. *That's* how his other three ships had disappeared. They were fighting much too close to the mined area!—and so was *he*! He grimaced as he cranked the Starfury into a vertical climb. How to warn the others without alerting the Leaguers? "Attention—all Starfuries," he broadcast to all channels, "keep well clear of the final target area! Repeat. Keep well clear of the final target area!"

Below, another great explosion where a Starfury had been moments before showed that at least one Imperial Helmsman hadn't heeded—or perhaps understood—the message. He was about to broadcast another, more pointed warning but shook his head. It was a trade off. Loiterers waited at definite points in space to which Leaguers would purposefully steer. If an occasional Starfury blundered into the same point *before* its designated Leaguer, then so be it. Statistically, the odds were highly in favor of Leaguers getting there first—*unless someone warned them off*. Biting his lip because he might *also* be sacrificing Eve Cartier, he switched the radio to LOCAL and rejoined the fray, bagging a Gorn-Hoff and damaging two Kreissels that had escaped the dwindling supply of Loiterers before the Leaguers again broke off their vicious attack and bolted off in disorganized gaggles headed for Effer'wyck.

Round two had also gone to the Empire—if one failed to consider the additional damage inflicted on Avalon by the attack ships that *did* get through. Its cost had been heavy for both sides, but Leaguers had clearly suffered the greatest loss of starships and crews. Loiterers destroyed as high as seventy-five percent of their attack ships and crews. Nevertheless, early returns indicated the Leaguers' force of killer-ship escorts had been reduced only by a little more than the "average" percentage normally lost during the heavy raiding of the last week or so.

Still, Brim reasoned, the zukeed bastards couldn't very well wage effective war against cities—or conduct interstellar invasions—with only squadrons of escort killer ships. So one way or another Hoth Orgoth was hurting in a big way. If the past were any indicator, Nergol Triannic was capable of seeing through any extravagant claims his fat Admiral might make.

While tired Imperial defenders regrouped to meet the Leaguers' next onslaught, Brim received word via scrambled data link that less than two hundred Loiterers remained—including those reclaimed by the second set of salvage operations. Not good, he thought to himself—but perhaps not that bad, either. It would be difficult for the Leaguers to conceal the horrendous losses sustained by their attack craft. When little more than a quarter of the ships returned home, people were going to notice—and word would spread. With *that* kind of losses, the next attackers were going to be spooked before they even arrived. They'd certainly guess that some sort of secret weapon was operating against them—but they wouldn't know *what* it was.

Because of the Imperials' *own* depressing-but-inadvertent losses to the Loiterers (Eve had once more checked in, tired but unscathed), all defending starships were now positioned in a thick arc out in the 'Wyckean Void to make early interceptions and keep themselves clear of the intersections area until the Leaguers had cleared out a few of the Loiterers. Of course with only two hundred or so Loiterers remaining, it wouldn't take long for *that* to happen.

The Leaguers' third attack followed the model set by their previous raid: waves of large formations with up to forty large attack craft in a group. Each wave consisted of three such formations with killer-ship escorts between them. Both main bodies of antagonists met in the 'Wyckean Void at about Evening:1:0 nearly a quarter of the way out from Avalon. Again, the battle seethed toward Avalon City, but this time, the attack craft taking off from Effer'wyckean bases appeared to be infinite. Wave after wave were reported on the way until Brim simply shut off reception from that channel.

The two lead waves soaked up the last Loiterers with devastating casualties. After that, the city began to take significant damage, especially the ancient city center and the Imperial Palace (Brim mumbled silent thanks that Hope had been taken deep underground). Within a half metacycle, two more waves of Leaguers had been literally ripped apart. Unlike the *total* destruction inflicted on individual attackers by Loiterers, Leaguer casualties were now simply damaged—yet damaged enough to put them out of the battle as if they no longer existed at all.

But on came the replacements, each wave succeeded by another in a seemingly endless stream of destruction coming from Effer'wyck. Brim—who had been fighting almost constantly since midday—was nearing the end of his energy. Having crippled or downed at least five Leaguers since the battle resumed for the third time, he was now operating mostly by instinct. Off to his right, a lone Defiant broke off and headed behind two Kreissels. He caught a glimpse of the Imperial's tail number: P9137; it was Aram—or at least the ship he had been flying the previous day.

Brim decided to cover him, avoiding several determined attacks by going into a tight spiral—the Leaguers were going too fast to follow him. He saw Aram's turrets flash as they fired . . . then his own proximity alarms went off. Abruptly, the starboard disruptor turrets swung and fired at the same moment that huge bolts of incoming energy crackled past in the opposite direction. Moments later, a Gorn-Hoff's enormous, heat-streaked wing flashed below them. The carcless Leaguer had missed Brim and was now going after Aram.

Instinctively, the Carescrian curved 'round to his left, listening to the gunlayers' litany behind him. In the winking of an eye, four big starboard turrets indexed outward, elevated their eight powerful disruptors infinitesimally, then opened fire at nearly point-blank range. Eight super-focused bolts of raw energy caught the Gorn-Hoff amidships, about thirty irals outboard of the main crew compartment, literally blowing it in half and venting its energy chambers to the perfect vacuum of space. Shaken in its course, most of the big starship skidded violently to the left, then literally disintegrated in a veritable cloud of fluttering hull panels and blazing parts that showered the Starfury with fragments.

Brim had hardly recovered from that close call when he was suddenly attacked by six more Gorn-Hoffs— how had he *missed* them?

Shoving maximum energy to the Starfury's six big Admiralty gravs, he tried to power out of the trap, but he was caught in a three-way crossfire. Even while his own disruptors fired broadside to counter the threat, a great, blinding flash darkened the Hyperscreens and a muffled clanging sound reverberated through the whole spaceframe. The starship bucked wildly as if smashed by some gigantic hammer. Readout panels flickered and gravity pulsed wildly, smashing him painfully against his mechanical seat restraints. Fighting the controls—which had taken on a powerful bias to port—he glanced out the Hyperscreens to see that the whole forward half of the left pontoon was simply gone—along with an entire turret and at least one of the ship's six gravity generators. *Everything* from the attaching "trouser" pylon forward was simply gone—and a serious-looking radiation fire was already gleaming evilly from the shredded forward stump of the pontoon.

Cranking the damaged starship into a vertical climb, he listened to the spaceframe creak and groan over the thunder of the straining gravs. The maneuver put him temporarily out of the Leaguers' range, but not for long. This time, it was going to be a *xaxtdamned* close thing. Lawrence threw up a constant fusillade with his remaining disruptors, futilely attempting to discourage the six Leaguers who had now taken up station astern and were slowly closing the range. Scant moments later, they opened up, turning space around the Starfury into a veritable hell of blinding flashes and concussion. Violent waves of raw energy smashed the big ship this way and that as if it were the gamecock in a racket match between a whole crowd of colossal opponents.

Just as Brim glanced into an aft-viewing display, one of the pursuing Gorn-Hoffs abruptly disappeared in a rolling cloud of radiation fire and tumbling parts—as if somehow it had run into a stout wall eight hundred c'lenyts above Avalon. Then a second Leaguer ship stopped abruptly, its graviton plume terminating in a great, glowing ball of flame. After that, the four remaining Gorn-Hoffs skidded off in four different directions, pursued by at least six Starfuries firing in salvo mode. Brim mentally wiped his forehead (encased for the moment in a battlesuit helmet). A *damned* close thing indeed! "Damage Control!" he shouted over voice circuits that were only now coming to life. "I want a report."

"Control here," a stunned voice replied.

"Report, xaxtdamnit," Brim growled.

A globular display flickered to life beside Brim's console showing the view into space from inside the ruined pontoon.

"We've accounted for eight dead, Admiral," the voice said wearily. "Our whole port generator crew. But we've got the radiation fires nearly under control, already." A silhouetted figure stepped into the display from starboard, pointing forward to the ragged, blasted edges of the hull where crews in battlesuits focused unwieldy, hoselike N-ray projectors on the blazing hullmetal while others dragged massive shoring clamps to secure shattered ribs and longerons from further damage.

"Good work, Belzer," Brim said, grinding his teeth. He checked the proximity alarms, then swung the view aft where he confirmed for himself that the Leaguers' fire had indeed carried away all three forward bulkheads, exposing the entire generator chamber to outer space. Surprisingly, however, the situation was much better than he'd even hoped. Welding sparks showed that repair teams were already sealing off the main power bus. For all the apparent damage, both surviving generators did seem to be operating normally, and the Starfury hardly seemed to notice the drop in thrust.

"What about the trouser?" Brim demanded, checking through the Hyperscreens at the battle raging around him. So far, nobody on either side seemed interested in his lone Starfury. "How solid is the pontoon attachment?"

"*Looks* all right, Admiral," Belzer said, moving back into view. "But we'll never know until you try somethin'."

"Thanks," Brim growled. "Stand by one." He then activated the blower. "All hands not on damage teams return to your action stations," he broadcast. "All hands not on damage teams return to your action stations!" With that, he cranked the Starfury around and headed for a new wave of Kreissels just lining up on the city. "Let's blast 'em, Lawrence," he yelled—just as his COMM panel flashed IMMEDIATE PRIORITY and Calhoun's visage filled the display.

"Attention, all Imperial ships," the Admiral's image intoned while the scramble/unscramble indicator on Brim's panel blinked furiously in time to some inner mathematical rhythm, "Attention all Imperial ships. You will clear the target area immediately. I repeat, you will clear the target area immediately."

"Holy thraggling Universe!" Lawrence yelled. "I've got a xaxtdamned Kreissel just comin' into my sights."

"Save it," Brim answered curtly. If Calhoun himself was on

the horn, something big was up. Dragging the Starfury 'round into a near-vertical climb, he angled out into empty space with every measure of speed he could muster. Everywhere he looked, he could see other Imperial ships had also taken the message seriously, breaking off a hundred individual fights and speeding away from the general area—with enemy killer ships in hot pursuit. To the Leaguers it must have seemed like the very mother of all routs. Far below, the Kreissels had begun firing from perfect formations gliding over the city as if they were on parade. There was no opposition anywhere. He grimaced when he imagined what it must be like in the streets below. Just after he spotted two Gorn-Hoffs sneaking into position astern, he glanced out to port and his jaw dropped. "Will you look at THAT!" he exclaimed. So did everyone else on the bridge. . . .

Off to spinward, some twenty big Sodeskayan cargo liners of the Morzik class were streaking in over the city no more than ten or fifteen c'lenyts above the Leaguers—as if they had never heard of the war. Just before the elegant starships passed over the target area, however, great cargo doors opened in their sides and for some moments, a shower of glittering objects tumbled along their flanks, flared up momentarily, then disappeared in the glare of the burning city.

"Loiterers!" Brim shouted happily while he flicked the Starfury over on its back and drove straight for the two skulking Gorn-Hoffs. "Thraggling Loiterers!"

Lawrence fired his disruptors at the same moment the first Kreissels began to disappear below in the same prodigious explosions that had destroyed so many of their kind less than a metacycle before. Astern, the left-most Gorn-Hoff skidded drunkenly into a diving turn trailing long showers of sparks while its partner turned tail and ran for it.

Brim frowned as he curved around seeking out slower targets for his partially disabled Starfury. Who *were* those Leaguers? Certainly not the talented professionals he'd faced earlier. They'd turned tail like frightened cadets and . . . ! That was it. They probably *were* cadets—or something like them. By Voot, it looked like even fat Admiral Hoth Orgoth had limits on his resources. Pulling astern of a plodding Zachtwager that had somehow eluded the new crop of Loiterers, he waited only moments while Lawrence blew it to smithereens, then flicked off in search of larger prey.

Below, the great Loiterer explosions had largely died down and harried remnants of Leaguer attack squadrons were making off in all directions, leaving the smoke-filled sky over Avalon nearly clear of enemy starships for the first time since before dawn. As he hurried toward Effer'wyck in search of fresh Kreissels, Brim watched the formation of Sodeskayan liners swoop back over the distant target area sowing what could be only a fresh crop of Loiterers. The next wave of Leaguer attack ships was really in for it, he chuckled—*after* he got in a few personal licks while they drove for the target area.

But they never came. The only Leaguer ships on the BKAEWs were those heading *back* to Effer'wyck. . . .

Brim quickly regrouped what remained of his tattered squadrons. Out of sixteen squadrons of Starfuries and Defiants that started in the morning, only seventy-one starships remained more or less intact—including Eve Cartier's, he was again relieve to learn. Reports of lifeglobe retrievals and successful forced landfalls somewhat mitigated these grievous losses, but realistically, those would be few and far between. For the next tense metacycle, every Imperial starship that could persist in space under its own power remained on instant alert with a tense crew at action stations, ready to meet the fourth wave of Leaguers.

After still a second metacycle of inaction across the 'Wyckean Void, half the Imperial starships were recalled to their FleetPorts for refitting while the remainder continued to patrol. Finally, after three full metacycles of clear BKAEW screens, all defending starships were recalled home.

Brim docked his mangled Starfury at FleetPort at precisely Night:2:64, little more than three metacycles short of a full Standard Day in space, most of it spent fighting desperately for his life. He waited until the wounded and dead were transferred to the sickbay, then he followed Barbousse from the bridge.

As closely as he could calculate, the day's losses for the Leaguers had been close to six hundred starships—a total disaster. Initial tallies indicated that the Imperials themselves had lost nearly half that many, with more than two hundred crews killed or still missing—another disaster if the battle were to continue. But for all that, the fighting had been wildly successful. Orgoth in this, his boldest move so far, had incurred the most grievous losses in the history of warfare. Now, if only Triannic would conclude that the all-important space supremacy he sought could not be won in time to save his invasion.

Bidding good night to Barbousse with a clap on the shoulder, he stumbled to the new Admiral's suite he had occupied for only one short night, then forced himself into his bunk. But it was a long time before he could force his racing mind into anything resembling sleep. Outside, maintenance crews were rearming and servicing his ship in preparation for a morning sortie, in spite of her condition. For all anyone knew, the next day would bring a full-scale Leaguer invasion, and anything that could fly and fire a disruptor would be useful—if only for a little while. . . .

Brim awoke with a start, staring at his timepiece in disbelief. He had slept more than *three metacycles* longer than he had planned. "Barbousse!" he shouted angrily into a bedside communicator. "How could you have let me oversleep so?" Struggling into his battlesuit, he ripped open the door and stormed into the hall . . . then stopped short in the quiet emptiness. Not a soul could be seen in either direction. It was like a holiday. . . .

Presently hurried footfalls sounded around the curve to his left and Barbousse hove into view, dressed only in fatigues and running for all he was worth. His index finger was across his lips.

"Sh-h-h," the big Warrant Officer puffed in a whisper.

"Beggin' the Admiral's pardon, but everybody's still asleep 'round here."

"Gum'pas H. Voot!" Brim exclaimed in disbelief. "What about the thraggling *Leaguers*? Am I to believe *they* are still asleep, too?"

"Um . . ." Barbousse stuttered. "I've no information about how many of 'em might be sleepin' at this time. But they're still over there in Effer'wyck, and our latest reconnaissance ships are reportin' no action *whatsoever*—um, Admiral, sir."

Astounded, Brim rushed through a warren of silent corridors to FleetPort 13's third new COMM center that month, where he contacted the Office of Fleet Intelligence in a bunker hundreds of irals beneath the Admiralty. After a short conversation over the scrambler, he shook his head in disbelief and took a seat beside the tired-but-grinning Barbousse. It was true. Not a single Leaguer ship was headed toward the Triad or any of its five planets. Nor was there ground activity anywhere in Effer'wyck to indicate that the situation would change in the next twenty-five metacycles. Moments later, a rare EYES ONLY text message arrived for him directly from Calhoun, and he took it into an empty decoding cubicle. Brusque and emotionless, it was notification that although the Leaguers had abruptly changed their code, the last message successfully deciphered contained the following from Headquarters Tarrott to Orgoth:

> ". . . The enemy space force is by no means defeated. On the contrary, it shows increasing activity. Advent of the new secret weapon against attack ships has destroyed much of our ability to support ground operations. The gravitological situation on the whole does not permit us to expect extended periods of calm during the next five Standard Months. Emperor Triannic therefore decides to postpone Death's Head indefinitely."

EPILOGUE

A Message from Effer'wyck

"Not beautiful child, Wilfooshka—*magnificent* child," Old Borodov cooed, cradling little Hope in his great furry arm.

Beside him, Ursis grinned and tickled her chin with a delicate, hirsute finger. "Bears are easy marks for cubs of all ancestries," he said absently.

"I would never have guessed," Onrad laughed. "Except I visited Knez Nikolas at the Great Winter Palace in Gromcow as a child." He looked at Brim. "You'll need to watch these two carefully in the years to come, Wilf," he said. "Bears can spoil even badly *pre*spoiled Crown Princes."

Brim looked around at the magnificent nursery "Uncle Onrad" had ordered for his little "niece"—complete with adjoining apartment to house "Nana" Tutti. He shook his head. "It appears that full-fledged Emperors are pretty talented in that department, too," he said.

Onrad frowned as color rose in his cheeks. "Nonsense," he said with a little grin of embarrassment. "It's just so she'll declare Imperial citizenship when the time comes for her to choose."

"She's a lucky lady," Brim said with a serious smile. "She's got three *very* unique uncles."

Ursis nodded toward the child who was now holding his finger in one of her tiny, dimpled hands. "She also has pretty singular 'special uncle,'" he said, nodding toward the Carescrian. "You must be very proud, Wilf Ansor."

"As I've said before, I can't take much of the credit," Brim said, feeling his own cheeks burn. "But she certainly had a splendid mother."

"Too bad Raddisma is not here to see," Borodov said, rocking the little girl gently in his arm. "I am certain she would have been pleased."

"I suppose I'll have to be pleased enough for both of us, then." Brim said.

Onrad nodded and grinned. "I suppose you will, Wilf," he said. "And if you don't, I'll make up the remainder." Then he frowned. "But back to facts, gentlemen. Wilf, you and your people at group-level agree with the general war prognosis, then?

"We do, Your Majesty," Brim affirmed as Borodov handed over his tiny daughter, who was beginning to fuss. He slipped a feeder into her mouth, and she relaxed, chuffing away contentedly. "For the past two weeks, now," he continued, "League attacks on all five planets have dropped to pre-Aunkayr levels. From what I've seen, they're back to concentrating on military targets now—with an occasional 'spite' raid on Avalon just to keep their hand in."

"And they are removing invasion equipment they stockpiled on coastal planets in steady stream," Ursis added, "taking it back to where they plan to start trouble next, one supposes."

Brim nodded agreement, lifting Hope in preparation for burping.

Onrad absently placed a pad on Brim's shoulder. "And where do you suppose that will be?" he asked.

Ursis looked at Borodov and sighed. "Is supreme top-secret information," he said, "but one supposes that Hope can be trusted."

"We shall trust her," Borodov said, suddenly looking very serious. "Please proceed, Nikolai Yanuarievich."

"After long deliberation," Ursis continued in a deep growl, "many of us Bears believe that the Tyrant's mind has turned to Mother Sodeskaya herself for his next victim."

"I rather suspected that." Onrad said grimly. "I take it there are some who do *not* share your views?"

"A few," Borodov affirmed. "Not like CIGAs, of course. All Sodeskayans understand who is enemy. But in their way, they often obstruct just as effectively. These particular featherweights believe that Triannic will go after other targets first."

"When, in fact, there are *no* other targets he can go for," Ursis added. "So long as *both* your Imperial Fleet and Sodeskayan land armies exist to make war together, he cannot risk attack anywhere else. He must eliminate one or the other first."

"He must also rebuild his Deep Space Fleet," Brim ventured.

"While we do the same thing," Onrad put in. "If Triannic had been able to rush a few more reserves to fat-boy Orgoth, he'd have come pretty close to pulling off his invasion. Right, Brim?"

"That's the way I see it, Your Majesty," Brim said. "Luckily, with the new Carescrian shipyards in operation, we'll be able to rebuild as quickly as he." He held his breath momentarily, trying to stifle a bit of partisan pride. "Maybe a little *faster.*"

"So, he's effectively blocked here," Ursis said.

"Yeah," Onrad agreed. "It's hard to fault that line of thought."

"Which means," Ursis said, raising a long index finger pedagogically, "that at present, *our* first priority is to build a fleet."

"What?" Onrad demanded.

"A S-Sodeskayan fleet . . . ?" Brim stuttered, switching Hope to his other shoulder.

Both Bears grinned. "Yes, my friends," Ursis assured him. "First time in history, we can no longer count on continuing to live as free Sodeskayans under sole umbrella of Imperial Fleet." He looked at Onrad. "During foreseeable future, you Imperials are going to be busy enough defending your own Triad, much less our huge network of star systems, too."

Onrad took a deep breath and held out his hands to Brim for Hope. "Times have *really* changed, haven't they?" he sighed, cradling the little girl in his arms. "Who would ever have thought we'd see the day the Imperial Fleet couldn't keep peace throughout the whole galaxy?"

Borodov chuckled. " 'Constant change is here to stay,' as we say in Mother Country."

"Yeah," Onrad said with a grin. "I guess it is." Then he looked at Borodov. "I take it that we have just passed into an official visit?" he asked.

"We have, Your Majesty," Borodov said. He laughed. "I now become Anastas Alexi Borodov, Grand Duke of Gromcow Lakes and special Emissary to Nikolas the August, Knez of Greater Sodeskaya and Grand Federation of Sodeskayan States. Is impressive title, no?"

"Damned impressive," Onrad replied with raised eyebrows. "So what can we do to help you and the Knez build that Sodeskayan fleet?'

"Thought you would never ask, Your Majesty," Borodov replied with an old man's grin. He turned to Brim. "We want *this* gentleman," he said.

Brim felt his eyebrows go into orbit.

Onrad smiled, placing a finger to his lips. "A moment, gentlemen," he said indicating Hope with his head. "Little Miss Brim seems to be asleep." Then he winced. "I've got to be *careful* calling her that."

"How about if I get Tutti?" Brim asked, summoning the beautiful redhead with a light tap on an adjoining door. Moments later, the four men were on their way to the Emperor's private lounge.

"All right, now," Onrad continued presently, "you want to steal Brim, eh?"

"We do, Your Majesty," Borodov said. "For we have a twofold mission before us in Sodeskaya. Not only must we establish new fleet, we must also develop starship suited to our type of warfare. Friend Brim has already been elemental in both kinds of programs."

Brim frowned. That sounded like a *big* change of duty station. He'd been spending a lot of time with Eve lately—in and *out* of bed. And feeling very comfortable about their growing relationship. Not to mention his new command. . . .

"What do you think, Wilf?" Onrad asked.

"*Well,*" Brim began, "I, ah . . ."

"We make certain you return to Avalon often enough to watch Hope grow up," the elderly Bear promised.

"And I think I could guarantee that this 'foreign' assignment would result in considerable enhancement to your service record, Admiral," Onrad said pointedly.

Brim glanced at Onrad for a moment with suspicion. *He'*d been convinced pretty quickly. Then it hit him! Of course! The three of them had been through the whole thing in advance. He'd been sandbagged again. . . . He grinned resignedly. "I'd be honored by such an assignment," he said—and excepting his feelings about Eve and Hope, he almost meant it.

Onrad nodded. "Thanks," he said with a *very* serious look on his face, then turned to the Bears. "You're sure you want to let yourselves—and your dominion—in for such trouble?" he asked with a spurious frown.

"We have considered dangers, Your Majesty," Ursis said with an outrageous grin. "Knez Nikolas has convinced us that they can be largely overcome."

"Then it's done," Onrad said, glancing sideways at Brim, "*after* we send for our Admiral here on a tour of his native Carescria."

"Carescria, Your Majesty?" Brim asked, now completely confounded.

"Yeah," Onrad answered, then acquiesced with an embarrassed little grin. "All right," he said, 'I'll admit that this Sodeskayan assignment is so important that you never had a choice—*and* that I discussed everything in advance with these two grinning, so-called friends of yours. . . ."

Ursis and Borodov suddenly took an abiding interest in the ceiling of the Emperor's study.

"But the Carescrian trip's a different thing," Onrad went on.

"I understand how you feel about your home sector, so I'll leave that one up to you. You just need to know that it's damned important, too. Those people out here broke their backs making the starships that just saved our Triad. They're important; we're going to need them a lot more before we finally whip the Tyrant and his bloody League." He smiled. After the war too," he added, his eyes ocusing somewhere off into the future. "We'll have a different Empire by the time that happens . . ." Then he visibly forced himself back to the present. "I'll give you time to think it over, Admiral," he said.

"I won't need to do that, Your Majesty," Brim said, in the now *very* quiet room. "It's a trip I'd like to take." This time, he *really* meant it. Especially since he was almost certain that Eve would need to come along as his "adviser."

Onrad's eyebrows raised. "That's quite a change of heart for you, Brim," he observed.

"I know it is, Your Majesty," Brim said as the faces of Eve Cartler and Nadia Tissaurd materialized in his mind's eye. "But I've had a bit of help lately. It's made me realize that . . . well . . . hating that one part of me has cost dearly over the years. I think I'm ready to move on, now," he said, "and clearly Carescria's ready to move on, too." Then he took a deep breath. "After," he added, "we *first* win a pretty serious war."

"Pretty serious indeed," Onrad agreed, glancing up toward the surface where much of Avalon lay in smoldering ruins. He glanced at an exquisite timepiece on a nearby table. "Which reminds me of the Cabinet meeting I must attend in a few moments." He stood. "Gentlemen," he said in a clear sign of dismissal.

Brim and the three Bears rose. "We thank you in the name of Knez Nikolas," Borodov said.

"You can tell the Knez I thank *him* for the Loiterers he sent the other day," Onrad said with a smile. "But I'll make certain he knows officially." Then a chime sounded. He frowned and touched a small, glowing panel on the arm of his chair. A moment later, the door opened and General Zapt appeared with a small leather pouch embossed with what a startled Brim recognized immediately as the royal crest of Effer'wyck.

"Your Highness," Zapt said, "this came for Admiral Brim through an intelligence channel—highly secret, and all that. Seems as if it was smuggled out of Effer'wyck by one of our operatives."

Onrad nodded. "You've had it checked?" he asked with a frown.

"Completely benign," Zapt said, handing the pouch over to Brim.

"You don't have to open it here," Onrad said.

"It's all right," Brim said, loosening the drawstrings and peering into the pouch. Then his jaw dropped. "It's my new *timepiece*," he said in amazement, "the one I bought at the terminal during your last trip to Luculent, Your Majesty."

"How'd it get *back* to Effer'wyck?" Onrad demanded, then suddenly closed his mouth. *He knew.*

"Um," Brim equivocated, "I was on a . . . secret mission, Your Majesty. We had a bit of trouble and I, er, lost it on the surface of one of their little starcoast planets."

"Harrumph . . . yes," Onrad said, his face reddening slightly. "They *do* send you on the damndest missions, Brim." He gazed at the pouch with fascination. "And the timepiece is all that's in there?" he asked, narrowing his eyes in curiosity.

Brim peered into the pouch again. "No. Your Majesty," he said, drawing out a folded sheet of thin plastic stationery. "It seems to have a note with it." Frowning, he unfolded the sheet . . . then silently closed his eyes in absolute bewilderment. He knew the handwriting as well as he knew his own.

Dearest Wilf:

I watched you drop this in the forest during your short, miraculous visit to Bra've with my outrageous cousin Onrad. How I wanted to touch you there among the trees that stormy night! But I could not without risking the compromise of your escape. Never forget me, Wilf. Perhaps one day when I have helped win back the freedom of my poor, violated Effer'wyck we can find each other's arms again. Until then, I remain,

Once your devoted lover,

Margot Effer'wyck